W9-ASR-642

MAY 1 8 2009

strange
nervous
laughter

strange

nervous

laughter

Bridget McNulty

Thomas Dunne Books
St. Martin's Press
New York

This is a work of fiction. All of the characters, organizations, and events portrayed in this novel are either products of the author's imagination or are used fictitiously.

THOMAS DUNNE BOOKS.
An imprint of St. Martin's Press.

www.thomasdunnebooks.com
www.stmartins.com

Definition of "debacle" on page 234 taken from MSN Encarta © Microsoft 2007

Library of Congress Cataloging-in-Publication Data

McNulty, Bridget.
Strange nervous laughter / Bridget McNulty. — 1st U.S. ed.
    p. cm.
ISBN-13: 978-0-312-54434-8
ISBN-10: 0-312-54434-0
1. Magic realism (Literature) 2. Friendship—Fiction.
3. Conduct of life—Fiction. 4. Durban (South Africa)—
Fiction. I. Title.
PR9369.4.M396S77 2009
823'.92—dc22

                                    2008046506

First published in South Africa by Oshun Books, an imprint of Struik Publishers, a division of New Holland Publishing (Pty) Ltd

First U.S. Edition: May 2009

10 9 8 7 6 5 4 3 2 1

List of characters

Beth

Mdu

Aisha

Harry

Meryl

Pravesh

Prelude

There are three states of love. In love, out of love, and on the precipice between the two. We all have a preference, and – surprisingly – in love is not always the hands-down winner. It is too messy, too all-consuming, too *much*. Then again, out of love can be a little lonely, and that teetering precipice – when you're no longer in love, but not quite out of it – exhaustingly dramatic.

Each is risky.

As life itself is risky. As the most mundane activities that fill our days are risky – crossing the street, withdrawing money, shopping for groceries.

Especially, you might say, the latter.

☼

It is all over in five minutes.

8.31 am: Beth, the cashier in a small supermarket, sits twirling a few strands of her hair and sucking on the ends thoughtfully. She seems to be floating above her chair, softly humming a love song, one of her feet pirouetting mid-air. There are only two customers in Handy Green Grocers this morning – Meryl, a woman with sleek, black hair and flawless skin, perusing the Weigh-Less Meals for One, and Mdu, a tall, dark, scowling man choosing a bunch of grapes.

It is a seedy little shop – dust particles hang suspended in the lattice of sunlight that creeps in through the burglar guards of the small window, and the *Today's Specials!* signs are clearly not today's specials. They're advertising Easter eggs in October. The overhead fan does nothing to move the stagnant air, and the display of mangoes seems to be ripening with each passing moment.

Handy Green Grocers is the kind of shop that only locals shop at. The kind of shop that has everything you could ever need, but only in small quantities for exorbitant prices. The kind of shop that somehow, always, seems to smell of curry powder and over-ripe bananas.

The kind of shop you wouldn't expect two men with hooded sweatshirts and hand guns to burst into at 8.31 am on a Tuesday morning and say, in voices thick with fear, 'Okay, get down on the floor! We don't want to hurt anyone, we just need some money!'

Beth screams, shattering a stand of All Gold tomato sauce bottles, each one exploding messily. The man in the blue hoody spins around and aims his gun at her.

'Shut up!' he demands, crunching tomato sauce shards under his feet, while the man in the red hoody starts chanting, 'Oh shit oh shit oh shit,' under his breath.

Sleek Meryl, on the other side of the shop, drops the Weigh-Less meal she is holding, then drops to the floor, silently, swiftly, as though practised in the art of hitting the ground.

Beth immediately bursts into tears, loud gasping sobs that leave her breathless as they fill the small shop, bouncing off the windows and landing in the middle of the tinned beans display, causing it to topple over and almost crush Meryl. Luckily, she is bound so tightly in a corset of cynicism that neither emotions, nor tumbling tin cans, have any effect on her. In fact, Meryl is amazed at how calm she feels; amazed at the almost Zen-like sense of clarity that descended on her the moment the men burst into the shop. She always thought she would fall to pieces in an emergency. But she didn't. Not at all. She simply fell to the ground, kept quiet and played dead.

She pretends not to breathe. She does not move. And when ten more cans of cheap baked beans fall on her back, she refuses to flinch; braced by her intricate, tightly woven armour.

Mdu is the only other customer in the shop. His hand, still stretched out to pick up the only good bunch of grapes in the pile, remains there, frozen. The rest of his body freezes too, except for his heart, which speeds up and pounds deafeningly in his ears.

Mdu forgets how to breathe.

His mind fills with the clamour of things the other people in the shop are not saying out loud. The words behind the words.

Underneath the plump cashier's repeated plea – *Please don't kill me, please don't kill me, please don't kill me* – Mdu hears, *I don't want to die, not now, not here. Please God, don't let me die, not here, not now …*

Just keep it together, keep it together, the dark-haired woman next to him tells herself silently, sternly, without any trace of emotion. She is still stretched out on the floor, buried under a pile of cans.

Not for the first time, Mdu wishes he did not have such exceptional hearing. Being able to hear the things that people are afraid of saying aloud is not always helpful. Like now, when he can hear the man in the red hoody thinking: *I don't want to have to shoot anybody, but, fuck me, if this woman doesn't shut up, somebody will hear. I'll shoot one of them if I have to, just to get away.*

Mdu does not want to be that one.

He knows his role in this scene; knows that he is the only man who can defend these two women; knows that he has to step forward and say, in a quiet but determined tone, 'Come on, guys, leave these good people alone.'

In his mind's eye, Mdu can see exactly what to do: disarm both men by grabbing the watermelon to his left and knocking them out, simultaneously signalling the hysterical cashier to call the police. He is young, he is strong; he has in many ways been waiting his whole life for this chance to prove that he is capable of doing something remarkable.

Instead, he remains frozen.

Frozen, as he watches the two men force the wild-eyed cashier to empty all the money from the till, watches as they wave their guns around, shouting, 'Shut the fuck up!' in increasingly loud voices, while she continues to whimper, 'Please don't kill me, please don't kill me, please don't kill me.'

He watches their hands shake as they silently tell themselves, unwittingly in unison, *Time to go, hurry the fuck up!*

And finally watches as they scan the shop one last time. Then the more confident man, the one in the blue hoody, grabs a Bar One from the checkout counter and tears it open with his teeth.

He grins mockingly at Mdu and takes a bite.

Pussy, he thinks.

The word echoes in Mdu's mind.

8.36 am: All over. Beth, still sobbing, still gasping for breath, dials the police and tells them to 'Hurry, please hurry, they might come back!'

Meryl, unharmed, stands up and makes pointed eye contact with Mdu. Then walks out calmly, past Beth who covers the phone with one hand and calls out, 'No, wait, you might have to identify them!'

Mdu finally picks up the bunch of grapes, crumples to the ground and slowly starts eating them, not tasting anything but the lingering bitterness of cowardice.

A bird starts singing outside the door. For a moment, the air in the shop stings with relief.

☼ ☼ ☼

Let's press pause for a minute. What do we see?

Beth, the cashier, hugging herself tightly with her arms across her chest. Eyes wide and still terrified, forehead crumpled in despair, mouth open mid-sob.

Mdu, the grape-eater, sitting on the floor with his elbows on his knees. A half-eaten bunch of grapes dangles from one hand as he covers his ears to block out Meryl's disdain.

Meryl, one hand on the door, the other tightening the laces of her stiff corset, glancing at Mdu with an undisguised look of disgust.

And outside the shop, outside where the world continues as if nothing has happened?

Pravesh, a young Indian man, sits on a bench under the large acacia on the opposite side of the road, reading the 'In Memorium' notices in the newspaper, his knees pleasurably tingling as they are wont to do in the proximity of death.

Aisha, a beautiful black girl, walks past on her way to work, staring dreamily at the clouds gathering overhead, wrapped up in a private dream world.

And Harry, the local garbage man, stands on the edge of his truck just over there, sifting through an overfull black plastic bag.

Sure, they all seem preoccupied. But without a doubt, if we could crawl inside each of their heads (just for a moment, without them noticing) we would find, amidst the cobwebs and jingles and completely forgotten New Year's resolutions, an opinion or two about love. A few thoughts on relationships. One or two fervently held hopes of not dying alone.

Because, despite its inauspicious beginning, this is not a tale about crime.

Nor about the daily woes of living in South Africa.

But rather about love; and what can happen to it when combined with the hottest summer Durban has ever known.

[Beth]

A week later that summer began.

A summer so hot it was (almost) all people could talk about.

Heat had a personality that summer. And it wasn't pleasant.

Every morning when she woke up, Beth lifted her blind, looked out the window and said, 'I wonder which exciting person I'm going to meet today!'

Sometimes she lay in bed for a few minutes, imagining various romantic scenarios – a man catching her eye from across Handy Green Grocers, where she still worked, so transfixed that he walked up to her in a love-smitten daze and asked, 'Who *are* you?'; a man who couldn't bring himself to speak to her because of the depth of his passion, and thus had to slip her little love notes along with the cash he paid for his groceries; a man who lingered outside the supermarket on his way to work every morning, just so that he could stare longingly through the window at her.

At the start of that hot summer, Beth had dreamt up thirty-seven different ways that men could ask her out at work.

Pravesh was the first man in real life to actually do it.

He arrived at her house in a hearse, which was perhaps not the best omen for a first date.

What was unusual about this particular gentleman, dressed in his best suit (the same suit he wore for funerals) was not so much that he arrived in a hearse, as that he didn't think it strange. Well, that and the fact that he was wearing a suit on what was, undoubtedly, the hottest day in a decade.

Surrounded by the relentless to and fro of death, it was easy to forget that there were others untouched by it; others who did not confront corpses, coffins and grief on a daily basis; others who might, when coming to their front door in a pale pink dress, screech with fright at the sight of a hearse parked in their driveway.

Those things did not occur to Pravesh the day he drove to Beth's house for their first date.

Perhaps they should have.

Luckily, Beth was a rather forgiving soul who, after the initial shock, quickly forgot about the ghostly apparition of a man in a dark suit standing next to a hearse. She had been nervously waiting for Pravesh to arrive – absentmindedly floating an inch above the ground while looking out the window – so the relief of not being stood up led her to forgive any strangeness on his part.

She even tried to joke about it. Beth was good at making jokes; it was her #1 Tool for Attracting Men. ('Always make them laugh,' her mother used to tell her. 'Make them laugh, or make them supper.') Beth had decided on the former as a rule of thumb – cooking was not her forte. She made Pravesh laugh within the first ten minutes of their date: a good sign. Actually, it was within the first three minutes, as soon as she opened her door and they had exchanged greetings.

'You know,' Beth said, 'a friend of mine and his daughter recently went to a funeral parlour to pick out a coffin for her goldfish. "Why is the coffin so big, Daddy?" the little girl asked. "Well, honey," her father replied, avoiding eye contact, "your goldfish is inside Fluffy, the next-door neighbour's cat!"'

Beth snorted, laughing at her own joke before Pravesh had a chance to.

He joined her with a short, sharp bark of a laugh that nonetheless made her eyes shine.

☀

Beth had never been in a hearse before.

Perhaps that wasn't surprising.

She stared at it curiously as they walked down the path, taking in the tinted windshield, the pink velvet curtains, and the extra-long rear section to distract herself from the nervous fluttering in her stomach. The outside of the hearse was black, as is customary, but it had large pink letters covering both flanks of the car that read, *Frankie's Funeral Parlour: The Finest Service This Side of Heaven.*

Following her gaze, Pravesh explained that it was, in fact, one of Durban's premier funeral parlours, and that his boss had kindly let him borrow the hearse for this special occasion.

Beth felt no need to question him – she was happy to be a special occasion.

It seemed like the perfect match: Beth was a self-confessed Saver, Pravesh a Man in Need of Saving.

She had a heart too big for her life, and he had a life too big for his heart.

Beth often wondered where her enormous capacity for love had come from; what aberrant gene in her had malfunctioned, causing her to always, always give too much. Little did she remember a certain Friday evening in the hot summer of her fourteenth year: at a school disco, being ignored by all the boys because she was slightly overweight, spotty, and dressed in a rather unflattering jeans and T-shirt combo. She felt ugly. She was unhappy. She overheard Tom du Plessis, the boy she was quietly, desperately in love with, saying to his friend, 'I just don't know how to talk to Andrea, she's so hot!'

And instead of fleeing to the bathroom and crying behind a locked door for the rest of the night, Beth decided to help Tom woo Andrea, even though it felt like weighing her shoes down with concrete.

So, you see, it was not so much an aberrant gene, as a conscious decision.

Her reasoning – subconscious though it was at the time – was that boys would like her more if she helped them; if she could make other people happy, it would make her happy.

Over a decade later, Beth's motivation hadn't changed.

In many ways, Beth was still stuck at that disco. Somehow, she still couldn't figure out why loving intensely – instead of drawing men towards her like a magnet – always scared them away. Magazine psychologists, love doctors, talk show hosts, and readers of romance novels worldwide knew exactly why, of course. They had (all, collectively) majored in Female Saviour Instinct; they had written master's dissertations on it, and had given lectures on the prevailing need of twenty-first-century women to Save Men.

This was easy stuff: Beth scared men away because she fell in love too hard, too fast, and insisted on constructing elaborate relationship fantasies in her head. Her sense of self was dramatically subverted for the benefit of the male of the species, and she relied too heavily on the necessity of a relationship in the construction of her identity. She also had a startlingly vivid imagination, and had spent many years watching romantic comedies. All of this blended together to produce a heady concoction called Beth's Recurrent Destructive Relationship Pattern (as those in the know would call it).

Those out of the know called it 'that thing she always does'. Time after time Beth would see a man from afar, or meet him casually, and something in his manner, or look, or speech (or lack of manner/look/speech) would endear him to her.

After even the briefest, most fleeting of encounters, Beth instantly layered her unwitting prey with everything she ever wanted in a lover, coated him with her romantic dreams and desires, and dressed him up as Prince Charming (tailor-made, of course). He would be funny, caring, sweet and loving, intelligent, witty, sensitive and spiritual, phenomenal in bed, endlessly thoughtful in everyday life, and – of course – smitten with her.

And then they'd go on their first date.

During that first date, Beth would pounce on certain key phrases to prove her fantasies were grounded in reality.

'I also like drinking tea,' translated seamlessly into, 'We have everything in common and will probably never fight.'

When he said, 'I once thought about getting a puppy,' she heard, 'I'm ready to settle down and start having kids.'

'What would you like for dessert?' really meant, of course, 'I will devote my life to making you happy.'

After they got to know each other a little bit, Beth would fall madly, deeply, hopelessly in love (the second date). This happened on every second date, regardless of whether the man was a catch or a dud or an unutterable bore; or maybe even potentially dangerous. The object of Beth's deep love would be (hopefully) somewhat intrigued by her, but (naturally) alarmed by her ardour so early on.

This was (usually) where their paths diverged.

If this week's Prince Charming was a fairly normal, mildly issued man who enjoyed her spirit, but found the intensity of a whole evening of constant talking a little overwhelming, he fled as quickly as his golden boots could carry him; pausing only when he found a cool, calm and collected girl who might someday deign to like him, but nothing more.

None of that emotional nonsense.

If, however, he was complex, depressed, heavily issued and near-suicidal, the Prince Charming inevitably saw sweet Beth as his guiding light –

finally The One who could change his life/pay his bills/cook his supper and generally get him back on track. Like a mom but with sex. And once this Prince Charming-in-disguise reached the back-on-track state (no longer suicidal, no longer socially inept) and had entirely sapped Beth of all her energy and will to live – after she allowed him to unload every doubt and insecurity onto her – she would be unceremoniously dumped.

Every time.

But Beth refused to get bitter about it, refused to admit defeat in the face of overwhelming evidence that each time she found a new Love it ended, and she recovered. She kept the candle of hope burning, and even though the flame wavered dangerously at times, Beth vowed never to grow cynical.

This is not to say that she didn't sometimes feel a little used. Beth was no idiot; she saw the furtive looks her friends gave each other when she said she was in love (again), noticed the false enthusiasm her siblings tried to muster when she gushed, picked up on the resigned tone her mom had started to use whenever Beth phoned in tears. But she just couldn't help it: each time she met a new man it felt like waking up to a new morning, a whole new day.

A whole new set of circumstances.

Or so Beth thought.

The trajectory of these doomed love affairs was fairly easy to follow, thanks to a little 'condition' Beth had had since birth. She floated when she was happy. Not high up in the air, not enough to notice unless you were staring at her, but definitely with her feet above the ground. Every time she met The One, she started floating, and usually stayed in a happily floating state until he started dumping on her, at which point she came back to earth with a thud.

Each of Beth's short-lived relationships followed this rainbow-like arc, with no pot of gold at the end.

Beth sometimes felt a little tired by the constant merry-go-round of emotions these relationships kept her on, sometimes wondered if she couldn't perhaps hop off and sit on a bench for a while, catching her breath. But whenever she reached that level of reasoning – the maybe-I-don't-*need*-a-boyfriend level – she found herself gripped by a panic so intense that it left her breathless.

Those thirty-second panic attacks always centred on the same scene: Beth, at thirty-five, single, overweight, smoking heavily and drinking glass after glass of red wine in a bar, on her own, until her teeth turned red. The fact that she neither smoked nor drank red wine made no difference to the scenario. And logically, sure, Beth knew that you didn't *have* to have one boyfriend after the other just to ensure you were never alone. But whenever she thought about being single for longer than a few weeks, she got that sick feeling that maybe, somehow, if she got off the merry-go-round it would speed up and leave her behind, and she wouldn't be able to get on again until all the good men were taken.

And then she'd be right back there in that bar, drinking wine, smoking, with ghoulishly outlined teeth.

This very real fear trapped Beth in a continuous state of checking-out.

Wherever she went she kept her eyes peeled for eligible guys.

In Handy Green Grocers.

In the dentist's waiting room.

At the Blood Donor Centre (he had to be a good guy if he was willing to donate blood).

Over piles of cantaloupes in Fruit & Veg City.

Walking on the beach.

Walking down the road.

Even walking down the aisle on Sundays, at the church she occasionally popped into to see if there were any new male converts.

Beth was constantly checking out men.

It was exhausting.

And often hopeless. Take last week, for example – even as Beth pleaded for her life, and sobbed her way through the robbery, she couldn't help noticing the tall, dark, handsome man's eyes on her, and briefly wondered whether he was staring at her because she was hysterical, or because he was somehow attracted to her.

She so hoped it was the latter.

All in all, by the time Beth had a gun held to her head and realised she was not quite ready to die, she was in trouble.

Big trouble.

Stuck on a highway to disaster and heading for a crash.

Which made the pink-dress-black-hearse-moment a lot more significant.

[Pravesh]

But what of Pravesh? What brought him to that moment, spruced up and ready for a date with our Beth? How did he come to be a man with a life too big for his heart?

What does that even mean?

Well.

Pravesh's parents, Nashikta and Poobalan, had always wanted six children, but for medical reasons could only have one. Both had come from large Indian families, with lots of children and various cousins sharing a house. Only having one child to look after forced them to lavish the attention and care meant for six onto their poor, precious Pravesh. Pravesh's mom baked him treats and sweetmeats every day, and on weekends she cooked huge curries and dozens of samoosas.

Whenever there were leftovers, Nashikta would lock herself in the bathroom, crying about her undeniable failure as a woman, so Pravesh felt obliged to eat until he was sick to his stomach. Although the stress of guilt-eating would make it difficult for Pravesh to stomach Indian food as an adult, he was unable to tell his mother how he felt, paralysed by her tears.

The smell of samoosas frying and incense burning filled the house like tear gas, and left very little space for oxygen.

When Pravesh was a young child, his mother had enthusiastically taught him how to sew and knit – frustrated at the lack of a girl-child, she even encouraged her only son to take up embroidery. On the rare occasions that Pravesh fell ill (and was too sick to hide it), Nashikta sat by his bed day and night. She called her sisters (who lived in various cities around South Africa) for medical advice, even if he'd just caught a cold, and refused to sleep for more than twenty minutes whenever Pravesh had a fever.

Pravesh's dad, Poobalan, played basketball with his son every afternoon, and wouldn't let him eat dinner until he sank five hoops in a row. They also played cricket and touch rugby and soccer, and he pushed his son to join the teams as soon as he was old enough for school. Once Pravesh reached high school, Poobalan encouraged him (strongly) to join the debating and chess clubs, and helped him with his science projects so that he always came first at science fairs.

They forced many musical instruments into his reluctant hands, but never managed to find one that he could play.

Usually, by dinner each evening, Pravesh sat immobilised by the feeling of desperate expectation that his parents wrapped around him like a heavy quilt in summer.

Come on, they seemed to say with their wordless glances and insistent, mindless questioning; *Come on, prove to us that we did something right.*

Swallowing became almost impossible for Pravesh.

Poor Poobalan and Nashikta – frustrated patriarch and matriarch of an imaginary clan – felt obliged to pour all their energy, love, attention, worrying and expectation into their one child.

He drowned in it.

Pravesh tried to rebel. He wore a custom-made necklace under his school uniform that had five silver letters spelling out the word S-A-T-A-N (as well as some shiny purple beads for colour) but no one ever noticed. He streaked around the neighbourhood wearing nothing but a green Speedo, but nobody saw him except old Mrs. Moodley, and she only clapped her hands and smiled toothlessly.

He even snuck out of the house to go to The Beer Bar, a renowned hang-out for prostitutes and loose women. But they all laughed at young Pravesh's puerile pick-up lines and patted him on the head.

It was maddening.

As a final stab at his parents' over-parenting, Pravesh took one of his mom's favourite religious prints (a particularly lovely rendition of Jesus Christ with a glowing sacred heart), removed it from its ornate gold frame and signed a devilish *JChrist* along the bottom in permanent marker. He reframed it to hang in his bedroom. Pravesh's mother and father, deeply and devoutly Christian, were so hurt they never mentioned it.

It wasn't the response he'd been hoping for.

Pravesh's true calling was eventually, inevitably, revealed: dead people, and the undertaking business. Once someone has died, they have used up their allotted words and gestures. Silence becomes the only option. Pravesh loved that about the dead, loved the peace he found driving his hearse, and the solemnity that greeted him at every corner, so different from the forced gaiety of his childhood home environment.

He carried this gravitas with him at all times, even as he made his coffee in the mornings, speaking to himself in the same hushed tones he used when dealing with bereaved families.

'Time to buy more milk,' can take on immeasurable weight when spoken in the right tone.

It was not just an act; the solemnity sank in deep under his skin.

Alas, as a direct result of his unusual upbringing, Pravesh found himself entirely incapable of feeling or receiving love. The problem was compounded by his highly developed death radar. No matter where he went, or what he was doing, Pravesh could sense death, in a very specific way. Usually, whenever this radar was triggered, he felt a slight tingling in the backs of his knees, and his ears grew hot. It was a distinct and pleasurable feeling – the tingling and the heat pulsed in unison, unlike anything else Pravesh had ever experienced.

Sure, you might not think it such an inconvenience – after all, how much death could there be in an average day, even for an undertaker?

You might be surprised.

For Pravesh could sense the death of not only humans (which would be disturbing enough) but also dead animals and road kill, dead silences, dead or dying relationships, dead air, deadbeats, deadlines and death wishes, dead languages, dead weights, dying hopes and diehards, dead ringers, deadheads, death marches and deadly sins, death-defying risks and all manner of dead ends.

Sometimes, as a treat, Pravesh hung out at SteinerWheatleyNdwana Attorneys, the divorce lawyers across the street. The rush of dying hopes and dead romance – that final deathblow to love – made Pravesh light-headed and giddy for the rest of the day.

✵ ✵ ✵

Now, you might be wondering why Pravesh was not constantly abuzz, what with the decaying social structures, dying family values and spiritual demise so rampant in cities the world over (and even more so in one deluged with street children and empty churches).

You might be wondering indeed.

And if you were to walk along this path of reasoning, surely, surely, in Durban, the city at the heart of KwaZulu-Natal, the province at the heart of Aids in South Africa, surely his sensor would be vibrating at sonic speed?

Surely.

Death that summer was so relentless it had outweighed the birth rate in Durban; the very air was infected with it. The colour, the heat, the intoxicating closeness of the city must inevitably have intensified the scent of fatality on the hot breeze.

Without doubt, Pravesh should have been humming like a loose electric wire.

Well, no. Yes, and no.

✵ ✵ ✵

At first Pravesh's radar picked up on the grander deaths in this life – the social demise, the spiritual casualties, the Grand Moral Decay. But he soon found that this constant white noise drowned out the smaller, more personal – and infinitely more interesting – fatalities occurring around him every day. And so he fine-tuned his gift, bit by bit, day by day. He took to spending large chunks of time in Point Road, notorious for its profusion of drug dealers, crack addicts, hookers and good-kids-gone-bad. But instead of sensing their moral destitution, instead of his knees tingling to the tune of their spiritual decay, instead of being thrilled by the Death of Society As We Know It, Pravesh sat in the doorway of an abandoned house, eyes closed, and found the tiniest casualty amidst the larger ruin. His extra sensor, as he liked to call it, picked up the vibrations of a dying cockroach on the third floor of a whorehouse. He felt the pull of a young boy thinking of suicide as he played on the roof. He heard one word of Latin – *Valedico* – spoken by a Nigerian drug lord.

The smaller deaths were more satisfying. They made Pravesh happy.

Now, it is said (by those who say things) that men choose girlfriends who resemble their mothers in some way. Were any man to recognise this disturbing trait, he would be horrified. However, it does seem like a perfectly plausible reason why Pravesh decided to ask Beth out for dinner.

But perhaps it was something else; something not quite so obvious. Perhaps it had more to do with one particular night the previous week; one night that just happened to be Pravesh's thirtieth birthday. A night which he chose to spend alone (rather than choking on curry with his parents).

The bells of change were ringing as Pravesh sat eating a Hungry-Man macaroni cheese TV dinner, and watching a documentary on whales, those highly intelligent mammals that live in stable social groups their whole lives.

[Mdu]

Mdu woke up with the niggling feeling that he was forgetting something, something important on this early October day that was, freakishly, the hottest day that Durban had ever known. The sheer effort of trying to remember what he was supposed to remember made Mdu sweat. With a sigh, he rolled out of bed and shuffled through to the bathroom. He wondered, staring at himself in the bathroom mirror as he brushed his teeth, whether it was just the heat that was giving him this strange sense of foreboding, or whether it had something to do with the lingering, dogged unease that had followed his every step each day for a week – each day since his pathetic cowardice in the Handy Green Grocers robbery.

Mdu looked, at first glance, like an ordinary enough man.

Appearances can be deceiving. He was, in fact, not even a little bit ordinary. Not at all. For Mdu had a voice with an unusual frequency that could speak to whales, and special hearing that could pick up their sounds. He worked out at sea, leaving Durban Harbour each morning and only returning at dusk. His specific task was to communicate with the whales and to chart their journey, so that whale-watching cruise ships would know where to go.

Mdu was a glorified whale tour guide. He tried not to dwell on it.

Now, if you think about it, being able to hear a frequency that nobody else can hear must have some deeper effect on a person's psyche; some Superman-like residue that lingers in normal life. Because Mdu was able to communicate in ways that others could not, and hear things that others couldn't hear, he found himself taking what people said with a rather generous pinch of salt.

There are so many layers to the things we say, so many meanings and unspoken opinions and thinly veiled double entendres – so many nuances to each and every word – that Mdu found it difficult to listen to people and hear only what they said, and nothing more. Uncovering the hidden layers became an exhausting, never-ending translation exercise.

He chose, instead, to keep to himself.

It had taken some time to reach this decision. Mdu had tried being an ordinary twenty-something-year-old. Just the night before, in fact, he had ventured out to a pub, Jimmy Fox's, one of those 'authentic' ye-olde-Irish places. He had tried socialising, but found it futile. His head hurt from the cacophony of so many people not saying what they really meant, combined with the relentless cheery Irish jigs and forced laughter from the bar. He saw some people he recognised from high school, and they asked what he was up to, and, not really listening to his answer, drunkenly replied, 'Oh, cool, man! We should hook up sometime.'

He also saw some people from work, and they tried to feed him shooters by the dozen, delighted to see him out. And then he saw the other woman from the Handy Green Grocers robbery – not the cashier, the customer. She was standing at the bar downing drinks and looking at the people around her with open scorn. Mdu pretended he hadn't noticed her, and left. He didn't need more of her disdainful words ringing in his ears.

That little jaunt reinforced Mdu's belief that he was simply not like everyone else.

He had known this from a young age. Mdu had always thought himself extraordinary, different in the best possible way. His parents encouraged him, strongly, to realise his potential, and he did not disappoint. Intelligent, and raised to believe that you define yourself by your achievements, Mdu was quirky and popular; a Golden Child.

Everyone wanted to be friends with the boy whose path to the future was straight and true, without any of the usual kinks, dead ends and delays normally caused by construction en route to adulthood.

His mom and dad scratched around second-hand bookstores and garage sales to find him every single edition of the *Guinness World Records* (from his birth year on), painstakingly reading through them before handing them over to Mdu, marking certain pages with helpful comments like, *Not particularly impressive,* and, *You could do this!*

In spite of himself, Mdu grew to love reading the *Guinness World Records,* and imagined himself on every page. Well, almost every page – the Animal and Plant Kingdoms, World Structures and Natural Phenomena were a little beyond him as a teen, but everything else was fair game.

In fact, some of those world-renowned records were such fair game that Mdu didn't even deign to imagine breaking them. There was an inherent flaw, as far as he was concerned; a number of loser ways of getting in, easy options that afforded the same fame and recognition without any effort.

Like the heaviest man in the world.

The longest moustache.

The most prolonged coma.

Please. Mdu spat on these vain attempts. He didn't even bother reading the Amazing Feats section. What was there to impress him in eating the most cockroaches in one minute (thirty-seven), the heaviest weight lifted by tongue (approximately twelve kilograms), the most live rattlesnakes held in the mouth (nine, but only for a measly thirteen-and-a-half seconds)?

Some records inspired not only scorn in Mdu, but anger.

The longest ear hair! (fourteen centimetres.)

The most body piercings! (seven-hundred-and-forty-six needles.)

The oldest male stripper! Some sixty-four-year-old geezer starts stripping to get in shape after recovering from prostate cancer, and they expect Mdu to applaud?

Not a chance.

Now, three-hundred-and-eighty-two days without any food, that was pretty impressive. Staying married for 86 years – well, Mdu could appreciate the skill in that. Even being buried alive for 100 days was no mean feat.

Mdu took to scribbling his own fantasised achievements on various pages in blue ink.

He was determined to be in the *Guinness World Records* by age twenty-five. Nothing would stand in his way.

At least, not until adolescence hit.

All of a sudden, Mdu felt constrained and trapped in his Golden Child Suit, which had not been altered since childhood. He was the cake of success that dissatisfied people ate to make themselves feel better, the heady sugar rush that made them forget their petty, ordinary lives, the secret indulgence that made it all seem okay.

Everyone wanted a slice of him – his friends, schoolmates, teachers, parents – even his parents' friends. Everybody fed off Mdu's success. And it had started to piss him off. Arbitrary people, who should have had nothing to do with his life, took inordinate interest in everything he did, and before long the enormous weight of carrying the hopes of the pharmacist's assistant and the preschool teacher and the doctor's wife and the check-out girl and the garbage man and the hobo and the entire staff of the Durban Municipal Library, began crushing Mdu, inch by painful inch. Everywhere he went he was expected to give a progress report on his various activities, while his mom stood by, smiling serenely, looking unsurprised as people oohed and aahed and said, 'I don't know how you do it all, Mdu!'

For a while, more out of habit and a vague sense of responsibility than anything else, he continued getting straight A's, playing first team in all school sports, acting the lead role in school plays, and consistently being awarded Best Speaker at public speaking competitions.

But then one day.

One day, Mdu woke up and shook it all out of the window. All the acclaim, all the praise, all the awards, all the labels that had nothing to do with who he was, and everything to do with who other people thought he should be. Mdu set them free, with a polite bow. He stopped being diligent, quit all of his extramurals and took to spending large amounts of time alone in his room, listening to loud music through his headphones.

He liked Nirvana. And Guns 'N Roses. He walked around with his hands in his pockets, singing, 'I used to love her, ooh yeah, but I had to kill her,' softly under his breath.

His parents, in panicked despair, sent him to a psychologist, forced him to go for drug tests and eventually decided to stage an intervention. They invited the pharmacist's assistant and the preschool teacher and the doctor's wife and the check-out girl and the garbage man and the hobo and the entire staff of the Durban Municipal Library over for tea, to try to talk some sense into him, but Mdu, although polite, was not swayed.

For a short while after, Mdu's parents continued heaping their expectations on him, piling them up like blankets on a summer's night. But Mdu no longer accepted his parents' vision for his life. He simply shrugged free from the blankets and disappeared into the night.

And so his parents resigned themselves to this new, less loveable child, comforted by the assurance that they had tried everything (except actually speaking to their son). They wrapped up their dream of a vicariously satisfying life in gold tissue paper, put it away in their cupboard, and started growing old.

[Aisha]

Aisha woke up flattened by the weight of her dreams. They lay on top of her, worn out after their night's adventures, trying to get some rest. As Aisha climbed out of bed, they too climbed out, clinging to her skin like oil to the surface of water.

Most of us, let's be honest, are rather impatient with dreams and portents and all that gobbledygook. Give us a horoscope that says something good about our love-lives and we're happy, but don't bother us with funny feelings and lingering fantasies and half-remembered omens. Most of us deny our dreams, dismissing them as soon as we wake up.

Aisha was not like most of us. She welcomed her dreams, invited them in, offered them a cup of tea. They were her chosen daily companions. For Aisha, living in her dreams felt like living in a fairy tale, the perfect way to avoid reality.

She was not always so accommodating. When her dreams first started to linger, she had tried everything to annul them, concerned that her over-active subconscious revealed something disturbing about her. Nothing worked: sleeping pills only made the dreams brighter, dagga – which was supposed to guarantee dreamless sleep – instead flavoured them with a soft peacefulness, staying awake simply caused them to visit her during day-light hours.

In desperation, Aisha had even taken an old woman's advice and slept with a dead fish in her arms – the coldness of the fish was supposed to chase away the dreaming unreality – but alas, she ended up chasing hordes of neighbourhood cats yowling at her door in the morning. The dreams grumbled softly at the noise, rolled over and went back to sleep.

So, finally, she accepted them. They became a new kind of reality, a slightly-less-real reality.

Isn't it often that way? Those things we feel we cannot change become a way of life, burglar guards around our lives that separate us from what's out there.

Aisha was quite happy to be disconnected from reality. She lived alone, in a newly built block of flats on reclaimed land – it used to be a tree-filled, empty space where squatters set up holiday homes, and where (apparently) a family of small duiker lived with the local monkeys and a few meerkats. That had all been razed to make way for the development.

Aisha sometimes felt tenant's guilt.

Her one-bedroom home was somehow always messy. A few cacti bloomed quietly in ceramic pots, and a painting of a whale hung over her bed. There were no photos, no knick-knacks, no mismatched sentimen-tal bits of junk, but still it looked ... neglected. Piles of junk mail spilled from the kitchen table – take-away menus and adverts for beauty salons rubbing shoulders with fake credit-card offers – forming a mound of rejection on the floor. There seemed to be too much stuff for one little flat to contain, as if she had no filter to help her decide what should be kept, and what should be thrown away. Dishes, with a bite or two of last week's dinner, lay forgotten next to chairs in the lounge and bedroom, waiting patiently to be scraped and cleaned. Half-eaten apples adorned her kitchen counter top and bedside table, slowly giving up hope that they would ever be eaten.

It was not that Aisha did not care about her home; she simply didn't notice.

Her mind was otherwise occupied.

She'd have liked to spend more time in the garden, but all twenty-six flats shared it, and the thought of neighbourly chitchat kept her cocooned in her flat. Her small veranda jutted out over the communal garden, and was home to a white plastic chair and a small table. The bricks laid into the floor retained the heat of the sun long into the evening. It was Aisha's favourite spot, the one place where the world quietened down and she could breathe freely.

Every segment of her daily life had been fitted carefully to form a cohesive puzzle – and yet. That was as far as Aisha's reasoning ever reached.

And yet. For no matter how meticulously her life had been assembled, the fact remained that something was missing, and it bothered her like a mild toothache – possible to ignore, but acutely worrying. There wasn't anything wrong, just something out of tune; only it had been out of tune so long that Aisha couldn't even remember the melody. And instead of facing the problem head-on – going to therapy, taking a pottery class, joining one of Durban's many activity clubs, listening to motivational CDs – she chose to step even further away from reality. It was easy enough to do; nobody stood in her way. She had a straight line to follow each day: walk to work, past Handy Green Grocers to buy lunch. Work. Walk home from work, past Handy Green Grocers to buy dinner. Home.

It was a risk-free tightrope, not even an inch from the ground.

Aisha felt happiest in a routine; it provided less opportunities for her dreams to intrude and cause a scene. And so each day passed in the same way. She always bought the same thing for lunch (two-minute noodles, a granadilla Yogi Sip, an apple), always bought the same thing for dinner (Rice-A-Roni, vegetables, chocolate milk). She smiled instead of responding to the cashier's friendly questions – 'Do you work near here?', 'Oh my! Did you see that hot guy over by the bananas?', 'Would you like a plastic bag?' – and, after a while, the questions dried up.

Aisha walked to and from work in a daze, not noticing the men whose eyes followed her when she passed them, not noticing the piles of garbage reeking in the summer sun, not noticing the air of shocked stillness one morning when she walked into Handy Green Grocers, stepping over the mess of tomato sauce spilled on the floor, past the collapsed display of Koo baked beans.

She had chosen to retreat from the world of noticing.

Her daily work was perfectly suited to this choice. It required no human contact at all; all Aisha had to do was type.

So that was what she did, in the long stifling days of that near-unbearable summer. Like a shadow stubbornly following one step behind, Aisha typed and typed and typed, following each word with the next until they were all used up.

And then she went home.

It felt a bit like living under water.

[Meryl]

Experts and scientists claimed the intense heat was due to global warming. Frankly, Meryl didn't care. It was the hottest day Durban had ever known, and she hated heat. Hated, too, that every day for the past week she had been woken by her heart pounding and her palms sweating.

It was always the exact same dream – back in Handy Green Grocers, when the two guys in hoodies burst into the shop. But instead of falling down as instructed, she turned her back and tried to hide behind the display of tinned beans. When the tins fell, as they had in real life, one of the startled men fired a gun in her direction. She could feel the bullet burning into her back as it hit her squarely between the shoulder blades. In that moment she woke up, gasping.

Her girlfriend Edna slept through all of this; never noticed anything.

With a disgruntled sigh, Meryl pulled the sheet over her head to block out the sunshine. Ten seconds later, she pulled it down again. Meryl had an intense fear of suffocation. She breathed deeply – in and out, in and out – then turned to lie on her back. Lying on her side her lungs felt squashed, which made it hard to breathe.

She had not always been afraid of suffocating, only in the last few years, since her corset of cynicism had developed. It was a bizarre condition, a self-chosen disability. It tightened her in every way; kept her hair shinier, her skin smoother, her expression more inscrutable. Emotions of all kinds bounced off Meryl without a trace; she retaliated to niceness in any disguise with blistering scorn.

Meryl felt exhausted, tired before the day had even begun.

It was those bloody nightmares, she thought, straining to breathe against her laced and knotted cynicism. They'd woken her up every night since the robbery. In fact, she couldn't remember the last time she'd slept through till morning – before the robbery nightmares, it was fearing that she might suffocate on her pillow that used to wake her up, gasping. Edna had not once woken up with her during one of these episodes; Meryl couldn't understand how someone could sleep through a panic attack happening right next to them.

Unlike Edna, she was a light sleeper who stirred at the slightest noise. It was a family trait – when Meryl was six, she started sharing a room with her brother Joe, and he woke up as frequently as she did.

'Let's talk,' Joe would say, and then not have the faintest idea what to talk about.

They would lie in the dark, making up stories until they fell asleep again.

They shared a room until Meryl turned ten, when she moved to her own room next to his. Sometimes, when she woke in the middle of the night, she would knock on the wall separating her room from Joe's. If he was awake (as he always seemed to be) he would slip into her room and lie at the foot of her bed, filling the room with his soft breathing. They repeated an old, familiar bed-time rhyme to each other before falling asleep: 'Good night, sleep tight, don't let the bed-bugs bite!'

'Love you!' she would always call out after a short silence.

The rhythm of those words echoed in Meryl's head as she tossed and turned.

Joe was the one person she had thought she could always depend on, any time of the day or night. But when her mother was dying and she needed him most, her brother decided he couldn't handle it, and moved to London. He sent her emails about all the bands he was watching, and about how easy it was to travel over there. Meryl read them and did not reply, resentment forming a barrier she could not imagine ever breaking down.

Meryl turned over onto her side again, hoping her exaggerated movement would wake Edna.

It didn't.

She knew that thoughts of Joe would not help her get back to sleep – they'd only cause her freckles to disappear. Meryl's mom had always been able to gauge her daughter's distress by the absence or presence of her freckles. Her face was usually chocolate-chipped with them, but when things upset or frustrated her, they faded dramatically, making her look pale and wan.

Meryl was more and more frequently looking like an insipid porcelain doll. It pissed her off.

☼

But Meryl had not always been this way.

Three and a half years earlier, Meryl's mom had been diagnosed with a brain tumour, and the cancer quickly spread. Meryl did not smile once for over half a year. They were inseparable, right up until her death – two olives in a martini – and Meryl missed her with a constant ache just beneath her heart.

The smell of the hospital – illness, medicine, overcooked food, blood, flowers, false hope – had haunted her all these years.

Once a week Meryl would wake in the middle of the night, heart pounding and gasping for breath, fearing that she was back at those cold doors. Only this time, they wouldn't open for her, and remained stubbornly shut, keeping her away from her mom. She pounded on the thick glass, imploring the nurses and doctors to let her in, but they just stared at her, uncomprehending.

It was just horrible. That was the only way she could describe it. Made worse by the fact that her father, who had always been a strong man, fell apart completely when his wife first fell ill. So, as well as tending to her mother, who asked (daily) where her son and husband were, Meryl had to look after him as well. He needed help with the simplest things: eating, washing, getting dressed, putting his socks on. It was as if his wife was the light that helped make sense of his world, and once she was gone, he couldn't see anything anymore.

Meryl, barely able to cope with her mother dying, lost all respect for her father and her brother, and soon afterwards, for all men. Meryl's boy-friend at the time didn't know how to handle her violent mood swings. One day she would come to him crying and wanting to be consoled; the next, she would be raging, furious at anything and everything – from the crappy service at the coffee shop to the ceaseless rain (that fell that year for nearly three weeks without stopping) to his futile attempts at calming her down.

Some days she would call him eight or ten times, just wanting to hear his voice, just wanting him to tell her everything would be all right; on others she would yell at him if he called her even once, not wanting to be disturbed, and just needing space.

One day she would look at him and see their future in his eyes; the next day she could not see past the clouds of anguish in her own.

To his credit, he tried. He supported, he consoled, he didn't fight back; he was understanding and sweet and steadfast.

Meryl despised him for it.

It was almost as if she was trying to drive him away, and once she succeeded, she felt her point had been proven about the incompetency of men.

It was during this traumatic six-month period that Meryl's cynicism was born, and burgeoned with such ferocity. Her freckles went on holiday, and did not return for almost a year.

By the time her mother died – a day just like any other, except that when Meryl walked away to fetch her customary cup of tea from the vending machine, she walked back into a room silent and breathless – she was hardened and unhurtable, or so she thought.

It was as if her heart had become a record player that got stuck on all the hurt, unable to play past it. And the more she focused on the hurt, the more it showed up for her.

※ ※ ※

What you expect of the world is what you see of it, each and every day.

It is possible that Meryl accidentally left a chunk of her heart in the hospital that day. Thereafter, every time someone managed to hurt her, she added another layer to her corset, until, by the hottest day Durban had ever known, it was thick and flawless.

If you think about it, though, don't we all walk around with thinly disguised armour? We hide behind our jobs, our partners, our reputations, our ability to make jokes, our circle of friends, our stylish clothes, our effervescent friendliness.

Behind anything that can hide the person we really are.

Meryl merely allowed her armour to thicken and knot by feeding it shovels of disdain every moment of every hour of every day

[Harry]

Harry lived in constant fear of someone knocking loudly on his front door.

What began, for him, as an amusing distraction, quickly grew into an almost frightening obsession, and the thought of his carefully constructed reality being crushed by that abomination called 'real life' made bile rise in his throat.

Harry was quick to defend his chosen quirk – only eating green food – to anyone he could convince to listen, arguing that it displayed a level of patriotism to his ancestral Ireland that few modern-day Irishmen shared. He was proud to point out that although at first he only intended keeping it up for St Patrick's Day, nineteen months had passed, and he showed no sign of stopping.

Harry was not Irish.

His great-grandfather on one side was, but Harry was undeniably, genetically, South African. Afrikaans, in fact. Still, in a country whose motto was *The Rainbow Nation*, he couldn't very well eat foods of all colours, now could he? That would be too easy. So Harry decided, as a pledge to his great-grandfather, for Ireland, to eat only green food.

The point? According to Harry, the Guinness World Records would be clamouring for an interview any day now. They should be – he had sent them enthusiastic letters every month since March, in the hopes that he alone was committed (read: imbalanced) enough to attempt limiting his diet to only green-pigmented foods.

It was not necessary to send letters, enthusiastic or otherwise, every month. In fact, it was only necessary to submit *one* application, as Harry was reminded each time he sent another letter. They assured him that if the Guinness

Book adjudicators thought his claim was suitable, they would draw up the necessary guidelines to establish a new record category. Harry knew all this; knew it off by heart, in fact.

But he persisted.

Persistence was one of his best friends.

☼

After the first month of eating only green food, young Harry felt violently ill.

No great surprise there.

The only green foods he could think of were fresh leafy vegetables and Granny Smith apples, a diet that soon turned his bowels into an active volcano. Besides, there were only so many ways to disguise Granny Smith apples – chopped up on a bed of lettuce, cooked in a pot of spinach, stuffed with broccoli and then baked. Before long, Harry's stomach started turning at the faintest whiff of a Granny Smith, and his Master Plan seemed short-lived.

But then he discovered jalapeno bread (conveniently a brilliant lime green colour) and hit upon the trick of adding whole limes to anything he cooked, giving most foods a greenish tinge. Beef was tricky to disguise. Sadly, Harry went a bit overboard on the lime-flavoured ice cream one sunny Saturday afternoon, resulting in a nasty puking episode that led him to believe limes were part of his Allergic Foodstuffs List (along with peas and gherkins, other green foods which he could unfortunately not eat).

Still, there were always beans and lettuce and green olives, spinach and cabbage and broccoli, unripe fruit of any description, green peppers and green tea.

He never stooped to tasting grass.

But the problem with all of these foods, as Harry all too soon discovered, was that none of them were carbohydrates. In the absence of potatoes, rice, pasta, couscous, bread (other than jalapeno) and any manner of other assorted starches, Harry found himself constantly hungry. He was eating vegetables all day, all night, having to stuff a Tupperware of green bean stew in his overalls so he could snack on it during work, waking up in the middle of the night for a bite of broccoli sans cheese sauce.

This gnawing problem consumed him until late one night, lying in bed and thinking longingly of creamy mashed potatoes, basmati rice, freshly baked bread – anything that would fill the gaping hole in his stomach – he finally dreamt up a solution: green food dye! Of course! It was genius. There was nothing in the *Guinness World Records* that said that his green food had to be naturally green (indeed, there was, as yet, nothing in it about green food at all).

The very next morning Harry rushed out and bought a small bottle of green food dye. By the end of the following day he had used it up, gorging himself on green spaghetti, green rice, green mashed potatoes and green white bread.

Harry's fear of someone knocking loudly on his front door was not due to hyper-hearing sensitivity, but in fact due to the disgraceful fact that Harry possessed an abnormally large stash of green food colouring (to rival any drug dealer's secret hoard). He used it each time he ate.

Were the Guinness World Records crew to come a-snooping (and each day he nervously hoped they would), they would be horrified. More importantly, Harry believed he would be disqualified. And rightly so. Although the rules didn't explicitly say that dyeing one's food was prohibited, Harry suspected that the sticklers from Guiness World Records would not approve of such a loose interpretation of 'green food'. Still, he wasn't quite ready to ditch the food colouring, so he lived each day in mild fear that they would discover his dirty secret and nineteen months of culinary repression would be flushed down the drain. Hence the blow-up swimming pool in his backyard, ostensibly disused and mouldy, but actually a convenient green hue so that were, say, large quantities of green food colouring to be dumped in it, no one would be the wiser.

Harry found the swimming pool at the dump. It was in good condition, apart from the few rips and tears that Harry had patched up with masking tape, and was one of the better finds from that month's shopping spree. Harry had cleaned it up well.

Cleaning things up was his vocation in life, initiated by a remarkable gift that Harry thanked his Lucky Stars for each and every day. He had been born with a curious smell that attracted broken things to him like a magnet. It wasn't a discernable smell – he didn't reek or stink or hum, he wasn't particularly malodorous or fetid – he just had an odour that broken things responded to; an olfactory dog whistle for the conked-out things of this world.

As a child, this dubious gift had been quite a health hazard. Walking to school on garbage day, Harry led a Pied Piperesque trail of broken appliances, cracked crockery and smashed toys. It looked as if he'd tied a string around the broken goods, and then attached the string to his shoes; a long line of useless items following him like ducklings follow their mother.

Broken glass was a problem.

So were broken dreams.

One particularly spiteful little boy, observing Harry's curious affinity for damaged goods (and not knowing it was the damaged goods who felt an affinity for Harry), nicknamed him Junky Monkey. The more Harry tried to explain that there was nothing he could do about all the broken things following him, the more his classmates taunted him, leaping around scratching their armpits, making 'ooh-ooh, aah-aah!' noises while throwing their rubbish at him.

The rubbish clung.

For a while, Harry tried wearing his father's strong cologne to hide his natural smell. But when the bullies at school started calling him Funky Monkey, and the broken things still trailed him – albeit a little uncertainly – Harry decided he had no choice but to accept his peculiar affliction. Eventually, he stopped feeling ashamed, and started picking out one or two treasures to fix up with his dad's help.

There were other side effects, of course, for Harry's smell attracted not only broken junk, but also broken people. Unhappy housewives on the verge of nervous breakdowns, junkies whose lives had shattered like misplaced wine bottles, young girls with ruined self-esteems, aspiring artists whose dreams had turned to dust and shambles, jilted lovers, estranged fathers, faithless priests, confused souls of all ages with split personality disorders – they were all drawn to Harry like hungry children to a bakery window; like flies to spoilt food.

☀ ☀ ☀

And really, isn't it true that there is something broken in all of us? If not a broken dream, then a broken heart, a shattered self-esteem, a not-quite-whole belief in our potential.

☼ ☼ ☼

These broken people approached Harry everywhere: on the street, in the shops, as he left school every afternoon, at the public swimming pool and even in the bathrooms at the cinema. Looking slightly befuddled, these damaged souls would wander towards him, shake his hand and say hello, and then hover nearby until he walked away.

From a very young age, Harry recognised that everyone just wanted to be loved; everyone was just trying their best, muddling along, waiting for someone to give them a secret thumbs-up or a small little nod to let them know they were doing okay. He tried to give that thumbs-up whenever he could; he always had a kind word and a look of recognition in his eyes that made these lost souls feel, somehow, that maybe one day they would manage to piece themselves back together again.

Harry's gift led him (naturally) to a job as a garbage man.

Of course.

Every morning he woke at 4 am, donned his green overalls and set out for the Durban Municipal Dump, the largest dump in the city. More specifically, Harry set out for the Durban Solid Waste (DSW) headquarters – aka the Pit Stop.

He was a pro at his work. While other garbage men spent their days nursing premature hernias, heaving heavy bags and boxes, running back and forth from the pavement to the van, Harry merely stood on the lip of the truck and waited for the garbage to come to him. All it took was one cracked mug, or a single shard of glass, to propel entire bags towards Harry, the broken goods perhaps recognising the affinity he had for wreckage, something in his smell that gave them hope.

Most of us discard things at the first sign of damage, unwilling to accept any imperfection.

Harry welcomed them all.

 and

Beth and Pravesh decided on dinner as the most sensible choice for a first date – it allowed time for talking and getting to know each other, but if awkward silences showed up uninvited (as they were wont to do) food would fill the gap until they could think of something to say.

Pravesh's favourite place was the Roma Revolving Restaurant, an old-fashioned Italian eatery with waiters in starched uniforms, where the gentle murmur of muted conversation perfectly intertwined with the subtle strains of a lone violinist. The funereal ambience made him feel at home.

Beth's favourite was Rowdy Ranchers, a busy steakhouse where the waiters dressed in cowboy outfits, and shouted their orders across the restaurant to the kitchen.

❁ ❁ ❁

At first glance this may not look like a successful recipe for love. *Why even continue?* I hear you ask. *Why bother?* They're clearly ill-suited, they don't have anything in common, and it's just going to end in tears – destined to be another random relationship that both parties will try to forget about in six months. One of those where you see the person and pretend otherwise, so you don't have to stop and talk to them or smile wanly while trying to think of something to say.

But (luckily for this story) it is not up to us.

❁ ❁ ❁

On that hottest night following the hottest day in Durban's history, Beth and Pravesh decided to take a risk. As yet, a small risk, but any situation that involves the heart has the potential to turn Risky with a capital R. And besides, something entirely unplotted and heartfelt had drawn these two towards each other – Beth knew that somehow Pravesh wouldn't be one of those guys, and Pravesh was tired of playing dead.

Pravesh never thought it would happen. Playing dead had, for such a long time, seemed like the most logical choice in life. Not that he had never dated or interacted with people. On the contrary, in his early-to-mid twenties he had gone out with a string of timid, pretty Indian girls (mostly his parents' friends' daughters). But they'd bored him. Either they hadn't had anything worthwhile to say, and therefore chattered inanely about nothing, or they'd been *too* opinionated, and always wanted to argue. And none of them, not even a single one, had even vaguely sped up his heart rate and ignited his death sensor.

31

This might seem unsurprising to you; Pravesh found it disappointing.

Eventually, he decided that people – and girlfriends in particular – were a waste of energy, an infringement on his personal space. But television (which *always* used to fill the gap) just wasn't rising to the occasion anymore. Even though there were shows for every occasion – comedies, dramas, horror, porn, documentaries, mysteries, soapies – and even though they were unemotional, dependable, and, unlike a girlfriend, could be watched on mute, Pravesh felt that something was missing.

☼

'So, do you watch much TV?' Pravesh asked as they drove to the restaurant, holding his breath hopefully.

'Well, no, not really,' Beth answered carefully, trying to gauge his feelings on the matter.

'Oh.' He paused. 'I like it. No matter how you feel, there's a show to match your mood.'

'Well, ye-e-es, I suppose. But, you know, my yoga teacher firmly believes that television is the number one cause of divorce, and directly related to the dreadful rate of relationship failure within the first two months,' Beth announced confidently, then listened to the echo of her words.

Pravesh was listening to the echo too.

A brief but significant silence followed, while both parties contemplated the chances of this relationship, above all others, lasting.

In the curtained containment of the hearse it seemed possible.

☼

Once they were seated in a booth at Rowdy Ranchers (he was a gentleman, and naturally deferred to the lady's choice) and had ordered a Loud 'n Proud 100% beef burger and onion rings for her, a Weeny Greeny salad for him (dealing with dead bodies tends to make one vegetarian), there was another brief silence.

Awkwardly, Beth and Pravesh stared around the restaurant. The decor was a strange combination of tacky cowboy paraphernalia and dim, oppressive lighting. Cowboy hats masquerading as lampshades hung low over each table, and furry cut-outs of horses galloped along the walls, desperate to get out. But instead of bright, synthetic lighting (to accompany the bright, synthetic decor) Rowdy Ranchers had invested in low-watt bulbs, which gave the place an uncomfortably claustrophobic edge. The air felt cloyingly thick, heavy with the smell of greasy chips-and-steak, and sodden with sweat from that day's unbearable heat.

Pravesh's eyes smarted from the cigarette smoke that hung like BO around their table. The greasy smell of cooking reminded him of his mother, and he felt his throat close up, suddenly worried that he wouldn't be able to swallow in front of Beth.

For the next few moments Beth and Pravesh surreptitiously checked each other out.

He was a handsome man, Beth thought, though not in the conventional sense. As he was the first Indian man she had ever dated, she felt ill-equipped to weigh him up against her other boyfriends, but he had lovely, thick black hair, and warm brown eyes. Although a little on the slim side, he was neat and well-groomed and tucked his shirt in, which was an excellent indication of character. She also liked the way his nostrils flared a little when he smiled.

As far as Pravesh could tell, Beth looked like a nice girl. She had mousy brown hair, tied back in a ponytail with a yellow scrunchie, and was wearing a lot of make-up – he had never been a fan of blue eyeshadow – but other than that she looked pleasant. He had not been on a date in years, and found the whole experience strangely exhilarating.

Perhaps it was time to grow up a little. Find a mate. Continue the species and all that.

Of course, the biggest turn-on was under the table. When he had picked her up earlier that evening, Pravesh noticed with a thrill that Beth was wearing open-toed shoes, and that her toenails were painted bright red.

Pravesh loved toenails.

After a few moments, Silence made its presence felt – sitting in the centre of the table, blushing furiously and chewing on its thumbnail. This was the moment of reckoning. Pravesh and Beth had decided to venture out on this date, had mutually agreed that there was a better than average chance that they would like each other, and now they had to face the music (which, in true Rowdy Ranchers style, was loud and discordant).

While on a date, Beth always felt a flash of fear at this point. Not, as you might imagine, from social anxiety, but rather from too many horror stories told to her when she was young and unattractive.

'You can't just say yes when a man asks you out,' her mother had warned a chubby, spotty Beth with no hope of a date for at least a few years. 'What if he's an axe murderer? He takes you to a nice restaurant, you sit down at the table, there's a slight pause … and then, *boom*! He's slammed an axe into your chest. You're dog food. Dead.'

Her mother was perhaps the slightest bit disturbed, Beth admitted.

Pravesh cleared his throat, releasing Beth from her bloody reverie of axes and hungry dogs.

'So,' he said hesitantly, toying with the large carnivorous steak knife that dominated the place setting, 'do you have any hobbies?'

Momentarily transfixed by the sight of an undertaker playing with a large knife, Beth took her time answering.

'Oh, well, yes, yes I do. I uhhmm … I like watching movies, and social-ising … I do yoga once a week.'

Those were safe, generic, characterless answers. Beth paused, evaluating exactly how much she could reveal to him so early in the evening.

Perhaps it was because he laid down the knife to listen to her that Beth softened.

'To be honest, I really only have one hobby … it's my passion. It's kind of dorky, so don't laugh. I usually don't tell someone until I know them better,' she said with a shy smile, leaning forward conspiratorially.

Glancing down, Beth took a deep breath and blurted out, 'I *love* lawn bowling.'

☼ ☼ ☼

Now, much as we all like to pretend we're not judgemental, and that we don't draw up a list of pros and cons during the very first conversation to decide whether a person is worthwhile or not, let us be honest. We do. Most first-date conversations are landmined with these challenges. Should a potential lover reveal a passion for scuba diving, for example, we are more likely to give them our special date eyes than if their passion turns out to be the lesser-understood art of killing small buck.

Or lawn bowling.

The delicate subtleties of date language – staring at the lips, leaning in closer than necessary, laughing when a mere smile would suffice – are reserved for those who pass certain tests. This made Beth's confession, by any dating standards, a bold move.

Luckily, a move that Pravesh appreciated.

☼ ☼ ☼

Pravesh's nostrils flared appreciatively.

There are few hobbies as quiet and calm as lawn bowling, and even fewer that involve people so close to death. Both of these won Pravesh's instant approval. Without meaning to, he broke into a wide grin and nodded vigorously. As far as he knew, not many young people chose to play bowls, and the fact that Beth was spending time in the company of so many near-dead every week just made her more attractive.

This unexpected response to her secret pastime filled Beth with a deep sense of satisfaction; here was someone who could love her for who she really was – not some tamer version, but the real Beth Ann Walters.

All pretences of playing it cool were cast aside.

'Have you ever played?' Beth ventured hopefully, and before Pravesh could reply, she started gushing. 'It really is the most super game, so relaxing, and a lot more challenging than you might think. And of course, the people I play with are marvellous! Most of them are old dears from Fading Roses, the old-age home down the road? And they are just super. Old people have so much time for each other, and they really listen when you talk. And even when they're partly deaf, they *pretend* so well, that it feels like they're listening? I have some of my best times with those folks. And the clothes we wear! It's a hoot. We have to wear all white, right? But instead of just wearing a skirt and a shirt, I usually dress it up a little. Fake fur, feathers, sequins, that kind of thing, you know? And you get to choose some *outrageous* hats if you want to. It's like a whole different world. The Lawn Bowling World. It's really something special, Pravesh ...'

And so she nattered on, and on, and on.

Beth talked through her enormous medium-rare hamburger, and his wilted lettuce salad (which made his knees tingle and his ears burn; the lettuce had been dead a long time). She talked all the way through her Death by Chocolate cake, and his surprisingly flamboyant choice of a Pardner's Pie, which came in a miniature pastry cowboy's hat, and required the waiter to shoot caramel sauce into it with a water pistol.

Beth talked like a tape on fast forward. Pravesh liked her pleasant, lilting voice; it sometimes went up at the end of sentences, changing mere statements into questions, causing ordinary words to sound like poetry. Pravesh couldn't be sure, but he thought he saw Beth floating slightly off her chair when she spoke about the beauties of lawn bowling, and how it had changed her life.

He wrote it off as a trick of light, and carried on listening.

If someone had initiated a worldwide Good Listener Award, and lined up Catholic priests in their confession boxes, Buddhist monks who had taken vows of silence, sweetly smiling mutes with thirsty ears, and young mothers waiting anxiously for their babies' first words, Pravesh would have beaten them all. He listened as only an undertaker can. He didn't need to interject, or tell his stories, or make his point of view known; he was simply content to absorb all there was of Beth, soaking up her stories like a sponge in a pool of vodka. Pravesh found her candour intoxicating; listening to her felt strangely voyeuristic, like watching an episode of reality TV. She had no filter, no sense of how much was too much information.

Over the years, Pravesh's daily diet of soapies and sitcoms had convinced him that dating was akin to being dangled over a pit of hungry crocodiles. *Au contraire*, he thought, smiling at Beth chatting away, all he had to do was sit and listen.

Easy peasy.

Beth suddenly laughed.

'My mom used to tell me that going to discos was dangerous, because one second you're dancing, and the next the DJ goes crazy from over-exposure to too many flashing lights, and starts throwing records like knives. If one hits you on the neck, it'll slice your jugular vein wide open.'

She shook her head, and mimicked her mother's voice. '*And then, you're dead.* That's how all my mom's stories ended … *and then, you're dead.*'

Pravesh felt a warm glow spread from where he imagined his sleeping heart lay.

Even though her mother had raised Beth on a diet of warnings and old wives' tales (the dog-meat date being only one of many), her childhood had been happy. She was one of five – two brothers and two sisters – and they were an extremely close and expressive family.

School was a bit of a shock, though, because up until then Beth had assumed that everyone was as affectionate and loving as her family. That she was clearly mistaken, she found out within five minutes of entering the school building, when she ran to hug her chubbily cheerful teacher. All the other little boys and girls, nervously looking for some distraction, started chanting, 'Teacher's pet, Teacher's pet, what a wet, you teacher's pet!' Actually, only one or two children started the chanting – those who had older siblings and knew what a teacher's pet *was* – but all the others joined in with gusto, eager to learn the joys of being one of the sheep.

Added to the difficulties that all young children experience when adjusting to school, was Beth's Condition.

'The doctors still aren't exactly sure what it is?' she explained to Pravesh in her lilting way. 'And it's completely harmless if I keep it under control, just a little embarrassing, you know?'

Beth bit her lip. She took a big gulp of white wine. She had secrets leaking from every pore.

'I, ahmm … I have a tendency to float,' she said softly.

'You float?' Pravesh was understandably confused.

'Well, yes. Since I was born – only I suppose nobody noticed till I started walking? Whenever I feel really happy, my feet leave the ground and hang in mid-air, only about an inch or so, but still. It's wildly embarrassing. As long as I keep focused, it doesn't happen, but as soon as I start feeling that giddy, light, happy feeling, I, well, I float? Just a little,' she amended hastily. 'Of course, all the kids at school thought it was hilarious. They called me Beth the Blimp. That always brought me back to earth with a bump. It wasn't very nice.' She took another gulp of wine and sighed.

☼ ☼ ☼

In some ways, Beth was luckier than most. So often we walk around holding our breath, crossing our fingers, waiting for some bolt of happiness to strike us so that we know: *Okay! This is how it feels.*

Beth simply floats. No doubting that.

❋ ❋ ❋

As first dates go – usually an exchange of stories, likes and dislikes, witty comments and little snippets of endearing information – Pravesh and Beth's First Date was doubtlessly atypical. It was none of the above. Or rather, it was all of the above, but from an entirely one-sided point of view.

By 10 pm, Pravesh knew almost all there was to know about Beth. But eventually, she stopped talking. When the bill had come and gone, and they were both sitting at the empty table, having ploughed through starters, mains, desserts and coffee, and when the waiters had cleaned up the rest of the tables and were standing, yawning, by the door, Beth guessed that maybe the time had come to say goodnight. However, because of the in-depth nature of her storytelling, they had only reached age seven.

Reluctant to let such an avid listener out of her grasp, Beth carried on chattering as they walked out.

'You know, Handy Green Grocers was held up a week ago?' she said, followed by three of Pravesh's favourite words: 'I nearly died.'

He stopped, and looked at Beth intently. She dropped her voice to a husky whisper and leaned in closer to him, her eyes round and wide as she recounted the story.

'These two men burst in with guns, and threatened me while I emptied the cash register. They held a gun to my head … I thought they were going to kill me. It was the most terrifying moment of my life.'

Then she fell silent, lost in the memory that haunted her far more than she would ever let on.

Beth had nearly died. No wonder he was attracted to her! Pravesh was aware of his knees feeling unusually tingly around her, but up until that moment he had been unable to figure out what had set his radar off. He had sensed it while talking to Beth in the supermarket, but put it down to the rancid meat on sale there. Although it didn't feel as strong as an actual death, her near-death experience definitely explained the distinctive buzz he felt around her.

Unwilling to divulge anything more about the robbery, and not (quite) ready to talk about the recurring nightmares she had had every night since,

Beth kept her silence on the drive home, like a strange pet she didn't know how to hold.

☼

There was no second world in Durban, Pravesh mused while driving. The third world rubbed shoulders with the first, and wondered where it had gone wrong. The lines had always been clearly demarcated; the crushing throngs of people in the city giving way to the sterile peace of the suburbs. But over the years the city and the suburbs had been involved in a dogged tug-of-war. Streets that used to be good neighbourhoods to raise children in were now good neighbourhoods to buy drugs in, and areas that used to be high danger zones were being developed into high-income zones.

It was like a real-life game of Monopoly.

The city centre – with all its late-night shebeens, homeless people sleeping in cardboard boxes, rank alleyways, overflowing dustbins, hookers in skimpy eighties outfits, fried chicken take-outs, tiny flats and council houses with Nigerians sleeping ten to a room – crept closer to the suburbs each day.

The suburbs – with all their book clubs, afternoon teas, art exhibition openings, dinner parties and strolls around leafy blocks – lived in denial. Being there felt like visiting a different country.

For the duration of the fifteen-minute drive home, Beth distracted herself from thoughts of the robbery – the look of scorn on the dark-haired woman's face as she walked out the shop, the hopeless way the man by the grapes sank to the ground once the robbers had left – by wondering how to broach the topic of their hopefully soon second date. Her usual tactic was to blurt out a desperate, 'Can I see you again? Please?' but Eranie, the night-shift cashier at the supermarket, had told her that that wasn't the way to do it.

'Just wait, honey, just wait. He'll ask, but in his own time. You don't want to go scaring him off now, do you?'

No, thought Beth, that was exactly what she didn't want to do. She definitely did not want to scare Pravesh off. So she waited, pressing her fingernails harder and harder into the palms of her hands until they broke the skin, creating thin, red crescents that marked her palms and would not fade for months. She pretended to look out the window, nervously fantasising about their goodbye kiss, hoping there would be one, worrying that her mouth tasted like hamburger, wishing she had eaten a mint.

Pravesh, too, was staring out the window. He had been too nervous to pay much attention when he picked her up earlier, but saw now that Beth lived in a pleasant enough neighbourhood, in one of the used-to-be-nice streets almost in the right area of town. The scent of yesterday-today-and-tomorrow shrubs, planted en masse in family gardens a decade before, lingered even at this late hour, and lent the air a sweet hopefulness. Although the paint was peeling from most of the buildings in her street, and the heavy bass of kwaito music filled the air, it was still the kind of neighbourhood where people chatted, where children could play on the road.

Beth estimated that they were no more than forty-five seconds away from her gate when Pravesh burst the silence in the dark hearse by saying, 'I'd love to hear what happened to you when you were eight, if you wouldn't mind telling me.'

She was thrilled! She had passed the First Date Test! He liked her. Eranie was right – wait, and he'll ask. At the last minute (typical male!), but he'll ask.

'That would be *wonderful!*' she gushed. Despite trying to contain her enthusiasm, 'I did *sooo* enjoy this evening!' nevertheless slipped out.

'I did too, Beth. Very much,' Pravesh replied solemnly, as he pulled up to her gate, then strode around the car to open her door and help her out.

The house next to Beth's was graffitied with the outline of a falling man's body, three floors up. Pravesh turned his head to look at it properly, fascinated. Squinting at it, it looked like the silhouette of impending death. As he turned back to face Beth, there was a moment of breath-catching awkwardness before he quickly kissed her hand, jumped back into the car, and sped off.

Too late, Beth realised that they hadn't decided on a date for their next meeting, but she was too happy about the kiss on her hand to worry.

How gentlemanly! How chivalrous!

Truly, of all the men she had ever met, Pravesh was The One, her very own Prince Charming. On cloud nine, and with no plans to descend, Beth floated off to bed.

※

At 9 am the next morning, Beth was still floating, this time just above her high green chair, oblivious to the humidity that hovered around her like a swarm of mosquitoes; her feet suspended in the air, tied with a ribbon to a chair leg. She was busy scribbling in a notebook, absentmindedly sucking a strand of her mousy brown hair, a look of unadulterated bliss on her face. Her eyeshadow that morning was pale purple.

The radio was playing a song by the latest pop sensation, Candy K. Something about love and doves, and Beth hummed along, reliving Pravesh's kiss on her hand over and over in her mind. It almost felt like she'd imagined it, it was that romantic.

How was it possible to be this in love in just one day, Beth wondered happily, just as Pravesh tapped her on the shoulder politely.

She turned around, startled.

'Good uhm … morning, Beth,' ventured Pravesh, noticing her exposed toenails with a shiver of desire. 'I was wondering if we could uhm … maybe go for a drink this evening?' He swallowed noisily. 'So you can continue your story …'

Entirely unused to speaking more than a curt morning greeting so early in the day, he trailed off uncertainly.

Beth's heart rate trippled, and her stomach flipped. He was real! She hadn't imagined him! Her cheeks stretched into an involuntary grin.

'Of course!' she replied enthusiastically, 'I'd love to! Pick me up at eight-thirty?'

A brief moment of mutual, idiotic smiling followed, interrupted only by a customer waiting impatiently to pay for her low-fat, hi-protein, added-vitamins-and-minerals Bread of Life.

Beth couldn't help feeling that she had been given Pravesh at just the right time in her life. It had been difficult coming back to work at Handy Green Grocers after the robbery. For the first few days she had felt constantly on edge, short of breath and jumpy, and she had yelped (on more than one occasion) when men in hooded sweatshirts walked up to her. This

anxiety was exacerbated by the strange behaviour of one of the two customers who had been in the shop that day – the tall, dark, scowling man.
He kept walking up to the doors of the shop as if about to enter, then
turning around and hurrying away. He did this for three days in a row,
until Beth decided to have a word with him if he came to the door again.
Much as she wished she could pretend he was only returning to the scene
of the crime because he was in love with her, and didn't know how to
approach her, she couldn't deny the fact that his eyes were fixed, not on
her, but on the display of watermelons.

But then, on the fourth day, Pravesh pushed past him and asked her for
a date. Since then, all thoughts of violence had been chased away by thoughts
of love. She was rather grateful.

※ ※ ※

And sure, if we were in the mood to point fingers, we could say that Beth
chose to throw herself into that relationship so that she didn't have to
deal with the inevitable life-questioning that walks around hand-in-hand
with violent encounters. And if it was true that Pravesh had asked Beth
on a date because the seismic plates that his life had been resting on all
his life were finally shifting, forcing change, and not because he was
smitten with her, well, so be it.

Really, who are we to judge? We're all dealing with things the only way we
know how, muddling along like blindfolded clowns, trying to do our best.

With this point thoroughly clarified, even if only in our minds, and not
in Beth's or Pravesh's, let us move on.

※ ※ ※

That night they began a series of sweet and successful storytelling dates.
Beth generally covered two years in one date, and eagerly anticipated how
– in later months – they would be able to look back on their courtship as
a highly organised, and well-divided saga.

Ages 8 & 9:
Cocktails at the Blue Waters bar (Pravesh's choice).

A tiny place next to the beach, still decorated with the original seventies
furnishings, and with a bar sunk so low they had to sit on mini-stools.

There were only three other people there, clearly regulars. The aircon was not working, and Beth glowed with a sheen of sweat all night. Afterwards, a long walk along the beachfront. Handholding, dreamy lighting, mutual ignoring of beggars and street children sleeping in oil drum dustbins. Beth's feet never touched the ground. Pravesh tingled satisfyingly the whole time from the abundance of dead fish scattered around the pier.

Goodnight kiss on the cheek. (Beth's cue to start bulk buying *Your Perfect Day* and *Beautiful Brides* magazines.)

Ages 10 & 11:
Funworld (Beth's choice).

Stories told in-between dodgem cars, roller coasters and various nausea-inducing motion rides. After all the rides – popcorn and pink candy floss on a much-graffitied bench on Durban's Golden Mile. Handholding, arms around each other, oblivious to teenagers smoking dagga behind the ferris wheel and vagrants camping out near the swimming pools. The pungent air around their bench was a potpourri of urine and old garbage. Neither Beth nor Pravesh noticed.

Quick goodnight kiss on the lips. Beth hovered mid-air hoping for another.

Later that night, Beth began cutting out pictures of favourite wedding dresses, and pasting them in a scrapbook adorned with hearts and flowers. She carefully wrote *P&B Forever* on the cover with her best gold calligraphy pen.

Ages 12 & 13:
Coffee and cake at a quaint coffee shop, The Antique Café, in the suburbs (Pravesh's choice).

They chose to sit on a loveseat on the same side of the table, held hands throughout (even though it made drinking coffee difficult) and indulged in plenty of sexual innuendos. The café doubled as an antique store, and Beth pointed out furniture she liked to Pravesh. He agreed with her choices. They were clearly made for each other.

The First Real Kiss as Beth leant across to undo her seatbelt. A little clumsy and slobbery, but neither complained. Soon followed by a less clumsy, yet much more slobbery Second Real Kiss.

Beth called her mother the moment she had closed her front door, and told her that she had finally met her future husband.

Ages 14 & 15:

Karaoke at a local pub, Cockle Jack's. (Beth's choice).

Beth sang 'I Will Always Love Yooou' by Whitney Houston, with a great deal of enthusiasm and a marked inability to reach even one of the high notes. All the way through the song, she looked meaningfully at Pravesh. The drunks at the bar stared at her floating feet, shaking their heads and rubbing their bloodshot eyes.

Pravesh sang 'Love Me Do' by the Beatles (in monotone) and Beth swooned. (He'd asked for 'Happiness is a Warm Gun' or anything else death-related, but the DJ – dressed in an oversized shirt with bright flames all over it – just looked at him sideways and put on the Beatles instead.)

Cockle Jack's was a sleazy little bar nestled in a residential area, and peopled entirely by middle-aged locals who resented Beth and Pravesh's intrusive presence, even though they clearly stood no chance of winning any of the prizes. These deadbeats made Pravesh's ears unusually hot, and his knees trembled so fiercely that he had to sit down. They found a quiet corner in the back of the bar, next to a window overlooking an industrial area, and made out until someone spilled a Hairy Belly cocktail on them.

Beth could no longer remember what life was like before Pravesh. She wondered how she filled her hours, if not by thinking of him. She created a screensaver from a series of photos of him, and made a mouse pad from a picture she took of them on her cell phone. The picture quality was poor, but Beth didn't mind.

Ages 16 & 17:

Sunday lunch at La Lampara, a sweet Italian farmhouse in the countryside, (Pravesh's choice).

After lunch, a long walk through the surrounding fields, dodging cowpats and plagued by flies because of the relentless heat. Pravesh was enthralled by Beth's high-school stories. On the drive home, they pulled over to the side of the road, and made out on the verge, hidden by the car. Pravesh licked Beth's toenails for the first time. She found it strange, but not unpleasant.

Beth decided to get a tattoo of a heart with Pravesh's name and finger-print inside. She spent two and a half hours drawing three versions of the tattoo, which she wanted on her left butt cheek, and resolved, as a special treat, to let Pravesh choose which one he liked best.

Ages 18 & 19:
The Drive-In (a mutual choice).

They ate Pop Rocks candy and listened to the movie on Pravesh's car radio, all the windows up to avoid interacting with any of the other patrons (who looked, to Beth, a little dodgy). Snatches of her story were interspersed by long, sweaty make-out sessions in the back seat.

The English Patient, a film touted by many as a great masterpiece, was chosen by the frisky couple for the sole purpose of being extraordinarily long. Pravesh was surprised to hear that Beth had not been that popular with men before she'd met him. This she revealed to him as he took off her bra.

'I always knew I was just waiting for the right guy, though,' she whispered soulfully. He bit her nipple in response.

Later that night Beth sent a group email to everyone she knew – Subject: **I've found the one!** It was a non-stop gush about Pravesh, and hinted, not too subtly, at their imminent nuptials. As she typed, her feet floated several inches off the ground.

Ages 20–22:
Lawn bowling at Kingfisher's Bowling Club (Beth's choice).

Beth could play a decent game; Pravesh was useless (which pleased Beth no end). The stories from these years were less exciting (Beth had been a checkout girl for many years) and she huffed out snippets between vigorous bowling moves. They made out wildly in the women's change room (one of Beth's many fantasies) and blessed the old ducks for not being able to hear that well. As far as Pravesh was concerned, the bowling club's change room was designed for sexual encounters. A small vestibule – with pale green walls covered with a porcelain-plate display – led to another room with a dirty pink velour couch and wall-to-wall vanity mirrors. As they stumbled in, Beth locked the door and drew the frilly curtains so that none of her bowling buddies could see inside.

After the make-out, they played another round of bowls. Pravesh, somewhat distracted by Beth's half-unbuttoned blouse, played an atrocious game. He was ridiculed by one of the old men, but didn't mind too much as the man's imminent death caused his radar to buzz pleasantly.

Beth's scrapbook was by then nearly complete, filled with wedding dress cut-outs, magazine articles on themed weddings, menu ideas, contact information for florists, hairdressers, caterers and venues, and even a provisional guest list.

She was just waiting for the right moment to show it to Pravesh.

Ages 22–24:

Dinner at Yossi's, a somewhat hip café-restaurant in the bustling Davenport District (Beth and Pravesh's choice, because of its charming combination of cozy dining and busy eatery).

Beth's life had changed very little since the age of twenty-two, so she had far less to tell. She purposefully kept it brief so that they could scoot off to her flat for 'coffee and dessert' – or whatever your euphemism for sex might be: the funky monkey, doing the wild thing, makin' babies, putting winkie, hiding the sausage, etc. etc. etc. – as soon as they had finished their Moroccan dinner.

Besides, Beth was twenty-five. She had no more stories to tell.

Pravesh, however, hadn't even started telling his.

'It's not that I don't like her,' Edna, who typed in the cubicle next to Aisha's, would explain to anyone who cared to listen. 'It's just that she's a little … well, weird, you know? I mean, has anyone ever seen her outside work? She wafts in here, looking like she's dreaming, types away all morning not saying a word, and then sits reading during her lunch break. Why doesn't she ever talk to anyone?'

Edna raised her eyebrows questioningly.

'I don't think she's ever said two words to me,' Andrea interjected, her short brown hair bobbing as she nodded. 'In fact, I don't even know if she's ever said one word to me.' She dropped her voice. 'And have you noticed that she smells a bit funny? It's not BO … it's a kind of weird, musky sea smell …'

Saveshnie, quietly making tea in the corner of the kitchen, looked over at Andrea as she pulled a face to punctuate her comment. Andrea was startlingly beautiful, even with spite etched into every pore. If she wasn't in a wheelchair, Saveshnie felt sure Andrea would be conquering one beauty pageant after the other with great panache – she brewed the perfect concoction of beauty, malice and charm. Sadly, her skills were confined to petty office politics.

'Maybe she's just shy,' Saveshnie said softly. 'Maybe she's waiting for an invitation. We've all known each other for years … she could be feeling left out.'

Shrugging her shoulders, she walked from the room, her blue sari trailing lightly on the floor.

'Saveshnie really needs to learn how to gossip,' Edna grumbled, her pale skin flushing as red as her hair.

Even so, just as Aisha was opening her book at the beginning of their lunch break, Edna popped her head around the cubicle division.

'Hi,' she said, somewhat clumsily. 'Phew, it's as hot as hell today, isn't it?'

Aisha did not reply. She looked faintly alarmed, her eyes wide with surprise. It was certainly as hot as hell; the stale air in the office hardly moving at all, the temperature a steady thirty-five degrees.

'Listen,' Edna continued, 'Andrea, Saveshnie and I usually go to Slammit Dammit, this little bar, for a drink on Fridays after work. Do you want to come with? I can give you a lift home afterwards.'

Edna chewed the inside of her lower lip and looked sideways out the window as she waited for Aisha's reply.

Aisha blinked once, and then again. Then she nodded her head.

※

The next day, from the moment she stepped into the office, Aisha felt trapped. Overnight, Andrea and Edna had undergone an attitude shift, switching from spitefully indifferent to cheerfully jocular, and the blast of unwelcome enthusiasm coming from them hit Aisha like a gust of warm air from an under-ventilated bathroom.

She felt as if she'd been secretly initiated into a club she had never asked to join.

'You've got to see this place!' Andrea whispered, wheeling her chair around the cubicle divide so that she sat right next to Aisha, and glancing over her shoulder to make sure the supervisor couldn't see them. 'It used to be a strip club, and they only converted it a few months ago, so it still has all the old decor! It's a hoot! You're going to love it.'

Aisha smiled weakly, and then slowly made her way to the bathroom and locked herself in, sitting on the toilet seat, hugging her knees and wondering how she could possibly get out of that evening's plans. She felt nauseous, and deeply tired, and wanted nothing more than to go home and be by herself. She took a few deep breaths to try to calm down, but it didn't help at all. The air smelt like potpourri toilet spray and other people's bodies, the one tiny window in the toilet bolted shut.

Aisha could suddenly not remember what fresh air smelt like. She wished there was someplace to hide, somewhere she could just crawl into until they forgot about their stupid plan, somewhere she could sit in peace, not waiting for the girls to burst in any second, wearing matching T-shirts and handing her one with her name printed on it.

Momentarily lost in this suffocating stillness, Aisha was startled by a loud banging on the bathroom door.

'Come on, Aisha, stop hogging the mirror!' Edna called through the door. 'You're pretty enough already, let us in to fix our make-up!'

With a sigh, Aisha opened the door, and a gust of perfumed air blew away the staleness of the moment before. In her haste to get inside, Andrea accidentally rode over Aisha's toes with her wheelchair. Shoving each other out of the way, they competed for mirror space as if they hadn't seen their reflections in months.

Saveshnie remained standing in the doorway, smiling at her friends' giggly antics.

'It's not as bad as it sounds,' she whispered as Aisha passed her, patting her arm consolingly.

☼

But Saveshnie was wrong. If anything, the girls' night out was even more unpleasant than Aisha's worst imaginings. She had never spent much time in bars, preferring her own quiet company to the crowds and noise, smoke and alcohol-fuelled familiarity that she imagined was part of the cover charge.

Most evenings, Aisha just slipped home and ate supper alone on her veranda, listening to the night sounds. She often talked to herself on those nights; a soft, murmured commentary about whatever glided into her head. Sometimes she simply sat, eyes closed, feeling the cool night air on her face, and inhaling the sweet smell of jasmine that seemed to intensify as the light diminished. At those times, Aisha liked to pretend that she was blind, imagining a world devoid of anything but darkness, dreams and scent.

A world diametrically opposed to Slammit Dammit, which seemed to operate on a different plane of reality from Aisha's everyday life. Although it was only 5 pm, and the sun still shone brightly outside when Aisha, Edna and Andrea arrived, the dimly lit bar was already full, and scented with a cloying perfume of liquor, sex and stale sweat. All along the walls the silhouettes of men's torsos and heads had been outlined, and filled in with graphic depictions of women's naked bodies.

The constant flicker of strobe lights hurt Aisha's eyes, and made strangers' faces loom suddenly and terrifyingly close; the whole place was lit with a garish UV light that tinged everyone's face a curious blue, and made their teeth glow, like something from a panic attack. Loud, thumping R&B with too much bass filled the smoky air with almost visible sound waves.

Barely a moment after they arrived, Edna thrust a bright orange drink into Aisha's hand.

'Try this,' she called over the loud music, 'it's delicious!'

Aisha sipped at the too-sweet drink as she glanced around the rest of the room. Tables and chairs were lined up along both walls, each with a pole attached from the tabletop to the ceiling.

'What are those for?' she asked Edna, whose only response was a lewd move around an imaginary pole.

To her dismay, Aisha noticed that Edna was on her fourth shooter already, and she started feeling panicky – hedged in by strangers and smoke and noise, and not being able to escape for hours. Her panic kept her stuck in a chair in the corner of the room, staring at the floor. She closed her eyes and pretended she was sitting on her veranda, blind. The effort made her head hurt.

The next few hours passed in a curiously distressing haze. Time stretched out like warm bubblegum on an endlessly hot day, and the idea that the world was carrying on as usual outside Slammit Dammit seemed prepos-terous. Many of the men there seemed unaware that it was no longer a strip club, and expected the women to dance for them.

Edna and Andrea clearly did not mind. Every time Aisha looked at Andrea, she had a new man sitting on her lap, utilising her wheelchair as the ultimate flirting tool, and more than once Aisha was sure she saw Edna snuggling up to her, too. In fact, as the evening progressed, Aisha realised that Edna and Andrea were a couple, although by no means exclusive. She wondered why they bothered subjecting themselves to this ordeal when they had already found each other. She couldn't imagine they enjoyed it, couldn't imagine that anyone would.

Aisha felt powerless, trapped in her seat by the airlessness, the noise, the darkness. Not used to socialising, she had no idea how to respond to drunken, leering louts asking, 'So, do you come here often?'; 'Can I buy you a drink?' and 'Have we met before?'

Her one-word answers – 'No, no, no' – left the insecure drunkards floun-dering, more willing to call her a stuck-up bitch than to initiate a real conversation.

Durban was too small a city to avoid bumping into someone you knew when you went out, but Aisha had not expected such a visceral response to seeing half-forgotten faces; it took her breath away. She kept recognising people from high school, and their over-familiarity made her feel, some-how, as if they were all still there, walking down those chalk-scented corri-dors towards another hopeless day.

Her reaction scared her a little, made her wonder if the only reason she normally felt fine was because she spent each day on her own.

※ ※ ※

Now, it could be argued that Aisha's view of a night on the town was perhaps a little too harsh, lacking the magical elements of fun and alcohol normally associated with such a rendezvous. It could even be argued that she was just being judgemental and not open to new experiences. But perhaps we need to remember that all the other nights of Aisha's life were silent and serene, peopled solely by dreams. Not surprisingly, the noise and confusion of the bar felt as dangerous as a night-time stroll through the centre of town; as intrusive as a stranger in her home. The smoke that she breathed in, instead of the oxygen she craved, smelt faintly metallic, a scent Aisha instinctively associated with danger.

☀ ☀ ☀

One man in particular made Aisha feel skin-crawlingly uncomfortable. He was a thin, weedy man with too much confidence and dull, brown skin, and his name was Pradosh or Pravin or Pravesh or something like that. Aisha couldn't hear over the heavy bass of the music.

His original opening line – 'Your make-up looks better smudged' – was answered with a simple, 'I don't wear make-up.'

Floored, he walked away, only to return a few minutes later with a new line.

And a few minutes after that with another one.

Eventually, Aisha was forced to hide in the bathroom until he wandered off and found a new victim.

Even Saveshnie was lost to her; her fiancé had arrived at the bar shortly after the girls had, and they spent the whole evening at a small table with their heads close together, laughing softly and whispering to each other.

Aisha's head throbbed in time to the beat of the oppressively loud music, and she wondered how the other girls managed to do this every week and not fall ill. Every muscle in her body felt tense, and she wished, achingly, for the soothing company of her dreams. Eventually, she chose a drink-stained seat in a deserted corner, and waited for Andrea and Edna to get tired. She kept swimming awake from an uneasy, dreamless sleep, opening her eyes to snapshots of Edna and Andrea: kissing, shunning a geeky-looking guy by pinching their noses theatrically, and drinking, drinking, drinking.

The song 'I Miss You So Bad I Could Puke' seemed to be playing every time Aisha surfaced from her stupor. The inane lyrics spun her head like a sickening merry-go-round.

Four hours later, Edna and Andrea jostled Aisha from her half-sleep, and dragged her out of the bar. The night air was muggy and warm, and smelt of overripe fruit. Aisha breathed in deeply, trying to remove the layers of smoke from her nostrils.

'That was *so* much fun!' gushed Andrea, and Edna agreed.

Aisha kept quiet.

Edna narrowed her eyes, pointed a long finger at Aisha and declared in the loud voice of The All-Knowing Drunk: 'You know what you need? You need some fresh air. Go to the beach for a walk! Buy an ice cream! Get your feet wet! *That's* what you need ...'

Her voice trailed off while she fumbled for the car keys.

Aisha wanted to offer to drive – opened her mouth and tried to – but the words stuck in her dry throat like fish bones. Instead, she clung to her seat in terror as Andrea and Edna tried to drive the car together, weaving across the solid white line, running red lights with abandon and singing, 'Ooohhhh ... I miss you so bad I could puke, yeeeeahhhh ... I miss you so bad I could puke!' at the top of their voices.

Aisha was amazed that Andrea let Edna drive drunk. Sometime in the earlier part of the evening, Andrea had pulled Aisha aside and confessed that she had been crippled from a drunk-driving accident two years earlier. She had been in the passenger seat of her boyfriend's car when they collided head-on with a car speeding in the opposite direction; spinning out of control over three lanes of traffic, before crashing into a tree.

Andrea's boyfriend was killed on impact. She lost her legs.

As soon as she had finished telling Aisha the story, Andrea laughed bitterly and called out: 'Who wants to buy me a drink?'

☼

It was after 1 am when Aisha finally arrived home, shaken and exhausted. She slowly sipped a cup of tea to try to soothe her aching head, and then fell into bed, longing for the comfort of her dreams.

Aisha threw the sheet off. The room was so hot that the fan felt like a hairdryer.

By 2 am she still had not fallen asleep, although her eyes were burning, and her head felt dizzy from tiredness.

Then 3 am passed, and still Aisha was not sleeping. She started to panic, wondering how it was possible to live for twenty-four years fully able to fall asleep within ten minutes of lying down, and then suddenly, one night, turn into an insomniac. She wondered if she would ever fall asleep again.

She put on a calming CD, drank some chamomile tea, made sure there were no cracks of light to disturb her perfectly dark bedroom. Her eyeballs felt as if they were made from sandpaper. It hurt to blink.

Soon it was 4 am. Still awake. Now it felt as if there was not enough oxygen in the room. How could there be? It was one small room, and she had been practising deep-breathing since 1 am. It was unbearably hot. Aisha's normally peaceful bedroom grew tiny and contained, uncomfortable, airless. Her blanket prickled, her pillow felt lumpy, she could not remember how it felt not to be awake.

How was she possibly going to survive the following day without her dreams?

It would be like walking around without a skin, exposed to whatever the elements decided to throw at her. The clock clicked over to 5 am, and the first grey light of dawn started brightening the curtains. The panic, which had been growing in Aisha's belly since 3 am, moved to her throat as she realised that she had not slept at all.

A whole night without sleep.

Even in her loneliest, unhappiest, most traumatised times, Aisha had been able to sleep every night. What if this was the beginning of a Condition? What if she could never sleep again? What if life as she had known it – peopled predominantly by dreams – was gone now, forcing her to live like everyone else?

Surfing a rising wave of panic, she grabbed her car keys from the kitchen table, and ran, barefoot, into the gathering light of dawn.

The Durban beachfront – usually abuzz with cool-kid skateboarders in baggy pants, sneaky-kid pickpockets with bare feet, street children holding polystyrene cups out for 'donashuns, please', volleyball players showing off their moves, old men in long socks going for a stroll, Shembe priests laden with chicken sacrifices and candles, Zulu women in clinging T-shirts taking photos of each other, sand sculptors sitting proudly behind their rugby-playing sharks, policemen cruising in their shiny cars, bikini-clad girls cruising the beach, tourists wearing socks and slops and expensive cameras, beggars wearing hopeful looks, surfers jogging into the sea, and fat men jogging into shape – was deserted.

Aisha's walk along the beach was meant to calm her down. But it didn't. The morning after her hellish night was one of those strange summer days when the heat had been building for so long that the sun didn't have the strength to rise. A band of dark clouds seemed to trap the humidity in a solid layer. The deserted beach – a mile or more of coarse, grainy sand, and a limitless horizon of grey water – looked like a house on moving day.

A haunted house on moving day.

The heavy clouds and impending thunderstorm kept even the most enthusiastic beach-goers cuddled indoors under their blankets, all thoughts of sunshine as fuzzy as a dream. The ice cream vendors were not ringing their bells. Even the palm trees drooped, weighed down with dripping condensation.

The beach smelt like salt. Not suntan lotion, or ice cream, or pineapples dusted with chilli, or excitement, or sweat, or sun-warmed sand, or holidays – just salt.

The wind picked up, stinging Aisha's legs.

Her chocolate skin stood out against the grey sky – the only variant of grey and blue for miles around – and the air was charged with that strange yellow glow that comes before a thunderstorm.

There was a hint of wildness on the salty wind.

Aisha stood on the concrete blocks that separated the promenade from the sand, and ached. Her eyes ached, her head ached, her heart ached, and the thought of a life lived entirely in everyday reality terrified her.

Then, appearing like some otherworldly sign (or, perhaps, just the weather clearing out at sea) she saw a strip of sunlight break through the clouds. She waded out into the grey water, letting the waves break over her toes, her knees, her thighs and her belly, kept on wading until the sand dropped from beneath her feet and she was swimming, effortlessly and strongly, away from the reality that she had tried so hard to avoid, away from the loneliness and the tiredness, away from life.

Aisha paused, once, far beyond the pier where nobody could see her, and only then released the sobs that had been trapped inside her for so long. Gut-level, open-mouthed, body-shuddering sobs. She sobbed until she couldn't breathe, until she had emptied herself of tears.

The ocean didn't even notice.

And so she carried on swimming. The lifeguards were too busy drinking coffee in their clubhouse, exchanging tales of daring and near-drowning, to notice a solitary figure swimming out to sea, and so Aisha slipped away, her sadness trailing after her as the rain began to pour.

Mdu sat outside the *Whale of a Time!* offices in the Durban harbour, waiting for the rain to stop, idly watching a teenage boy argue with his dad over whose turn it was to use the better fishing rod. The boy's vehemence reminded him of his own teenage angst which had plagued him, day and night, during the months following his decision to give up his Golden Child role. They were difficult months, fraught with bottled-up emotion, loud silences and constant, high-pressure guilt.

The only problem with partial self-realisation, as Mdu realised too late, were the parts that were not revealed. Although he saw quite clearly, even as a teenager, that he had always defined himself by his achievements, he took no responsibility for this choice, and duly went to the other extreme. Mdu gave up all the activities that he had once excelled at, and chose instead to do nothing. Nothing at all.

The ensuing boredom ate away at his soul.

He listened to music. Read the newspaper from cover to cover. Sat around doing nothing. All the friends who had hitched themselves to his coat tails for years dropped off one by one, bored by the less-exciting ride, and commiserated with their parents about how Mdu had always seemed too good to be true: his Golden Child suit turned out to be spray-painted, not real gold at all.

Mdu spent more and more time alone. He didn't have anything to talk about with his classmates – most of them were obsessing over girls, or their matric results, or new cell-phone designs, and he had little to contribute to these conversations. He wasn't interested in discussions about arts and culture or politics either, nor about tricky mathematical equations. There was no gap in which he could fit, no social subset engaged in a similar, prolonged existential drama with which Mdu could compare notes.

To make matters worse, it was around this time (possibly due to some overactive hormonal changes) that Mdu developed his extra-sensitive hearing. He was not a mind-reader; he could not sense thoughts as they passed through a person's mind. But he could hear – distinctly, clearly – those deeply felt, hidden thoughts that were never spoken out loud, for one reason or another (usually out of social politeness). Mdu nicknamed them 'loud thoughts' and hated being privy to the inane content of the ones that constantly emanated from his classmates.

So he kept to himself. He grew his hair till it started to dread, and stopped washing quite so often, stopped wearing deodorant and wore the same clothes without even noticing. He couldn't see the point of choosing a new set of underwear every day.

It wasn't that he felt superior to his classmates, exactly, or that he was consciously trying to create a cooler-than-thou image. Mdu just felt, quite simply, that much of high-school life didn't apply to him. He strolled around with a faint smile on his lips, humming a nondescript tune while looking into the middle distance, blind to the fact that he was irresistibly cool.

It was in the final year of high school, when the promise of freedom lent a vitality and danger to the air (a combination that somehow smelt like fireworks, and made his nose itch) that Mdu became interested in whales. It all started with an article in the *Daily News* that focused on two separate incidents of whales in captivity displaying unusual behaviour. Both whales were orcas, which were not known to harm humans in the wild.

The first incident happened at SeaWorld in Florida, when a mentally ill man climbed into the orca tank after-hours and was found draped across the whale's back the next morning, nude, dead. An autopsy showed he died of hypothermia.

The other incident occurred at SeaWorld in Texas, where an orca pushed its trainer of ten years underwater for several minutes.

These stories haunted Mdu. Why did the whale drape the nude lunatic over its back? Was it trying to save him? Keep him warm? What had prompted the other whale, after ten years, to try to drown its trainer? Mdu couldn't figure it out. So he started researching orcas, trying to find some key to unlock that seemingly irrational behaviour.

He learnt about the orcas' complex interactions, near-photographic memory and unique problem-solving abilities. He read about their tendency to live in stable social groups their whole lives. But it was only when he read that their brains had a weak connection between the two hemispheres that he really started liking them. Every one of Mdu's numerous aptitude tests as a child had shown a poor connection between the two hemispheres of his brain – although intelligent and resourceful in practical matters, Mdu displayed a startling lack of imagination. His doctor suggested art therapy. Mdu balked at the idea; only losers needed therapy.

The longer he researched the orcas, the deeper his understanding of whales grew, until he read the one sentence that would define the rest of his life: *The orcas' complicated behavioural and vocal structures have no parallel outside those of humans.*

Mdu knew then that he had to find some whales.

☼

It all started on a Friday afternoon in the middle of a cold July.

School had sluggishly staggered towards the finish line, as it always did on Fridays, and when the final bell rang Mdu couldn't bear the thought of going home to his falsely upbeat mother, asking him about his future plans while surreptitiously sipping neat whisky from a tea cup.

Mdu headed straight for the beach, taking a route through the heart of the city, which forced him to execute some nifty bike moves as he dodged minibus taxis, jaywalkers, trolleys laden with tin cans and refundable bottles, and hordes of people walking in every direction. He flew past a man jogging on a busy corner, dressed in an immaculately pressed white karate uniform, a legless woman sitting on a brightly checked blanket playing a recorder, fresh oranges for sale piled up in boxes, and a pair of youngsters trying to balance a fridge in a wheelbarrow.

He held his breath as he passed rotting garbage lurking in the gutters, meat cooking on open braais outside butcheries, and piles of unwashed clothes for sale, mixing with the usual fetid city cologne of sweat, car fumes and mielies roasting on the paint-can fires on the pavement.

The wind streaming past him tasted like adventure.

Mdu held his breath until unexpectedly (in a burst of sunlight, it seemed) the sea opened up before him, framed by palm trees with street children lounging underneath, and flanked by the rundown remnants of Art Deco buildings. He turned and biked north, passing old women selling bright beadwork, woven baskets and Chinese toys, passing mimes posing like white-painted statues, passing young teens working out their issues on the skate ramp.

The beachfront always smelt like holidays to Mdu – suntan lotion and ice cream and sand. He didn't like it; it made him feel anxious. And so he carried on cycling until he reached the furthest chunk of land he could find, right next to a steep drop-off into the churning Indian Ocean, home to killer whales.

Orcas. His new family.

He slowly ground to a halt, dropped his bike, loosened his school tie and took a deep breath. And waited. After half an hour or so of standing on the edge of the rocks, straining to see anything in the constantly shifting sea, Mdu heard a strange clicking sound. And then a series of clicks, a clicking train, a few high-pitched whistles. Mdu had read all about echolocation, the high-frequency sonar communication in whales, but had never once imagined that he would be able to hear it. Hesitant at first, but soon gaining confidence, he responded to the whales' calls. They came to him like kittens to a bowl of milk.

From that day on, Mdu visited the whales every day after school.

When he arrived, he would close his eyes and take a few deep breaths, allowing the strain of being boxed up in a confined classroom, where nobody understood him, to leak out slowly, like stress into a hot bath. He stayed there until the sun set, casting long purple shadows over the water, intensifying the strong smell of fish and salt and sea, the atmosphere his lungs seemed to crave constantly. Lying back on the rough beach stones, his feet dangling over the edge of the broken-down pier, he spoke and listened to the playing whales below, inhaling as deeply as he could, trying to store up oxygen so that later, trapped in his airless house, he would have some saved away.

In the whales Mdu found what he had struggled to find in people – extraordinary intellect, and the unreserved acceptance that he was not normal. It was all he'd ever looked for in a relationship.

Their company kept Mdu from breaking into pieces.

☼

Mdu's parents had long since given up trying to follow their son on the strange path he had chosen for his life (there were too many brambles and not enough signposts, and they could never find anywhere to stop for a drink). They had resigned themselves to living with a reticent stranger, accepting that somewhere along the Parenting Road they had taken a wrong turn into a dead end.

It wasn't their fault, they reasoned; their map was faulty.

But still a small flame of maternal instinct continued to burn inside Mdu's mom, a flame fed mainly by nosiness and an intense desire to gain access to forbidden places, but maternal nonetheless. This flame smouldered at the edges of her thoughts during her bridge mornings, and her beauty salon afternoons, and her cocktail evenings, until it began to wear a hole in her mind, a hole through which she slipped, quietly, one afternoon, when she decided to investigate her son.

Why was Mdu consistently coming home each day after nightfall? His mother was determined to find out, so she took the first step down an unforgivable path, and followed him after school. She had watched one too many late-night B-grade crime films, and followed the classic disguise formula: a scarf wrapped around her head to conceal her curly black hair, a winter coat to bulk up her trim figure, and dark glasses to cover her eyes. She hoped, of course, to find Mdu at a girlfriend's house, making out while her parents were at work, or at a friend's place, smoking joints behind the garage. She hoped that, without her noticing it, her son had stumbled into some boulevard of normality, some avenue of ordinary teenage life.

❁

Mdu cycled, dreadlocks flying out behind him, in the direction of the sea.

But not to the beachfront, filled with other young misfits on skateboards and surfboards, dreadlocks and underarms stinking, clothes stylishly ragged, eyes suitably angsty. No, instead his mother struggled to keep up as Mdu cycled to a rocky outcrop that could only be reached by a narrow pathway intended for emergency vehicles. It was completely deserted – the lighthouse that stood there long since abandoned, its red and white paint dulled to a vague pink and grey.

Mdu's bike was the only sign of human presence for miles around. The desolate outcrop was furiously windy, and the sound drowned out the crunch of his mother's car tyres as she pulled up a few metres behind the lighthouse.

The wind blew away the sound of her cautious footsteps as she crept up to hide behind the faded tower, the sound of her handbag dropping from her hands in surprise, and her gasp as she saw the enormous whales gathered around her son's dangling feet.

☼

By that time, Mdu had managed to carve out a simple, confrontation-free routine that seemed the best possible route through potentially conflicted territory. When he came home in the evenings, he let himself in, called hello to his parents (they had usually retired to their bedroom by the time he came home, and did not answer) and then had a quiet supper alone in the kitchen.

This self-enforced seclusion began just a few weeks after Mdu's parents finally gave up on him. The disappointment that seeped from them, combined with their unspoken rage at his refusal to cooperate with their vision for his life, turned the air in the house sour. It made Mdu gag. Whenever he had to be in the same room as his parents, the space between them bristled with all the things they had not said to each other. He couldn't help but hear all the things they dared not say out loud. At dinner, he frequently looked up from his plate to see them looking at him with eyes filled with bitterness. The food tasted burnt each night. Before long, it became unbearable for Mdu to spend any time with them at all, as he found it impossible not to translate every word they spoke into litanies of disappointment. And so, day by passing day, he excused himself from their lives, until he was little more to them than a lodger.

☼

When Mdu arrived home that evening, he was surprised to see their house lit up like a Jack o' Lantern, light pouring from every door and window. His parents were waiting for him and looked as if they had been for quite some time – sitting on the edge of the couch in the living room, brimming with excitement, their eyes unnaturally bright.

'Sit down, *mntanami*,' his mother said, gesturing frantically to one of the empty chairs, and calling Mdu by the term of endearment he had not heard in years.

'No, thanks, I'd rather just eat my dinner and go to my room,' he replied softly.

'Hlala phansi, Mdu! Do what your mother tells you!' demanded his father in an unusually brusque voice, and Mdu reluctantly complied.

'Manje, let's talk about your little secret,' his mother began in a cajoling tone. 'Why didn't you tell us you could talk to whales? *Hawu, kodwa,* you could be famous! Just imagine – The Wonderboy Who Spoke With Whales. *Umfana okhuluma nemikhomo.* They might even make it into a movie! *Hawu!* This is so exciting, Mdu! Why didn't you tell us?!'

His mother's voice rose steadily in pitch until she was forced to stop for breath, and her skin, usually pale brown, flushed bright pink as the oxygen returned. Mdu's face had steadily been growing more ashen as his mother spoke, and, when at last she paused, he exploded. Pent-up frustration burst from him so violently that his words shot out like electric sparks.

'This is why I didn't tell you! I don't want to be on television, I don't want to be made into a freak show! Why do you think I dropped out of so much at school? So that I could stop walking this path that I didn't choose! I refuse to let you tell anyone, *anyone* about this! It's none of your business. You hear me? None! Just leave me alone!'

Mdu stormed out of the room, leaving his parents reeling with shock, staring at the small, red burn marks on their hands and arms and legs, where his words had struck home.

The next morning, Mdu was woken by his father pulling him roughly out of bed. He was a small man, impeccably dressed in a waistcoat and tie, his black hair neatly trimmed, his moustache straight and tidy. Anger gave him the strength to wrench Mdu into a sitting position.

'Lalela manje, you *scabenga,'* he said in a dangerously cold voice. 'You cannot ... you will not treat your mother and me in such a disgusting way. You give us no respect, no gratitude ... you do what you want, and you don't work at school, and then you expect us to let you throw your life away? Well, my boy, the free ride's over. From today, *uzosebenza,* and we already have the perfect job for you.'

He looked at Mdu with open revulsion.

'You have an hour to cut those disgusting dreadlocks, and wash properly for once, and then you're going to that sightseeing ship at the docks. You're going to lead them to the whales. I don't care what you say. If you refuse, you're out of this house, and out of this *umndeni*. I'm sick of dragging you around like a useless lump of meat.'

Mdu was trying to absorb this harsh information, his mind still wandering back from a dream where he was a tightrope walker, when his father threw a pair of scissors at him, narrowly missing his leg, and stormed out of the room.

And so, with a heavy heart, Mdu took the scissors to the bathroom and started cutting his dreadlocks off; one by one. Then he washed each one carefully, and walked outside to hang them on the line so they could dry in the sunshine. There was no way he was throwing his dreadlocks away. That would be real defeat.

After he had showered and dressed, Mdu looked presentable; his dark skin offset strikingly by the white shirt his father had thrust into his hands, along with a blue-and-white striped tie. His parents remained tight-lipped and tense, their skin still pockmarked from the night before, their anger cold and satisfying.

Silently they drove Mdu to the docks, where his father shoved him out of the car, leaving him standing there with an indifferent air, waiting to hear what he had to do next.

☀

Three years later, Mdu's indifference towards his job remained intact. The positive side of his work – being able to spend time conversing with the whales – balanced out having to put up with the tourists taking trips on *A Whale of a Time!* He worked as though sleepwalking; neither the whales nor the tourists seemed to notice.

Over the years, Mdu's adolescent angst seceded to the much stronger opponent of apathy. His dreadlocks were carefully preserved in a shoebox on top of his cupboard, and he sometimes took them down to stroke them absentmindedly, but in all other ways he had put aside his younger self; his golden achievements only a vague tickle in the back of his mind.

Until one particular day; a strange, stormy Saturday, when a lone swimmer struck out into the ocean, unwittingly heading straight into his life.

Harry had to agree with the general consensus amongst DSW employees that that summer was the worst in recorded garbage removal history. It was, by all accounts, and in every weather report, the hottest summer ever chronicled in Durban. And it was still only October. Harry dreaded to think what would happen once February hit. It was as if the whole city had been sitting in a sauna, and all the trapped smells were being drawn out and fermented by the heat.

The midday garbage collections were already steaming early in the morning, as their contents rapidly decomposed, and on more than one occasion the black bags had sprung gassy ruptures from too much internal pressure.

To put it mildly, the back of the garbage truck was growing a little overripe.

For Harry to notice the stench, it had to be unbearable.

There was only one house that did not reek; a small gem tucked away in a quiet street, which always seemed to smell like honeysuckle. It offered a slipstream of lingering pleasure in an otherwise distasteful olfactory experience.

Harry looked forward to passing it every week.

It had not taken him long to learn that some houses had better garbage than others. Those that recycled and had compost heaps were not as squidgy as those that didn't. Those with dogs tended to leave less meaty off-cuts, and those who had been raised right knew how to tie a garbage bag without it coming undone and spilling all over the pavement for some poor sod (aka the Garbage Man) to pick up the contents, piece by piece, even though that wasn't his job, and all he was supposed to do was collect the *correctly sealed* bags, and not run around like a preschool teacher making sure all the rubbish landed in the right place.

It could get somewhat frustrating.

Harry loved his work, loved making other people's lives cleaner, loved feeling like a magician who miraculously removed all evidence of everyday existence. Garbage removal was, to Harry, a mystical experience. He lived one of the four DSW core values every day: Honest work never hurts.

But more than the work itself, he loved the opportunity for treasure-hunting at the end of each day. Sifting through mounds of rubbish at the dump was Harry's favourite hobby. Time slowed, and then stopped, as soon as he pulled on his yellow rubber gloves and started digging through the piles of debris, exclaiming under his breath at the folly and waste of modern living.

The wastefulness of it sickened him.

But it also furnished his house, which was soon full to overflowing with carefully chosen treasures from the dump.

Harry's unique smell gave him a great advantage, of course. Although he still had to dig through the mounds of rubbish, he was not blindly sifting, but rather creating a special kind of oxygen, as he saw it, for his newly-found broken friends to breathe. He was a pheromone for damage. Each new treasure was cleaned thoroughly before being carried home, where he placed it in the perfect spot. Perfect spots were, regrettably, running out. If Harry had had any friends, he would have boasted about each of these acquisitions; but in the absence of friends, the stray cats that wandered in and out of the house – grateful for the green-tinged titbits he so willingly provided – were a suitable replacement.

After his parents had died, leaving him homeless, Harry's insatiable need to treasure-hunt forced him to buy a cheap ramshackle house right next to the dump, so that he would always have first pick of other people's cast-offs. The house wasn't on the dump, of course, but it was so near it might as well have been

Finding the house had been something of a miracle. Walking home one afternoon with his armload of loot, he noticed a bumpy dirt track overgrown with weeds and long grass. Nestled in these very weeds hid a disused care-taker's dwelling, conveniently out of sight of any prospective dumpers. It was love at first sight. The lingering aroma of rotting garbage in the air, the rats that scurried around the garden at night, the absence of neighbours or neighbourhood shops, or passersby (apart from those who were dump-and-running) did not bother Harry in the slightest.

Au contraire, he relished the proprietor status his house gave him over the dump.

Harry could spot a Promising Dumper from three-hundred metres away. As soon as he did, he slipped unnoticed from his house, crept through the tall grass to the edge of the dump and crouched there, waiting, until the PD moved away from his/her discarded belongings, and drove back to his/her newly clutter-free life. Certain that the coast was clear, Harry would pounce on the pile, sifting through it with the expert hands of a garbage man on the prowl.

One man's trash is another man's treasure, was Harry's daily mantra.

He was, by all accounts, an unusual individual.

Of course, there were some disappointing dumpers. One group in particular really got Harry's goat. That entire hot summer they charged in late at night, driving too fast, with screeching tyres that woke him with a jolt of anticipation, only to leap out of their car with armloads of posters, shouting, 'Boobs! Boobs!' over and over again.

These episodes flummoxed Harry. And infuriated him – disrupting his peace, and raising his hopes. Although, to be honest, dumpers who came screeching in late at night rarely had good treasures. In fact, sometimes they intimidated Harry just the teensiest bit, and caused him to break his Every-Bag-Is-Worth-Searching Rule.

The three shifty characters, who always wore black leather jackets (even during that scorching summer), sported well-developed stubble and surveyed the dump through slitty eyes, gave Harry the heebie-jeebies. These men only ever dropped off heavy canvas bags that needed two men to lift, and they always threw them as far as they possibly could. Now, rationally, Harry knew that the bags were probably just full of potato peels, and that the only reason they were in canvas, and not in plastic bags, was because one of the men happened to be a canvas manufacturer, and the reason they threw them so far, was because one of them used to throw shot-put in high school, and wanted to keep his arm exercised, and the reason they only came so late, was, of course, because they all had busy schedules.

Rationally, Harry knew all of this. But still, he chose never to open those canvas bags.

Just to be on the safe side.

Just in case.

※ ※ ※

In the normal, everyday course of things (things being, of course, life and the living of it) we don't often come across too many weirdos. Well, we probably do, but they have developed their disguises to such an extent that we don't recognise them as weirdos. They strap themselves into different types of armour, invisible corsets that conceal their true natures. Not many people are brave enough to reveal their inner quirks, to expose them to light and air and judgement.

Why? Because then they will be called names. Names like *creep*, *freak*, *junky*, *funky monkey*.

Knowing this, it is quite courageous that sweet Harry not only revealed his quirks, but chose to develop them. Instead of mocking this choice, perhaps we should applaud the bravery of a man unconcerned (or possibly unaware) of society's judgement.

Perhaps we should be taking tips from Harry here.

Perhaps, perhaps, perhaps.

Maybe this is a good place to mention that Harry was quite good-looking. Somehow, that makes everything better, doesn't it? Oh, he was a little eccentric, perhaps; a little unusual, but definitely with more than a hint of good looks. (He just needed cleaning up.)

Harry found most of his clothes on the dump, not seeing the point in buying clothes when he could get perfectly good ones (if a little torn or mouldy) absolutely free. And perhaps he hadn't shaved in a year or so, since his mother last reminded him. But his hair was a lovely deep auburn, and his beard had flecks of red-gold nestling in the dark brown curls, and he was in surprisingly good shape from lifting rubbish bags all day.

To add to his charm, Harry had an impish smile that showed off his wonky tooth (third from the centre) and crinkled his eyes into slits. Were he any other guy, he could even have passed as a bit of a ladies' man.

Unfortunately, being Harry, this was not the case.

※ ※ ※

Although Harry always found a day of good, clean work ultimately satisfying, he often wondered – sitting in his patchy green armchair at night, the stray cats prowling around his feet and yowling for more food, the day's treasures clean and shining on the floor – if he wasn't missing out on something. Increasingly, he found himself chatting out loud to nobody in particular, wishing he could answer himself with words he couldn't anticipate. Sometimes he even wrote himself letters, and posted them just so that he could receive something in the post box that wasn't junk mail.

He tried playing Scrabble by himself, but it wasn't much fun.

He always won.

Harry missed his parents dreadfully. They were the only people he had ever felt entirely comfortable around, a charming old couple, both slightly deaf and entirely unable to smell (psychosomatic, perhaps). They had raised Harry in a traditional Afrikaans way, and although he had not picked up their accent, he sometimes peppered his English with Afrikaans words. It was his family's secret language.

It just felt, Harry thought to himself as he sat listening to the crickets on the dump, like time for a change. And instead of initiating Great Change – which can be quite troublesome, and disrupt the natural order of things – he managed to cultivate two bad habits: an addiction to James Bond reruns (which he borrowed in succession from the video store, all twenty-one of them, watching them repeatedly at a steady rate of three a day) and a minor addiction to petty theft.

Harry started stealing tips from Mike's Kitchens. He drove around Durban, from Mike's Kitchen to Mike's Kitchen (all three of them), stealing the waitresses' small change from the tables while they weren't looking. The more worrying aspect of Harry's behaviour was that recently he had started to combine these obsessions, by humming the James Bond theme tune as he tipped the small change into his palm. Although he never quite managed to reconcile the image of James Bond pinching petty cash, it nevertheless made him feel debonair and suave, especially when he wore the bottle green (only slightly stained) corduroy jacket he'd found at the dump. This jacket had a distinct advantage – its last owner (someone with appalling body odour) had worn it on many a hot day, and although Harry would usually have scrubbed away the stench, on those sticky-finger occasions he wore it with pride. The strong smell it held hostage within its creases masked Harry's natural odour better than any other scent he had ever tried, thereby preventing broken cups and plates from trailing him (all too common in restaurants) and drawing attention to his activities. The smell also caused people to turn their heads away in disgust when Harry walked past, thus allowing him the few precious seconds needed to filch the spare change.

It was, all things considered, an outfit of pure genius.

Initially, Harry's stealing was under control. He only pocketed tips once a week, rationalising his actions as stress relief from the many demands of his high-powered job (it was, after all, no mean feat to make the evidence of peoples' extravagant existence disappear). Kind of like yoga. Or *Fight Club.* Tallied up, it wasn't much money, and the guilt was minor in comparison to the intense thrill he experienced from sidling in, pocketing the cash, and sidling out unnoticed.

Harry loved the anonymity of these restaurants. They all had the same synthetic look, no matter what time of day – a fake, caffeine-fuelled cheerfulness blanketing the tables in various states of disrepair, and overweight, underpaid waitresses fast approaching the jagged corner of middle age. A certain *Yebo!* flavour, not quite in alignment with the interior design, added to the charm.

The steamy summer nights of that hot summer scented the air with infinite possibility, and as Harry began frequenting those three restaurants more and more, he started to feel invincible, invisible almost. Shivers of glee ran down his spine when he heard the waitresses complain about stingy customers, and he began to adopt a supercilious attitude towards those who served him, feeling that he deserved the tips far more, because of his superior skill and expertise. They carried burgers and melktert to tables; he carried the pride of legions of James Bonds on his shoulders.

It was on one of those (by then nightly) jaunts around the three MKs (as he liked to call Mike's Kitchens, thrilled by the freedom-fighter overtones) that Harry found the flyer on his car. He had just walked out into the humid night after another successful stint as undercover secret agent Harry, the night air vibrating with the singing of cicadas, when he saw it. Trapped under the windscreen wipers, the flyer looked harmless enough, similar to those advertising Cheap Soup Bones, or Super-Effective Hair

Regrowth Cream. A simple piece of paper, really, with just a few words printed in black:

Tragedy Club
For those who don't see
the fun(ny) side of life.
6 Fenton Lane. 8 pm.
Every night.

Looking around, Harry noticed that none of the other cars around him had been targeted. The parking lot was fairly full – at least ten cars surrounded Harry's green Mazda, among them, a long black hearse with *Frankie's Funeral Parlour* written in hot pink along both sides. If any car deserved this flyer, he thought, surely it was a hearse. It leaked tragedy from every hinge.

But no, Harry seemed to be the only one invited to the Tragedy Club.

Logically, he knew, there were many possible reasons for this. Perhaps the other cars had only just arrived; perhaps the Flyer Man was lazy, and had only chosen to target every fifteenth car; perhaps he had unwittingly been entered into a flyer lottery; perhaps they had run out of flyers, and chosen to give the last one to Harry; perhaps the car had to be green to get a flyer (there definitely weren't any other green cars around, as far as Harry could see).

Despite all these perfectly plausible reasons, Harry couldn't shake the feeling that he had been specially singled out by some mysterious protocol, and nervously glanced around for a black-cloaked figure in a sinister hat to explain it all.

Finding no one, he pocketed the flyer next to that night's stolen tips.

Not long ago, on a particularly black day, Harry had gone to a comedy club, thinking it would make him laugh. It didn't work. Not a chuckle. Not even a snigger. Not even – and this was saying something about the poor quality of the comedy – not even a *smile*.

Comedy clubs weren't his cup of tea. But a Tragedy Club? Harry couldn't help but wonder, as he drove back to his comfortingly cluttered home with all the car windows open, trying to chase away the tangy sweat smell that clung to his jacket. A hint of coolness blew in with the tepid night air.

✶

Initially passing it off as a strange new fad (akin to cappuccinos and wild rocket and egg sandwiches) all thoughts of the invitation to the Tragedy Club were chased away the following afternoon. Another hot berg wind was blowing, filling the air with expectation and dust. Harry was sitting in his green armchair, wearing his green boxers, and rereading some of his pa's old *Garfield* comics.

And then the phone rang.

Harry's phone did not often ring.

Thanking his Lucky Stars that most people were directionally challenged when it came to navigating the dump, he was warned well in advance by the Guinness representatives, who were three blocks away, completely lost.

He managed to direct them to the house whilst simultaneously throwing one hundred and twelve bottles of green food colouring (his ma had always told him to Buy Bulk and Save) into the blow-up swimming pool.

Having trained each day for the last nineteen months, Harry was a pro at Speedy Bottle Top Removal (or SBTR, as he liked to call it). He knew that throwing the bottles whole into the pool would do nothing for his chances, so he painstakingly practised, bit by bit becoming increasingly adept at unscrewing each bottle in turn, pouring the liquid into the pool, and throwing the empties neatly over the wall onto the dump (whose borders crept closer and closer each day).

You might be tempted to point out that he could have just thrown the full bottles onto the dump?

Harry never thought of it.

Sad, but true.

With the successful completion of SBTR – in record time, Harry was pleased to note – he greeted the two representatives in a state of high excitement, bouncing from one foot to the other, unable to believe that one of his dreams was in the process of coming true. Clapping his hands softly at a rate of about ten claps per second, Harry opened the door without fear, secure in the knowledge that his secret was safe, his claim legitimate, his months of abstinence about to pay off.

The meeting was brief and to the point. Mr Collins, one of the official Guinness Book adjudicators, stared down his nose at Harry in a practised way, flaring his nostrils and looking stern. This was intended to strike fear into the heart of any chancers. It worked every time. He had voluptuous, bushy eyebrows and thinning hair, and liked to purse his lips together when he spoke, creating the impression that he had just taken an accidental bite of lemon, and was trying not to gag.

His assistant, Meryl, was a striking woman. A little thin, Harry thought, but with beautiful, shiny black hair, smooth skin and bright red lipstick. Just looking at her made him want to sit up straight; her posture was so perfect. The pair spent the first few minutes looking around Harry's house – Mr Collins with a look of professional disdain, and Meryl with one of cynical detachment – before sitting down and asking him a few questions.

Mr Collins pulled out a slightly stained hanky, and mopped his brow before beginning.

'It's as hot as hell out there today,' he grumbled, looking around in vain for a fan. 'You understand, of course, Mister … er … Harry? May I call you Harry?' he continued, before Harry had a chance to nod nervously.

'You understand, that by investigating your house, we are not in any way implying that you are up to any funny business,' he said, raising his remarkable eyebrows, convincing Harry that he was not so much implying as accusing.

'It's just that we have to check, you see. You never know, these days. All sorts of oddballs all over the place.'

He gave Harry another stern look, the second one in five minutes.

'Heh-heh …' Harry laughed nervously, afraid that his voice, if he tried to speak, would give him away.

His temperature had risen dangerously, and slowly – so slowly it was almost imperceptible – all the not-yet-mended plunder lying around his living room started to inch towards him, drawn by the smell that intensified with each drop of sweat.

'So, if we could just ask you a few questions, we'll be on our way,' Collins continued, giving Harry another funny look from beneath his eyebrows. 'What exactly is your claim? Just for the record … excuse the pun.'

'Well, uhm, the St Patrick's Day before last – 17 March to be exact

– I decided to see if I could eat only green food for that entire day. And since then, it's been more than nineteen months and I'm still only eating green food.'

'Hmm … yes, I recall hearing about you at the office. Rather insistent chap, aren't you? Been sending us letters for over a year now. And why is it, precisely, that you only eat green food, Harry?'

His assistant, Meryl, busy inspecting her nails, had glanced up briefly when Harry spoke of his green food fetish. Not many things made Meryl glance up, her disdain was absolute; the world did not interest her.

But at least, Meryl thought, this green food freak sounded slightly more interesting than the other claims they had investigated that day – a man who purported to have grown the longest tomato (alas, he was short by two centimetres), a woman with the smallest mice ever bred (the size of cockroaches, running all over her house and scampering underneath her clothes. Meryl was *not* impressed), and a mother convinced that her child was the only one in the world with perfectly curled ringlets. They were almost fooled, until Mr Collins discovered a curling iron underneath her bed in a locked box.

At least the green guy had some imagination, Meryl thought. Unless he was insane – a definite possibility given the state of his house. While Collins further interrogated him, Meryl checked for possible suffocation dangers (flying plastic bags, towers of books ready to collapse on her and cut off her airflow, pillows, suspiciously low ceilings, highly flammable materials, large mounds of wool, etcetera). She carried this fear around with her at all times. She kept it in her handbag next to her lipstick, in the cubby-hole of her car, tucked underneath her bra strap, wrapped in a handkerchief in her pocket, and underneath her pillow.

This man's house was definitely a fire hazard, but other than that, the only thing that made her uncomfortable was the strange smell that lingered over everything. She couldn't quite identify it. She worried that it would get in her hair.

It was when Harry told Collins that he only ate green food because his great-grandfather was Irish, and that he felt a sense of responsibility towards his heritage, that he really caught Meryl's attention.

Surely, *surely*, she thought, this eccentric little man had to be joking?

But no, he wasn't. In fact, he seemed to be warming to the subject, divulging to Collins how he felt a closer connection, somehow, to his roots now that his diet had changed.

He *had* to be barmy, Meryl thought, barmy or a fantastic actor.

For the first time since the robbery, something piqued her interest.

She didn't particularly like the feeling; it made her itch underneath her corset.

Harry was really enjoying himself. What a pleasure to have a captive audience to listen to the woes and triumphs of his green food crusade! An audience that could actually relate to the hard work necessary to achieve world-record fame; that was not a cat. As his temperature returned to normal, he noticed with satisfaction that he had managed to slow – if not halt – the broken goods' inevitable journey to his feet.

Without pausing for more than a breath, he continued.

'Of course, it was difficult at first, finding that much green food, you know, and then thinking up different ways to prepare it each night. It's no picnic only eating food in one colour; you're cutting out a lot of essential nutrients that way.'

Harry paused, and took a deep breath, looking out to an imaginary horizon, his eyes misting up a little.

'It's been a difficult road to follow, I don't mind telling you, and if I had been less dedicated to my cause, I would have given up long ago. But luckily I feel the spirit of my grandpappy very strongly, and he's helped me through the rough times.'

Harry's hand rested on his heart. For a moment he was sure he saw Meryl's eyes twinkle, and the faintest glimmer of a smile brightening her face.

With newfound confidence, he was about to launch into his theory of the superiority of green food over orange or red, when Collins interrupted him by standing up, snapping his notebook shut, and saying promptly, 'Right then, we'll let you know. Thank you.'

He then turned on his heel and walked out the front door, not even waiting for Meryl to pick up her bag and files.

As she brushed past Harry to catch up with her boss, he offered a friendly, encouraging (but not desperate, he hoped) 'Goodbye! Speak to you soon!'

Meryl snorted. It was a polite, ladylike snort, but a snort nonetheless.

She couldn't help it.

Alas, Harry knew the Female Derisive Snort (FDS) far too well.

☼ ☼ ☼

There was nothing wrong with Harry, per se, it was just that he had somehow managed to reach his late twenties without ever having had a girlfriend. This was, you must understand, not at all on purpose; he had *thought* about having a girlfriend many times, but he just didn't really know how to go about getting one. There was no General Girlfriend Store (your One-Stop Companion Shop), no dump on which potential girlfriends lay waiting to be discovered, no convenient list of girlfriends looking for boyfriends that he could peruse. Well, there was that 'Companions' section in the newspaper, but he had called one or two numbers from those ads, and they were *not* the kind of girls he was looking for.

Indeed, you must agree that in the absence of the usual social initiation most of us receive in our teens, the whole dating game can become a bit indecipherable; like a board game with only Chinese instructions.

Like Hansel and Gretel without the trail of breadcrumbs, green or otherwise.

☼ ☼ ☼

Harry was uncomfortable around most women – he could admit that quite openly. He felt they knew something that he didn't, and it made him nervous, like swimming without a noseplug. In the presence of women, Harry's temperature rose exponentially, and he began to sweat. Violently. And in this way the vicious circle began: as soon as he started sweating, his special pheromone was released, intensifying his magnetism, and attracting broken things to him with even greater force.

Which, in turn, made him sweat even more.

Try chatting nonchalantly to a stranger – a female stranger – whilst smashed beer bottles snuggle around your feet.

Not easy.

Nothing in particular had happened to make Harry feel this way – there was no single ego-crippling incident that caused him to fear women, no deep-seated Freudian complex to overcome, not even an embarrassing childhood memory involving his winkie and a blonde girl; he just didn't have much practice with the fairer sex.

Of course he was attracted to women. Like any other local hot-blooded male, Harry kept the *Daily News* Valentine's Day poster of Candy K under his bed. She was his favourite pop star, and although his copy was just the teensiest bit torn and damp from its time on the dump, he treasured it. The only problem was that Harry couldn't quite figure out how to get her out from under the bed. More to the point, how to get her on top of the bed.

Harry liked women, he liked them very much. He liked the soft way they smelt, and the way their eyes crinkled when they smiled, and he especially liked the way they always knew what to do when someone hurt themselves. He liked most things about women, in fact, but he didn't see the point of going to unnecessary lengths to meet them, assuming the right one would just pop up in his life.

And while his parents were alive, the chances of finding anyone as delightful as the pair of them were so slim, that he simply didn't try.

It was only in the year following their death that Harry decided to attempt a normal social life – venturing out to bars and movies, and trying to talk to women. This proved far more difficult than he had imagined. First of all, he didn't find either bars or movies very conducive to conversation. Harry wished he could find a quiet Scrabble hoo-ha instead. All the bars in Durban were smoky and over-crowded, playing music with too much bass and whiny girl singers, and only serving alcohol, no tea. It was difficult to hear anyone, or be heard. There seemed to be some kind of unwritten social code regarding how you started conversations, and, 'Hello, my name's Harry. I'm looking for someone to play Scrabble with,' wasn't part of it.

Movies were just as bad. Trying to meet someone during a movie was like patting your head while simultaneously rubbing your stomach. Sometimes Harry tried starting a conversation in the refreshments aisle, waiting to get a Creme Soda.

'I used to love popcorn, but now I only eat green food,' he blurted out one day. 'I'm hoping to be in the next *Guinness World Records*.'

The women standing in front of him in the line pretended they hadn't heard, giggling while looking over their shoulders in disbelief.

They snorted. Derisively.

It was very hurtful.

Amazingly, too, most women did not view garbage collecting as the fine and noble profession that Harry believed it to be. They liked their garbage vanishing, but they didn't want anything to do with those involved in the vanishing act.

Harry felt like a magician whose audience only wanted to see the rabbit. Each time he met a new woman, he would immediately mention his profession, hoping to break the ice and start an easy flow of conversation. After all, everyone creates garbage. As far as Harry was concerned, it was one of the Unifying Factors of Humanity (he had written a whole speech about UFH).

But none of the women he mentioned it to wanted to hear much about it. They ignored him, or made rude comments – 'What smells? Did somebody forget to take out the garbage?'

And if he lingered, they threw more insults at him.

Poor Harry, minding his own business, trying to initiate some good old-fashioned conversation, was repeatedly attacked with comments like, 'Back off, you creep! Why don't you go and take a shower, instead of showering me with your BO!'

The insults stung.

And he found the smell comments totally unfair. It wasn't that he was dirty, not at all! His vocation in life was to clean things up, so naturally he ensured that he, too, was clean. However, when one works for eight hours a day picking up garbage bags, many of them suspiciously damp and oozing, leaking or spilling open (which, he felt like pointing out, was not his fault, but the result of incorrect garbage bag closure – one of his pet peeves, and the mark of an uncivilised race), the inevitable side effect was a certain odour. And when this odour was compounded every day, it could become a bit difficult to remove.

Harry's mum had never complained.

It wasn't that he never met women, either. He met women all the time. They were always walking up to him – in Handy Green Grocers where he bought his weekly groceries, at the beachfront where he went for strolls, even while he was working.

They constantly came up to him, and said their timid or brash hellos, but three-quarters of the time, that was the extent of their meeting, especially if the woman was attractive. Harry had a penchant for attracting young models – their appetites broken, their sense of self in shards – but as soon as they felt that strange, inexplicable magnetic pull towards him, they turned nasty.

'What are you looking at?' they'd ask, even as they chose to remain directly in his sightline.

He would try to initiate a conversation, try to find out if he could heal their brokenness in some small way, but invariably they lashed out at him, as if suspecting that it was somehow his fault that they had approached him.

Which, in a way, it was.

Of course, there were other, nicer women. Usually not quite so pretty, nursing a broken heart or a crushed self-esteem, battling to find their way out of a wrecked dream. These women walked up to Harry shyly, unused to initiating conversations with strangers, but once they saw that he was kind and interested, they gladly dumped on him, unloading their sad stories as if to say, *See! It's not my fault this happened! Tell me it's not my fault!*

He always told them it wasn't their fault; always listened, even when it meant holding a bag of rapidly defrosting green beans in his hand for minutes on end, because he didn't want to interrupt them.

Oh yes, Harry listened. But then, once they had finished their rant/confession/defence/saga; once it became time to let go (so that perhaps Harry could talk for a little bit), they thanked him for listening, and quickly walked away.

On the rare occasion that Harry plucked up the courage to suggest a second meeting, he was met with, 'Oh, I don't think it's the right time for me to be starting anything new,' or, 'I'd love to, but I'm just really busy at the moment,' or the inimitable, 'It's really not you, you're the kind of guy I should be going out with … I really just don't …'

Harry knew how that sentence ended – *she just didn't feel that way about him.*

No woman on earth seemed to feel that way about him.

And sure, sometimes he felt a little used. Sometimes it felt as though he was performing a service that usually accompanied gainful employment (priest/psychologist/undertaker) without remuneration of any kind.

Harry wasn't looking for money; would have refused it flat out if it had been offered, in fact.

All he was looking for was a bit of companionship.

It seemed impossible to find.

Harry blamed all-boys schools, personally. When one is constantly surrounded by males, it often seems as though the female of the species is from another world; a world where one is expected to speak and act differently, always smell good, and know everything there is to know about hair products. Harry didn't know anything about hair products. Or about how to partake in a two-way conversation. He was a fantastic listener – the absolute best, top of his class, a rival to undertakers the world over – he just didn't know what to say once the women had finished talking.

※

This convoluted explanation brings us to why, when Harry received the Tragedy Club invite under the windscreen wipers of his car, he was a little reluctant to accept it.

Bars, as we now know, were not his buddies.

Still, there was something about the mere idea of a Tragedy Club that clung to Harry's mind like the crusty bits in the corners of his eyes when he woke up. Maybe, he thought (a spark of hope entering through the back door), maybe this bar would be different; the bar he had been waiting for all his life, the bar that had weekly Scrabble nights!

Harry hardly dared hope, even though for a brief moment he saw himself walking down the street, whistling a happy tune, passing bar after bar until a man popped his head out of the doorway of one of them and called out, 'This is a fantastic bar! You might want to come in!'

Harry wished for a bar like that; where he could just walk in and it would feel like home.

So far, he had not even met one friendly barfly.

※ ※ ※

I wouldn't blame you if there was a little niggle at the back of your mind about this whole Tragedy Club set-up: How did they know which sad individuals to invite? Where did they find them? What measure of misery did they use? Who were they?

All good questions. Regrettably, there are certain things in this world that are deemed to remain mysteries – the chemical compound of love, the appearance and disappearance of ladybugs, the Tragedy Club guest list.

Believe it or not, some things can't be looked up on the Internet.

☼ ☼ ☼

Summoning all his courage on the night of the Guinness World Records inquisition, Harry decided to celebrate.

'By golly!' he said to himself as he ate his broccoli and green bean stew. 'If anyone deserves to celebrate, it's me! The Guinness World Records popped in today!'

Harry loved the way it sounded; loved that he now had some rightful claim over enunciating that hallowed title as often as he wanted. He repeated it a couple of times out loud as he washed up his dinner plate – 'The Guinness World Records popped in today, the Guinness World Records popped in today, the Guinness World Records popped in today!' – a song he couldn't kill, no matter how many times he listened to it.

Still repeating his lucky mantra softly under his breath, Harry spent a good ten minutes carefully choosing an outfit, trying to look as inconspicuous and relaxed as possible. Eventually, after discarding a grey T-shirt with pink and green sleeves, a blue and yellow striped shirt and an orange vest, he decided on a pink, flower-splashed Hawaiian shirt, tight stonewashed blue jeans, and brown cowboy boots.

Harry felt confident he'd blend right in.

Of course, when he arrived at 6 Fenton Lane, a small bar down a little alleyway near the waterfront, he didn't blend right in at all, but stuck out like a man wearing a loud Hawaiian shirt at a funeral. Every other person in the club was wearing black.

Too late, Harry made the connection: black = tragedy.

Alas.

It was a hot, sticky night, and he felt uncomfortably warm in his tight jeans and cowboy boots. The tacky decorations in the Tragedy Club hadn't been changed for years, not since its days as a seaman's pub, and dusty ships' steering wheels and foghorns hung from the walls; a distinctly Old South Africa feel.

The air was weighted down with disappointment, heavy with sighs.

Harry found a dark spot at the bar, near the back of the club and away from any obvious lights, hoping that the shadows would tint his shirt a dark shade of grey. Fat chance. When the barman finally ambled over, he ordered a fizzy green Creme Soda, extra ice, and looked around the club.

At first glance there wasn't much to distinguish it from the comedy clubs he'd been to: the same small, round, candlelit tables (although these were covered in dark black velvet shrouds, not cheery red-and-white check tablecloths), a similar stage with a single microphone and a spotlight, and the same long, horseshoe-shaped bar. On closer inspection, however, Harry noticed that the bar top – which looked at first like harmless dark wood – was in fact black marble, and that the slabs used to construct it were in the rather sinister shapes of tombstones.

The design was highly impractical, plagued by frequent gaps where a careless soul could accidentally place his drink, only to watch it tinkle to the floor; further confirmation of his tragic alignment with the stars.

Harry was about to inspect the club for other telltale signs of death, destruction, despair, demise, or even mild depression, when a light smattering of applause announced the first tragedian. Tragician? *Tragedosaurus?* He wasn't sure what to call the man climbing the steps to the stage; slowly, sighing.

His gait was heavy, his arms limp at his sides. In a monosyllabic tone, without the merest hint of enthusiasm, the unsurprisingly stoop-shouldered and droopy moustached man began narrating his life story.

'Everything was just dandy,' he started, 'until I was six days old. My mother was carrying me to the hospital for a check-up, and on the way there a woman defrosting her freezer on the ninth floor of a block of flats threw the half-melted chunks of ice out of the window, not thinking to look before she threw. I was struck by sharp, freezing cold chunks of ice (or so I'm told) and when we finally arrived at the hospital, the doctors found that I'd gone temporarily deaf. Somehow, nobody could determine the exact reason – something to do with exposing my newborn ears to such extreme cold – that the temporary deafness turned permanent, and, to this day, I can't hear a thing.'

He paused, filling his lungs with stale air, and sighed loudly into the microphone. Harry blocked his ears with his hands.

'My childhood was happy enough,' the deaf man continued, using the same monotonous tone, 'filled with the usual taunting and bullying, people stealing my hearing aid and my lunch, tripping me after class, and beating me up on Fridays; no worse than any other average hearing-disabled kid. But there were good times, too – mute classical music concerts with my parents, long silent phone calls to our overseas relatives, dinner around the radio every night. Seeing my mom and dad chuckling as they listened made me as happy as if I'd heard the voices myself.'

The man tried to smile. He managed a half-grimace.

'After school, I got a series of poorly paid, menial jobs – car guard, street sweeper, dishwasher – until I finally landed the job of my dreams: managing a McDonald's Drive-Thru.'

He lifted his head momentarily, as if looking at a distant, dream-like horizon. Then dropped it again, his chin resting on his chest.

'Unfortunately, due to severe vandalism, my branch had to close, and I was retrenched. But I remained hopeful that something better would come along.'

He gave another huge sigh that crackled through all the speakers in the club, causing one or two startled patrons to drop their drinks.

'You see, the tragic part of my story actually only happened a few months ago. I had been going out with this lovely girl for about two weeks, when she threw herself off a bridge, and died. At the same time, heavy flooding destroyed the contents of my first-floor flat, and the damage-costs were much more expensive than I could afford, so now I have nowhere to live … my best friend, Pooky … he is, or should I say, was, a hamster … drowned in the flood, and while I was trying to find his corpse, I lost my hearing aid, and I can't afford to buy another one.'

The room fell silent as he paused, catching his breath.

'Of course, I'm sure things are going to pick up soon. I mean, compared to some people, I'm living a life of ease. And my parents are still alive, although they're both senile, and neither of them recognises me. What goes down must come up, though, hey? Always look on the bright side of life, that's what I try to remember.'

He looked out over the audience, as if searching for some hint of affirmation that his positive thinking would one day pay off. Dour faces looked back at him. There was an awkward pause.

'So. That's my story,' the man finished lamely. 'Thanks for listening, you're a great crowd.'

He turned to trudge off the stage.

Harry was horrified. He wondered briefly if the man was making it all up, unwilling to believe that anyone could have so much misfortune in such a short space of time. In comparison to that poor blighter, he realised, his life was unparalleled bliss. In fact, he wondered if he had any right or reason to be in the Tragedy Club at all. He felt, suddenly, as if he were faking a family tragedy to get a discounted bereavement fare on an airline, or playing sick to get off school, whilst all around him people dropped to the ground with diphtheria.

Harry had a rather vivid imagination.

Deeply shaken, he glanced around cautiously to see if anyone else was as affected by the story. It seemed not. In fact, he could have sworn he saw one or two people scoffing to their neighbours, unimpressed.

But Harry felt quite ill.

He was just about to claw his way out of the pit of depression the man's story had thrown him into, when a young, slightly overweight woman limped onstage, leaning heavily on a cheap plastic walking stick.

'Hi,' she began in a soft voice, 'thanks for being here tonight … my story began when I was about five.'

Harry's nausea intensified; he felt himself slipping back into the dark pit as she spoke – both parents and all seven siblings killed in a car crash; orphanages without enough food, numerous freak accidents that left her without two fingers (a clown juggling knives), without eyebrows (an over-zealous street vendor cooking sausages), and with severely impaired eyesight (a welding display at a fête, without the customary warning not to look straight at the welding rod).

The limp was not even mentioned.

Things were just looking up when she was demoted at work from being the Porta-Potty coordinator to being one of the Porta-Potty cleaners. And because her eyesight was so poor, she often misjudged where to aim the contents of the Porta-Potty bins, which resulted in a large portion of the excrement-urine mixture splashing up into her face. This had caused a rare allergic reaction that often left her short of breath, and with severe heart palpitations. She had no medical aid, so she had to wait in line for four hours every time she wanted to see the medical students at the monthly clinic in her area. They had no idea what to prescribe yet, but she was confident they'd find something soon.

When the girl had finished talking, she remained behind the microphone, as though waiting for someone to rush onstage and say, 'Don't worry! I've got the answer!'

No one moved. The hardened crowd was a little put off by the whole excrement-in-her-face part of the story, and hoped she'd get off the stage soon.

Undeterred, the girl pursed her lips, swallowed, took a deep breath through her nose and started singing – '*Cliiimb* every mountain, *fooooord* every stream, follow every *raiiiiinbow*, till you find your *dreeeeam*' – in perfect atonal pitch.

Harry was beginning to suss out the Tragedy Club situation.

He was the only one who clapped.

People were invited here to tell their stories, similar to comedians' acts, except that this was real life, entirely devoid of humour, and, it seemed, moderately to intensely humiliating.

Curious about the incentive to get up on stage and reveal the most depressing secrets of their lives to absolute strangers, Harry whispered to the barman, 'Is there a prize for the worst story?'

He quickly wished he hadn't.

The barman, who (judging by the huge bags under his eyes and the lifeless expression on his face) had a depressing story of his own to tell, glanced at Harry with what would have been scorn if he had had enough energy to muster it.

'No. That would provide hope. We tend not to do that here.'

Chastised, Harry ordered another Creme Soda, and sat twirling his straw in circles, surreptitiously wiping away the wet rings left by other people's drinks. He hoped there was an intermission before the next act. Surely, he reasoned, so many depressed people all in one concentrated spot, could act as a breeding ground for some kind of unnameable contagious disease?

Harry started breathing shallowly through his mouth to avoid the cloying scent in the air – a potpourri of despondency: musty, mouldy bedrooms, unaired hopes, and neglected washing baskets.

He was beginning to feel just a little bit claustrophobic.

Lately, he had found himself repulsed by smells that had never bothered him before. Even the green jacket, his genius disguise, was beginning to sicken him, sticking to the insides of his nostrils for hours after his clandestine MK trips.

Although Harry's dim spot at the bar had been deserted when he arrived, a cluster of people had by now gathered around him, and were casting furtive looks his way. This always happened when he went to bars – they accumulated more profoundly broken people than anywhere else – but the pressing cluster of bodies at the Tragedy Club was far larger than at other bars, and Harry felt them closing in on his space with ever-increasing insistence.

※ ※ ※

You have to wonder at Harry's patience with broken things; his refusal to get mad and shout at the pile of refuse that followed him with the persistence of a slightly dim pet. Most people would flip, just once, and yell obscenities at the accumulated hoboes and drunkards, broken men and confused, shattered souls that always hovered near him.

A normal person might even consider going to a doctor for some kind of olfactory-gland-removal operation.

But not Harry.

Perhaps it was because, in an oddly mature way, and from a very young age, Harry simply knew that broken things were people too; they also had feelings to consider. Or maybe he just understood that each one of us was here for a reason, to do something with our lives. Harry knew that his mission was to connect – if only for a moment – to the brokenness inside so many.

Some might call him the most altruistic of men.

※ ※ ※

As the night wore on, Harry became thoroughly absorbed in his clandestine cleaning operation, carefully wiping away every droplet of moisture from the marble top, and startled when a woman plonked herself down on the barstool next to him, calling out, 'Double-vodka-and-gin on the rocks, pronto!'

She looked at him boldly, clearly deciding whether or not he was worth the energy of initiating a conversation. As most women found that he was not, he was about to help her out and say, 'Don't bother,' when she stated, in an entirely expressionless voice, 'You're the green food guy.'

Harry looked up in slow motion, a glow of light surrounding the face of this woman who somehow knew and understood his daily passion, who saw through his Hawaiian shirt, to his green-tinted soul.

Only to find that it was Meryl, the cynical Guinness Book assistant, who had snorted so derisively at him only a few hours before. She wore a tight, low-cut black dress, and her dark hair was swept back.

She looked ravishing.

Harry gulped.

'Oh, heh-heh, yes,' he replied softly, cursing himself for the strange, nervous laugh in the middle of his two-word sentence.

Seemingly satisfied with his response, Meryl launched into a detailed explanation of how she came to be at the Tragedy Club that evening, recounting how she had found the flyer on her car at the end of the day, after leaving Harry's house, in fact.

Dying to ask what her boss had said about his chances, Harry wasn't given even the faintest whiff of an opportunity. Each time Meryl took a sip of her drink, Harry opened his mouth to interject, but even after her fourth double-vodka-and-gin (a drink that left him mystified – wasn't vodka one drink, and gin another?) he was still battling to get past the open-mouth stage of his question.

It seemed that although drink loosened Meryl's tongue, it did nothing to loosen her tight corset.

'The trouble with love,' she explained, her words slurring ever so slightly, 'is not so much the falling, as the landing.'

Meryl's voice dripped with poisonous sarcasm as she whacked the heel of her hand on the hard marble surface of the bar top to emphasise her point, causing three unfortunate souls' drinks to spill.

They stared at the mess, and sighed resignedly.

'Falling in love can be quite pleasant – finding a person whose wonder has no depths is like finding a drug that obliterates all sense of reason.'

She took another slug of her drink.

'Until it starts to fade, that is, as it inevitably, constantly, painfully, does. And then the landing begins. Landing in love is all about unsexy panties, unexcused belching, and callous inattention. The relationship sours, the sex life dies, and conversations turn to rat poison and household repairs.'

Momentarily satiated, she leaned back on her barstool, and ordered another double-vodka-and-gin, which she half-emptied in one large swig.

Meryl's words were so bitter that they caused the air around her to wither and crumble. As she spoke, a cloud of fine, black dust seemed to settle over everything – undoing all Harry's hard work – coating the shiny bar top, muddying the wet rings left by people's drinks, and taking all the fizz out of Harry's Creme Soda. But he didn't mind – for a change, he was not the object of scorn; the inconvenience of a flat fizzy drink seemed a fair price to pay.

'The trouble with love,' she elucidated, 'is that as soon as you think you have it in your sweaty grasp, it fucks off.'

Meryl smirked, the ugliness of the expression marring her otherwise pretty face. Her frown deepened the premature wrinkles around her mouth.

'Maybe it's got something to do with forces greater than mere human emotion refusing to be confined to the petty margins we try to squeeze them into – *If you loved me, you would've washed the dishes* – or maybe it's something far less cosmic. Maybe it's just that every person turns out to be human after all, and not the god or goddess they appear to be at first – everyone has ugly days, and spots, and strange smells.'

She briefly glanced at Harry as she spoke the last words.

He sensed that her naivety and trust had been violently broken.

'The trouble with love,' she concluded bitterly, 'is that it blindsides you out of nowhere, wrenching you from your perfectly contented life into a melodrama worthy of soapie scripts; complete with tearful goodbyes, furious, whispered conversations, and long hours spent dreaming of some marvelous piece of flesh.'

She downed the last drops of her drink, black dust and all.

☀

But most of all, the trouble with love was that it had taken an unannounced vacation from Meryl's life. Along with her friends, and her will to do anything interesting and/or worthwhile. All Meryl was left with was a pile of half-remembered snippets on once-sticky memos, a book with pages of *Words That Rhyme With –*, and a signed paper serviette from an old boyfriend that stated simply: *You are talented.*

Meryl had meant to have it framed as a reminder that she was first and foremost a Poet, someone of extraordinary worth and insight, but instead, in a drunken depression one night, used it to wipe congealed tomato sauce from a cold pizza off her cheek.

It wasn't so much apathy that she was suffering from, as crippling self-doubt disguised as bitterness – the inability to do anything but wake up late, complain to her goldfish, and watch bad B-grade movies on TV. And sometimes go to work, doing a job that interested her less than the five-second memory-span of said goldfish.

Meryl just couldn't see the point in caring about things when they were inevitably going to disappoint her.

Take her friends, for example. She had stopped trying to keep in touch with them months ago. They couldn't handle her telling them the truth all the time. Besides, Meryl couldn't shake the feeling that they were only spending time with her out of pity. Whenever they called, she could hear the strained sighs behind every, 'So, how are you doing?' and the forced enthusiasm that lurked beneath each, 'Let's meet for coffee!'

None of this was Meryl's fault. In her head scrolled a litany of wrongs the world had committed against her; all of them entirely beyond her control.

※ ※ ※

Have you noticed how many people living dead-end lives are living them entirely out of their control? You have to wonder who, exactly, is controlling these aimless, drifting, thoroughly disagreeable lives. Is there perchance some Grand Master Planner who handpicks a couple of people and takes away all sense of responsibility? Some large poker game in the sky, where the chips are human lives?

Or could it be that denying ownership gives you an unending list of things to complain about, without ever having to take action of any kind?

Meryl would spit on this kind of philosophising. She didn't care one way or the other. As far as she was concerned, her friends had changed, and it was a pity, but there was nothing she could do about it. Each day her corset – a seamless construction knitted out of endless moments of bitterness, cynicism, sarcasm and negativity – pulled her body and soul tighter and tighter, keeping her in a constant, mild state of near-suffocation (and terror). This garment fitted her so tightly that anything pleasant simply bounced off it, warping any compliment into something patronising, condescending, or simply stupid.

But somehow, that night at the Tragedy Club, Meryl found the strength to wade out of her swamp of scepticism, and elucidate the trouble with love to Harry, and in that we must see some small glimmer of hope.

Debate is better than denial.

As they say, denial is not a river in Egypt.

☼ ☼ ☼

Harry felt as if he had been ironed flat by the onslaught of sardonic truisms that he was in no way equipped to respond to (having had no experience with love of any kind, save maternal and paternal). He remained seated at the bar when Meryl fell silent, staring fixedly into the depths of his dusty, flat Creme Soda, and wishing, for the eighty-seventh time since his parents' death, that he was one of those men brimming with self-confidence. One of those men who knew what to say in every situation, and could say it without sounding like an idiot.

Harry never knew what to say. This was the longest time he had ever spent with a woman who wasn't his mother; he felt almost ready to suggest starting a relationship. Of course, he thought, absentmindedly chewing at the green straw from his drink, this probably wouldn't be the right time to mention it, seeing as she had just finished outlining the trouble with love in such bold, dark strokes. Still, this was the only woman in more than a year who didn't seem to mind that he smelt faintly of garbage, and Harry (desperately) felt he couldn't let Meryl slip through his (scrubbed clean) fingers.

In a sudden rush, he took a deep breath, fixed his eyes on a spot midair (five centimetres from Meryl's right shoulder) and blurted out, 'Would you like to go for coffee one day, maybe, if that would be okay with you, or maybe not, if you're not keen … I totally understand, I mean we don't really know each other, you know, I just thought that perhaps if you liked coffee and I liked coffee, we could maybe one day drink coffee sitting next to each other. Although I don't actually like coffee, I only like tea, but not normal tea, only green tea, heh-heh … obviously. So maybe we could go for tea sometime, or tea and coffee, or a milkshake or something, a lime milkshake, I mean, it wouldn't be a date or anything, just two people sitting next to each other, maybe drinking a beverage of some description, maybe talking, maybe not … I guess not, though …'

Harry trailed off, a little winded, a little pale, certain that when a woman started writing on a napkin while you were busy asking her out, it had to be a bad sign.

So that when she handed him the napkin with *Meryl – 031 2017762* written on it in her confident scrawl, he didn't quite know what to say.

As it turned out, he didn't have to say anything.

After she had handed him the napkin, Meryl stared for a moment into her empty glass, stood up and walked away.

Why Meryl had given her number to the oddball with the green fetish was almost beyond her.

Almost.

Yes, he was strange and smelt funny, but there was something magnetic about him. There was no way for Meryl to know that she had been drawn to Harry because she not only had a broken life, but also a broken heart and a broken shoe. (Its high heel had snapped off – bringing her down a notch – as soon as she'd stepped into the club.)

Very inconvenient. Although not for Harry.

If Meryl chose to be brutally honest, her reasoning behind the napkin-number fiasco was crystal clear. She had given him her number not because she felt strangely attracted to him, not because he had asked for it so sweetly, not because he actually looked like a good guy; but because she was very, very pissed off with her latest lover, and looking for that sweetest of all fixes.

Revenge.

Few of Pravesh's stories were pleasant, as Beth too late discovered. When she thought about it, it seemed inevitable that someone drawn to the business of death would have some unresolved issues with life – dealing with the dead on a daily basis is not what most people would call a good time. To compound this, Pravesh had not really had anyone to talk to for, oh, say a few years.

Unskilled as he was in the Relationship Arts, he naturally assumed that Beth was now his dumping ground, and that he, by virtue of the fact that he had listened to her stories, could now indulge in a massive off-loading of every miniscule neurosis he had ever entertained. Not even vaguely aware of the effort and skill Beth had employed to make her life-story entertaining, the phrase *your best foot forward* did not occur to Pravesh. Nor did *keeping the romance alive,* or *retaining some of the mystery.*

Added together, these painful conversations probably amounted to about as much time as Beth took delineating her youth, but Pravesh's sad soliloquies had no storyline, no plot, and all revolved around the same issues in a number of poorly thought-out disguises.

While they were still getting to know each other (during Beth's storytelling phase), Beth thought she had Pravesh figured out: shy, sweet, considerate, a fabulous listener and a real gentleman. What a catch! Not surprisingly, it was not an entirely accurate judgement, based, as it was, on the few monosyllabic responses he offered to her stories, and the four or five sentences he managed to squeeze in before or after she started talking.

Hugely relieved to have at last found someone to talk to who was actually alive, Pravesh's issues initially dripped out, then flowed, then poured. He was a veritable ocean of problems – from the aforementioned 'not being able to love', to his minor obsessive-compulsive tendencies (having to shower three times each morning, and only ever eating food from the right to the left-hand side of his plate), to the constant, exhausting minutiae of his difficulties with relationships.

Their relationship in particular.

They went over and over and over the numerous ways that Pravesh didn't know how to 'do' a relationship, even though his very participation in these conversations (plus the ensuing sex) guaranteed his role in doing it.

Part of the problem was that Beth knew he was right. He didn't know how to do a successful relationship. How could he, when his only example growing up had been his parents, who had subjugated their romantic love for the adoration of their only child? And, certainly, there comes a time when blaming your parents for your bad relationship skills is in bad taste (and for Pravesh, that time had come and gone a long time ago). Still, he had never been in love long enough to outgrow their influence. At least, that's how Beth rationalised it.

And so she buoyed up his insecurities, flattered his poor self-confidence, and listened, time after time, to how strangled with attention he had been as a child. These conversations smelt like stale, oxygen-deprived air; they made Beth yawn. The weather was so humid and sticky that some days she battled to breathe. For a month and three days her feet never left the ground.

For some reason, it never felt like the right time to mention wedding plans, but she kept the scrapbook in the cubby-hole of her car, just in case.

It was just a phase. Beth felt sure it was just a phase. Didn't everyone have them? Times when every conversation centred around you, when you needed other people to acknowledge each and every moment, every miniscule detail of your day.

Pravesh's phase was just lasting a little longer than most.

Until, after two months, when her thoughtful advice and loving hints brought nothing but the same old stories again and again, Beth began to feel somewhat annoyed. A little frustrated.

To be perfectly honest, downright pissed off.

It was not just the boring talks.

It was the lack of romance, the cessation of all excitement, the total absence of fun … and the fact that Beth had somehow turned into Pravesh's maid. In too much of a funk to wash his dishes, make his bed or sweep his floor, she did all of Pravesh's chores. He couldn't even manage to take out his rubbish.

Beth soon found herself, week after week, tearing after the rubbish truck in her clean work clothes. On the rare occasions that she left Pravesh and his rubbish to fend for themselves, she was assaulted by overflowing dustbins, not only in Pravesh's kitchen, but also in his bedroom and bathroom. Adding even a scrap to these bins threatened a landslide.

Overflowing dustbins were not part of Beth's picture of a Happy Home; she preferred the early morning chase. Luckily, there was a strange, gentlemanly garbage man who seemed to lighten her load by waiting for her every week. He always waved kindly when she came running down the street, and Beth felt drawn to him like a headache to a painkiller. Somehow, no matter how stressed she felt when she was chasing the rubbish truck, by the time she met his eyes, she felt calmer. The morning's peace was less broken.

Regardless, this chore-filled farce was not what she called a relationship. Where were the flowers, the candlelit suppers, the long hours spent gazing into each other's eyes? Where was the chocolate body paint?

Why had they stopped driving around in the hearse? What did that mean?

It was as if Pravesh was a patchwork quilt, Beth rationalised (only to herself, she would not admit the relationship was less than perfect to anyone else). It was as if he was a patchwork quilt pieced together with all the little things she loved about him. Only as soon as he opened up to her, the quilt ripped a little. And all the stuffing started leaking out, until all she was left with was this bit of old rag.

Every now and then, her palms tingling, she suppressed the urge to slap him, just once, across the face, so that he'd snap out of his funk and turn into the man she knew he could be; the man she had (foolishly) assumed he was.

But, of course, Beth didn't. Nice girls don't slap their boyfriends. Or voice their discontent. They figure out how they can do better, and then patch things together as neatly as if there had never been a tear.

Many nights, she stayed at home trying to dissect their relationship, lighting candles all over her tiny flat, playing soulful music and lounging on a large purple beanbag. The candles made her flat even hotter on those claustrophobic summer nights, and no matter how wide she opened the windows, the air did not move.

Although Beth called it a flat, it was more like a large room with an en-suite toilet and shower. The 'lounge' was a small, rectangular section at the base of the 'bedroom' (a bed and side table), and from her bed she could reach over to the 'kitchen', which was really just a countertop with a portable stove-top and a bar fridge. There was no dining room, per se, but Beth liked to call the kitchen table a dining-room table. She had painted the walls herself (sky blue with sponged-on clouds, each with a silver glitter lining), and hung cheap Indian fabric instead of curtains over the two small windows. The walls were covered with bright, cheery paintings (mostly of couples in love) that she found at garage sales. Every inch of the flat happily shouted, 'Beth!'

She loved it.

Often, she would listen to Sheryl Crow's old albums on repeat, full volume, singing along at the top of her voice, 'Are you strong enough to be my man? My man ...'

Music blaring, candlelit Beth would stare into her large, fake-flower-festooned mirror, and say all the things she wished she could say to Pravesh in real life, without the strict censoring she usually imposed on their relationship. She had latched onto the Mirror Technique, as her high school guidance counsellor called it, so that her inner bitch could say anything she wanted, without causing her sweet Pravesh, or her relationship, any emotional damage. It was genius.

'Pravesh?' Beth would begin, brushing her hair from her face, and looking herself squarely in the eyes.

'There are a few things I would like to say to you. I love you, but ...' and then she paused, took a deep breath, and spewed forth.

'I don't know why you've turned into such a useless excuse for a human being. I feel like you do nothing but eat, sleep and complain, and I am so freaking sick of hearing about your childhood and your parents and your unresolved issues and giving you great advice that you never ever take. You never take it! And it's such good advice. And then you have the cheek to come back and complain to me all over again the next day, about all the same things, even though we've come to a conclusion the day before, and the conclusion is that you need to start taking control of your life, and taking responsibility for the way you feel, and not always take it out on me, because every time you dump on me I feel like shit for the rest of the day while you go off feeling fine!'

Beth took a deep, shuddering breath. Her cheeks were bright pink, her eyes shiny with unshed tears.

'And I also want to know why there's no romance in our relationship anymore, and why we hardly ever make love, and when we do it's always all about you, and not about me, and why you never tell me that I'm beautiful anymore even though you did when we first started going out, and why you never notice when I try and look nice for you, and why you never try and look nice for me, and why things were so good in the beginning and now I can't even remember the last time you made me feel happy!'

She breathed in deeply through her nose, and then out again.

'I love you, Pravesh,' she said calmly, 'but I just think it's time we made some changes.'

Beth was often surprised at what came out in the Mirror Technique. Much of what she said felt like a rush of diarrhoea – maybe necessary, but uncomfortably messy. Sure, things got exasperating at times, but it wasn't that bad, she quickly reassured herself. At least her teeth weren't stained from one too many glasses of red wine; at least she had someone to save her from that nightmare.

Sometimes, she continued to reassure herself, she had a tendency to get a little over-dramatic, that was all.

A breeze entered her open window and the suffocating heat lifted, just a little. As soon as she caught her breath, Beth took out her fluffy pink diary and sat down on her bed.

Pravesh is the reason I was born with such an enormous heart, she wrote in firm, confident strokes. *Here I have found a man I can really love, and who needs me as much as I need him. That's what all good relationships are built on – mutual need. Look at Snow White and the Seven Dwarfs. Look at Cinderella and Prince Charming. Look at the Three Little Pigs. And although I do sometimes feel that we're sort of going round in circles, he just needs someone to give him the space and understanding to get over his childhood issues.*

And once he's over them, we can start planning the wedding properly. It's just a phase he's going through. I just need to pour all my love into him, so that he can get through this.

To celebrate her newfound clarity, Beth made a big cup of hot chocolate, with extra marshmallows and whipped cream, and watched *My Fair Lady*, a film she had seen forty-seven times. She sipped her hot chocolate, and said all the lines along with the characters. Sometimes, while watching the film, Beth found herself absentmindedly chewing her toenails; a disgusting habit that she knew would repulse Pravesh, but that she'd never managed to break. After the final credits had rolled (and she had sung along with the medley that accompanied them), she pranced around the room singing, 'I could have daaanced all night!' while waltzing with one of her many teddy bears.

This was Beth's Special Time, the only time of late when her feet had left the ground.

⚘

The next evening, when Pravesh arrived at Beth's door to pick her up for their date (they were going to watch the French film, *Amélie*), he looked morose. A scent of crushed flowers and despair preceded him, sucking all the oxygen out of her flat.

'Do you mind if we give the film a skip?' he asked, before saying hello. 'I just want to talk.'

Pravesh didn't even bother looking at her, just crumpled onto her purple beanbag. With a thinly disguised grimace, Beth decided to test out her previous night's revelation.

'Yes, honey, of course, what do you want to talk ab–' Beth began, the very picture of the Understanding Girlfriend, but then something inside her revolted.

'Actually, no, I don't really feel like talking,' she retorted, flinging the words at Pravesh.

He looked at her over his shoulder, surprised.

'I'm sick of freaking talking, Pravesh, that's all we ever seem to do!'

Flooded by an unaccustomed rush of power, Beth felt giddily light-headed.

'Well, I'm sorry if I have some issues that I need to work through, Beth. Not all of us are as balanced and together as you think you are!'

He spat the words out scornfully.

'Although from some of those stories you told me, especially about your other relationships, I'm not so sure that you aren't even more fucked up than I am!'

Spite lent a shine to Pravesh's eyes that had not been there for weeks.

'Ooohhh, trust me Mister My-Parents-Loved-Me-Too-Much-So-Now-I'm-An-Undertaker, *I'm* not the screwed-up one in this relationship! At least I had the … the … gumption to use my imagination, instead of going over and over and over the same, sad, pathetic story every single time I spoke.'

There was a long pause that slowly inflated, like a hot air balloon, smothering them. Her words seemed to hover in the air, taunting Pravesh, poking him, laughing in his face. His eyes smarted as if he had been slapped. With a whimper, he turned his back to her, and curled into a ball on the beanbag.

Beth sat down on the bed, and sighed. *Here we go again,* she thought angrily.

But then she looked at poor, vulnerable Pravesh, curled up like a little child, and her heart softened. How could she have done this to the man of her dreams? What kind of demon had possessed her to speak such cruel and heartless words, when she really didn't mean them? Really, she didn't!

Beth's remorse covered Pravesh like a soft blanket.

'Oh, baby, baby, I didn't mean it. I was just angry, just upset 'cause I could see how much you were hurting, and I couldn't make it better. Come here, baby, come on, it's okay …'

As soon as Pravesh started crawling towards Beth, her heart sank.

☼

Much as Beth loved Pravesh, his lovemaking left a little to be desired. Well, more than a little. He followed the same formula every time, and it was by no means a winning one – starting with her feet, he would lick her toenails, and suck each toe individually, lovingly. That was where the gentle loving stopped.

Moving to her face, he would kiss her over and over, each time pushing his tongue deeper inside her mouth, making it difficult to breathe. Sometimes she wanted to gag. Next, he would move to lie on top of her, carelessly throwing her teddy bears to the floor, one by one. (Beth winced with each thud.) And finally, with one short, swift movement, he would pull up her skirt, and get out of his pants and his underwear. Half-naked, Pravesh shut his eyes tightly, and pushed, shoved, thrust.

Nothing more than rutting.

It was as though Pravesh knew everything there was to know about bodies, but nothing about the sexual act. Beth never had time to ponder this conundrum for long, because he usually came very quickly. And that was it: no romance, no sensuality, none of the violins and fireworks she had been promised.

On the contrary, making love to Pravesh felt a lot like a brief visit to the dentist: someone probing a cavity. His 'technique' frequently made Beth feel quite sore, quite used. She hated feeling so disconnected from her body, hated having to lie there hoping he would soon be done, trying to think of something (anything!) that would get her to feel relaxed enough to get some kind of pleasure out of the experience.

But she never could.

❁

One day soon, Beth resolved as Pravesh rolled off her, when the time was right, she would suggest they work at their lovemaking.

Afterwards, to add further punishment to her pain, Pravesh needed to talk. He wasn't one of those men who fell asleep straight after sex, but became garrulous, and talked and talked until Beth fell asleep, usually out of boredom.

But she didn't mind, not really. Beth still believed that these post-coital talks helped Pravesh. Admittedly, a part of her hoped that he had actually listened to her earlier outburst, and that he might just possibly, maybe, perhaps choose to alter his behaviour ever so slightly because of it.

Alas, no.

'Babes?'

'Mmm …?' murmured Beth, her head face-down in the pillow.

'I just, I keep feeling like it's all too hard, you know?'

'Unnn …' grunted Beth.

'Like, how am I possibly going to get through all of this? I mean, most mornings when I wake up, I feel like there's nothing to get out of bed for.'

Beth's stomach lurched involuntarily. She was suddenly wide awake. What about her? Wasn't she worth getting out of bed for?

'I just … I don't know how to *do* this relationship thing, you know? I mean, we've been together for two months now, and I still just don't know how to do it …' he trailed off.

Beth picked up her largest teddy bear from the floor and held its paws over her head, trying to block out his voice.

'And then, well, there's something else that's really been bothering me,' Pravesh continued, staring at the ceiling, his forehead creased in consternation.

'What is it, honey?' Beth asked, trying to muster some enthusiasm, her voice muffled from talking into the pillow, her yellow 'Love Me' bear still draped over her head. 'Let's talk about it.'

'Well, I've never told anyone about it before, so I'm, you know, a little shy ...'

As the air around these words settled, Beth's mind started running away. It wanted no part in this conversation; somehow sensing that it was going to be the moment their relationship changed forever.

In a thin little voice, her heart inching up her throat, Beth lifted the teddy off her head and said, 'Pravesh baby, you can tell me anything, you know that.'

'Well, I uhhh ...' he paused and swallowed, avoiding eye contact, 'I have this thing I do, and it's kind of weird, but I can't stop doing it.'

'Okaaaaay,' Beth said encouragingly, turning to lie on her back and praying to God (Whom she didn't believe in) that he wasn't about to say something heinous; something she couldn't possibly deal with.

Pravesh coughed. 'Well ... you know how it's my job to prepare all the dead bodies for their funerals?' he began.

Oh God no, oh God no, oh God no, Beth thought, her head beginning to spin.

'Well, I have this thing I do, where I uhmm ...' Pravesh took a deep breath. 'I, well, it's a little embarrassing, but I just, I can't stop doing it— '

'What *is* it?' she whispered hoarsely, her heart moving from her throat to her mouth, unable to handle the suspense a second longer.

He turned to look at her. Coughed again. 'It's become an ... an obsession for me, you know? I might as well just say it, I don't know why I'm dragging it out so much. I ... I like to paint corpses' toenails.'

Stunned silence stretched between them like a tightrope. Pravesh paused to gauge her response, and then, unable to read her utterly blank expression, continued.

'I paint the men's a dark brown, and the women's bright red or pink, depending on their colouring. Nobody ever sees it, except me, because they're put into their coffins wearing shoes and socks, but I just feel that if I was going to meet my Maker, I'd wish my toenails looked nice. And really, I know I should check with the families, and not tamper with dead bodies, and that it's none of my business, but I just can't stop.'

He looked imploringly at her stony face.

Then the tightrope-tension snapped, just like that, as Beth began to giggle, snorts of laughter bursting from the back of her throat.

'Beth! Get a hold of yourself. *God*. This isn't funny. I've never told any-one before! Beth! Come on now.'

Pravesh looked strained; his eyes bulged, and a vein in his neck was pulsing dangerously.

'Sorry,' Beth squeezed out in-between giggles, then tried to pull herself together, sitting up and smoothing the sheets over her legs. 'Sorry, Pravesh honey, I'm just, well, relieved! Sorry, baby, I didn't mean to make light of your … obsession, it just, well, it could have been a lot worse, hey?'

'I don't know how,' Pravesh sulked.

'Well, that's all right then, isn't it?' Beth said soothingly, finally calming down. 'Come on, let's have a bite to eat, then you'll feel better.'

'Okay,' replied Pravesh grumpily. 'I still can't believe you laughed at me. I don't know what's gotten into you today, Beth. Maybe you need to get your head checked out.'

With that, he retreated to the darkest corner of her living room where he kept a pile of well-thumbed copies of the *Guinness World Records* inside a large box. To her dismay, one night, Beth found they were only well-thumbed in one section: 'Died in the Attempt.'

Living records, it seemed, were of no interest to Pravesh.

※ ※ ※

Now, I wouldn't blame you for wondering, at this point, why Beth did not run – shrieking just a little – from Pravesh. There are certain things in life that warrant the termination of a relationship: surely, *surely*, painting dead people's toenails is one of them?

Well.

Perhaps it should have been a warning sign.

Beth may have been firmly ensconced in her Saviour Quest, but she was no fool. She knew it was pretty weird that her boyfriend felt compelled to paint the toenails of corpses. And yes, Beth wished that he was obsessed with cricket rather than cadavers, but she was also deeply committed to their strange relationship, deeply certain of their impending future together, and she couldn't quite forget the initial image of Pravesh as her Prince Charming.

Couldn't forget, either, that there was a perfectly complete scrapbook waiting in the cubby-hole of her car. She couldn't just throw away all those plans.

Beth had decided, quite resolutely, that this was the man she was going to marry. She was done with dating, done with kissing random guys, done with worrying how her hair looked whenever she saw a man. Since she had started going out with Pravesh (albeit only two months before) she had not had one alone-at-thirty-five panic attack. Not one. She had cashed in her ticket for the merry-go-round, she had chosen her horse and she was holding on for dear life. So Beth pretended Pravesh had never told her about his strange habit, and went on adding to her (already extensive) scrapbook, imagining his glee when she finally showed it to him.

※ ※ ※

The change in Pravesh, however, was remarkable. Within two days of his confession, his metamorphosis began. All of a sudden, the formerly quiet sad sap became confident and brash; a man's man who went out for beers, and who didn't want to talk at all. Beth tried in vain to find a glimmer of recognition in his eyes, a hint of the deeply troubled soul she'd finally decided to love, but he was on extended leave (without permission).

Without admitting to it, that guilty secret had governed every aspect of Pravesh's life, keeping him in a constant state of insecurity and unworthiness. All of a sudden, all of that was gone. Unleashing his darkest secret transformed him into the man he had always wanted to be; a very, very different man to the one he had been, leading up to that moment.

Though positive for him, the change in Pravesh was devastating for Beth. For the last two months, she had been his (sometimes reluctant) twenty-four-hour confidante – he had needed her like water, like air! He had been her (bad) lover, her (inconsiderate) best friend, her (somewhat dull) daily companion. But despite his obvious shortcomings, Pravesh had also been Beth's project and full-time hobby; she had even given up lawn bowling, because he needed her to be available all day, every day.

Now, all of a sudden, Beth saw him maybe three times a week (as opposed to seven) and, when she asked how he was feeling, he scoffed and replied, 'Feeling? Fine … why wouldn't I be?'

If she tried to push the matter any further, he would get pissed off, and start sulking.

Beth couldn't remember the last time his nostrils had flared as he smiled at her.

All she was looking for was for somebody to return the love she so freely bestowed – was that really so much to ask? Wasn't that what relationships were for? You found the one who satisfied (almost) every need on your list of desires, and once you'd found him, you hung on tight, and never let go.

Beth felt tired, tired, tired. Tired of having to try so hard when he didn't even seem to notice.

☼

And then, one morning, things started to die. Just like that. It was a discrete moment – the beginning of the end – and yet, as it unfolded, Beth refused to recognise it.

It is amazing what impaired vision we can give ourselves if we really want to.

Beth's favourite Pravesh memory was from their first month together. He had woken up before her, snuck out of bed quietly, and prepared breakfast in bed for her. It had been pretty basic – no homemade pancakes or sausage, egg and bacon – just cereal and toast and tea; but the fact that he had gone to all that trouble just for her, melted Beth's heart. It puddled around her lungs, and made her gasp for air (gleefully).

Pravesh gently kissed her awake, and then placed the carefully laid tray (complete with paper serviette and perfectly milky tea) on the bed next to her. He looked so pleased with himself, so delighted that he had managed to delight her. Whenever Beth thought of him from that day onwards, it was that look on his face that swam into her memory.

So, when Beth woke up in his dark apartment early on a hot summer's morning not long after his toenail-painting unburdening – the air still and pregnant with humidity, the smell of toasting grass on the breeze, her nightie stuck to her back with sweat – and found that Pravesh was not next to her in bed, Beth naturally assumed he had slipped off to make her breakfast.

She grinned, her first grin in a long while, and began floating ever so slightly above the bed. What a relief! Things weren't that bad after all. The Pravesh that she loved – that sweet, slightly dorky man who knew how to balance a breakfast tray with one hand while opening a door with the other – was going to shuffle in any moment, with that pleased smile on his face.

She even thought she could hear plates clattering in the kitchen.

Slow excitement fizzed in her veins as Beth lay in bed and stared at the flawless blue sky outside the window. Her heart was filled with a sense of deep satisfaction. What a funny little frog she was! She had almost convinced herself things were going sour.

Twenty minutes later, the fizzing sensation had receded, and a slow, numbing dread was beginning to creep into her heart. Was it possible that Pravesh had not snuck off to make her breakfast, but had merely woken up, and not bothered to wake her? They had woken together every morning they had ever spent together. The significance of Pravesh getting up alone (if that was indeed the case) was so huge, Beth didn't think she knew how to comprehend it.

With a ripple of nausea spreading from her stomach, she quietly opened the bedroom door and walked through to Pravesh's small kitchen. He was sitting at the table, reading one of his Guinness annuals, already showered and shaved.

He glanced up briefly. 'Morning,' he said, 'you had a nice long sleep,' then went back to his reading.

Beth stumbled through to the bathroom and locked the door, switching on the shower so that he wouldn't hear her sobbing. She cried her tear ducts dry. It wasn't even anything explainable, really. She couldn't ask him why he hadn't been making her breakfast, why he hadn't woken her up when he woke up.

Couldn't ask why he wasn't amazed by her anymore.

The very fact that he hadn't thought of it was what hurt so much.

Beth feigned illness and cried all that day, the soggy edges of her heart slowly disintegrating. The oppressive heat that had been building for weeks lent the morning a suffocating stillness that completely enveloped her. Someone had sealed the envelope; she couldn't breathe.

Within half an hour the sky turned black, with dark clouds so low they seemed to touch the lampposts. The air was charged with a strange kind of electricity that day, a prickling, uncomfortable static that erupted suddenly into a freak midday storm. It rained torrentially for an hour, interspersed with marble-sized hailstones and lightning that flashed like strobe lights. Beth could feel the thunderbolts shaking her apartment as she sat wrapped up in her flowery duvet at the window, transfixed.

It felt like an omen.

Their love was dying.

But she refused to hear the death rattle.

☼

To make matters worse, Beth didn't feel that she could confide in anyone. Her friends at the supermarket, her parents and her siblings, had all voiced relief that she had finally found herself a nice man. She couldn't bear annihilating that relief.

And yes, at times it did feel as if she was forcing the relationship, as if she was the only one calling and making dates; the only one saying, *I love you*, or making any effort at all. And yes, every magazine she read told her that if you tried too hard, love would retreat faster than a blind mole in daylight (although in less creative terms). But Beth was terrified that if she stopped forcing their quality time together, Pravesh wouldn't even notice.

The main problem, she admitted to herself, was that their relationship used to be based on mutual need, and much as Beth still needed him, Pravesh seemed suddenly self-sufficient. Somehow, while she wasn't looking, they had moved from being on the same page, to being in entirely different books. He made new friends, bought new clothes (in different colours, not just black) and started talking about rugby.

Beth had little to contribute to these conversations.

She mourned the loss of their time together – even the exasperating moments – desperate to resurrect it. It didn't seem possible that Pravesh could have a life without her when she felt entirely incapable of doing the same. She had always been chirpy, bubbly – irritatingly cheerful, even. She was the kind of person who answered every 'How are you?' with a 'Super-fantastic, thanks!', who drew smiley faces where no smiley faces belonged, who grinned so much her cheeks sometimes hurt.

But throughout those unhappy days, she longed for sore cheeks. Every grin felt like a grimace.

Beth's grimace would have turned to a groan had she known her Prince Charming had been taking off his crown for somebody else. Or his doublet. Or whatever it is that Prince Charmings have to remove before engaging in hanky-panky.

Yes, the two-timing nitwit had continued the pattern so recurrent in her love life: working through his issues with her, wringing her large and beautiful heart dry, and then – fully restored – venturing out on the road to less needy pastures.

The whole sordid tale began on one of Pravesh's (by then habitual) Tuesday-night bar crawls. The intense heat of the past few days acted like a garlic press on the city, squeezing all the flavour out of the surrounding restaurants and bars, and the scent of meat cooking, fish frying, and tequila pouring was intoxicating.

Pravesh and a few of his new cronies were (literally) crawling from bar to bar along Florida Road, Durban's party street for yuppies and other assorted not-quite-so-youngsters out for a good time. The night was stiflingly hot, the air thick with the promise of sex, and the warm wind carried just a hint of desperation. (Beth's alone-at-thirty-five panic attacks were always located here.)

Beggars and their babies slept on old blankets on the side of the road, ignored by drunken rich kids more concerned with finding the next beer than listening to the street kids' pleas. Inebriated drivers swerved to miss stumbling party boys and girls, and a sense of drunken urgency kept everyone moving down the road, in search of the bar that never closed.

The New Pravesh had developed an intense passion for bars, especially those in the Florida Road area. He loved the extreme tingling activated by people drowning their morals and their sorrows. (The death of resolve was one of his favourite fatalities.) Countless times Pravesh's heightened sensitivity picked up on stray women who walked in with firm resolutions not to hook up with a random guy, only to leave a few hours later, drunkenly hanging onto a stranger. Or men who came in for 'just one beer', and left when the bar closed. Alcoholics who tried sipping soda water, and then succumbed to the lure of the Jägermeister.

These casualties mixed into a heady cocktail of sensations, and Pravesh greedily lapped it up.

He soon found that he loved getting drunk, using sleazy pick-up lines and lusting after girls far too young for him. It was the fulfilment (at last!) of his fifteen-year-old attempts at rebellion at The Beer Bar. The dissolution of Pravesh's morals left him feeling as if his veins were flooded with champagne, his sensor dangerously overloaded.

He welcomed it with a leer.

The fourth bar Pravesh and his friends stumbled into that night was a double-storey olde Irish pub called Jimmy Fox's, adorned with Irish flags of all sizes and colours (except for one which was hung upside down, thereby officially making it the flag of Côte d'Ivoire). There, amidst the drunken pseudo-Irish cheer, Pravesh met his Dream Woman.

She had long, blonde hair, wore an obscenely short skirt, and answered Pravesh's calculatingly casual, 'So, what do you do?' with a giggle.

Then she flicked her hair and said, 'Well, I'm a part-time beautician. I specialise in pedicures, you know, painting toenails and stuff?'

Pravesh's heart stopped. A few seconds later, it started again. It was a direct sign from God. This luscious beauty – Tracy by name – had to be the girl for him.

'You know,' he said, with a practised leer, 'your make-up looks better smudged.'

Later that same night, Pravesh took her back to his apartment. It was the first time in his life that he had managed to pick up a woman in a bar, and take her home. And not just any woman – a hot blonde! Pravesh's arrogance bloomed like a seedling after the first spring rain.

The whole drunken drive home he kept up a running commentary.

'Baby, you made the right choice tonight,' he told her. 'Oh, yes … you won't regret coming home with Pravesh, I'll tell you that right now.'

His smooth, slippery voice turned the words into sleaze, oozing from some untapped, primal source.

At last they arrived at his flat. It was not in a nice neighbourhood. Tracy felt a little nervous walking to the door while Pravesh's neighbours, loitering outside the building and drinking beer, stared at her lasciviously. Pravesh, too intent on getting her upstairs, didn't notice.

The air in the stairwell smelt rank with other people's sweat. Tracy crinkled her nose. She was not a snob, not by any definition, but this was just a little too close to the industrial part of town. She liked the suburbs, where factories hadn't yet muscled in on the houses. A liquorice factory lay on the west side of Pravesh's apartment, a fertiliser factory on the east; depending which way the wind blew, his apartment smelt strongly of one of the two.

Pravesh had come to count heavily on a liquorice-scented day being a good omen.

But that night he didn't care about omens. His apartment was a dingy place – dark and dank with no clutter, no plants, no pictures, and dark grey walls barely lit up by a lone light bulb hanging from the ceiling. It looked utterly uninviting, unlived-in.

Tracy felt a moment of fear, walking down the long corridor leading from the kitchen to the bedroom and bathroom. The place reeked of a grisly newspaper story: this Pravesh could quite easily be a serial killer, she realised with a chill. He had been pawing at her all the way up the stairs, trying to slip her thong off as she walked, and all of a sudden his touch gave her goose bumps. Shaking her head to clear the thoughts, she walked into the bedroom and lay down invitingly on Pravesh's bed. It was long and narrow and he slept on black velvet sheets, even in summer.

Tracy was understandably a little disappointed that his inflated ego didn't translate into a similarly inflated talent in the bedroom. But she found that if she told him exactly what to do, it was moderately satisfying. And at least he didn't slice her up with a carving knife, turning her into dog food.

Pravesh told Beth that his pub-crawls were nightly (Beth didn't argue, she didn't have the energy) and spent every night with Tracy. The relentless heat of those summer nights slicked Tracy and Pravesh's bodies with sweat, made them slippery and lithe, made the velvet stick to their backs and thighs. Tracy left promptly at 11 pm each night – to go home for her beauty sleep, she told him – after which Pravesh fell into an exhausted slumber.

He was so worn out from these nightly sessions that he had no energy left for any sexual activity with Beth.

She was secretly relieved.

☼

The problem, of course, was that Pravesh ceased not only sexual activity with Beth, but *all* activity.

Usually Beth loved the beginning of summer because it meant trips to the beach, or lounging by the local swimming pool, or late sundowners at the Bat Centre next to the harbour. But this year, Beth simply sat inside her flat and sweated. The heat seemed to press in on her, giving her tension headaches, and the air in her home was so thick with humidity, she wished she could part it like a curtain and stick her head through, and breathe.

Something was definitely off that summer. Wherever Beth went, flies buzzed constantly around her head, and she couldn't shake the feeling that things were rotting. No amount of cheerful suggestions to Pravesh ever led to a summery outing, no matter how hard she hinted. Whereas before they had gone on all manner of interesting and delightful dates (during the well-documented courtship phase) now Beth could not remember the last time they had done anything even vaguely romantic. Her brave suggestion that they play a game of lawn bowls was met with scornful laughter.

Beth missed lawn bowls dreadfully, and kept meaning to pop by the clubhouse. But somehow the days turned into weeks, and she found herself still sitting on her couch in the sweltering heat, still sweating.

In fact, the only date they *ever* went on during those muggy post-confession days was to the local Mike's Kitchen to eat, and Beth suspected that was only because Pravesh was hungry, and it was his turn to cook.

The first time he suggested going to Mike's Kitchen, Beth was delighted. A date!

At last. She could just picture it – snuggling up on one of the long, comfortable booth seats, sharing an ice-cream sundae, and staring into each other's eyes. The burst of energy this hope gave her was enough for Beth to change into a dress (instead of the sweatpants and T-shirts she had recently adopted as her sole wardrobe), put on some eyeshadow, and even slip on her 'special' panties. She had been wearing stretched, beige cotton undies for days now, but the promise of a date led her to her black satin ones with little red bows.

They made her feel pretty.

The sound of Pravesh hooting from outside (he never came up anymore, just waited in the car, hooting impatiently), sent a thrill up and down Beth's spine. Perpetual hope was her new best friend. Her only friend. Maybe she had just imagined that they were having problems? Maybe it was all in her head, and things were actually still as wonderful as those first days.

Maybe she would start floating again!

Maybe not.

As soon as Beth opened the door and slid into the car, Pravesh started driving. Her attempt at a hello kiss was met with a cold cheek. Determined not to be put off, Beth persisted.

'So, how was your day?' she asked cheerily.

'Fine,' Pravesh replied.

'I was thinking,' she continued, looking out the window and refusing to be dragged down by his gloominess, 'maybe we could go and watch a movie after dinner? We haven't been to a movie in ages. It's still early.'

The hope that flowed out of Beth filled the car with tiny pink butterflies. Pravesh opened his window, and the gust of wind that blew in splattered the butterflies against Beth's closed window.

'I'm busy,' he said.

A hot wind was blowing that night, a wind that smelt somehow of foul eggs and felt like a portent more than an ordinary berg wind. Beth chose to ignore it, although it buffeted her skirt around her legs and messed up her carefully brushed hair.

When they walked into the restaurant, Pravesh headed straight upstairs without asking Beth where she wanted to sit. She slid into one of the leather booths and smiled at him invitingly, but he avoided eye contact as he sat down opposite her. She realised that he had not changed out of his work clothes, or shaved. She sniffed the air. He had not even bothered to put on deodorant that day, it seemed.

Pravesh deliberately placed his cell phone between them on the table, then stared at it longingly, willing it to ring. No matter how many interesting conversation starters Beth dangled in front of him, he did not bite.

'Hi, there! It's as hot as hell out there tonight, isn't it?' a smiley-eyed, middle-aged woman, wearing a too-tight uniform and too much pink eyeshadow, commented. 'What can I get you two love birds?'

Against her will, Beth felt tears welling up in her eyes, and turned her head away. There would be no shared ice-cream sundaes this evening, she could tell.

Pravesh looked up at the waitress and smiled.

'I'd love a bacon cheeseburger, if it's not too much bother,' he said in an unfamiliar, slippery voice, not waiting for Beth to order.

She looked up, startled. When had he started eating meat?

'Oh, and if you wouldn't mind, could you ask someone to switch on the TV, please?'

The waitress gave him a conspiratorial wink.

'No problem,' she said.

Turning to Beth with a kind smile, she asked, 'What about you, honey?'

Beth looked at the dessert menu disconsolately. She would have loved to order some Kiss Me! Italian Kisses, 'the lover's thing' as the menu called them, but she didn't think Pravesh was in the mood.

'I'll just have Mike's Famous Cheesecake, please,' Beth said in a choked voice, wondering for the hundredth time why her boyfriend was nice to everyone except her.

As soon as the waitress had left, Pravesh switched off the charm and leant back in his chair (as far away from her as he could, Beth thought sadly), playing games on his cell phone. A few minutes later, the TV screen – two metres from their table – was switched on, and Pravesh asked to swap seats with her so he could watch the news.

Slow, reluctant tears started trickling down Beth's face. Soon, her nose blocked up, and she had to breathe through her mouth. Pravesh stared right past her and didn't notice a thing. She tried humming the restaurant's catchy theme tune to lift her spirits – 'Mike's Kitchen, you couldn't eat better, even at twice the price!'

It didn't help. Looking at Pravesh only made her cry harder, so she turned in her seat, and looked around the restaurant, noticing the cheery black and white colour scheme and the rather pathetic porcelain plate display on the walls. It made her think of the porcelain plates at the Kingfisher's Bowling Club, which made her remember those first blissful weeks with Pravesh, when he had been attentive and sweet and smitten with her.

Just then the song changed, and Whitney Houston's 'I Will Always Love You' started playing. Beth had to bite her lip to keep from sobbing.

It was then that she noticed, through the iron balustrade next to their table, a familiar-looking man below, wearing a green corduroy jacket and humming quietly to himself. Beth blinked the tears from her eyes and looked again. Yes, humming, and *stealing money* off the tables downstairs – tips that people had left for their waitresses. The little man seemed to have perfected his technique; casually sidling up to a table, he pocketed the cash in a flash, and carried on walking.

One seamless, obviously practised, movement.

He was fairly inconspicuous, Beth reasoned, although, judging from the way people covered their noses and turned away as he walked past, he must have smelt pretty bad. Luckily, her nose was blocked. He looked very familiar, and she struggled to figure out where she might know him from. Handy Green Grocers? High school?

Beth smiled. She liked him, she decided, liked anyone who was daring enough to go out on a limb and do something dangerous. She hadn't done anything dangerous for months, she admitted to herself with a sigh, and a whole litre of fresh tears sprang to her eyes. She escaped to the bathroom, so she could cry in peace. (Pravesh didn't even notice her getting up.)

The bathroom was mauve and stank of cheap, pink liquid soap and fried onion rings. The smell overwhelmed her. Beth sat on the toilet seat, staring at someone's blue-penned graffiti on the back of the door: *Ugie 4 Snoeks 4eva*. Between that sweet confession of love and a bright baby-changing cushion next to the sink, it took her a good ten minutes to stop the flood of tears.

On her way back to the table, she bumped into a woman who had just walked into the restaurant. Beth recognised her immediately from the day of the supermarket robbery, but although they made eye contact and Beth could swear a glimmer of recognition sparked in her eyes, the woman promptly turned around and hurried away.

Beth remembered with dismay how intrigued Pravesh had been with her when she first told him about the robbery. But lately, it seemed, he couldn't care less – she could be choking on her cheesecake and he probably wouldn't lift his eyes from his stupid cell-phone game.

By the time she got back to the table, red-eyed and blocked-nosed, Pravesh had finished his burger and was tapping his car keys impatiently against the table, ready to leave. Beth had to take her cake home in a doggy bag.

The evening ended dismally, as anticipated, with Pravesh dropping Beth at her flat and abruptly leaving, just as the hot wind finally delivered its promise – a brief rain shower that coincided with Beth's slow walk to her front door.

With wet hair and a heavy heart, she sank into bed, exhausted. She used to fantasise about different romantic scenarios to relax before she went to sleep. These days, it felt like too much effort.

※ ※ ※

So, if things were so very bad, why did either party bother? Well, that's a rather interesting question, isn't it? A question that could apply to some people you know, you might even say, people who find themselves stuck in a relationship so comfortable and passionless it might as well be an old armchair left in the corner of the living room. But Beth and Pravesh's situation was perhaps somewhat unique. (Although, in all honesty, don't we all like to think our situation is unique? Just before we hear, repeated in a romantic comedy on TV, the very same words we've spoken to our ex-lovers. And then the sad truth sinks in.)

Beth, as we already know, had made up her mind that this relationship was It, for better or worse.

Pravesh, on the other hand – well.

Pravesh had no doubt that It was over, but had decided (in his new, confident frame of mind) that simply killing the relationship would be a temporary pleasure far inferior to the lingering benefits of keeping Beth around, so that he could continue to enjoy the buzzing sensation and rush of adrenalin generated by her dying hopes, the death of his love for her, the death of his sensitive side, and, especially, the inevitable decay of her self-esteem.

It was a veritable crackpot of death. Pravesh felt high on it for days.

※ ※ ※

It was two weeks before Beth started adding up how many pub nights she thought there had been lately (fourteen, Pravesh went out every night) and then calculated how many beers he must have drunk during those fourteen nights (at least three a night, therefore at least forty-two beers, at five hundred millilitres each, which rounded off to approximately twenty-one litres of beer). Beth's calculations confirmed her fears that Pravesh was turning into an alcoholic.

That simply would not do.

Ever since that night at Mike's Kitchen, when Beth had glimpsed the sleek-haired woman from the Handy Green Grocers robbery, the night-mares had returned. Every night, the same scenario – Beth was back in the supermarket, back with the two men pointing guns at her, only this time she couldn't speak, couldn't say 'Please don't kill me' over and over again, couldn't convince them that they could take anything they wanted, if they would only leave.

Beth woke up just before the guns fired, but she was absolutely certain that they did fire, every night, and that because she had not been able to speak, she had been shot. Every morning began this way, whether she had the nightmare at 1 am, 4.30 am or 7 am, because once Beth had woken up, she refused to go back to sleep, in case the nightmare returned. Bedtime turned to dread.

The sticky summer nights exhaled fear.

She did everything possible to stay awake late, to avoid sleep, to soothe herself into a half-sleep so that she wouldn't dream.

Nothing worked.

By the time she detected Pravesh's problem, Beth was hanging on by her last, frazzled nerves. And so she resolved (perhaps not entirely in a clear-headed and sensible way) to *do* something. She was not going to let her precious Pravesh throw his life away on booze! Oh no. She was, after all, his Saviour. The one who gave him meaning in life, and helped him navigate the dark swamps of his issues.

She decided to go over to his apartment and talk some sense into him.

She just had to wait for him to get back from the pub.

So, after a couple of hours, sweet Beth traipsed off to Pravesh's apartment, seven blocks away, sure that at almost 11 pm, he would be home. Walking the streets of Durban at night as a single female is not a clever thing to do. In fact, it's downright stupid. As the heat of the day finally lifted, slime-balls and crooksters started emerging from dark doorways like rats from sewers. Once or twice she heard someone following her for a few steps.

But Beth believed so strongly in her Guardian Angel Status that she chanced it, smiling sweetly at dodgy men offering her a score and ignoring the suggestive comments of bored drunkards loitering on street corners. The night air was chilly for the first time in weeks, scented with tragedy and the smell of burnt rubber, but Beth chose to ignore the obvious, and whistled a happy tune as she passed red traffic light after red traffic light.

When she arrived at Pravesh's apartment, more than a little out of breath, she rang the bell. There was no answer, so she rang again. And again. And then resolved to wait on the cold, hard pavement.

The air outside smelt like fertiliser. Chicken shit. Beth breathed through her mouth. Not five minutes later, the front door of the apartment block opened and a tall, curvaceous blonde in a tiny mini-skirt walked out.

'Are you going in?' she asked Beth, in a friendly voice.

'Oh, yes, thanks awfully,' replied Beth, 'it's a little nippy out here. Nice wig, by the way.' Beth was not being sarcastic. She really liked the wig.

'Thanks,' said the wigged woman casually (let's call her 'Tracy', shall we?).

She paused to shake out her sleek, black shoulder-length hair, moving into the circle of light spilling from the street lamp, just as Beth stood up into that same golden light. Both women paused, motionless. Beth's gasp caught in the back of her throat, Tracy's eyes momentarily unmasked by surprise. Then, breaking the stare, Tracy hurried off, leaving Beth with one hand on the doorknob, and the other half-raised, as if to call her back.

How was it possible, in a city the size of Durban, to run into the same woman twice in one week? What was the Universe trying to tell her?

In retrospect, the events that followed condensed into one, long, sticky reel in Beth's mind – walking up the stairs, stepping over a purple thong, entering the apartment, seeing Pravesh, and knowing, even before he said those fateful words – 'Beth, we need to talk' – knowing that it was over.

Somehow, once he had spoken, time reverted back to normal. A spell had been broken. The air smelt of sweat and an unfamiliar, musky perfume, and something else Beth couldn't name. Pravesh sat down at his tiny dining-room table and gestured to the only other chair, opposite him. With a mounting feeling of panic, Beth sank into it.

'I … well, I hate to do this to you, Beth, but I'm afraid it's over. I've met someone else, and I think I'm in love.'

The words *I'm in love* absorbed all the air in the room. Beth nodded, concentrating too hard on trying to get enough oxygen, to reply.

'I'm sorry. I didn't mean to hurt you. I couldn't help myself. It's not you, it's me.'

Pravesh's words, spoken in monotone, hung sullenly in the air in front of Beth, like trails of cigarette smoke. She looked at them carefully. The dark grey walls closed in on her and Beth longed to turn around and run away, out of the flat, down the stairs, out the front door, and all the way back to her cosy, warm home, where she could curl up on her purple beanbag and watch *My Fair Lady*, and pretend she had never heard these words, never had to hear these words, never would hear these words coming from Pravesh's mouth.

He waited, staring at her in a disinterested way.

'How can you do this to me?' she asked at last, in a small, vulnerable voice. 'After all I've done for you, how can you do this to me? I've bent over backwards for you, Pravesh, for us!'

She breathed in through her nose.

'This can't be happening,' she said softly.

Pravesh also took a deep breath, and sighed.

'It's just not working, Beth. I need my space. I don't feel the same way anymore. I think you're a wonderful person. I hope we can still be friends.' He delivered the lines in a deadpan voice, looking over Beth's shoulder and out the window at the night sky.

Beth closed her eyes and breathed in and out. It felt as if she was watching the scene from the outside, wishing she had the power to stop it, or at least change the dialogue. How had they reached this point? Her heart was pounding so heavily that she felt like vomiting. She squeezed her hands together tightly, clenched her jaw, and tried to keep her voice calm. Perhaps he could still be convinced to change his mind.

'I just don't understand why, Pravesh. I did everything right!' She tried to smile. 'We were going to get married!'

Pravesh laughed disbelievingly, and then stopped himself.

'No, Beth, we weren't,' he said, and stood up.

Beth stood up too, walked over to him, and tried to hold his hand. He pulled it away.

'I don't want to rush you,' he said, in a tone that implied that that was exactly what he wanted to do. 'But I need to be up early for work in the morning.'

That was it. It was over.

Beth had only one weapon left. 'Why? So you can paint dead people's toenails, you *freak*?'

The last word surprised her as it escaped from her lips.

There was a silence so sharp it cut into their skins.

Pravesh paused.

His whole body stiffened.

Through pursed lips, and with eyes full of hatred, he said, 'Don't you ever, *ever* tell anyone about that, you hear me? Never! It never happened!'

And with a final look of scorn, Pravesh sent Beth out of his apartment and out of his life.

☼ ☼ ☼

Pravesh was not trying to be an ass. In his head, in fact, he wasn't being an ass at all; he was being kind but firm, gentle but straightforward, letting Beth down in the easiest possible way. I would go so far as to purport that most of the time, if we were able to get inside a person's head, nobody thinks he's being an ass. Nobody thinks she's a total bitch. Nobody thinks they're Satan Personified.

Therein lies the beauty of the human animal – we can reason our way out of any behaviour.

It's either that, or we're all just trying our hardest, making the decisions we feel are best, even if they regrettably end up hurting others.

The point is, Pravesh didn't think he was being particularly roguish.

Beth, naturally, did.

What she didn't understand (and it probably would not have helped if she had) was that Pravesh was truly – at last – in love. All those years of blaming his parents for his inability to love had been only part of the problem. Pravesh could not love because (drum roll please) he found himself unlovable. He couldn't imagine anyone accepting his corpse-toenail-painting fetish, and so he cordoned off the section of his heart reserved for love. Beth accepting his little hobby allowed him to take down the barricade.

Alas, not for her, but for Tracy.

☼ ☼ ☼

Pravesh woke up smiling the day after breaking up with Beth. The first time, he reflected, that he had ever woken up smiling, but he felt certain it was the first of many. He was in such a chipper mood, in fact, that he didn't even talk to himself in his funereal voice that morning, but hummed instead. Yes, hummed!

And the humming quickly turned to a tone-deaf whistle on his way to work. Pravesh only knew one happy tune – 'Don't Worry, Be Happy' – and the only reason he knew it was because his mother had given him a singing doorbell once. He had disconnected it after just one day, but the tune popped involuntarily into his head that morning, and for once he didn't wish for some quick neurosurgery to remove it.

When Pravesh arrived at work, he made a big decision. Tracy was clearly the girl for him – his Dream Woman – and he was pretty sure she felt the same way about him. Totally sure, in fact. Now that they didn't have to sneak around all the time, they could enjoy a proper relationship. Dinner, visits at work, maybe a pedicure or two.

That last thought sent shivers down Pravesh's spine, and he grinned suddenly, confusing the grieving parents he was busy interviewing. When Tracy came over that evening, he decided, he would have a romantic, candlelit dinner waiting for her. Over wine and roses, Pravesh would break the good news to her, gently, so that she didn't get too excited. And then they could carry on with their usual, frisky evening activities.

For the rest of the day, he dwelt in a happy daze, mixing up bodies and coffins, placing corpses upside down, and almost sending the wrong body to be cremated. He sang the 'Dooo-doo-doo-doo-de-de-doo' part of 'Don't Worry Be Happy' over and over again under his breath, until his colleagues looked at him awry. But one of the great advantages of working as an undertaker, as far as Pravesh was concerned, was that nobody ever asked questions.

Undertakers learn this early on.

Pravesh had the whole evening planned – what to eat, drink and wear, and exactly how to phrase the wonderful news to Tracy. There were three options: 'Well, baby, your prayers have been answered! I dumped my girlfriend, so now I'm all yours.' A bit coarse, perhaps. 'Tracy, baby, I've been thinking. I don't want to be with anyone else, ever again. Your wish has been granted, we don't have to hide our love anymore!' Maybe a bit over-the-top. 'At last we are free to love each other, wherever and whenever we want! All day! All night! Your wishes and prayers have been answered! Tracy, baby, I'm yours!'

Perfect.

That evening, Tracy arrived at 8 pm on the dot, wearing an even tinier skirt than usual. Pravesh took it as a good sign. It was a hot, humid night, and the air in the apartment smelt sweetly of roses and liquorice. He had a table set up in the middle of the room, covered with a black tablecloth, red roses, two long candles, and a bottle of red wine. Tracy loved red wine, and gladly accepted the glass that Pravesh poured for her.

The dinner had taken Pravesh ages to prepare (cooking was by no means his forte) and Tracy oohed and aahed over the food and the candles, although she did seem a little put out that they weren't heading straight for the bedroom. She even tried spilling food down her cleavage so that he would be forced to clean her up, and thereby skip dinner for 'dessert', but it didn't work.

Pravesh was a man on a mission. He couldn't treat his girlfriend like a slut, only his mistress.

Mustering all his self control, he tore his eyes from her and said, 'Tracy, baby, come and sit down. I've got something to tell you, before we go to the bedroom.'

Tracy pouted beautifully. 'But, Praveshy-pooh, I don't want to talk, I want to fuck!' She unbuttoned her dress as she spoke, and Pravesh had to close his eyes and shake his head vigorously to resist crawling over to her.

Eyes still closed, he said sternly, 'No, Tracy, just this once we need to talk, baby. It won't take long.'

Pravesh waited till she was seated before he took a deep breath, ran the line over in his head one more time, and blurted out: 'At last we are free to love each other, wherever and whenever we want! All day! All night! Your wishes and prayers have been answered! Tracy, baby, I'm yours!'

There was a dead pause. Not shocked or delighted or flabbergasted, just dead. Pravesh sensed it straight away, his heart rate sped up, and the backs of his knees tingled painfully.

He suddenly felt a little nauseous.

'*What?*' Tracy said eventually, a profound look of contempt in her eyes, and every hint of the playful seductress gone in an instant.

'What did you do? What the hell do you mean 'my wishes and prayers' have been answered? What wishes and prayers?'

Her voice was dangerously soft.

Pravesh didn't pick up on the warning sign. How sweet, he thought, she really is rather dim. She doesn't understand the magnitude of what I've just said.

'Tracy, baby,' he repeated gently, patronisingly, 'what I'm telling you, is that I've broken up with my girlfriend, so that you and I don't have to sneak around any more. You can be my girlfriend, full-time!'

Tracy looked at him like he was a hideous form of gecko, grown to human size.

'What on God's good earth gave you the idea that I wanted to be your girlfriend?' she asked scathingly. 'To be perfectly honest, I couldn't imagine anything worse.'

She watched as the poison of her words sank in, turning Pravesh's skin pale, and his eyes bloodshot.

His mouth fell open in disbelief.

The sweet smell of roses and liquorice turned sickly.

Tracy took a deep breath and leaned forward, enunciating each word carefully.

'Let me spell it out for you, Pravesh – you are not good enough for me.'

Then she sat back in her chair, and smoothed her dress down over her hips, pulling it nice and tight, satisfied that she had made her point clear.

'In fact,' she added as an afterthought, 'I think you and your mousy girlfriend are a perfect match. I saw her yesterday, and she looked like just the kind of girl you should be going out with.'

A suffocating cloud of confusion settled on Pravesh, blurring his vision and dulling his senses. Where had his Tracy, his dim-witted, giggly girl, gone? And who was this spiteful shrew masquerading in her place? Was it possible that she had a twin? His mouth still agape, his eyes even more bloodshot, he stared at her, wordless.

'I have a fiancé, Pravesh,' Tracy explained, sounding tired.

She leant over to pick up her handbag, preparing to leave.

'You were never anything more than some last-minute random sex before I settle down.'

She stood up, and looked at him with a mixture of disgust and annoyance.

'Honestly! Why do men have to screw things up every time? I was looking forward to some kinky sex in our last week together.' She shook her head and sighed irritably. 'Thanks a lot.'

And with that, Tracy stalked out of the room, pulling off her wig as she left and slamming the door behind her. Secretly, she was relieved. Besides the obvious perk of not having to return to that sleazy apartment, she did not like the proximity of Pravesh's girlfriend to her own life. She didn't need any reminder of the robbery.

Astonished, Pravesh slumped down in his chair. He was in love! *They* were in love! That wasn't the right response at all! He had imagined a few possible versions, but that certainly wasn't one of them. It was all too much for one evening.

Pravesh needed some solace, some comfort.

He needed to go to the morgue and paint some toenails.

☼

Pravesh usually felt happiest in the morgue, but not that night. That night he felt like a fool.

An aging, useless fool.

All that time he had been thinking Tracy was with him because he was cool and attractive and suave; he had been making all those plans for their future together (outlined in great detail in his head). He cringed when he thought of all the nights he'd treated her like an imbecile.

That night, Pravesh painted eight sets of toenails without pause: a new record. Unfortunately, there was nobody he could boast to. He had rarely been in the morgue at midnight – a long, metal room, filled with bodies in various stages of disrepair that would usually make his knees and ears go berserk, and his heart race in a pleasantly excited way.

But that night his detectors were malfunctioning.

In fact, all his senses seemed to have shut down. Pravesh sniffed, and couldn't smell the strong tang of formaldehyde that usually clung to his clothes; blinked, and battled to differentiate between the pink and brown nail polish in his hands; swallowed, and could taste nothing but despair.

The stifling humidity of that hot Durban summer had inched its way inside the morgue, and Pravesh found himself sweating profusely. Soon, his clothes were drenched. He took off his shirt and pants, and spread

119

them neatly over the back of a chair, considered lying down on the cold floor, but decided against it.

When he had finished the first round of toenails – three males (brown nail polish), three females (pink nail polish), two females (red nail polish) – he paused, and took a deep breath.

He still didn't feel any better.

And so Pravesh returned to the first set of toes, and painted them all again. The eight cadavers were lined up in a row, their shoes and socks neatly placed on the floor at their feet, their toenails bizarrely fresh and alive in comparison to their waxy skins. But it was a messy pedicure. Pravesh's hands were too shaky to paint neatly, and the guilt of sending the dead to their graves with untidy toenails made him cry even harder. He lost track of time, circling the corpses like a lone dancer in a strangely spotlit room.

It was a peculiar sight.

Which nobody should have seen.

Unfortunately, due to his extreme emotional distress at the time of entering the morgue, Pravesh had forgotten to take his usual precautions – double-locking the stainless steel door and putting a chair under the handle. He had, in fact, been particularly careless, and merely closed the door behind him.

Big mistake.

When the head undertaker, Frank Simmons (not the Frankie of Frankie's Funeral Parlour, but his great-grandson) popped in for an early-morning survey of the work to be done that day, he found Pravesh, in his best green undies, crying while painting Mrs Naidoo's toenails a shocking fuscia.

'Pravesh! What the *hell* do you think you're doing?' he asked, his incredulous gaze travelling from Pravesh's red-rimmed eyes, to his pale, pantless legs, to the line of eight barefoot corpses, over and over again, trying to comprehend what he was seeing. His face turned a dangerous shade of puce.

There was a long pause as Pravesh turned around, registered his boss's presence, what that meant for his undertaking career, and tried desperately to think of a plausible explanation. Unsurprisingly, he hit a blank; couldn't speak even if he wanted to, because the air he was trying to breathe stuck in his throat like a wad of chewing gum.

Mr Simmons was breathing heavily through his nose, and his eyes bulged.

'You're finished, Pravesh,' he said at last, quietly, through clenched teeth. 'Get out of my morgue!'

His eyes flashed sparks at Pravesh, who scampered from the room in his underwear, running down the passage, and onto the street outside.

☼

The funeral parlour was in the heart of the city – street vendors in need of a bath set up shop on the pavement with small pyramids of oranges and apples, hawkers with shifty eyes tried harassing passers-by to take a look at their cheap-cheap watches, and medicine men sat serenely behind displays of innards, monkey skulls and animal hides that reeked in the heat. A layer of smog, sadness and shortage hung over everything like a sickly yellow cloud.

☼ ☼ ☼

Sometimes in life (rarely, yes, but sometimes) there are moments that act as doorways into another kind of reality. Moments, for example, that make you realise how easy it would be to abandon all semblance of normality by the wayside, pick up a trolley from Pick 'n Pay, start loading it with tin cans and random bits of crap, and slowly begin losing your mind – talking to robots as if they were people, trying to unlock the secrets of the tin can, entertaining ideas about prophecies.

Pravesh was in the midst of one such moment. His heart rate sped up so fast he started seeing black dots dancing before his eyes, an iron clamp squeezed all the air from his lungs, and he started getting severe cramping along both arms.

There he stood, convulsing on the busy pavement in his underpants, surrounded by early morning commuters.

Nobody looked at him twice.

☼ ☼ ☼

After a few moments, the panic subsided. The smell of not-so-fresh fish and sun-ripened meat hit Pravesh across the face. He hardly noticed. Men with Polaroid cameras mimed taking his photograph, shouting, 'Passport photo! Passport photo!' Women with babies strapped on their backs displayed their tables full of underpants, safety pins and hopes while children with torn pieces of cardboard and stray dogs played make-believe with the breeze.

The children were the only ones to stare openly.

Dazed, Pravesh randomly chose a direction and stumbled down the street, bumping into people and being pushed off the pavement into the open gutter, which was swimming in a murky film of liquid. The heat that lay like a blanket over the city wrapped him up, and he broke into a feverish sweat. Mini-bus taxis hooted at him, drivers cursed from still-moving cars, and one or two people on bicycles rode over his toes.

Nobody seemed to notice him, too intent on running the red robots that confronted them at every turn.

For the rest of the day Pravesh wandered the streets of the city – down lanes that sold saris and bindis and Mother-in-Law Hellfire spices, up alleys peddling cheap Chinese plastic goods and traditional Shweshwe fabric, and along suspiciously vacant roads where every window had double burglar guards and women peeked out of their front doors nervously.

Fear hung in the air like smoke. The smell of too many people all living together mingled with overcooked curry and exhaust fumes, soaking up all the oxygen in the air.

The yelping *umgodoyi* in the area started following Pravesh, sensing that he was in need of man's best friend, but uncertain how to approach someone with death in his eyes. He passed old men playing chess on the side of the road, impromptu hair salons set up with just a painted sheet for privacy, and swindlers shuffling cards while a huddle of hopefuls crowded close. Their hope smelt like freshly baked bread and Pravesh tried to linger so that some of it would waft over to him. The crowd gave him dirty looks. He accepted them graciously.

If Pravesh had had anything to steal, he would have been mugged. As it was, naked except for his undies, he was ignored, left to burn his feet on the hot tar and turn his usually light brown skin a dark reddish brown from the relentless sun. By the end of the day, the normally neat and tidy Pravesh would have passed for a hobo down on his luck – his black hair messy, his body filthy, his eyes tinged with that distinctive, crazy look usually reserved for lunatics running naked along the freeway.

By late afternoon he was being trailed by thirteen mangy *umgodoyi*.
Pravesh was a mess.

As night fell, he managed to turn around and head back in the general direction of his home. Lost and bewildered, Pravesh couldn't help wondering how he had fallen so far, so fast. Just yesterday he'd had a job, a girlfriend *and* a mistress, and now, by some cruel blow of fate, he had nothing.

(Well, let's be honest, it wasn't so much a blow of fate as his own stupid fault, but trudging along a highway in your underpants in the middle of the night tends to make one's thoughts a tad melodramatic.)

Pravesh did get home at last, around 3 am. He crawled up the stairs to his apartment and spent ten minutes weeping over the discarded purple thong on the sixteenth step. Then he used the spare key under his mat (the one he had planned on giving to Tracy) to open his door, and fell into an exhausted sleep.

For the next three days, Pravesh tried everything possible to convince Tracy to speak to him, but to no avail. Eventually, he gave up, and slept for a week, waking only to use the toilet and eat uncooked rice (the only food he could find in the house). He woke to a pounding headache every time he opened his eyes. Most days, he didn't open the curtains or switch on the lights, and, gradually, his world shrank until he could not imagine anything outside his dingy home.

He started to think he had made Tracy up, but then pulled out the purple thong she had left (which he kept under his pillow) and stroked it softly, trying to remember how her voice had sounded when she said his name. He found himself absentmindedly sucking his thumb again, a habit he had painfully outgrown at age seven.

Somehow it made him feel a tiny bit more human.

※ ※ ※

And Beth?

Beth was also a mess. She had cashed in her ticket to the merry-go-round, only to find herself deposited halfway down the road to her alone-at-thirty-five panic attack. Sure, you might say that she had brought it on herself, what with her unhealthy delusions of Grand Love and all that, but let us try – just for a moment – to imagine how Beth must have felt: to trust that Pravesh was The One, and then have that trust demolished, without any hope of salvage.

Life without that one guiding belief – the belief that had kept her buoyed up even in the absence of friends and lawn bowls and romance – felt like living without a central nervous system.

※ ※ ※

Beth woke up in the mornings and didn't know what to do.

Not having to think about Pravesh, or worry about Pravesh, or try to get hold of Pravesh, took away all meaning from her days. Going to work was too much of an effort, as was getting out of bed and showering and combing her hair. Any time she fell asleep, it was a desperate, hot, feverish sleep that circled only and always around the nightmare of the robbery. Her dreams left her constantly exhausted, constantly on edge, constantly in a state of fear.

She couldn't bear the thought of leaving her flat.

So Beth's home slowly filled with the thick fog of depression, and her toilet bowl slowly filled with snotty tissues as she battled to do anything but cry. She looked through her beautiful, completed scrapbook, and cried. She looked at photos (and screensavers and mousepads) of Pravesh, and cried. She lay on her bed, looking out the window, and cried. She traced the outlines of the thin, red crescents marked into her palms from their first date, and cried and cried and cried.

She cried until her eyes puffed up into slits.

And then, one night, Beth woke up for the third time in two hours, gasping and panicky from the same nightmare, and made a sleep-sodden decision: It was time to let go of the robbery.

She had not died.

They had not killed her.

It was time to let go.

Exhausted and achey-eyed, Beth thought about the robbery head-on for the first time in months; thought about it, and pictured it exactly as it had happened, and then, when the bottled-up feelings in her stomach made her retch, she blew, as hard as she could, out the window.

She blew away the nausea, and the panic, and the injustice; and the fear and the fear and the fear.

She blew it all away.

And then Beth fell back onto her pillows, and slept through till morning.

 and

On that day – the day when the air was charged with electricity, and the sky dark and brooding – Mdu's life changed forever. Oh, I know people bandy that little phrase around, that 'life-changing' phrase. Give someone a heartbreaking CD, a really good bar of chocolate or an excellent episode of TV and you'll have 'changed their life'. But this time it was for real. The habitual lonesomeness that he threw on every morning like a heavy overcoat was interrupted by a girl so full of sadness, it seeped out of her like water from a sponge.

Now, you might want to argue that it was nothing profoundly cosmic that drew Aisha and Mdu together. That it was, instead, the strange magnetism that had lured Aisha's dreams, since childhood, to linger after their allotted time. You might want to argue that, yes.

You might be right.

＊

After swimming a slow breaststroke for four hours, Aisha heard, somewhere in the back of her mind, a strange clicking sound. Then the water around her erupted in an oval of small fountains, and a pod of five whales revealed themselves briefly before sinking back underwater. They were unperturbed by her presence.

She continued swimming with just the faintest smile playing across her face. The whales' soft cries lulled her into a deep slumber, where her dreams were able to find her again. She swam in a trance, her slow breathing the only sound in her ears. She swam in the rip tides created by the whales' huge bodies, and so, without entirely meaning to, she swam straight into Mdu's life.

There is a moment that happens once, if ever, in a person's life. A moment where everything radically shifts under the surface – unnoticeable to the outside eye – and nothing is ever the same again.

Mdu, with only the merest trace of foreboding, was on the brink of such a moment. He was standing on the cruise ship deck, listening idly to the whales' chatter and daydreaming, as he did every day while out on the ship. It was a stiflingly hot morning, the dark clouds pushing the heat closer to the sea, the air heavy with moisture. The air was electric, and made the hair on his forearms tingle, warning him that an epic thunderstorm was on its way.

As Mdu turned to face land, he saw a bank of clouds rolling towards the ship at a steady pace and could glimpse, even from that distance, a sheet of lightning flashing from their heart. He only just had time to usher all the passengers below deck before the storm hit, littering the ship with hailstones, deluging the deck chairs and tearing the fabric off the large sun umbrellas. He watched the rain pelting down for a full hour until, as quickly as it had come, the storm moved off with a last flash of lightning that seemed to quicksilver across the water, giving the air an unearthly glow, searing the image onto his eyes and making everything smoulder at the edges of his sight.

The ship looked wrecked in the bruised light that followed the storm. Pieces of umbrella and deck chair were strewn about, and everything swam in a foot of water. But the air, for the fist time in weeks, was breathable and cool, and the sea shone calm and eerie in the golden afterglow. A shaft of sunlight broke through the leftover grey clouds and lit the water just as Mdu noticed five large whales surfacing not ten metres from the boat.

He recognised them immediately as a transient group of killer whales. When they surfaced again, this time much closer, Mdu saw what he had not noticed before – a small shape wedged between them; a small shape that was not whale, but human.

For five full seconds Mdu froze.

He knew exactly what he had to do in this situation, knew that there was nobody else above deck who could jump in and save that person, knew that to be this far out in the open sea, it had to be a matter of life and death.

But he froze. Just as he had done in the supermarket. And then, in a supreme act of will, fuelled by every moment of self-loathing he had had in the past few weeks, he threw on a life jacket and jumped feet first into the water, in what he hoped would be a life-defining, life-saving incident.

As Mdu swam closer, he saw that it was a woman, and frantically called out, expecting her to start flailing about or to slip under the surface at any moment. But the beautiful girl just kept swimming, rhythmically, calmly, in a deep trance.

It was only when he came within reaching distance of her, treading water and wiping the salt from his eyes, that he saw that she was crying. Trickles of teardrops dripped softly down her cheeks and fell silently into the vast ocean. She seemed not to tire as he swam next to her for ten minutes, until his arms and legs began to ache, and the cruise ship started fading out of sight. Her face looked exhausted – flat and colourless, pale and wan, excused from reality, as it were. But there was something about her that Mdu could not pull away from.

It was then that Mdu made the biggest decision of his life – although how much of it was rational and how much because of a maddening scent that infused the air surrounding her, he could not tell. Gently, he turned her around so that she faced the prow of the cruise ship. This was her journey, he had just chosen the destination.

Time slowed as they moved towards the boat; slowed, so that Mdu could see, for the first time in his life, how it looked when sunlight pierced the water, could feel the slimy caress of a fish flitting past, and smell the heady wildness of salt and unfathomable deep. He felt infinitesimally tiny, adrift in a vastness that seemed to reduce his life – up to that point – to irrelevance. To keep from succumbing to the eerie unreality that had seeped into his pores soon after diving in to save the girl, he focused not on the water, but on her; and yet, the flash of fear he felt at being out so deep flared brighter when he looked at her.

And then, like the lights being switched on at the end of a heart-wrenching movie, the spell broke. In a rush of sound and colour, time sped up as two bright orange lifebelts were thrown overboard by the crew, hauling Mdu and Aisha up by thick ropes. The harsh droning of the ship's engines, the sound of passengers and crew chattering like mynah birds, the clanking of chains and the rising wave of hysteria grated Mdu's nerves. He longed for the silence of moments before, wished there was a mute button some-one could press.

One of the crew members was dispatched to find two dry towels and while they waited, a shivering Mdu studied Aisha more carefully. He realised that she was the first person he had ever met who did not have a chorus of voices constantly debating in her head. She had not yet spoken a single word and seemed unaware of the cold or the wind or the excitement her arrival had caused. With a slight, faraway smile, she stood staring calmly out to sea.

As the sun emerged from behind the clouds and shone warmly on them, she glanced up for a moment. A gaggle of cruise-ship passengers huddled a few feet away taking photos. Aisha did not notice. They passed a fishing boat laden with reeking, sun-baked fish, and all the passengers gagged. Aisha did not flinch.

※ ※ ※

You might be thinking that instead of just studying her from a distance, Mdu should have been asking Aisha questions, checking her vital signs, ensuring that her eyes were not damaged by the long exposure to sea water. You might be thinking that that's what you'd be doing, what anyone with half a brain would be doing.

Why was she swimming with whales? How long had she been out at sea? Was there anyone who needed alerting that she had been found? Was she injured, harmed, scared or psychotic?

I totally see your point.

※ ※ ※

But Mdu chose not to. He simply stood behind her, guarding her like a bulldog, his broad shoulders and sharply defined face making him look far sterner than he felt. The setting sun lent a fiery glow to his dark skin and the cruise-ship passengers – all foreigners – felt as if they were facing a reincarnation of Shaka Zulu: an image to be stored in a little box in their minds, only to be opened when they were old and partly senile, and reminiscing over the few truly remarkable moments of their lives.

When they reached the harbour, Mdu was the first one off the ship, leading Aisha tenderly by the hand. She followed him meekly, still in a daze, and he helped her gently into his car and then drove her to his house.

This tender kidnapping felt like the most logical thing to do in a clearly illogical situation.

Aisha's silence was complete. She did not speak as they drove to Mdu's home, staring mutely out the window with that same vague air of confusion, and when she stubbed her toe on the step leading up to Mdu's front door, her mouth opened briefly, but no sound came out.

Her dark eyes were filled with clouds and they continued to drip a steady flow of tears. Aisha walked wherever he led her and sat down when he gave her a chair, but otherwise it looked as if she was still in the ocean, floating contentedly.

Mdu's house was small and rundown, cosy in a lived-in kind of way. The paint was peeling in the bathroom, the kitchen cupboards hung off-kilter, and there were large bubbles in the bedroom-ceiling paint. A few steps led from the sparsely furnished living room to a shoebox garden, which was overflowing with wild flowers – a chunk of veld contained by a red brick wall. There was a constant fragrance in the air from all the flowers. It was Mdu's favourite spot.

But that evening he led Aisha straight to his tiny kitchen, where he fed her Pronutro cereal like a baby, spoon by spoon. He couldn't think what else to do. He was working largely on intuition, on gut feel, on a strange hunch that may or may not have been based on an old TV commercial.

Afterwards, he tucked her into his own bed, drew the curtains, and quietly turned out the light. Her breathing was so light that had he not known there was someone in the room, he would have thought it empty. He still could hear no inner whisper; not a single loud thought escaped her mind.

Later that night, when he was sure she was asleep, Mdu made himself a pot of tea and then walked outside to sit on the back steps, his view obscured by masses of flowers and weeds. He poured a stream of tea into the green china mug he always used and sipped it thoughtfully.

Aisha was certainly the saddest person Mdu had ever met – she cried so constantly that he worried she might soon dissolve, like a cube of sugar in a cup of tea. There was no way of finding out why she was so sad, or who she was, or why she had been so far out in the ocean. And although she smiled vaguely at him when he spoke to her, she had yet to utter a single word.

Perhaps it was the total acceptance with which Aisha treated each moment that allowed Mdu to believe that somehow, against all logic, it made sense for her to be staying in his house, rather than in a police cell, waiting to be claimed.

He couldn't shake the feeling that there would be nobody to claim her.

But he knew that underneath his rationalisation, like a pass-the-parcel surprise, lay another, more honest reason. This stranger was the first person he had ever welcomed into his home. From the moment he escaped his parent's stranglehold, Mdu held his personal space sacred, never again wanting to allow other people to suck the oxygen out of it.

But this girl, he thought, amazed, somehow made the air lighter, sweeter even.

It sounded ridiculous.

With a sigh, Mdu drained the dregs of his now-cold tea and stepped back inside, closing the door softly behind him.

☼

For three scorching summer days, Mdu treated Aisha like a small injured bird – conscious of her every sound, dozing next to her bed in a large easy-chair in case she woke up scared, and stroking her hair in his sleep when she whimpered in hers. Occasionally, Aisha woke with a start, surprised to find herself not swimming, but in a bed in a room, yet at the same time completely accepting, as if it was all just a dream.

As far as Mdu could tell, she had no recollection from one day to the next. She did not recognise him or the room or any of her surroundings, and stared at it all each day with the mild curiosity of a newly awakened coma patient.

She did not complain about the heat, either, although it turned the room into a steam bath and beaded her skin with sweat.

Mdu occasionally worried if she wasn't perhaps brain-damaged from too much time in the ocean. That seemed possible: dehydration and excessive sun exposure could blight normal functioning. But, as on the first day, he remained reluctant to take her to a hospital – he couldn't bear the thought of subjecting her to all that cold metal machinery, scanning, intrusion, questioning, of having to admit that he knew nothing about her.

Some might call it hubris.

He preferred to think of it as subjective reasoning.

Aisha never complained. She lay in bed, sleeping or dozing or staring out the window, totally oblivious to the tears that had started forming shallow grooves in her skin from their constant trickle. As each tear finally slid from her face, it changed form, turning into a tiny iridescent bead, smooth and cool to the touch. When Mdu woke up that first morning, he found his bed covered with these tear-beads, turning the large, soft mattress into a shimmering series of undulations not unlike the sea.

He collected them and put them in a large bowl, not wanting them to bruise Aisha as she lay in bed, not wanting to throw away her tears. They seemed to pulse, slightly, as they lay at the bottom of the bowl. Sniffing them, he thought he could detect – ever so faintly – the smell of deep ocean, of seaweed and of sunshine.

They spent a large part of that first day asleep, and the next, and the one after that. Mdu wasn't used to sleeping so much, but in the presence of someone so surrendered to sleep, he felt no need to resist. An uncanny silence had settled over the house. The phone lay unplugged and word-less, and the television sat stunned into stillness.

It had never seen anything like this.

His bed, covered with a soft blue duvet, faced a large bay window that looked out over the garden and the rooftops beyond. Each time he swam awake, Mdu glanced sleepily at the window to see what time it was – that view was the only hint that time was passing outside – the sky changing from orange to yellow to blue and purple, and then to black.

If it seemed to be somewhere near an ordinary meal-time, he would stumble downstairs to the kitchen. After her initial bowl of Pronutro he had tried in vain to tempt Aisha to eat something other than fruit. She managed to be exceptionally stubborn in a sweetly sleepy way.

Mdu had vague intentions of snapping out of it, making some decisions, figuring stuff out. But then, almost against his will, his eyelids would grow heavy and he would slip, slowly and inevitably, back into sleep. Before long, the somnolent pair was adrift on a small floating island. The air in the house dropped in atmospheric pressure; a languid heaviness enveloped them. No disturbances from the outside world intruded and, bit by bit, Mdu slipped away from his familiar world and into one whose whimsical unreality was beginning to feel very normal.

He was never quite sure when Aisha was awake or when she was sleeping, but he was almost certain that she was dreaming all the time. Whenever he spoke, she turned her head towards him and smiled her distant smile, but it felt as if his words came out in bubbles and floated away before she could catch them. Her eyes were always half-closed and her movements so fluid that she seemed still submerged in water.

He could sit and watch her for hours, transfixed.

It sometimes felt as if he was watching a really long modern-dance piece. But for some reason, it didn't infuriate him (as even ten minutes of real modern dance would). Her tears, which had flowed so ceaselessly the first night, continued to fall, spilling small iridescent beads all over his bed and floor. After three days, Mdu had collected two large bowls and two tall vases of tears, and their scent was so strong that he often felt, on waking, that he was somewhere distant – out at sea, perhaps – far away from any human contact.

It felt as if the air they breathed in that little house was one part oxygen, three parts dreams. Just enough to keep them conscious.

Mdu soon found himself talking in his sleep, to the whales, and even that did not seem so strange.

A warning sign he chose to ignore.

And then, on the fourth day, they ran out of fruit.

At first Mdu was not too concerned. He had raisins and dried apricots, and even a tin or two of pineapple slices and peach halves. But when he presented these to Aisha, gently placing the tray next to her on the bed as he had done every day prior, she simply smiled her distant smile, turned over and fell asleep again. Three hours later, the food lay untouched, and Mdu began to worry.

Usually, as soon as she saw fruit, Aisha would devour it with an intensity that surprised him. Perhaps it was in these brief moments that her physical body regained some control over her sleeping, dreaming mind, and asserted its need for nutrients.

This lethargic refusal to eat was entirely out of character, and Mdu had no choice but to leave the house and buy fruit.

❋ ❋ ❋

You might wonder why Mdu hesitated at all, why he waited, in fact, for all the fruit to run out in the first place, and why he hadn't simply popped out to the shops the day before.

Laziness? Absentmindedness? Perhaps a reluctance to visit Handy Green Grocers?

Well, no.

Rather, three full days and nights trapped in one long fever dream.

Thinking rationally was as far-fetched as waking the girl.

❋ ❋ ❋

Mdu pulled on his shoes and jeans in a daze, buttoned up a fresh shirt (instead of the T-shirt he had been wearing since they came off the ship) and left the house, armed with his wallet and keys. The moment he stepped out of his front door, noise and activity assaulted him.

They leapt from the bushes lining the pavement and pummelled him about the head. Cars driving, dogs barking, music playing, people calling out to each other: all the usual Friday morning cacophony imploded in on him. In the space of thirty seconds, Mdu swam from the tranquil lake of his dreams into the shark-infested paddling pool of reality.

In other words, he woke up.

The smell of car fumes and sweaty people, mixed with that of overripe garbage bags waiting to be picked up in the midday sun, flared Mdu's nostrils as he stumbled down the road in search of fresh fruit. Handy Green Grocers was only two blocks away, and he walked there in a stupor, his mind racing at a dangerous speed. Mdu had tried to avoid the shop since the week after the robbery, preferring to drive to the much larger Pick 'n Pay than be reminded of that morning, haunted by the display of watermelons, unable to look the cashier in the eyes.

But today it was the only option.

In the space of those two blocks Mdu managed to do a lot of thinking. The beautiful girl asleep in his house, seemed, all of a sudden, like a strange fantasy, the plotline of a fairytale that he had read somewhere, something which clearly had no basis in reality.

Clearly. He was (almost) sure of it.

He could not possibly have spent three days half-asleep next to a complete stranger. Things like that did not happen. How could they, when, as now, he stood touching a poster with the headline 'Two Dead in Police Shoot-out' emblazoned in black writing? How could he walk into Handy Green Grocers as he had done a hundred times before, as if everything was normal, when a girl he did not know lay asleep in his bed at home?

With a confused frown on his face, Mdu stared in bewilderment at the orange papaya in his hand as he tried to marry the two realities, avoiding the pile of grapes instinctively (as he would for the rest of his life, never able to chase away the bitterness that lingered whenever he ate one).

⚙

It is a strange, little-documented fact that our bodies can function quite well without our minds, at least for a few hours. Well, maybe not so little-documented if you look at the legions of people who leave their brains at home, wrapped up in tissue paper, while they go to work, only taking them out to do the crossword or answer quiz-show questions, or maybe, sometimes, on other special occasions. Thus, even as Mdu's mind fought off the gang of conflicting thoughts in his head (much more effectively than he had dealt with the real robbers), his hands picked out a handful of oranges and a bag of apples, while discarding a few overripe guavas. He chose pineapples and naartjies, even some nectarines, and had them weighed with a preoccupied scowl.

It was only after he had paid and left the shop that Mdu managed to reach some kind of conclusion. He realised, with a shiver that ran from his knees to his fingertips and bore a strong family resemblance to raw fear, that unless he did something very soon, there was a good chance they would never leave the house.

The scorching heat outside the shop brought sanity – inside his house, he lost his head around Aisha, lost all sense and reasoning.

And so, as soon as Mdu walked through his front door he dropped the bags of fruit in the hallway and marched upstairs, heading for the bedroom before the sandmanesque effect of the slumbering house and its Sleeping Beauty could overwhelm him.

Gently, Mdu shook Aisha's shoulder, and then turned her onto her back and pulled her into a sitting position, supporting her shoulders with his hands. She smiled vaguely at him as he held her by the wrists and pulled her upright.

A small river of tears cascaded down her front as she stood up.

Then, slowly and carefully, Mdu walked her down the stairs, guiding her through the doorways and down the short flight of stone steps into his flower-filled garden.

☼

Aisha jerked awake with a sudden, brief movement, as if a loud bell had rung somewhere. Listening intently, breathing fast, her eyes grew large and dark as molasses as she stared at Mdu nervously, a petrified meerkat caught in a net, searching for an escape. When he approached, trying to speak, she started and backed away trembling until she bumped into the wall surrounding the wild garden. Her hands began to explore the sun-warmed bricks, her fingertips searching as they glided over the uneven surfaces, as if trying to discover some code that would unlock the strangeness she found herself in.

She found only biting ants.

Mdu, startled at this change in the dreamy girl he had come to know, stepped forward.

'My name is Mdu,' he said carefully, speaking in a soft voice. 'You've been staying with me for the last few days. I found you swimming in the ocean with a pod of whales.'

At the word *whales* a smile flitted across her face. A radiant, light-emanating smile.

And in that instant, something profound happened to Mdu.

The curious attachment he had felt since the first moment he saw her finally revealed its DNA.

It was Love.

Every romantic cliché he had ever heard turned out to be true – the birds' chirping soared, the sunshine felt warmer, the sky glowed a more glorious blue, his whole life made sudden, perfect sense, he felt complete, the flowers gloriously opened to full bloom, and from somewhere in the distance, a faintly familiar melody started playing (he was later to find out it was the ice-cream truck).

✵ ✵ ✵

Oh please! I hear you say. That stuff doesn't actually happen. There's no sudden transformation, no validation of a thousand cheesy Hallmark cards, no selfless passion, just a slow, cautious walk up an unfamiliar, bumpy path that may or may not be peppered with landmines, and once you reach the end of the path, there's a nice comfy armchair.

If you're lucky.

I challenge you to fall in love.

✵ ✵ ✵

To Mdu it felt as if something hard and solid inside of him melted, and the very act of melting made his life more vivid, more lucid, more real. It had been a long time since his life felt real, a long time since it had any meaning or beauty in it at all.

In fact, until Aisha swam into his life and turned it inside out, it had been as predictable as a bad soap opera. Her arrival broke a long frieze of days spent on the sightseeing ship, and nights spent alone at home – eating, sleeping and watching trashy talk shows. The latter was Mdu's secret passion, a habit he would admit to no one (were there any people in his life to admit things to). He loved trashy talk shows, the trashier the better – Jerry Springer, Ricki Lake, Judge Judy – Mdu devoured them all. He knew they were probably slowly rotting his brain, but they were addictive and satisfying and juicy, all at the same time.

An irresistible combination.

Had Mdu been more analytical by nature, he probably would have understood why he enjoyed watching total losers spill their innards on TV – their weak characters reaffirmed his specialness.

For, much as Mdu had cast aside all the glory of his younger days, he had not lost the taste for it. There was an itch, a call to greatness, which had never completely dissolved, no matter how much apathy he dumped on top of it. And underneath that itch was a very real and tangible fear that he might have turned into someone ordinary, a mediocre somebody just like everyone else.

This fear rose in him in the middle of the night, when he would wake up sweating, tasting bile. What if he had given up his only chance at doing something exceptional? What if greatness withered if you didn't pay attention to it? What if he faded into obscurity?

To stave off a total panic attack, Mdu watched late-night reruns of his favourite talk shows.

Other people's idiotic behaviour always calmed him right down.

☀

That first day, after Aisha had woken up, things felt a little weird.

Naturally. Aisha found herself not in her cosy little flat, but in a strange man's home. She couldn't quite understand the why and how, or grasp the order of events, couldn't really remember anything but an overwhelming need to get away from her life. There was a faint echo of not being able to sleep and being forced to spend time in airless, smoky darkness.

And so she spent the first day in silence, trying to figure out the Rubik's cube she found herself trapped in. Mdu respected her silence, respected her space, and spent the rest of that day in the garden, while Aisha sat staring out of the bedroom window. He was polite and quiet and unobtrusive. Inside, his emotions were raging. All he wanted to do was talk to her, open her up like a long-awaited book, and savour each word and line. But he restrained himself, remaining among the flowers and pretending to pull out weeds.

Even though the day was dry, the air smelt like rain falling on hot earth.

As he sat there, Mdu realised that the funny feeling in his stomach – a mixture of nausea and exhilaration – the feeling he had guessed was love, needed an outlet. He needed to do something with it. Without particularly intending to, he found himself scribbling words in the sand, and then piecing the words together and forming sentences and lines.

In the glow of the setting sun, for the first time in his life, Mdu used his imagination.

It was thrilling.

It felt as if a deep well of frustration had been blocked within him, only now he'd found the plug and pulled it, so it could all gush out.

It felt like plunging a blocked drain.

Lifting the lid off a boiling pot.

Learning to speak.

When Mdu ran out of dirt, he moved inside and picked up the pen and writing pad he kept stuck on the fridge. He wrote and wrote and wrote, filling the pages with words and descriptions, unexpectedly exhilarated to have finally proven his primary-school doctor wrong.

He could integrate both halves of his brain!

And although Mdu could admit that his writing was little more than sentimental pap, he knew he could get better.

Would get better.

That first day after Aisha's awakening passed in a strange, awkward harmony. But Mdu didn't want to give her much time to piece together her puzzle – he didn't want her to realise she could leave him (not now, not ever) and so he opened the game of love with a bold move the very next morning.

As soon as she woke up, Mdu, who was still sleeping on the easy chair next to his bed, knelt at her side and reached out his hand to stroke her cheek. A trail of a blush sprang up behind his touch.

Taking a deep breath, he blurted out, 'I love you. More than I thought it was possible to love someone. I can make you happy, I know I can.'

As he spoke, Mdu's words flew out of his mouth and into Aisha's ears. They flew, not invisibly and without scent, as most words do, but in a golden-orange stream of light, scented with honeysuckle. And as this light poured into Aisha, it seemed to fill her from the bottom up, as an empty glass is filled. Her pale hue was replaced by a vitality, an energy, a quickening.

It looked as if a light had been switched on inside her, and all her features sprang into relief. After only a moment's hesitation, Mdu reached out and pulled her close, feeling her heart beat against his chest. Aisha's arms, which at first hung limply by her sides, gradually moved to rest on his back, and he thought he saw a glimmer of something in her eyes.

Thus began Aisha's resurrection.

❀

Each morning when Aisha woke up – before their morning cups of tea, before they brushed their teeth, before they even stumbled out of bed to pee – Mdu held her, and told her how much he loved her. The blush that had trailed his fingers that first morning now spread throughout her body, from the tips of her toes to the tips of her ears, as if something inside him heated her up like a hot-water bottle. The initial stream of his love continued to flow whenever he spoke to her – the colours and scents different each time – and these differences were heady, and unexpected, and delicious. The deepest purples and oranges, reds, blues and yellows entered Aisha's body and transformed her.

Her cold vacancy started to disappear, melted by Mdu's love.

Some days his love was jasmine-scented, some days mangoes ripening on a windowsill, on others it was the pungent aroma of fresh coffee brewing.

But no matter what the scent, it conjured up a plethora of healing images – the smell of earth as it begins to rain, a crusty loaf of homemade bread, the crisp texture of sun-baked grass – which helped Aisha to remember life.

Or, rather, to know it for the first time.

But still she spoke no word.

Aisha and Mdu lived in silent harmony – gestures, looks and guesswork making up for what words usually achieved. It made Mdu realise the limitations of his gift: he could hear what people chose not to say out loud, but only when they thought it, but did not say it. Aisha had nothing to say, out loud or otherwise. Her mind seemed to be utterly at peace with itself – a blank slate.

He couldn't hear a word.

He accepted this obstacle as generously as a man in love.

And he wrote. Every day for at least an hour, he wrote. About the irresistible girl, and feeling alive for the first time in years, and anything else he could think of. Word by word, line by line, Mdu lost the melodrama, and found the heart.

Each night they lay in each other's arms, their breath mingling and their dreams colliding, until, after a week, Aisha emerged as clear as the first day after rain. The ferocity of Mdu's love dissolved the shimmering layer of imaginings that had clung to her for as long as she could remember, and gradually, one by one, the nerve-endings linking her mind to her body reconnected.

Slowly, like a sculpture being carved out of wood, her mind cleared, and she arrived, distinct and real, into the world.

It took only a week.

Her whole life had been waiting for that one week.

But still Aisha cried, every night, her tears spilling over the side of the bed to scatter on the floor. They were not tears of distress: she did not sob or wail or weep – they simply slipped from her eyes each night, as naturally as her sleeping breath.

※ ※ ※

It might seem, from our outsider's perspective, that Mdu would grow exhausted from this never-ending filling up process.

How did he manage to feed her, day by day, with such a constant stream of love without anything flowing back?

You need only fall in love to tap into such boundless energy.

Only fall in love.

As if it's the easiest thing in the world.

※ ※ ※

One hot morning not long afterwards, when their sheets were damp and sweet with sweat even as the sun rose, Aisha turned on her side to look at Mdu, outlined his face with her finger and whispered, 'I love you.'

The first words she had ever spoken to him.

Their effect was electrifying. Mdu opened his eyes immediately, still dragging himself back from a dream where he was a lion tamer, battling five lions without a whip. He had these dreams every night – always a different circus performer, always having to prove his courage in the face of adversity.

His delight at hearing Aisha's declaration was so great that he momentarily lifted off the bed, levitating three inches above the mattress. When Mdu landed (with a soft thwump) he smiled at Aisha, a long, slow smile that made her fingertips tingle.

They made love for the first time that morning, and it was slow and beautiful. Mdu gently undressed her, covering her body with kisses and soft caresses, running his hands along each curve and contour. She, in turn, moved with him instinctively, pulling him towards and inside her with a force that surprised him. They clung to each other like survivors of a shipwreck.

Afterwards, when they lay wrapped in the magic of pure connection, Aisha started crying once more, tears streaming down her face and dripping onto her naked breasts.

Mdu, afraid he'd hurt her without knowing, rocked her gently in his arms.

'My love! What is it? What's wrong?' he asked, but she just shushed him, and continued sobbing.

And then, just as suddenly as her tears had begun, they ended. In the same way the storm had cleared over the sea as he rescued her, her crying passed. She dried her eyes, nestled into Mdu's chest, and fell asleep, her breath steady and even, her smile contented.

'I don't even know your name,' Mdu whispered a moment later, lifting his head to look at her.

But Aisha didn't hear him; she was fast asleep, one arm flung over his chest to keep her afloat.

It was midmorning, and the sheets were tangled around their legs when Aisha stirred, waking Mdu. The bed once more saturated with their sweat. Turning on his side to face her, he lightly stroked her brow, placing the gentlest of kisses on the faint thinking lines that creased her forehead.

She opened her eyes and smiled, the same hesitant smile that had first woken his heart up. And then she started to speak; the words pouring out of her as unexpectedly as water from a broken dam wall, as intimately as a confession.

'My name is Aisha,' she said.

Mdu smiled. 'Hello, Aisha,' he said.

'I never knew either of my parents. They died when I was just a few days old ... it was a freak accident ... they were taking a late afternoon stroll along the beach for my mother to get some fresh air, and as they walked out on the pier, it just collapsed. They were the only people on the pier that evening. Before anyone could rush to help them, they were swept out to sea. Three days later a couple on a yacht found them, buoyed up by dolphins, but they had given up ... they were dead.'

Mdu guessed that Aisha, trying to make sense of the tragedy, had turned the story into myth over the years.

'My parents were both without siblings, and my grandparents had all died years before, so I was sent to an orphanage when I was just a week old. I spent almost a year there ... at the Valley of Sunshine Children's Home, until I was placed with my first foster family.'

Mdu kissed the top of her head. She smiled.

'I was lucky with foster families. I stayed with the first family until I was seven, and then with another until I turned seventeen. Neither family mistreated me, neither abused me – '

Mdu's gift told him that Aisha was leaving parts out of her story, but he could not tell what, and didn't want to push her to reveal more than she wanted.

After a small silence she continued.

'And neither loved me … my first family already had four children, and only fostered me as a good deed. They were staunchly religious, and I often heard them discussing how, if one ordinary good deed sent a brick to heaven, then fostering me was building them a heavenly mansion. It wasn't that they couldn't love me, it was just that we were so different that they didn't know how to. Well, to be honest, they never really tried to find out how. Their own children were boisterous, very loud, sociable, sporty types, and, of course, I was the exact opposite. I liked to read. So I faded into the background, and after a while they seemed not to notice whether I was there or not … it's not even that I wanted to be included in anything they were doing; I just wanted to be invited.

'So, I spent my early years living their cast-off lives until I turned seven. They had to send me to school then, and I think they realised, all of a sudden, how much I was costing them, and how unsatisfying I had turned out to be as a Good Deed Child. So they let me go. I suppose they resigned themselves to a smaller mansion in heaven.'

Aisha sat up in bed and leaned against the headboard, hugging her knees.

'Because I was quiet and never caused any trouble, I was quite easily placed with another family. It wasn't too different from the first – a smaller house, so less personal space, two children instead of four, but I was still the odd one out. My foster brother and sister grew closer because of me; they suddenly had a common goal: to make me cry.'

A thin layer of scorn in Aisha's voice just managed to cover the despair and longing she had been hiding for so long.

She did not yet know that Mdu could hear her unsaid thoughts.

'I just wanted to be on my own!' she said.

The air around this statement echoed a warning.

'I used to try and escape the house for as long as possible, but because

I went to school with my foster siblings, it was always tricky. They knew exactly where I was supposed to be … there was this one spot, though, a strip of abandoned wasteland behind our house, dusty and rocky with a few shrubby trees. I often climbed over the fence, and found a hiding place there, where I could sit, alone, by myself. That's where I first started drawing.'

For the first time since she began speaking, Mdu glimpsed a real smile lurking beneath Aisha's lips.

'I love to draw,' she added.

Her smile quickly disappeared as she continued.

'I managed to finish school just after I turned seventeen, and from that moment on I was finally free of foster families. I thought my life was finally going to take off –'

She shook her head, a small involuntary movement.

'I remember them trying to give me some kind of send-off, with pink cupcakes and little viennas on sticks, but I didn't even glance at the table. My bags were already packed, my forms had been filed months before, and I couldn't wait to walk out of that house and into freedom. And then I tried to get a job – in an art gallery, as an apprentice to a painter, working in an art store, selling art magazines – anything to do with drawing, really. But nobody needed me. Nobody wanted a girl with a matric certificate and no noticeable people skills.'

With each word she spoke, Mdu pieced together a little more of her puzzle, understood a little more why she had gone swimming that day, not planning or wanting to return.

'And so, again I found myself stuck in a corner, unnoticed, only this time there was nobody to blame but myself.'

He reached out to touch her. She didn't notice.

'So I got a job as a typist, the first job I interviewed for that accepted me, and the sadness that I had swum in since I was a few days old grew more and more suffocating. The only thing keeping me afloat was my drawing. And then, one day, even that slipped away from me. I couldn't draw any more.'

Aisha caught her breath.

'It felt as if the whole world spoke a different language to me … no matter what I said, people misunderstood me and cast me in a bad light. Do you know what I mean?'

Mdu nodded gently.

'Everyone always described me as having my head in the clouds, and it's true. I always felt as if I was fighting against succumbing to my dreams, trying to keep them only for night-time, trying to keep it together during the day. But then, once I started doing that awful typist-work, surrounded by awful people, unable to draw, there didn't seem much reason to be fully present. So, more and more, I allowed the dreams that had always lingered when I woke up, to stay. And I slowly started slipping away into a world of my own imagining.

'It was a way of coping, you know? Everything else just felt like too much. But then, one night, I couldn't sleep. And the thought of living a life without dreams was just –'

Aisha paused, lost in her reminiscing, in a faraway place that Mdu felt he would never be able to find. She looked at him and continued.

'And the rest you know … I woke up here, with you, and found that somehow you speak my language.'

☼ ☼ ☼

There are many people in this world who will make a real effort to understand others. They'll listen to their stories, hear the nuances behind their words, and will be able to explain away any unfortunate character quirks as a result of their unfortunate circumstances.

There are also many people who will make no effort to understand others at all. They'll listen to the same stories, and think that they are hearing the same old thing. They will allow for no variation in the way they feel life should be lived; no excuses or deviations from the norm. They are the kind of people who frequent the Tragedy Club, only to scoff at people's misfortune.

These folks will look at Aisha and say, *Please! Give me a break! So she was a lonely child. Get over it.*

But the first group will look at Aisha, and think, *Hmm … how interesting. So that's why she acts the way she does. It all makes sense to me now.*

☼ ☼ ☼

What was so interesting about Aisha's story was not, in fact, what she had told Mdu, but the details she had chosen to leave out.

That merest hint of a mention of the Valley of Sunshine Children's Home actually referred to the place where Aisha spent three years in-between foster homes; three years of being stuck in a room with twenty other kids, twenty-four hours a day, having to eat with them, and sleep with them, and do her homework with them, and play with them, and go to the toilet with them, and pray with them, and live in all ways as one segment of a very long caterpillar. Aisha was taught, along with all her fellow orphans, not to question her circumstances.

But, in her head, she questioned everything, constantly. From the ages of seven to ten, she was surrounded by the stink of kids who had not learned how to use the toilet properly, or who were physically disabled and had no choice but to defecate into nappies. Every meal was exactly the same as the day before, and it always looked grey and lumpy, no matter what they told her it was supposed to be.

For three years she didn't own a single thing.

Her possessions from her former foster home were distributed amongst the girls who were the same size as her, marked *7-10 yrs* in black permanent marker and handed out at play time, and school time, and dinner time, as if they had never been hers.

Love was handed out at these times, too, but only in small portions, and only to those kids who were willing to fight for it. One care-worker amongst twenty orphans could not possibly give each child enough affection, so it was given to those who looked the cutest, or tried the hardest, or cried the loudest.

Aisha did none of the above. She retreated into her imagination, with her dreams from the night before as company, and chattered to herself as she played with whatever toys the other kids had left lying around. If someone decided they wanted the toy she had, she gave it to them: no biting, no scratching, no yelling. Aisha never tried to get love from the care-workers, and they were too busy to notice that she never asked for it.

And so it remained, month, after month, after miserable month.

Aisha turned into a children's home child.

But she didn't discuss any of that with Mdu. Nor did she tell him how, once she was settled in her second foster home, she started stealing small items from her foster brother and sister, little things that they didn't really notice, or assumed they had lost: hair bands, pens, toy cars, sweets, sometimes 50c or R1 coins. She didn't tell him how she hoarded these items in a shoebox, hidden on top of her cupboard. She didn't tell him that she did not know how to share, and found it physically impossible to give anything away. She didn't tell him that she worried constantly that she was too damaged for this world, and that that was why she retreated from reality.

She didn't tell him any of these things.

In her defence, it was not that Aisha was trying to be sneaky or mysterious. She had simply never learnt the art of confiding. Most little girls will tell their mothers secrets; small treasures that no one else will ever hear. Most will turn to their moms for advice, for opinions, for a little light cast on a new situation. Aisha had been raised motherless; had never learnt how to confide in anyone, or reveal even a small part of herself to someone else.

The very idea terrified her.

☼ ☼ ☼

We could wonder at the necessity of Aisha editing out her less loveable parts to a listener as willing to love as Mdu. Clearly, here was a man besotted enough to hear the whole truth. But, as all children raised in orphanages, Aisha learnt early on the value of holding on to what you are given.

She did not want to lose Mdu. And so she placed (as we so often do) every single thing she ever wanted on him. All her hopes. All her expectations. All her love.

He accepted it without question.

And in him Aisha thought she'd found what she'd felt missing all her life – someone to return her love.

Perhaps, she thought, this is what relationships are all about: finding that one person who can fill that gap inside which you can't possibly fill yourself.

☼ ☼ ☼

Over the next few days, Aisha and Mdu grew into their love. They grew into the feeling, and the feeling grew around them, covering them like a vine.

They would make love in the strangest of places and at the strangest of times – on the breakfast table, lying on a bed of cornflakes; outside, whilst cutting the grass, stray bits of leaves and twigs sticking to their sweaty bodies; or in the middle of the night, both half-asleep and fuzzy with desire.

Aisha gathered strength and vigour each day; the colours that continued to pour from Mdu's words gave her a vivacity she had never known before, and she became, to her surprise, playful. She started speaking in funny voices just to hear Mdu's laugh, and often ran up behind him where he sat writing, to cover his back with kisses.

Until, on a Tuesday not long afterwards, when the sun was pouring down heat like syrup, the unthinkable happened. It was one of those sparkling afternoons that follow rainy mornings, and Mdu was planting some seedlings as Aisha made tea.

'Mdu!' she called out the window overlooking the garden. 'Tea's ready!'

As he turned to the sound of her voice, Mdu's feet slipped in the mud lining the path, and he fell backwards into the flowerbed. With a gasp, Aisha laughed, a clear ringing sound, and then clamped her hand over her mouth, uncertain about what had just happened. Mdu struggled to find a foothold in the muddy bed, and just as he staggered to his feet, he slipped again, and Aisha laughed again.

It was the first time Mdu had heard her laugh.

The look of wonder on her face as he walked into the house made Mdu forget everything but the tiny freckle on her top lip, and they made love again, on the kitchen floor, covered in mud while the tea grew cold.

That evening, while stretched out on the couch reading a book of poetry, the night air finally cooling down enough to breathe easily, Aisha found a pen of Mdu's stuck down the side of a cushion. She sucked the end of it while she read, and then, without meaning to, absentmindedly started doodling on the corner of the page. The doodle spread out to the margins, then slowly started covering the words, growing into a picture.

Aisha laughed softly to herself. She was drawing again!

Without even trying.

It felt like being able to breathe underwater.

☼

Mdu felt excited when he woke up in the mornings. Sometimes he kept his eyes closed as he listened for Aisha's breathing, just to make sure he had not dreamt her. He had boundless energy, and laughed freely. He could think of a hundred things he wanted to show her, a hundred experiences he wanted to share with her. She had placed all her expectations and hopes on him, and instead of feeling overwhelmed by the full plate she handed him, he cooked up a whole new batch for himself.

Every day felt like a new adventure as they got to know each other better, even the days they argued or misunderstood each other, or moved in different rhythms. Every day they fell more and more deeply in love. But the only problem with discovering something you love intensely, as Mdu discovered too late, is that suddenly there's so much to lose. For the past few years, Mdu had had very little to lose. He had achieved an almost Zen-like detachment from life – didn't love his job, didn't love his house, didn't particularly love his car or any of his possessions.

It was called indifference.

Aisha stole it from him forever.

He lived in constant fear of their love ending.

And so Mdu devised a plan, and brought it up as casually as he could. It was a blessedly cool day; the only one that whole summer, a drizzly, misty day that let all of Durban catch their breath. He was staring out the window, waiting for the kettle to boil so he could make their morning cup of tea, while Aisha sat at the kitchen table, doodling on an old shopping list.

'Aisha, I have an idea,' Mdu said.

(What he didn't say, was, *If you say no to this, I don't know what we'll do.*)

'What is it, love?' Aisha said.

(What she didn't say, was, *I'll do anything not to lose you.*)

'I think we should travel around South Africa; I'll write poems, you can draw, and we'll send the pieces to various newspapers around the country to fund our travelling,' he said.

(*I need to find a way to keep you with me forever,* he did not say.)

'Okay,' she said.

(*My life without you is no life at all,* she dared not say.)

On the surface, Mdu's idea had been to find an ingenious way to keep them both employed, without having to do work they didn't enjoy. Below the surface, the idea was to keep Aisha interested and constantly engaged, so that she never got it into her head to return to the sea and swim off again, leaving him bereft and loveless on the shore. (Scoff all you like at the words *bereft and loveless,* but they were the words Mdu used, daily, when he ran through the nightmare in his head.)

☼

Three days later the pair set off, shrouded and protected by the mist of love that followed them wherever they went, raining down the scent of honeysuckle and mysteriously covering them in tiny, sweet-smelling flowers. They travelled far, and they travelled wide – Mdu reasoned that if they saw a new place every few days, Aisha would be so caught up in the excitement of it that she wouldn't even dream of returning to the sea.

He would make her forget he had ever plucked her from it.

 and

In the years before her mother's death, Meryl had had one too many messy, lingering, heartachey break-ups.

Each time a relationship ended, she went through the same rigmarole of crying for a fortnight, feeling like her world had shrunk and that she would never enjoy anything again, losing weight from not being able to eat, dyeing her hair to illustrate how much she'd changed, finally feeling strong, and then seeing her ex out, and starting from square one all over again. It was exhausting.

Every failed relationship resulted in this three-month glut of emotions that left her feeling weak and useless, and washed out and sad.

And then she got over it.

Totally over it.

What a waste of time.

So Meryl decided to shortcut the whole process by never getting into it in the first place, so that she'd never have to get over it.

She simply stopped caring.

Or so she told herself, and anyone else who cared to listen.

In other words, she chose the bitter option.

As part of her newborn resolve, Meryl decided to experiment a little. Tired of men, and thinking that perhaps a woman might be less of a wanker (in more ways than one), Meryl had decided to indulge in a once-in-a-lifetime lesbian relationship. Men just weren't doing it for her. ('It' referring to a long list of requirements that Meryl felt she inherently deserved. More on that later.)

The point being that once Meryl decided to fall for a woman, she found just the right one, and fell hard.

When they first started dating, Meryl thought it possible to return to her younger, sweeter self with Edna. She hoped that the barriers she had been erecting around her heart were merely temporary, waiting for the right person to call off construction. She decided to give love one last chance, unlaced her corset, set it aside, and fell for Edna.

And then she landed. For numerous reasons, not least of which because Edna (the perfect girlfriend) had recently slept with a beautiful, handicapped woman that she worked with, only days after promising to never, ever cheat on Meryl.

Ever.

The deed being done, Edna claimed the old, 'I couldn't help myself, it just happened!' excuse, and swore she'd never do it again.

Meryl, trusting in the profound, intrinsic bond that all women share, believed her, and flew into a white-hot rage when, answering the phone late one night, a sultry voice on the other side whispered, 'Edna, I've been waiting naked in bed for half an hour, where *are* you?'

The (dis)advantage of same-sex relations.

Meryl put her corset of cynicism back on that night. She reinforced it with the disappointment of Edna's shallow love, stitched it with betrayal, and knotted it with distrust. Another reason not to open up, she seethed; more proof that the world had let her down.

As well as the philandering, however, Edna made Meryl clench her teeth for a number of reasons. She was the only one in the world, it seemed, with a difficult life, and every two weeks or so she crumbled into a pit of alcohol-assisted depression, where she wallowed, while contemplating the kitchen knives with a gleam in her eye. Meryl sometimes wondered whether it was all just an act for her viewing pleasure.

They were never allowed to talk about anything that bothered Meryl. Even when she had been in the Handy Green Grocers robbery, Edna had given her no more than five minutes of sympathy ('Ag, shame') before moving onto what a difficult day she'd had. On top of this, since Edna refused to do any grocery shopping, Meryl had no choice but to go back to the scene of the crime, over and over again. It wasn't even that Edna could plead ignorance – Meryl had said to her, 'Edna, please will you do the shopping? I don't want to go back there.'

Edna's response? A flat no.

Meryl had purposefully started shopping in the mornings to avoid seeing Eranie, her ex-best-friend who worked as the night-shift cashier, but now that she didn't want to run into the over-friendly day-shift cashier (who had been in the robbery with her) she was forced to shop at night again.

That wasn't all. Edna had a habit of being obscenely absentminded, making dates with Meryl and then forgetting, or cancelling at the critical moment (with Meryl dressed as Godzilla, standing outside an apartment block, waiting to go to Edna's friend's fancy-dress party, and being harangued by young louts).

And then there were the more insidious, poisonous ways that Edna liked to undermine Meryl: at a recent dinner party, Edna casually remarked, 'I had a girlfriend once, who'd never had an orgasm before she met me. She said she'd felt too nervous to open up that way in front of someone, too scared of what might happen!'

Six of the seven women sitting around the table laughed. (Meryl did not. That girlfriend was her.)

Often, Edna would simply stop talking to her. For no particular reason. She'd just wake up one morning and ignore Meryl, sometimes for days. Other times she would make snide comments about Meryl's figure, or dress sense, or hair. Couched in concern, she released one stinging barb of criticism after the other, which, at first, brought tears to Meryl's eyes. ('Huh, so *that's* why you haven't worn that dress in a while … it's too small.')

Somehow, Edna always managed to swing the situation around so that it was Meryl apologising for hassling Edna, or for not understanding her. She was the first-time lesbian unsure how things worked, she was the one trying to chain Edna down, and she was the needy one who demanded constant reassurance about their relationship. (The fact that Edna flirted with everything in high heels, male or female, seemed not to feature under the heading of 'Ten Reasons to Worry About Your Lesbian Relationship'.)

They had done the usual yo-yoing many a time: breaking up, getting back together, breaking up again, getting back together again, all at Edna's insistence.

All that to- and froing made Meryl motion sick. So much so, that when Edna called her, crying and professing great love after the brief affair had ended, Meryl cooked up a foolproof antidote to motion sickness. Reluctant to board the emotional rollercoaster once again, she laced up her corset extra-tight, padded it with her newfound distrust of Edna, knotted it several times, and acquired a written promise from Edna, stating that under no circumstances would she ever terminate the relationship again. The only way they could ever break up was if Meryl decided it was over.

✿

All of this happened four months ago.

For the last two weeks, Meryl had been finding well-thumbed girlie magazines lying around the house in strategic spots: in the bathroom, under the bedcovers, on top of the fridge, behind the couch cushions. Subtlety had never been Edna's strongest point. Meryl felt Edna's affections lagging, knew that she wanted to end their relationship, could sense that Edna might even honestly care for her beautiful co-worker.

But instead of giving her an easy way out and breaking off the relationship – as any sane person would – Meryl decided to make her suffer. Hurt after hurt had thickened her defence as it pulled tighter and tighter with each passing day. Her distrust was so tautly fastened, so intricately tangled, that sometimes she battled to breathe. Her fear of suffocation grew daily. It was only fair, Meryl reasoned, after all the torture Edna had put her through, all the discomfort she had caused her – it was only fair.

A little revenge to leave a bad taste in Edna's mouth seemed like a good plan.

So now it was payback time.

Edna was a member of the man-hating Gay Women's League, and it would cause her untold anguish to see Meryl with a man. She was convinced she had converted Meryl to the grass-is-greener other side, and took great pleasure in mocking heterosexual couples. (Edna had gone so far as to convince herself that heterosexuality was obsolete.)

Meryl wasn't quite so sure.

Harry presented himself just as she was worrying about the nuisance of finding and seducing a man. He was the perfect tool for revenge – quick and harmless to date, no doubt thrilled at the prospect of sex without payment, and easy to dump.

Or so Meryl thought.

⚙

Meanwhile, four blocks away, Harry sat at the Tragedy Club in exactly the same position as Meryl had left him in – napkin lifted in farewell, eyebrows raised in surprise. The very act that had so liberated Meryl's scheming mind had paralysed Harry's. He was battling to process the fact that there was a woman out there (not his mother!) who didn't despise him. Some motor reflex made him cling to the napkin like a winning Lotto ticket, but all other brain functions shut down momentarily.

After a few minutes, the bartender slouched up to him.

'You going home to call that number?' he said. ''Cause we don't take well to getting lucky in this place. You better skedaddle.'

As if released by a magic word, Harry sprang to his feet and left the place running. He vowed never to return to the Tragedy Club. Some men, delighted at how easy it had been to pick up a woman on their first visit, would have chalked it up as a cool place to meet hot babes.

But not Harry.

He had already decided that Meryl was the woman for him. Not schooled in the gently vicious art of dating, he assumed that some Supreme Intelligence matched the right people together (like salt and pepper). And once matched, they would meet, and then Love would take over.

Wedding bells, etcetera.

Harry was, by all accounts, a remarkably naive man.

⚙ ⚙ ⚙

The temptation is, of course, to put on your unbelieving face (the one that brings out all your wrinkles) and say, 'Come on! Ease up already! There's no way this guy managed to get to twenty-eight with all his innocence intact. I don't buy it,' or something along those lines.

But contemplate, if you will, the enormous impact of a life lived with hardly any friends, and no television. No romantic comedies or soapies or sitcoms to pollute the mind, no teenage boys to mock you for being a sap. Simply an overactive imagination, and two doting parents. With such a strange recipe, the possibilities are endless.

❋ ❋ ❋

Harry and his parents had lived, always, in the same house, a sweet old-fashioned place with wooden floors and peeling paint and a large, grassy garden. Harry loved it. His ma used to make his lunch every morning, wrapping it in cling wrap, with a paper serviette and a toothpick tucked inside, and his pa loved to cut out comic strips from *Die Beeld* to give him each night, mostly *Garfield*. They chuckled over them together: all 9 324 strips, collected in 14 shoeboxes under Harry's bed. The three of them played Scrabble into the early hours of the evening (they started at four o'clock, once Harry had finished work) and drank copious cups of strong black tea, three sugars each. They finished each other's sentences, and cups of tea, and laughed before the punch lines when they told jokes.

It was bliss, of sorts.

Some might have found it claustrophobic, or suffocating, or even down-right weird, but it was all that Harry knew of happiness. In his memory, those years with his parents were lightly scented with jacaranda blossoms from the large purple tree that grew outside his bedroom window.

Jacarandas always made him feel happy.

Until that Tragic Day.

Harry was on his way home after work with a special treat for his parents – an old kettle with a broken cord, and without a lid. It was a real find, and Harry could hardly contain his excitement. Straight away, his pa started fiddling with the cord, Harry hopping from foot to foot and clapping his hands together softly. Within an hour it was fixed, just in time for their second cuppa of the evening, so Harry's sweet old ma disinfected the newly mended kettle and filled it with fresh water. (Tea was Harry's only exception to the Green Food Rule, his reasoning being that green food didn't necessarily include green drink.)

'Oh, you are such a *liefling*, *boykie*, bringing us gifts all the time! You

spoil us, you really do,' his ma gushed. She still called him *boykie*, an endearment that had lasted for over twenty-five years.

'*Kom nou*, and I'll make us a nice cup of tea to have with our *beskuitjies*.'

'*Ek weet nie* if it's quite ready yet, dear,' Hannes, Harry's pa, called out.
'There might be something loose still, perhaps we should test it out later.'

He had been a proofreader for the Afrikaans daily newspaper, *Die Beeld*,
and always liked to double- and triple-check everything.

'*Kak*, man! My *boykie* didn't go to all the bother of finding us a new
kettle, just so we can carry on using our old one! It's working, I'm sure …
come, feel the water, I think it's getting hotter.'

Caution was not one of Harry's ma's many good qualities. (Gerda had
been known, in her youth, to speak longingly of bungee jumping.) Hannes
warily dipped a finger into the kettle full of water, right next to Gerda's
finger, which was busy tapping the element on the base of the kettle.

'*Ek weet nie* if that's such a clever thing to *dooooooooooooooooooooooo!!!!!*'

And with those words, Hannes died, along with his wife; electrocuted
with one violent spark.

Harry thought they were joking. They had both fallen to the floor in
such a perfectly synchronised way, Gerda's head landing with a heavy
thwump on Hannes's belly, that he thought they were playing a little trick
on him. He laughed till he cried, tears streaming down his cheeks. Honestly!
Those parents of his! What would they come up with next?

But when his laughter slowly bubbled to a stop, and he said, 'Okay,
lekker grappie! You can get up now!' his parents did not move. And Harry
noticed, with a stab of anguish so intense it left a permanent scar over his
heart, that his ma's head was not rising and falling as it lay on his pa's
stomach. It was totally still.

His pa was not breathing.

The sound that rose from Harry's belly was not quite human. It was a
wail. It was the sound of a heart collapsing in on itself. He dropped to his
knees, and felt frantically for a pulse at their necks and wrists and chests.
But nothing. They both lay on the kitchen floor with slightly surprised
expressions on their faces, their eyes mercifully closed, their eyebrows
raised as if they did not quite know how they had arrived here, dead, on
the kitchen floor.

Harry sat with them all through that night, stroking his ma's hand as it slowly started growing cold, patting his dad's arm every few minutes, and chattering about anything that crept into his head.

'You know, they've put up *nuwe* bus stops around town,' he told them around 1 am, when he was desperately searching for any words to fill the silence that pressed in on him like a rapidly shrinking oxygen tent. '*Jislaaik*, but they look cool. Kind of like they're from the future.'

Harry paused to brush a hair off his mom's face, carefully smoothing it back behind her ear.

'Only the *domkop* designers didn't think about which way the buses come, so whoever sits on one of those seats can't see the street, only the pavement! There are some dummies out there, hey?'

He laughed a little, then stopped.

As the microwave clock ticked over to 2.14 am, Harry began to cry. He couldn't help it. Slow tears dripped down his face and formed a puddle on the floor between his feet.

'*Ek weet nie* why I'm crying,' he said to his parents, 'there's *niks* to be done now, hey? I just don't really know what I'll do without you two …'

The tears came faster then, and Harry sobbed until he could sob no more, his eyes swollen and red and sore.

Then he rested his head on his knees and fell asleep, still holding his mom's hand.

Harry never quite recovered. The only way he could think about that day was to turn it into a story in his head. He found himself unable to use a kettle, and whenever he had to boil water, he did it on the stove. Most nights he talked out loud to himself, as if his parents were still with him, and he felt as if a section of his heart was permanently closed down.

He never once let himself feel like an orphan. Harry was wise enough not to blame himself entirely (his parents had always told him not to mix water and electricity) but nevertheless the guilt plagued him like a swarm of mosquitoes. He couldn't quite get past the thought that he had inadvertently contributed to his parents' death. Any time he heard the word '*boykie*', he teared up.

This, fortunately, wasn't often.

※ ※ ※

You might wonder why Harry had not gone to therapy after his parents' death, why some well-meaning relative had not pointed him in the direction of a trained psychotherapist, where he would be able to talk to, cry over, and eventually shake hands with his feelings of guilt. The answer is quite simple: there were no relatives. Both Hannes and Gerda were the last surviving members of their families (may their collective souls rest in peace).

Left to his own devices, one does not have to wonder long why Harry didn't go to therapy.

He simply didn't think of it.

How many of these people are out there? Living solo lives with minimal human contact, following a rigid dot-to-dot method of existence, waiting for the day when they Connect (at last) with someone else, and learn how to colour in the picture. How many of these people slip past us as we picnic with our friends, argue with our lovers, despair of our families?

Many more than we could ever recognise.

※ ※ ※

Back home from the Tragedy Club, as Harry settled into his creaky armchair with a cup of green tea, he couldn't stop grinning. It was the first time since his parents' death that he had felt more than a fleeting moment of happiness (usually sparked off by a particularly good find at the dump). He allowed himself a moment or two of fantasising about Meryl coming over for Scrabble dates and all-green meals.

'You'd really like her,' he said out loud. 'You know I'd never date anyone who I didn't think you'd both really like. She's lovely.'

Then Harry fell silent, wondering if that was entirely true. Would his parents really like Meryl? He didn't know anything about her, except that she was really pretty and that she could talk and drink a lot.

But Harry felt that he had to make decisions based on an internal guidance system of what his parents would and would not deem appropriate. It was his little way of assuaging the guilt – if he lived a life they unequivocally approved of it was almost as if they were living a little themselves.

There was a strange logic to this decision.

It was the same reasoning, though, that kept him listening to his pa's *sakkie-sakkie* records even though he despised *sakkie-sakkie*, and it made him irritable and jumpy; the same reasoning that kept him using the Sunlight soap that his ma had always used to wash her hands, even though Harry far preferred Lux. He felt it necessary to create, as much as possible, a life that his parents would have enjoyed, even if that enjoyment wasn't in alignment with his own tastes.

Harry kept rose-scented potpourri sacks in his sock drawer as a nod to his ma, used Old Spice aftershave in homage to his pa, ate dinner at 5 pm, even though he was hungry again by 8 pm, and still, even at his rather advanced age, refused to own a television, because his parents had believed so strongly that TV rotted family values.

Had Harry experienced the miraculous cessation of loneliness that comes from having a talking box filled with people whose lives you can participate in (even as they marry their half-brothers, and bear children to their long-lost step-uncles twice removed) he might have questioned this last lifestyle choice a little more extensively.

As it was, he lived the life of a sixty-year-old Afrikaans couple.

He just happened to live it alone.

Although Harry managed to restrain himself from calling Meryl that night (it was past 9.30 pm and he thought she might be in bed), he did call first thing the next morning, at 7 am, leaving a message on her answering machine. Harry had no doubt that the Edna of 'Hi, this is Meryl and Edna, leave us a message, and we'll listen to it!' was just a giggly roommate. Not realising that lesbianism existed outside of schoolboys' fantasies, Harry would never have guessed that giggly Edna was about to become his arch-nemesis.

❄ ❄ ❄

What is it about the human animal that simply will not let go? Oh, you might like to think you're the exception; the one who has managed to walk away from all your past relationships with a clear heart, and a firm resolve.

I don't believe you for a second.

And if you have managed to walk away without pain and torn fingernails from hanging on so tightly, then I'll bet there was an Incident when you were younger that devastated you, and turned you into the unfeeling slab of marble you are today.

I understand; don't take it personally.

For the rest of us, though, there is a definite tendency to clutch onto whatever shred of the relationship is left over from the arguing, the heartache and the spite. And even if this shred is dirty, and smells funny, and is really very obviously *not* what we want in our lives, we reserve the right to hang on to it, and if anyone else even *thinks* about touching our snotty little shred of leftover love, we will injure them in any way we know how.

It's called not letting go.

Not moving on.

Being human.

※ ※ ※

Edna knew the feeling well. Especially when she heard the message left at 7.03 am that morning: 'Hi, Meryl, it's Harry here. Just wanted to set up that coffee date of ours. Call me back on 031 4398452 when you get a chance. Or I'll call you. Either way, no bother. Okay. Looking forward to it. Bye now.'

The advantage of Harry's rock solid belief in instant soulmates was that it gave him a quantum leap of confidence where Meryl was concerned. Displacing his father's affection for his mother onto Meryl, he assumed the role he'd wanted all his life, in the most stereotypically Freudian way.

Meryl, in his mind, became his mother, and he imagined many a long, happy evening together, drinking Chinese tea and laughing softly over his *Garfield* comics. It was that simple. Never mind getting to know each other, potentially disliking certain aspects, finding out over the course of a few years that you may not, in fact, be entirely compatible.

Harry didn't consider any of that; only that there seemed to be a woman out there who could take the place of his mother.

Case closed. Signed, sealed and (about to be) delivered.

Edna, of course, took it upon herself to sabotage this happy scenario from the start. Erasing the message from the answering machine with a little snigger of satisfaction, and only the merest hint of a twist in her gut, she didn't count on Harry's blind persistence and ignorance of the subtleties of playing it cool.

He merely kept calling throughout the day until Meryl answered. Edna arrived home from work that evening (after working late, to cover for one of her co-workers who had gone missing) to find a note from Meryl on the fridge, stating simply: *Gone out, back later. M.*

For a moment, Edna's shoulders slumped. It was only fair, she reasoned. She had done the same thing to Meryl on more than five occasions, and had been just as obvious and heartless about it. It was only fair that Meryl should have the chance for a side-order of sex, she thought gloomily. She just had to accept it; accept it and perhaps eat a litre of ice-cream to cool down the fiery ache in her belly.

Sighing, Edna took a tub of double-choc-fudge-ripple ice-cream out of the freezer, and slouched to the bedroom to have a little lie-down. But, as she turned, she caught a glimpse of her reflection in the window, and in that instant she looked old, and ugly, and useless. She looked like a washed-up hag. The air in the apartment suddenly smelt like talcum powder and urine, like old-age home.

Edna was not ready to die, not just yet. With a rapid shake of the head to clear the fuzziness from between her ears, she slapped herself twice on each cheek, picked up her keys and stalked out of the house.

The night air was hot and angry, and smelt of veld fires. With each kilometre Edna drove, she grew more indignant. Without her, Meryl would be a boring, lame, characterless frump. She had given her life! Vivacity! Guts! Women! This was not the way to repay a benefactor, by running off with some ... some (she battled even to think the word without feeling nauseous) some ... *man*!

By the time she'd parked the car, Edna was drenched in quiet fury. She stalked from one coffee shop to the next, working up quite a sweat as she traversed the Musgrave coffee district, stepping over beggars who pleaded from empty doorways, paying scant attention to the waiters who ingratiatingly asked if she wanted a table for one, not even noticing that the summer heat had soured that evening, soured into something that smelt suspiciously like vinegar and made her eyes water.

Edna sweated in the night-time funk, sweated and cursed and raged so that she didn't have to listen to the still, small voice inside her that had quietly started crying.

Eventually, in a cosy corner of the seventh shop, Mama Cappuccino's, Edna spied Meryl holding hands awkwardly with a man. They were sitting at a small, round table, almost entirely surrounded by obviously fake, large, green pot plants. A few giant, plastic-pink flamingos lurked in the foliage. Their table was covered with a pink feather tablecloth, and the glass that Harry was holding (sipping his mint milkshake) was also pink, with a flamingo's beak for a straw. A large Mexican hat-shaped lampshade, covered in (you guessed it) pink feathers, cast a warm, slightly stifling glow over the table. Meryl's hair was so sleek it reflected the pink flamingo glow.

This profusion of pink made the air inside the coffee shop far hotter than it should have been. A note on the window declared that it was *Under New Management*, explaining the uneasy name-decor relationship. (It used to be called Frappe & Flamingos, and did so poorly that the owners couldn't even pay the fake feather suppliers.)

Tragic.

But convenient for Meryl, who claimed that pink things made her feel ill, so she couldn't stomach her milkshake. A milkshake was equivalent to two full loaves of white bread, according to Meryl's Convenient Calorie Counter (which she carried with her at all times) and there was no way she was going to get fat as well as unhappy because of Edna.

Meryl's milkshake stood melting on the table, untouched, next to their limp hands. For although Harry could now manage to talk to Meryl, physical contact was a whole other, deeply rooted issue. Although affectionate, his had been a surprisingly undemonstrative family, preferring to show their love through second-hand prezzies and quality time together, and, as a result, Harry had never learnt how to touch people naturally.

Sitting opposite her, he battled to bridge the divide between his space and Meryl's; it seemed too much to ask that they should coincide. Harry's hand, held in Meryl's, sweated profusely, inviting a small family of broken cups to nestle at his feet.

Spite had made Meryl's breathing shallow, and she felt slightly dizzy. The conversation centred, unsurprisingly, on Harry's passion for green food. Meryl thought that if they spoke about him the whole time, he would be more easily snared (not realising that this was one man who needed no snare to step into, and that he was already planning where they would live when they were married with children).

Meryl faked interest so successfully that Harry began divulging Deep Green Secrets. He worried, at one point, that he was talking too much, but the relief of having someone to talk to was so great that he didn't really feel like stopping. Harry had feared, over the last year, that he somehow spoke a different language to everyone else. The thrill of finding someone who seemed to understand his every word made his heart swell, and his tongue loose.

Still, admitting that he added tons of limes to his cooking was not quite part of the Guinness World Records rules, he was sure. Had Meryl not spied Edna's curly red hair, and decided to take a dangerous plunge, no doubt Harry would even have told her his Deepest Secret (that of the shameful food colouring).

'I know it was a terrible thing to do, and I don't add limes to –' he started saying, when Meryl leaned over the small, round table, looked Harry in the eyes, and planted a big, wet, passionate kiss on his startled lips, which melted underneath her warm touch, opened involuntarily and deposited a large amount of shocked spittle into her mouth.

Keeping up the act admirably, she discreetly spat into her water glass as she faked a sip, and smiled adoringly at Harry, relishing with vicious glee the incredulous fury she saw on Edna's face as she attempted to hide behind a pot plant.

Normally pale to the point of transparency, Edna had flushed bright red.

She stood transfixed at the sight of Meryl kissing a man – repulsed, yet unable to take her eyes off them. How was it possible that her Meryl was kissing someone other than her? How was it possible, when six months ago, Edna had woken to a small, yellow card on her pillow – the first of a delicious series – sending her on a treasure hunt through the flat? (*I just thought I'd let you know that you are …* was followed by another card in the bathroom, next to her toothbrush, saying, *The most beautiful thing I've ever seen.* A third one next to the kettle in the kitchen exclaimed, *So totally unique.* The fourth one, hidden in her handbag, declared, *Undeniably sexy.* The last one, still inside Edna's wallet, finished with *Just wonderful.*)

Edna shook her head, but it didn't help to clear the fug of her thoughts. She couldn't take her eyes off the two of them.

She felt suddenly nauseous and weepy, and wanted to go home.

Meryl, so caught up in the delight of revenge, didn't even consider that Edna might *feel* something. She just knew that for Edna, kissing her from that moment on would be like licking a public toilet seat, because of the contaminated male saliva that had entered her mouth. Edna was no wishy-washy man-hating Gay Women Leaguer; she had been president for three years running. Accordingly, Meryl felt it wise not to push her too far, in case she did something rash.

Had she known that the only rash thing Edna felt capable of doing was bursting into tears – all anger having rushed out of her like rice out of a torn bag – she might have considered her job done.

Much as Meryl's corset cut her off from the world, it did not make her inhuman. Actually, if you think about it, the very fact that she needed a layer to protect her against the world, suggested that the Meryl inside was too sweet and tender to deal with emotions that most people take in their stride.

Oblivious to Edna's anguish, Meryl slipped her arm through Harry's and led him out of the coffee shop, pausing only for him to pay for both of them, and leave a generous tip (which he secretly longed to steal back).

As they passed Edna's pot plant, Meryl leaned even closer into him, brushing her breasts against his arm (an action that made him jump, visibly) and asked in a clearly audible voice, 'Shall we go to your place for some … dessert?' whilst fluttering her eyelashes seductively. Luckily for Meryl, they were outside by the time Harry had a chance to reply. The hot, vinegary air slapped them across the face as they stepped onto the pavement, and travelled languidly into their lungs.

Harry took a deep, warm breath and said, 'I don't really have any dessert, nothing much is green, you know. I had some green jelly for a while, but for some reason all the green jelly is lime-flavoured, and you know how I feel about that! Anyway, it's almost my bedtime … early to bed, early to rise, makes a man healthy, wealthy and wise!'

Harry grinned, pleased at his clever rhyme, not knowing that in a recent survey it had been voted one of the most over-used rhymes of all time.

'I suppose we'll have to give dessert a skip, but how about dinner tomorrow night? I can cook for you. Come over to my place at about seven, shall we say? I may just have a little surprise for you.'

After this rushed monologue tumbled out at double speed, Harry stepped forward (inadvertently crushing Meryl's toes) and kissed her.

It was a nice gesture.

It was a terrible kiss.

Half his mouth landed on her left cheek, and he stuck his tongue out as far as it would reach, intending passion, but achieving, alas, disgust. Then he turned around quickly, and trundled off into the night. Meryl breathed a sigh of relief, mopped her cheek with a tissue from her handbag, and traipsed off to lurk in a bar just around the corner so that she could arrive home suitably late to fuel Edna's jealousy.

She was stuck on a one-way street to vengeance, no U-turns allowed.

❁

When Harry woke up the next morning and stumbled through to the kitchen for his early morning pick-me-up of green juice, he felt happier than he had in a long time. Absentmindedly humming the James Bond theme tune softly under his breath, he flopped into his favourite green armchair and stroked the stray cat sleeping on the floor with his foot.

The air felt ripe with possibility, smelt ripe with sun-warmed garbage.

'Well! Things are certainly working out wonderfully all of a sudden. Meryl's coming over tonight, and I'm going to cook her a dinner that will knock her socks off,' Harry told the cat, the photo of his parents or thin air, depending on your interpretation.

Just in case he and Meryl ran out of things to talk about, he had prepared some after-dinner entertainment: six shoe boxes of comic strips huddled expectantly next to the couch. Harry thought they could read them to each other by candlelight – reading by candlelight was one of the top ten tips in 'How to Spice up Your Love Life', an article he had found in one of the old newspapers recently. In the article they suggested reading something called the *Kama Sutra*, which Harry imagined was an Indian comic strip.

He preferred *Garfield*.

As soon as he'd drunk his green juice and done twenty push-ups (a habit his pa had instilled in him at a young age), Harry set off to do the shopping for that night's feast. He decided to go to Sparks Road, the Indian market area not far away. They always had the freshest vegetables.

Only the very best would do for his Meryl.

Harry loved the market, loved that he could arrive and instantly blend in, despite his pale skin, because there were so many people crammed into such a small space. The air smelt like curry twenty-four hours a day, and especially on Saturday mornings, when the apartment windows in the blocks surrounding the market exhaled their scent of pots on the simmer. Harry could also pick up the sweet smell of incense from the mosque at the top of the hill, and he loved the call to prayer that echoed through the neighbourhood as the sun began to set.

It reminded him of his childhood, when they had lived three streets away from a mosque.

Harry found parking a few blocks from the market, so he could avoid parallel-parking in front of a crowd, and slowly wound his way down the hill, with a large (slightly broken) basket hanging from his arm. He read every sign as he passed it, playing one of his favourite games by turning the words into a softly spoken chant, to the vague tune of 'Nkosi Sikelel' iAfrika': 'Universal Prayer, your one stop prayer goods shop, Radio Al-Ansaar, Half-Lamb on Special, All Occasions Bakery, Mangoes Cheap Cheap, Aah!! Chithibunga Family Funeral Brokers, Unfried Samoosas only R12.99.'

The times he managed to fit the words into the actual tune were rare, but special. That morning was not one of them.

He liked to imagine that he'd just popped over to India on these trips to the market. A shimmer of heat made everything more exotic, piles of fruit and vegetables spilled out of shops scented with spices, and every doorway seemed to hold a wrinkled old Indian man with gaps in his teeth wearing a faded cotton shirt.

Hardcore young Muslim boys, clearly adopting the gesture from their hip-hop heroes, grabbed their crotches as they crossed the road, and flocks of dirty-grey pigeons cut across the sky, searching for less crowded spaces. Indian almond trees lined both sides of the street, their huge waxy leaves green all summer, although that morning they looked parched and dusty in the stifling heat. Just up the road, a queue of people, at least ten deep, waited outside Johnny's Rotis (aka the Sunrise Chip 'n Ranch) for arm-length rotis filled with beans, chips, orange cheese and curried dhal sauce. The queue remained constant throughout the night and into the early hours of the morning.

He had always meant to visit Johnny's for a green bean bunny chow with his pa - it had been on their To Do list for that summer, in fact - but they never got around to it. Now Harry didn't feel he could go, chalking it up as a sacrifice due to unfortunate circumstances.

They had planned their first trip to a game reserve, too, and had decided to take up fly fishing. Harry vowed he would never do any of it. Not without his pa.

He tried to stay focused that morning, crossing items off his shopping list one by one as he stocked up on fresh green veggies, green bread, green biscuits. It certainly made shopping a lot quicker, only having to hone in on one colour, Harry thought with a smile. The young boy packing his vegetables into a box smiled back, wondering what trick the strange-smelling man used to keep the broken bottles, conked-out appliances, and cracked mugs from the rubbish heap outside the shop so firmly attached to his feet, without tripping over them. He wished he could learn it.

Finished with his shopping, Harry slowly made his way back up the hill, nodding to the stray dogs who stopped to sniff at him hopefully; taking care to step around an ancient man feeding the pigeons day-old crusts of bread, while smiling sweetly at a group of women walking towards him, wearing burkhas, shyly turning their eyes towards the pavement as they swerved and passed him.

The heat increased as he walked up the hill, lending an almost unreal intensity to the bright colours of the roadside flea market (with its second-hand clothing, imitation technology and bulk plastic goods), the vivid saris of Indian women doing their morning shop and the bright flags decorating the mosque.

Walking back to his car, Harry breathed in deeply, absorbing the mélange of fresh watermelon, incense, curry, sweat, car fumes and perfume, before knocking his feet against the side of the car door to dislodge any residual damaged goods, muttering a quiet, 'Sorry.'

⚙

Meryl's early morning pick-me-up was not green juice, but a cocktail of satisfying vengeance. The night before, she had arrived home late enough for Edna to be asleep on the couch in front of the television, and snuck off to bed without waking her. Had Meryl bothered to look closely at Edna, lying in the foetal position, her arms wrapped tightly around her waist, she would have seen that her eyes were swollen and red from crying.

Their apartment was tiny, no more than a series of small, linked rooms: lounge leading to kitchen leading to bathroom and bedroom. Edna had painted each room a different colour – the lounge was orange, the kitchen green, the bathroom red and the bedroom purple. Every time Meryl walked through the apartment, her head began to ache. Usually it just irritated her, but that night it added fuel to her vindictive fire.

What kind of a pathetic woman painted her apartment to resemble a row of Jelly Babies? Meryl snorted.

A few hours later she felt Edna creep into bed, but her attempts at spooning were unsuccessful. Meryl lay on her back on the edge of the bed all night, inched over by Edna's insistent cuddling endeavours, determined not to succumb.

For the first time in her life, Edna felt truly wretched. Every relationship up until this point, this very point, this moment in the middle of the night when Meryl flinched each time she reached out a hand to touch her, every relationship had been entirely in her control.

She could not possibly have imagined how awful losing that control would feel.

Three times that night she got up to go to the bathroom and retch, but nothing came out. Meryl didn't even ask her if she was feeling okay, assuming she was just trying to get attention, not believing that she actually had the power to hurt Edna.

The following morning Meryl woke up early, brewed some coffee and deliberately taunted Edna by not telling her anything about the previous night. She simply smiled a little cat-stole-the-cream smile, and giggled to herself while picking out sexy lingerie for that day: transparent black lace.

It was only fair, Meryl reasoned, locking the bathroom door to brush her teeth and talk to herself in the mirror. She could feel her corset loosening again, easing open ever so slightly, out of pity for poor Edna. She knew exactly how it felt; it was pure torture watching the woman you cared about running around with someone else.

The slight loosening gave Meryl a headache; a pounding headache, and a sensation that felt like vertigo. Very unpleasant. But it was only fair, she reminded herself, squeezing a few small pimples to help her clear her head, thinking back to the many times Edna had done the exact same thing to her.

Yes, she was ready to admit that she was only using Harry for a bit of R&R – Revenge & Retaliation. But wasn't that what relationships were all about? Using other people to get what you wanted, and in return giving them something that *they* wanted?

Besides, she concluded, dabbing her squeezed pimples with a tissue, it could be seen as proactive self-defence. If she didn't fool around with someone, Edna would, and Meryl simply could not bear being on the receiving end again.

'Life isn't some funfair ride,' she reminded herself sternly, 'you have to be constantly on your guard.'

Meryl licked her fingers and smoothed her hair down carefully.

'There's no room for wussies in the game of love,' she said, pointing a stern finger at her reflection.

Convinced that she was doing the right thing, the only thing to be done under the circumstances, Meryl winked at herself in the mirror, walked out past Edna without speaking, and went to her favourite shopping centre to window-shop for a couple of hours, biding her time till dinner.

That evening, Meryl took two full hours to get ready. She ran a candlelit bubble bath and locked the door, blocking any attempts at seduction Edna might be concocting. As she lay in the bath, a warm glow of vengeance spread from her belly outwards, and she thought she could detect a hint of roasting meat on the breeze.

It was most probably just someone having a braai, but Meryl liked to think that it was the scent of revenge. After her bath, she moisturised every inch of her body and spent half an hour on her make-up, perspiring lightly in the muggy summer air. Carefully, Meryl then chose some stunning new lingerie, and her tiniest, sexiest dress. It just so happened to be the dress she had worn the first night she slept with Edna. The cherry on the cupcake, though, was when Meryl slipped some condoms into her hand-bag as she passed Edna, sulking and pretending to watch TV. She was watching a show called *Cheaters*, where the presenter provided solid proof that some poor individual was being cheated on, filming their response.

Meryl smirked at the uncanny timing.

Let her have her beautiful handicap, she thought cruelly, as she smoothed the tight dress over her hips and checked her lipstick in the mirror on the back of the front door. *I've got a man … and there's nothing she can do about it – she's contractually bound to this relationship.*

Meryl's corset was so tight she could hardly breathe.

※

Nine blocks and years of experience away, Harry was preparing a green feast. He hummed to himself as he chopped and boiled and sliced and diced, hummed a medley of James Bond tunes, and grinned, somewhat stupidly, into the pot of soup he was stirring.

'This is it,' he said. 'This is the moment I decide to grow up. About time, I think.'

Harry was absolutely certain that Meryl would love the meal. For starters there was green bean soup with basil crackers (a super new invention – crackers flavoured, shaped and coloured like basil leaves), and then for the main course, there was spinach pâté, brocolli and pea stew, a large green salad (lettuce, cucumber and green pepper) and a fresh loaf of jalapeno bread. For dessert (she had hinted at her sweet tooth last night) Harry had discovered, to his delight, mint choc-chip ice cream! He didn't know how it had escaped his notice before, but he was thrilled. Of course, he had to pick out the choc chips, but that was a small price to pay for a new item on the Green-Friendly List.

Now, had Harry known Meryl at all, he would have known that this meal was not, in fact, in alignment with her dietary habits.

The lettuce in the salad, perhaps.

Everything else – not at all. Meryl dieted as fastidiously as nuns pray. Harry had no idea.

As he cooked, a small gang of damaged things collected at his feet: the broken chair he'd been meaning to fix, a teacup without a handle, a bent-out-of-shape lampshade, and a wind-up clock without a winder – or a clock face.

They huddled in a hopeful pile, like a puppy-dog waiting to be petted.

Harry kicked them. Unintentionally, of course – there was a knock on the door and he whirled around, tripping over the pile of broken goods, and falling flat on his face.

For a moment, lying there on the cracked grey linoleum, he felt the familiar twinge of panic; but then he remembered that he had dumped all of his green food colouring. Now that Guinness was officially investigating him, he was going clean. Harry had said goodbye to his dirty past. Besides, the food colouring had made his vision go funny; for a period of three weeks everything Harry looked at had a greenish hue.

It made choosing the right food very difficult.

Any thoughts of food and funny vision were supplanted by thoughts of a very different nature when Harry opened his front door.

Meryl was dressed to kill; Harry was quite happy to be annihilated.

The tiny dress she had chosen was made of red lace, with two strategically placed narrow strips of red fabric over the bust and buttock areas. Harry had never, ever, seen a woman looking this good. His sweet old ma had certainly never worn a dress like this. It was as if the poster of Candy K under his bed had come to life, changed her outfit, and knocked on his front door.

He gulped. The full moon just rising behind Meryl cast a silvery shimmer over her skin, and the dust particles in Harry's house seemed to cluster around her admiringly.

She sneezed.

'Hi Meryl, you look, uhm … incredible!' he swallowed, trying to form more words. For some reason, the blood supply to the part of his brain involved in verbal functioning was experiencing a temporary malfunction.

'Thanks, honey,' Meryl answered seductively, slowly licking her lips.

'Can I, uhhm … get you a drink? I only have green juice, or Chinese green tea, sorry, there's not much variety when it has to be green …'

He trailed off as Meryl moved towards him, her hips swaying slowly, her movements catlike and predatory.

She leaned forward, kissed him full on the mouth, and said in a husky voice, 'I'll have whatever you're having, honey,' and then she strolled away, satisfied that Harry looked suitably flustered, his gaze suitably fixed.

'Green juice it is, then!' he croaked, his voice cracking mid-sentence. He moved quickly through to the kitchen, where he fetched not only the green juice, but the green bean soup, the green basil crackers, and his composure (also, unsurprisingly, green-tinted).

All of a sudden it didn't seem like quite such an easy task to seduce and destroy Harry. He was a really nice guy – every cluttered inch of his house proclaimed that he was a nice guy – from the bowls of cat food left out for the strays (she had seen them lurking outside), to the table he had so sweetly set for her, and the carefully arranged pictures on the wall (many of them of puppies and kittens, with cute catchphrases scrawled underneath), the old-fashioned *sakkie-sakkie* music playing on the record player, and the large, framed photographs of his parents next to a burnt-out kettle on the mantelpiece (strange, but nice).

Meryl briefly massaged her temples to relieve the headache that had been building ever since she walked into Harry's house.

What was wrong with her? she worried. *Another headache?*

Twice now, in the last two days, she had had moments of grave doubt; loosenings in the cynicism that had been firmly laced and knotted for the past three years.

It was very disconcerting.

Meryl sighed.

She wondered if it wasn't some kind of early-onset menopause that was making her hormones go crazy.

'I hope you like your greens!' Harry called out as he walked back into the room, balancing everything on a big tray, with a look of intense concentration on his face and his tongue sticking out just a little.

'I wish you could have met my parents, they were the sweetest, most caring and supportive people in the whole world,' he said, placing a bowl of mucky green soup in front of Meryl with great pride, making sure not to spill.

'When I told my ma about my green food resolve,' he continued, keeping his eyes firmly focused on the table as he spooned the soup into his mouth messily, 'she went straight out to look for green cake recipes! She didn't have much luck.'

He looked up suddenly, making earnest eye contact with Meryl for the first time since she'd arrived.

'She's the reason I carried on with it for so long, you know. I could never disappoint her, and she was so pleased with the whole project, that I just couldn't give it up. She would have loved you.'

He sighed, his eyes drifting to the large photograph on the makeshift mantelpiece.

'I really miss both of them, it's just not the same without them, you know …' and so Harry continued, throughout the whole meal.

Meryl noticed that when he spoke about his parents, Harry seemed more comfortable than at any other time, and it made her think of her own parents and the cobweb of emotions that clung to them. She fell silent, wrapped in memory like a young child wrapped in a blanket, sleepily carried to bed after a long car trip.

Harry, sensing something broken, asked gently, 'What about your parents? Are they still alive?'

'Oh, it's a long story … I'll tell you one day,' she said casually, quickly steering the conversation to one of his many pieces of clutter – a rocking chair without a seat, entwined with broken fairy lights. Meryl dodged the question with a mixture of grace and cunning, as if shaking off the attentions of an unwanted stranger.

Harry, falling for her ruse, didn't push the subject and traipsed off to the kitchen to arrange Meryl's Big Surprise. He was so excited that he hopped from foot to foot, almost dropping the two bowls of mint choc-chip ice cream which he brought out with the air of a novice magician producing something extraordinary.

Seeing how important it was to him, Meryl stretched her face into a thin smile and oohed and aahed and said how much she loved ice cream (usually, she would have made a scathing comment about her diet, raised one eyebrow scornfully or simply kept quiet).

Another stitch in her corset popped.

Meryl wondered if there was some kind of hallucinogenic dust in the house, something that accumulated only on the ley lines of certain places – places of great clutter, maybe – something that was unzipping her control a little more with each passing moment.

Her corset was no namby-pamby construction; it was old-fashioned and sturdy, like those made with whale bones, built to last a lifetime.

And now, within days of meeting this odd little man, it was falling apart on her.

Harry didn't notice her momentary confusion, so determined was he to avoid stuttering and stammering again like a fool.

'When you suggested dessert last night, I thought to myself, *this young lady has a sweet tooth!* So I decided to get something special,' he said proudly. 'Eat up!'

Meryl's fanatical diet didn't usually allow for anything with sugar in it, but she could see that Harry would not take maybe for an answer, so she reluctantly popped a spoonful of ice cream into her mouth.

As she did, Harry said significantly, 'My ma would really have approved of you, Meryl.'

The ice cream left something hard and circular on her tongue, and with an alarming foreboding Meryl delicately opened her mouth, stuck out her tongue and pulled out the ring that she had narrowly missed swallowing.

The next moment excused itself politely from the normal time frame. It stood up and stretched, and stretched, and stretched.

Meryl watched it, spellbound.

Harry just smiled.

'I know we've only just met, Meryl, but we're right for each other, I know we are. Will you marry me?'

He was earnest and honest, heartfelt and sincere, direct and decent and true.

In other words, irresistible.

For ten long seconds, Meryl's corset of cynicism, which had kept her constricted and breathless for three years, came undone. Every knot that she had tied, every layer she had added, every inch of armour she had constructed around her sweet and tender self fell away, as if by magic.

Harry's honest certainty reached through it all, and spoke directly to her heart.

In a flood of romance (or something that felt like it), without any semblance of rational thought, and in the light of the full moon, Meryl whispered, 'Yes.'

✸ ✸ ✸

You may well be thinking, *What the hell?* Or, possibly (if there are children around), *What the heck?* How did *that* happen? What was she thinking?

All very good questions.

But much as Meryl tried to rationalise it afterwards, she couldn't come up with any logical answers. Blame spur-of-the-moment, blame rash responses, blame split-second dementia, if you will.

Perhaps it was something much more basic, and, at the same time, much more profound. Perhaps it is in these moments in our lives – the moments when we take leaps of illogical abandon – that we are nudged out of a rut by our impatient souls.

If we are here to do something bigger than the everyday slog of work, TV, banal relationships and tasteless food (and I would argue that each of us is), then perhaps, on occasion, when the ruts we are living in start resembling complex mole holes more than shallow dips, our souls get edgy.

Put more simply – perhaps, when it is time to change, we are governed by something deeper than common logic. And at the same time, deep down, don't we all secretly want to be swept off our feet? The still, small space within (many of us) dreams of meeting someone who will dare to say, after three encounters: 'You are amazing.'

Don't we all want that?

Meryl, surprisingly, did.

Of course, this desire was buried so deeply that she hadn't looked at it since she turned sixteen and decided to grow up; but it was still there, and it yearned to meet someone and just *know.* No five-year relationships figuring out if your living habits are well-matched, no extended comfort cruises resulting in a seemingly inevitable destination, no long and drawn-out test periods.

Meryl, in her heart of hearts (a cold and disused place, almost suffocated by cynicism) was ripe and ready to be swept off her feet.

You might say she had attracted the perfect man into her life. If you were being a smarty-pants, that is.

✸ ✸ ✸

After a few moments of hugging Meryl so tightly that Harry squeezed almost all the air out of her, making her feel panicky, he trundled off to the kitchen.

'Now for a celebratory cuppa of green tea!' he said, beaming, and Meryl was left alone, reflecting on what she had just done.

She regretted her decision immediately, of course. Her headache had intensified to a steady thud, and the clutter in the room seemed suddenly too much, the space too overwhelmingly littered with stupid little bits and bobs; too crowded, too claustrophobic.

Meryl started hyperventilating. It felt like the early stages of suffocation. She cupped her hands over her nose and mouth and breathed deeply, trying to calm down.

It will be fine, of course it will be fine, it will be fine, she repeated, silently, over and over again.

She wasn't dying after all, she was just a little confused. She would have to break off 'the engagement', but not now, not with this headache.

Tomorrow, definitely tomorrow.

There was only one thing left to do now, the one thing that always made her feel better. At that moment, Harry bustled back into the room, beaming and carrying two steaming cups.

'Here you are, my love,' he said sweetly, holding the boiling hot cup so she could grasp it by the handle, 'I can't tell you how relieved I am you said yes. I thought maybe I was rushing things ... I don't have much experience, you know.'

Meryl just smiled, her sore head raging. She sipped her green tea as Harry looked at her adoringly, his eyes starry, his grin unstoppable.

'Oh,' he said, suddenly looking worried, 'do you like the ring? I was going to find something at the dump, because I usually get everything from there, but I thought to myself, *No!* Meryl would want something new! So I went to the jeweller in Smith Street and picked it out. I thought green would remind you of me.'

Harry was waiting anxiously for an answer, so Meryl studied the ring sitting so presumptuously on her finger. It was very nice. Not spectacular, but delicate and lovely, a silver band with a large green crystal of some sort.

The cynic finally quieted for a moment – no doubt off in search of hard liquor – and Meryl was able to thank Harry sincerely.

'It's beautiful, Harry,' she said, and smiled a rare, true smile that made all the blood rush to his head.

They drank their tea on the couch, which had piles of half-broken furniture, pictures, birdcages and knick-knacks on it that had to be cleared first. There were a few loose springs sticking out of the cushions, and it took Meryl a good few minutes to relax. Her headache was quietly spinning into a severe case of vertigo.

Harry sat sipping his tea quietly, looking contentedly around the room and wondering if now would be the right time to bring out *Garfield*. He was jostled out of this happy thought by Meryl turning to him and kissing him, hard, on the mouth, so unexpectedly that he spilled tea down the front of her red, lacy dress. She didn't seem to mind, just took the cup from him and dropped it on the floor (it broke with a soft tinkle and immediately started its slow pilgrimage back to Harry).

Still kissing him so hard it bruised his mouth, Meryl mounted Harry, placing both legs firmly on either side of his body and wrapping her arms around his neck. Pinned down and defenceless, he placed his arms around her, unclear about what he was supposed to do.

She was clearly the leader in the lovemaking, and led Harry (willingly) into the bedroom, handed him a condom and slowly started undressing him. He let her, gulping and breathing hard, every now and again reaching out a hand to touch her hair, or her shoulder, or to stroke her arm.

Meryl saw that he had a thick red scar over his heart, and wondered where it came from.

Once Harry was completely naked, she sat him down on the bed and started undressing herself, slipping first one sleeve and then the other off her perfectly shaped shoulders, turning her back to him and bending over to wriggle seductively out of her dress. Noticing how Harry's breathing quickened, Meryl slowly, ever so slowly, slipped her underwear off until she, too, was totally naked.

Harry leapt forward and started sucking her breasts with a fervency that surprised her, and almost hurt.

Still, there were worse things than pain, she thought. Battling a bit to keep in the mood, and more than a little distracted by the persistent sucking, Meryl pushed Harry down on to the floor, and he let go of her nipple in surprise.

'I uhh … I think we should wait until after we're married, uhhm … don't you?'

Harry's voice squeaked as she stood over him with a lascivious look in her eyes, more than ready to give herself up to the pleasures of hormonal release. At least this would quiet the confusion. It always did.

'Well, heh-heh,' he muttered nervously, 'I suppose maybe … if we'll be married soon anyway … that's okay then, isn't it?'

If Meryl had had any friends left, she would have told them about Harry's sexual performance. It was, without exaggeration, the worst sex she had ever had. He pumped away for a short while (not providing an ounce of satisfaction or pleasure for Meryl), did not follow her lead as she tried to guide him into a more pleasurable position, insisted on his excruciating sucking the whole time, and then ejaculated prematurely and quickly went flaccid inside her.

After a few moments, an elated Harry turned to Meryl with a look of wonder in his eyes and said, 'It was my first time … how did I do?'

Now, Meryl may have been naked, but her cynicism was still intact – albeit a little looser than she liked – and she could instantly think of at least seven scathing come-backs for this single, heartfelt question. Instead she just smiled at him, which seemed enough.

The awkwardness Meryl felt after this particular sex act was worse than any post-coital awkwardness she had ever felt before. Even when the sex had been with a complete stranger, and they had both regretted it imme-diately afterwards, even when it had been with her best friend's fiancé, and her best friend had walked in on them, even (and this was the cracker) when it had been with a gay man who stopped midway and said, 'Nah, I can't do this,' and then wanted to talk about it (while Meryl was still highly aroused) even *then*, she didn't feel as bad as she felt at that moment

Meryl had done some sleeping around. She was lucky not to be infected with any nasty diseases. But Meryl had never slept with someone she was engaged to (even by mistake), someone who loved her (so soon!) and who couldn't perform (at all).

She had definitely never slept with a foolishly proud virgin.

Her head was now pounding so ferociously that small black dots kept flashing in front of her eyes, and she realised that she had to leave imme-diately or she would throw up.

So she left.

Harry fell into a content and exhausted sleep. As far as he was concerned, the evening had been an absolute success. The dinner was delicious (even if he had to say so himself), Meryl had agreed to marry him, and they had had fantastic sex, right there on his bedroom floor! He looked at the spot with a proud grin. And if she had left rather quickly, and if they hadn't cuddled – well, maybe she had to wake up early the next day.

He wasn't going to argue about silly things like that.

As Meryl drove away from the dump, she could feel the panic lifting, just a little. Her lips were swollen from his fumbling kisses, her skin strangely scented with his smell, her normally seamless composure rumpled and stretched.

The inside of her car prickled with confusion, it filled the air with tiny buzzing gnats that got under her dress and into her hair, and made her itch. Meryl's mind raced, and her heart beat too fast. Glancing in the rear-view mirror, she noticed that her freckles had all but disappeared.

Going home in that state was out of the question, so Meryl drove to the one place she knew she could be by herself. The night, although no longer muggy, was still as warm and comforting as a lukewarm bath.

She parked carefully, the tyres of her car crunching loudly in the still night air, and walked along a narrow path to the graveyard. Two yester-day-today-tomorrow shrubs had been planted at the entrance and their fragrance filled the air, reminding Meryl of how, as a child, she had made little bouquets from their purple, mauve and white flowers, handing them out to strangers walking past her house.

She smiled weakly at the memory.

It was pitch dark and the gravestones loomed ominously against the cloudy sky, creating the familiar jagged skyline that Meryl had come to recognise whenever she walked up that hill. The full moon, which had risen along with Harry's hopes at the beginning of the evening, was now clouded over with confusion, and there wasn't even the faintest starlight to see by. Luckily, Meryl knew exactly where to go. Her mom was buried here and it was the only place where Meryl ever felt at peace. The grave-stones were like old friends, constant companions on her frequent visits, steadfast and reliable like no one in real life ever was.

It was not for lack of trying.

At first, Meryl's friends tried being tender with her, tried encouraging her to let her vulnerable side show and talk about her feelings, but she wasn't interested.

'How are you feeling?' they'd ask, and she'd invariably reply, 'Fine. Good God, did you see what X was wearing last night? Is she trying to look like a cheap whore, or what?'

The names were interchangeable: clearly Meryl thought the whole of Durban dressed like cheap whores. She was spiteful, she was angry, she was deeply insulting. Only her two closest friends, Saveshnie and Eranie, didn't give up on her. They kept calling, inviting her to dinner and out for drinks, to watch bands or go dancing.

Meryl got horribly drunk every time they saw her, drunk and belligerent, and for a few months, every time they went out, she would end up swearing at them by the end of the evening.

'Come on Meryl, time to go home,' they'd say, gently leading her away from whatever guy she had chosen as her prey for the night.

'Fuck you!' she'd answer them, and there was real meaning behind her words, real anger, real scorn. She never apologised the next day, never thanked her friends for the support, never let them in, no matter how persistently they tried.

'She's not coping,' Saveshnie said to Eranie one night, watching Meryl pick a fight with a stranger who had accidentally stood on her toe in a nightclub.

'I just don't know what to do anymore,' Eranie replied. 'I keep thinking it's a necessary phase, that it's just her way of coping with her mom's death and that she has good reason to treat me so badly, but it's really starting to get to me.'

Eranie's eyes filled with tears, and she brushed them away with a self-conscious little smile. 'I know she doesn't mean it, but I don't remember the last time I saw her when she didn't call me a bitch. I *hate* that ... she knows I do, I've told her so many times, but she still does it. With this look in her eyes, this satisfied look.'

She sighed. 'I don't know how much longer I can take it.'

Saveshnie rubbed Eranie's back consolingly.

'I know what you mean,' she said, 'it just starts feeling like too much after a while. Like she'd actually prefer it if we left her alone.'

They both turned to look at Meryl, just as she slapped the girl who had stood on her toe. She slapped her hard – hard enough to bring tears to the girl's eyes – and Saveshnie and Eranie had to rush to the ugly scene to lead her away before more damage was done.

Meryl didn't thank them.

She cast her friends as the villains in her life story, and eventually they accepted their roles and left her to it. Tired of her angry SMSes, spite-filled phone calls and hateful emails, tired of explaining away her appalling behaviour and misdirected anger, tired of this new person who in no way resembled the friend they loved, they gave up.

☼ ☼ ☼

So that was that. Left without friends, without family, and without freckles, Meryl turned to her lover, who, as it turned out, didn't love her.

Alas, we know too well the consequences of that action.

Sure, this seems like a simple-to-solve problem: Meryl just needs to change her attitude, put on some fresh lipstick, and apologise to her friends. Easy peasy. The barriers will come crashing down, the cursed corset will unbind, and the phase will be filed away under *I was going through a difficult time*.

Only, it's not quite that easy to do, is it?

Especially when you're smack bang in the middle of it, and nothing is clear or obvious or in any way understandable.

☼ ☼ ☼

As she reached her mother's grave, Meryl's corset ripped, just a little, under the right armpit. She slumped down next to the gravestone, with a sigh that reached to the tips of her toes, and started talking.

'Oohh, mom, I wish I could have you back, just for one night. I don't know what to do … all I want is some advice. Dad's no good, he's been in the loony bin since you died, and all he ever talks about is macaroni cheese. And, as you know, I haven't really been getting on that well with Saveshnie and Eranie lately. It's just, I've just, things have just been pretty unhappy for a while now. I haven't written a poem since you died, and I'm just feeling so *flat*.'

Meryl sighed.

This was no exaggeration. Meryl's imagination had deflated. Rapidly.

It wasn't that she didn't have ideas for poems, or the desire to write them (she did, every day); it was just that any time she had a flitter of inspiration, instead of it filling her until she simply had to write it down or burst, the idea punctured. She didn't have the *oomph* to carry it through. It frustrated her to the brink of tears.

'So, anyway. Here's the dilemma: I randomly meet this guy on a job for work – don't ask, he has this weird green food thing going – and then I see him again at this strange club, and we get talking, and he asks for my number. So, I gave it to him, I admit, for all the wrong reasons. You know I told you about Edna, my girlfriend? Well, she went and cheated on me *again*, and I just, you know, I just wanted to make her realise how terrible it feels to be passed over like that.

'This guy, Harry, calls the next day and we go out for coffee, and it's okay-ish. Then he offers to cook me dinner tonight – an all-green meal, it's totally weird. And he lives in this ridiculously cluttered house near the dump, 'cause he's a *garbage man* … did I mention that? Thank God my sinusitis has been acting up lately. So, I go over for dinner and he proposes! He says we're soulmates, and I'm the one he wants to be with! After two dates!'

Meryl snorted.

'But I'm thinking about you and dad, 'cause he's been talking about his parents, and I'm thinking about how much I miss you, and how I went window-shopping today, on my own, and that made me think about you and Nanny, and that got me thinking about Nanny and Grandpa and how they only knew each other for two weeks before they got married, and there's actually always been a part of me that wants to do just that: to meet someone, and just *know*, and then to just do it.'

She paused for breath. The night sang with crickets and the humidity that had smothered the city lifted a little, blown away by a light breeze scented with memories.

'So, my head's full of all these thoughts, and he says to me all sweetly, "Will you marry me?" and I say yes! To this guy I hardly know!'

Meryl paused again, trying to come to terms with the words she had just said, before continuing.

'And my mind's racing, and I'm thinking a zillion things all at once, and there's this voice saying, *Well, now you can* really *get back at Edna, this'll show her!* but that's not who I want to be. I'm so tired of constantly being on guard, Mom. I don't remember the last time I felt comfortable around someone, like I could relax, and be myself.'

She sighed deeply, stretching her legs out in front of her.

'Oh, and then it gets worse,' she continued, leaning back against the gravestone and looking up at the clouds. 'We make love. Only it's the worst I've ever had. He has *no* clue what to do, no clue whatsoever. It was almost painful, it was that bad.'

Meryl ran her fingers through her hair, mussing up its sleek perfection, and pulling at it anxiously.

'So I've just left after this horrific sex, and my mind's spinning, and my head aches, and I don't know what to do. Well, I do know what to do, I just don't want to do it. I have to tell him, tomorrow, about Edna, and how I was just using him for revenge. But he's a good guy, Mom. A freak, but a good guy.'

'I don't know, I suppose there's a little bit of me that feels like maybe it's time for a change? I just don't know what kind of change. And anyway, I feel like I have all these requirements, things that I want out of a marriage that I've never had in a relationship. Besides, he doesn't even know me.'

Meryl clasped her hands around her knees, her knuckles white, her face drawn.

'Maybe,' she said slowly, 'maybe there's an easier way out. Maybe instead of me ending it, I can get him to – I can scare him off, you know? I'll give him this impossible list of demands, and then he'll call it off, and I won't have to do the dirty work.'

She nodded her head vigorously and got to her feet.

'Of course! It's that simple, really.'

Meryl stood for a moment, one hand resting on top of her mom's gravestone, and stretched, her muscles cold and aching from sitting on the hard ground. As she walked down the hill towards her car, Meryl thought she could detect the faintest shadow on the ground in front of her, the faintest glow of moonshine emanating from the clouds.

※

The problem with late-night clarity is that so much of it is contingent on that special combination of moon and dark stillness. The next morning it is often much less clear. The thought of facing Harry – so soon after the engagement/sex debacle – scared Meryl more than anything else she could think of. So she pretended to be asleep when Edna woke up, switched off her cell phone, and took the day off work.

Meryl stayed in bed all morning, dozing, reading trashy magazines and moping around. She felt at one with the numerous pop divas and movie stars who had been dumped, gone off the rails, got fat, puked up their lunch, chosen a bad outfit.

She felt their pain.

Even Candy K, who was usually on top of things, had been caught crying when her supermodel boyfriend dumped her.

What hope did Meryl have?

The weather didn't improve her mood. It had been oppressively, suffo-catingly hot all morning (conditions that were sure to make Meryl feel panicky) and then, around midday, the sky turned as dark as midnight, before erupting into a freak hailstorm.

Rain, hail, thunder and lightning for a solid hour.

There was a power failure, and Meryl could do nothing but sit in the dim light and stare out at the sheets of rain. And then it stopped. Just like that.

So she dressed up in a long blonde wig and a tiny black miniskirt, and traipsed off to drink in bars for the rest of the day, calling herself Tracy. She chose to be a beautician specialising in toenails, and swore not to think about Harry for at least the next 24 hours.

☼ ☼ ☼

Now, before you put your judging boots on, remember that Meryl was operating alone: she had no one to confide in, no one to tell her she was being an idiot, no one to shed a bit of light on the conundrum she found herself trapped in.

So she did what she thought best. With a grimace, Meryl zipped up her emotions like a too-tight dress, hyper-aware of the rip in the stiff panelling of scepticism on the right-hand side of her corset, yet unwilling to cast it aside.

She thought perhaps her freckles were starting to show just a little.

How often in life do we hear the call to change, and choose to ignore it? Our selective hearing kicks in, and we pretend that gut instinct to shake things up was simply indigestion, our imagination, the product of one too many drinks, or TV shows, or long nights spent alone. There is something so comfortable in our destructive patterns.

☼ ☼ ☼

For the first few hours, Meryl's blonde distraction technique failed miserably. She quickly grew drunk and maudlin at the first bar she walked into – an Irish pub called Jimmy Fox's – and asked every person who came near if they thought there was such a thing as a soulmate, and if there was, then how come so many people were unhappy, and if there wasn't, was it all hopeless, or were there a few people you could be equally happy with, and why were there so many fucking questions, anyway, how come you couldn't just find somebody and know that it was right?

The air felt sodden with her questions, thick and humid as the night outside.

Then a weedy-looking guy, with far too much confidence, sauntered up to the bar and sat down next to Meryl, bought her a Fuzzy Navel, and said, 'Your make-up looks better smudged.'

To which she drunkenly replied, 'Is my make-up smudged?'

'No, but it will be when I'm finished with you,' he said, with a slimy grin.

That was just the line she needed to forget about the Harry Dilemma. Meryl refused to feel even a twinge of guilt as they stumbled out of the bar, arm in arm, to go back to his place. She had been missing the comforting cynicism she usually felt towards everything, and was determined to re-activate it asap.

Random sex with this guy – what was his name? Pravesh? – would do just that.

He had told her he was an undertaker.

Perfect.

When Beth woke up after her cathartic experience, she was able to breathe through her nose for the first time in days, and felt a tiny bit better. Better enough to take a long, hot shower, and put on clean clothes. Better enough to open the windows to let in some fresh air. Better enough to take her full-to-overflowing garbage bags down to the pavement to get collected.

As she turned to go back inside, something shifted. Beth remembered running after the rubbish truck in her clean work clothes, lugging Pravesh's rubbish that he had forgotten to take out. And then she remembered how she had to clean his flat, and wash his dishes, and do his laundry, because he was in too much of a funk to do his chores himself. And that made her think about how he had always been in too much of a funk to do anything except sit around and complain about his childhood.

For the first time since the break-up, Beth's solemn face cracked into a tiny smile.

Those had been bad days!

She had hated those days! Constantly feeling weighed down, worried about Pravesh's issues, wondering if he was going to be depressed (again) and unable to leave the house (again), tiptoeing around him so that she didn't make him feel any worse, even though the tiptoeing made *her* feel worse.

Slowly, long fingers of light crept through the fog that had surrounded Beth since the break-up.

She could admit, now, standing on the pavement with her hair wet and her heart still tender, she could admit that it was totally fucking strange that he liked to paint dead people's toenails. So strange it didn't bear thinking about. She could admit that he had treated her like shit for the last few weeks, that going out every night and only taking her to that crappy Mike's Kitchen had been wrong of him.

And that cheating on her had been unforgivable.

As the fog lifted, and her thoughts cleared, a flood of memories and opinions poured into Beth's mind, memories and opinions she had kept dammed up for fear of what they meant to her relationship.

She hated the way Pravesh never made her feel special, hated the way he smelt in the mornings, hated the vague creepiness that clung to him like dandruff.

She hated the way he made love!

Beth grinned and shook her head in disbelief. Two schoolchildren walking down the road grinned back at her.

Truly, Pravesh was the worst lover she had ever had.

The toenail thing was nasty.

He was whiny, and irritating, and selfish.

He was not in great shape.

The rush of releasing all these pent-up feelings made Beth giddy with relief. The morning air smelt like jasmine. A butterfly flitted past. The shards of her heart – finally, infinitesimally slowly – pieced themselves together again.

In future years, this was the instant Beth would describe as her epiphany moment.

Outlined in gold.

It was a moment made for the movies; it validated all her tears.

Beth knew then, with complete certainty, that Pravesh was not the right man for her. She realised that she was stronger than him, had always been stronger than him. How ridiculous to have wasted so much time on a man who was not man enough for her.

Beth started to giggle, and soon the giggle turned into a laugh, and the laugh into a belly laugh. She laughed till her sides ached, and her eyes streamed, and her mind cleared.

Good Lord, what a waste! All those years spent worrying and thinking and obsessing over guys, and for what?

They weren't worth it!

They had all been idiots.

She had wasted her life away on love. And not even real love! A cheap, no-name-brand version of it.

Two-minute noodle love.

Beth strode defiantly to her apartment to fetch her fluffy pink diary, sat down at the kitchen table and started writing; writing so fast she had to massage her hand every few minutes to keep it from seizing up.

What a fool I've been! she began, *all these years spent with guys as my main focus. You know, I think I've been obsessed with love for ten years!*

This was no exaggeration. Beth, at fourteen – spotty, podgy, and inse- cure – had decided at that long-ago school disco that boys would like her more if she helped them find their own true loves, gave them lots of attention, and didn't ask for too much in return. She had never wavered in her decision.

That's it! I'm done, she wrote. *Relationships have been my number one priority, and what have they brought me? A whole lot of heartache. No thank you! I am sick to death of other people's issues being dumped on me.*
I AM NEVER GOING TO TRY AND SAVE ANYONE AGAIN.

With this last defiant statement, Beth closed her journal, dried her eyes and decided to change her life. Much as she found the check-out business satisfying and enjoyed utilising her people skills, there was something bigger for her on the not-too-distant horizon.

She just had to find it.

In that tender spot underneath his left rib where Pravesh had a feeling his heart lived, he knew exactly what was wrong – he was lost.

Totally lost.

His whole meaningless life had been leading up to this sorry point, and he had no idea what to do next. Any decision-making felt insurmountably difficult.

How did anyone know what to do when they woke up in the mornings? Did they just not think about it, and blindly follow whatever they had done the day before? How were they not immobilised with terror about making the wrong choices, screwing it all up?

Or was it just him, just now, who had no idea?

He sat slumped against his wall, sucking his thumb and staring disconsolately at the floor, disabled by the death of his purpose, the death of his future, the death of his self-respect. Until eventually, with a particularly vicious shudder, his death radar also conked in. Pravesh hardly noticed. He was, as you might have suspected, prime fodder for a charismatic religious sect. Alas, none came aknocking.

Pravesh knew that he needed something momentous to happen, something so grand that it catapulted him out of his life. What he needed was a vision.

By a stroke of tremendous good luck, filtering through the thin walls like the voice of God, the lyrics of Candy K's latest song 'I Miss You So Bad I Could Puke' alighted on Pravesh, and brought him hope. He found himself identifying so strongly with its message that he was certain she had written it just for him. Unfortunately, the adolescent next door was unaware of his revelation, and callously played some other pop song after Candy K's had finished, so the momentary high that Pravesh experienced was short-lived.

But what a high it was!

Fuelled by a feeling similar to the thrill of painting toenails, Pravesh ran outside and jogged three blocks to the nearest music store, his bare feet bruised from the sharp gravel by the time he got there. But it was undeniably worth the effort, for there, displayed in the window for all to see, was the luscious Candy K.

Well, a luscious cardboard cut-out of Candy K.

Pravesh spent the rest of that afternoon playing the CD on repeat, singing along with the chorus as loudly as he could, oblivious to the fact that he was totally off-key:

Baby, ever since you went away,
Every day is cold and grey,
Ohhh, I miss you so bad I could puke.
Yeah, I miss you so bad I could puke.

After the seventeenth repetition, Pravesh's neighbours started knocking on his door, asking him to please, *please* play another song. Pravesh didn't hear them: he was in a blissful daze, stretched out on the floor under his window, staring up at the small patch of sky he could see, and rejoicing at the remarkable turn-around his life had taken.

He had meaning again! And his meaning was a pop star named Candy K.

Pravesh vowed then and there to go to every one of her concerts, buy every magazine she featured in, tape every song of hers that played on the radio, and make all future life-decisions with her in mind.

Candy K was the compass to guide his lost soul.

His was a pure and undying love.

☼ ☼ ☼

Being dumped elicits a number of responses in people. Some go off the rails and take up drinking, drug-taking, all-night partying or unhealthy amounts of meditation. Some rush out and find a new partner. Some embark on a soul-searching odyssey that requires many leather-bound journals and cups of green tea.

And some develop an obsession, funnelling all the break-up angst into one single vessel.

Pravesh had found his.

The best that can be hoped for with an obsession is that it is killed, swiftly and suddenly; a machete to the brain. Anything else just invites disaster.

※ ※ ※

Alas, Pravesh's first glimpse of Candy K did nothing to dim the bonfire of his love, as she was, if possible, even more vivacious and beautiful in person. She sang at King's Park Stadium, in the blistering heat, to a crowd of rich, young white kids. Outside the stadium, beggars stood with their hopes on outstretched palms, but the stream of fans going in or out didn't seem to notice.

Nor did Pravesh.

He was so starry-eyed he could hardly see anything. Candy K's rendition of his song brought sincere tears to Pravesh's eyes, although he wasn't sure if he was crying for Tracy or Candy K. They had melded into one in his mind – the voice and body of Candy K, and the wild bedroom antics and toenail-expertise of Tracy. Twice he saw Candy K winking at him, and twice he felt like the luckiest man on earth.

With a strength and determination he had rarely felt, Pravesh elbowed his way to the front row in time for Candy K's encore. Standing next to thirteen-year-old teenyboppers, Pravesh stood out like an undertaker at a pop concert. As she finished her encore, she blew kisses to the audience, waving and smiling for the hundreds of flashing cell-phone cameras.

Perhaps it was those kisses that prompted Pravesh, in a momentary lull, to shout out, 'I love you Candy K, you're the girl for me!'

A few derogatory laughs followed and a wave of sniggers passed through the theatre, even as Candy K looked Pravesh straight in the eye, and said in a sultry voice, 'Well, honey baby, I love you too!'

Then, with a toss of her fantastically shiny blonde hair, she flounced off the stage, waving to her adoring crowd.

Pravesh stood as if touched by the hand of God. No matter how many people pushed, shoved and spat on him (Candy K's fans didn't like intruders), he stood his ground with a euphoric grin on his face, happier than he could ever remember being.

Out of an enormous crowd, Candy K had picked him, Pravesh, and professed her love for him even though she hardly knew who he was.

She had chosen him! It was almost too good to be true.

Well, it *was* too good to be true, obviously, but Pravesh, in his heartache-induced loss of sanity, couldn't know that.

That's all very well, but what of sweet forgotten Beth?

Well.

Since her defiant discoveries whilst journaling (in summary: *Saving others is a waste of time, Must Do Something Big*), Beth rushed out and bought a stack of magazines. Oh, how readily pop culture sprints to our rescue! And rescue her it did. Within the pages of *Maverick, Intelligence* and *Money Maker's Monthly*, she found story after story of ordinary people who had done extraordinary things just because they believed in themselves. Beth decided to become one of those people. They knew a secret, and she was determined to weasel it out of them.

There wasn't too much weaselling to be done. In fact, there was an article in *Intelligence* entitled 'Ten Steps to Success with a capital S!' that pretty much outlined the general practices of these über-successes.

Beth swallowed the theories whole. They made her feel satiated for the first time in weeks. All at once she understood the importance of grati-tude in daily life, of being aware that your thoughts create your reality, of the link between how you think and how you feel.

She read and reread the article until she knew whole sections off by heart, and could toss them randomly into the salad of her everyday speech.

'Do you know your thoughts create your reality?' she found herself saying to a customer in Handy Green Grocers, 'Now, how about a plastic packet?'

And once, to the waitress at her favourite coffee shop, 'I'd like a pot of tea please … and by the way … have you ever thought that maybe loving yourself a bit more will help others to love you?'

Unsurprisingly, not everyone was impressed by her forthright approach, and, at the best of times, the only response these comments elicited was one of polite indifference, the safest mask we can ever hide behind. Clearly, Beth needed a better vehicle for her newfound wisdom; preferably one with hot-pink interior and zebra-skin seats.

※

And so, on a late Tuesday night in the hottest summer Durban had ever known, when even the walls seemed to sweat and the air was so humid it felt like a steam bath (and smelt like a men's change room); when the lights of the city burned holes in her curtains, and each hole exhaled a stale breath of pollution; when the steady hum of late night shady dealings was undercut by the sighs of thousands of sweating sleepers, Beth sat down to finally figure out what to do with her life.

Yes, it is true that many people take years to figure out what to do with their lives. But Beth was sick of being just like other people. In a journaling session that lasted five hours and thirty-seven minutes (with a few breaks for tea and chocolate), Beth dissected and analysed and scrutinised the reasons why she had always felt the need to save men (seeking affirmation from without rather than within), why she had settled for such a mediocre life (not believing in her limitless inner power), and why she was always attracted to losers.

She explored how the thought patterns she habitually returned to had created the circumstances of her life – even though she didn't particularly like the circumstances of her life at that moment – and how she had not, for a long, long time, felt grateful for anything outside of a relationship.

She said 'Huh!' a lot, as bubbles of understanding burst gently on her forehead. And she listened to white noise on the radio, to drown out the sounds of the city.

Then she fell asleep at her desk.

And woke up with a sore neck and a Plan.

She would become a motivational speaker!

Of course! *Of course.*

※

By the end of that day Beth had written her first speech, jotting down notes at the supermarket, and testing out certain key phrases on unsuspecting customers. It was incisive, informative and quite incendiary, entitled: *Do Me A Favour, Don't Be A Saver!*

For the first time in a long time, Beth started floating. She did a little dance of glee to celebrate.

Clearly not in the segment of the world's population that feels death is preferable to public speaking, Beth needed no encouragement. Left to her own devices (as we already know) she could monologue for hours on nearly any topic. Forty-five minutes was a piece of cake, a slice of pie, a chunk of chocolate.

By the time Beth phoned the first on her list of women's clubs (The Women Who Wicker, a group fascinated by wickerwork of the seventeenth century), she was one hundred per cent confident that she would be invited to speak.

She was not disappointed.

In three short weeks, Beth spoke to over twenty groups around town, including the prestigious Durban Scottish Country Dancers, the nationally-recognised Regional Optimist Club, the Durban Bat Interest Group, the Durban Budgerigar Club, the Durban Go! Club and the Birman Fanciers Group.

Church committees from the Holy Grail Church of the Lamb of God, and meditation classes from the Hare Krishna Door to Enlightenment Temple, raved about her to their congregations, and The Compassionate Friends, The Serenity Group and the Wafflers Speakers Group all booked Beth as the keynote speaker for their monthly meetings. Even the Natal Toy Dog Club and the Durban Association of Miniature Enthusiasts – who were usually very specific about their speakers – invited Beth to join them.

She was a hit at the Yabba-Dabba-Doo! Centre for Creativity, an instant winner with the Jolly Outings Club, and a runaway success at both the Primrose Carpet Bowling Clubhouse, and the Wahoo Diving Clubhouse.

Soon, Beth's diary was so pencilled in she had no choice but to hand in her resignation at Handy Green Grocers.

As soon as she left, the robbery nightmares stopped.

There was a moment, a very distinct moment when someone 'got it'. Beth liked to think of it as connecting to pure energy, being lit up like a bulb. She fed on this feeling like a chocaholic on Easter eggs, and soon found herself mildly addicted to switching people on. It kept her in an almost permanent floating state, and she often had to read the newspaper to bring herself back to earth.

It usually only took a page or two.

Of course, not everyone chose to be switched on. Not everyone loved Beth. Not everyone thought she had even one iota of sense in her. Give me a group gushing unadulterated praise, and I will give you a sticker that says *Delusional*.

It is human nature (that nature of ours that clings no matter how desperately we try to shake it off with esoteric/philosophical/religious enlightenments) to doubt what we are told.

For every light bulb Beth switched on, she had a power failure to contend with.

Interestingly enough, two of her most vehement critics were men who had been dumped after their girlfriends heard Beth speak and realised that their relationships had a thinly disguised mother/maid dynamic. This pair became the leaders of an opposition club for men whom Beth had 'maligned' by 'brainwashing' their significant others into a break-up, and they stood at the back of halls during her speeches, booing loudly. In a display of great maturity, they called themselves BOOBS – Boys Outrightly Opposed to Beth Speaking – but failed to have much impact. In fact, they became a source of ridicule as they were escorted from her speech venues (after paying the entrance fee) and battled to find any women to listen to their propaganda. Perhaps it was the name, perhaps the fact that thirty-somethings should not still be calling themselves boys.

In desperation, they started a clandestine mission to ruin Beth's advertising campaign – driving around town tearing down all of Beth's *Do Me A Favour, Don't Be A Saver!* posters, drawing moustaches and horns on them, and dropping them off at the dump, chanting 'Boobs! Boobs!' the whole way.

☀ ☀ ☀

You might question the effectiveness of this plan, as nobody ever saw their defiant dumping or the defaced posters that had already been removed.

You might be tempted to call it foolish, even.

I might join you.

☀ ☀ ☀

Before long, Beth fell into a practised rhythm. She waited backstage in the hot, stuffy church halls (although 'backstage' was perhaps a glamorisation of those poky rooms crammed full of religious knick-knacks) and then, once the murmur of assembled hopefuls reached a certain pitch, and she felt that she couldn't breathe in the potpourri of dust, incense and wood polish any longer, she emerged, walking up the (usually) short staircase to the impromptu stage. These church halls – wallowing in a shallow pool of neglect – were always small, hot and inadequately aerated by a lone ceiling fan.

Beth didn't mind. With a deep breath and a radiant smile to hide her pinkly sweating face, she plunged in, the poetic lilt of her voice even more pronounced when she spoke into a microphone.

'When I was younger?' she would begin, 'I used to think that my sole purpose in life was to save men. I chose the most confused, screwed-up losers I could find, so that I could give them meaning in life? Only it turned out the meaning I was giving them, was *my* meaning, my idea of who they should be? At the same time, I was waiting – anxiously, desperately waiting – for Prince Charming to ride into my life and save me.'

At that point there were always a few murmurs of agreement from the audience.

Beth nodded her head.

'Well, let me tell you something!' she exclaimed, leaning forward on the podium. 'Maybe instead of all of us waiting around to be saved, we should go ahead and save ourselves! Maybe instead of blaming other people for the things we don't like in our lives, we should take responsibility for ourselves! How about *that*?

Come on now, repeat after me: *I am brave, I don't need to save! I am brave, I don't need to save!*'

At first, everyone would be a little reluctant to chant along with Beth, but soon, as one or two began, more and more people joined in until the church hall resounded with the defiant statements of women no longer trapped in the whirlpool of denial.

That was one of Beth's key phrases – *the whirlpool of denial.*

Six months previously, had anyone told Beth that she would be motivating people not to make their relationship the only source of fulfilment in their lives, she would have snorted. Derisively. Beth didn't think such a thing was possible. But soon – to her relief – she found that not expecting the world (and all its contents) from one person, outweighed the pleasure of having a confirmed Saturday night date.

Resigned to the fact that her career choice (*Helping people to liberate themselves from unhealthy relationships* was the tagline she had settled on, doubling as a quick answer to, 'So what do you do?') could be construed as a little intimidating to most men, Beth had quietly given up on relationships. Not forever, you understand, but just until her career plateaued a little. She couldn't imagine meeting anyone who would fit into her new life.

Sometimes life proves our imaginations underfed.

That is to say, proves us wrong.

Mistaken.

A little thick.

Beth was not looking for love, was not expecting it, had not even invited it for tea.

So when it came aknocking, it took her by surprise. And yes, there was a small, reluctant element which prevented her from gleefully climbing back on the merry-go-round, a small part of her heart which (to her surprise) whispered, *Don't do it.*

She was finally happy in herself, she realised, happy and content and entirely without turmoil. Having to once more care about someone else seemed a lot to ask.

But then this man arrived. This man who spoke the same language of love as her, this man who had mastered the fine art of the unexpected gift, a man who baked her cakes, and took her dancing, and prepared sunset picnics on the beach.

Finally she had found someone with a heart as big as hers. And combined, their hearts were not too big for their life together.

Still, there was a moment, after their third date (what is it about third dates?) when Beth stood alone on the fire escape leading to her apartment – the moon full in the night sky, the air hot and hopeful – and wondered if it was too late to turn back. She knew already that it would not be a light-hearted fling, knew the consequences could be heartbreak, could see her heart and his becoming intertwined. And, knowing all of that, she took a deep breath – in and out – and dived in.

Beth had not thought it possible to fall in love again.

It gives me great hope in the human heart, she wrote in her journal that night.

As Beth rode the escalator of success (no ladders for her!), Pravesh plunged ever deeper into the abyss of obsession.

It was not intentional. He did not plan it.

Listening to and looking at Candy K were quite simply the only things that made him feel remotely okay. It was as if a dead weight was permanently pressing down hard on his chest, and only when he thought of Candy K, did the weight lift slightly.

So he thought of her all day.

He booked tickets to all her shows, subscribed to her seventeen fan clubs (official and unofficial), read every magazine she featured in, watched every talk show she appeared on, listened to every radio interview, song and jingle he could find.

Pravesh carefully cut out her pictures from magazines (skilfully removing any men she may have posed with) and stuck them up on the wall next to his bed. To that he added lists of her likes and dislikes. (Likes: cupcakes, aerobics, funfairs and TV. Dislikes: asparagus, running, hairdryers and fire.)

He took to talking to the poster of her he had stuck up on the back of his toilet door. He did not work, or interact with anyone, or think of anything except Candy K. She was his daily purpose; his point A to point B, his compass and road map and life goal all rolled into one.

And yes, she was ruining his life.

Pravesh watched his bank balance dwindle with resigned dread. Before long, all the careful savings from his years of undertaking had evaporated into a cloud of adoration, and he had to move out of his apartment.

You might think this would act as a wake-up call.

But no. Not even a little bit.

For Pravesh's obsession had, at its core, a painful truth: the moment he had decided, at last, to love someone, that someone had taken his love and thrown it away.

He would do anything to avoid dealing with this truth.

Even face his worst nightmare, all packaged up and tied with a bow.

☼

Pravesh moved back home.

His parents lived in a secure complex, a group of twelve houses within the same high wall, where everyone knew everyone else.

And everything about everyone else.

He was forced to greet every one of his parents' friends each day, and if, by some lucky chance, two days went by without some chitchat, the friend in question would pop in for a cup of tea and a catch-up.

'So Pravesh, how is everything and all?' they'd ask, sitting on the pink sofa with the floral cushions that perfectly matched the curtains and the perfectly pale pink shag-heap carpet.

Pravesh felt numb, immobilised, trying desperately to find an excuse to vacate the room, which closed in on him like a giant, pink fluffy teddy bear wanting a hug. The house felt oppressively small and obscenely cluttered with all the pictures and porcelain ornaments that Pravesh had tried to avoid in his minimalist apartment. Every room looked like a very finely detailed painting in an old English country home, only his parents were modern-day South African Indians. It didn't fit. His mother had collected seven-hundred-and-three cutesy ornaments over the years, mostly bunnies and small children, and she dusted them all, every day.

She spoke to them, too, in soft baby talk, and had named each and every one.

His parents were absolutely thrilled to have him back. With nobody to fuss over and look after for years, they were even more emotionally frustrated than before. But moving back to that childhood prison – full of pointless conversation, too many hugs and twenty-four-hour cheer – plunged Pravesh into an even darker depression.

His mother started waking up at 5 am to prepare sweetmeats and launched a major curry-cooking campaign.

'Making curry for two is a pain, but for three it's a party!' she told him, three times a day (at least).

Pravesh was in too much of a funk to remind his mother that curry made him nauseous.

He swallowed it like penance.

Everywhere Pravesh looked he saw framed photographs of himself in various sullen poses, and sometimes he had to remind himself that he was no longer a child, and could actually do whatever he wanted with his days. The reminder held little weight when what he chose was to watch TV, avoid his mother, and sulk.

He was constantly hot, constantly sweating. He frequently felt like screaming, for no particular reason, and began to wonder if his parents were piping in low-quality oxygen to keep him in a numb, vegetative, captive state.

He felt certain they were slowly suffocating him.

But then Pravesh would hear one of Candy K's songs, and suddenly the whole world would make sense again; even the curry-infused air tasted sweet when he thought of her. Pravesh had his dream scenario all mapped out: very soon she would beckon to him from the stage, and the bouncers would give him a boost up, and then she would announce to all her fans that Pravesh was her man. He would smile and shrug his shoulders, unsurprised. Then they would go backstage, canoodle a little, and begin their life together. That little fairytale played out in Pravesh's mind every night before he went to sleep.

Hope remained his constant companion. He woke up with it, ate meals with it, watched TV with it, and cuddled it while he fell asleep.

Without hope, you see, Pravesh's life looked alarmingly like a failure.

☼

This unhealthily obsessive behaviour continued for quite some time (far longer than it should have) until one day Beth and Pravesh's paths collided with a somewhat sickening thud.

It was one of those late-summer afternoons that thinks it's a mid-summer afternoon. The sun was scorching, baking the city's filth into a hardened crust, and everyone walked around in a shimmer of sweat. Beth waited to go on stage, quietly glowing as she thought back over the past month. She was feeling rather giddy about it all – the boyfriend, the wild success, the fact that she now effortlessly floated every day. The air was filled with the smell of baked grass that afternoon – the ground still warm from a whole day of oven-like heat – and there was a hint of ripe mango on the breeze.

At last, as the buzz of the crowd reached a crescendo, Beth stood up and walked to the outdoor stage usually reserved for bands, because of the stadium's capacity to seat hundreds of audience members. She floated up the stairs. Behind her, on a gigantic screen, her face grinned knowingly, replaced, as she started speaking, by a PowerPoint presentation of inspiring quotes, interlaced with images of flowers, stars and fireworks. Her new favourite quote (coined in the past two weeks) was *Love is not a two-minute noodle.*

It was profound, yet accessible. She wanted it made into a bumper sticker.

'Everyone always speaks of the grand power of fate,' Beth began, looking out at her audience, 'Oh, it's *fate* that'll decide whether you get that new job/lover/house/nose or not. Well! Let me tell you something,' she grinned, 'I don't believe in fate! I believe in people taking control of their own lives, and making their unconscious choices conscious, so that they *know* what to expect from life! I have devised a four-step plan that will allow *you* to be the master of your own destiny; that will give you the tools to determine your *own* fate. I call it *Fate Is A Four Letter Word.*'

She paused for emphasis, and pointed to the screen.

'Step one: Find your forte. Step two: Accentuate your abilities. Step three: Take ten steps towards your treasure. Step four: Embrace the effusive excellence of everything. Now, if you take a look at these four steps, you will see that they spell out FATE. Why? Because using these easy steps you *too* can take control of your life!'

Without even noticing, Beth had lost the lilt that had turned her statements into questions every year since she was fourteen.

She no longer needed to question the world.

She felt she knew the answers.

Afterwards, whilst chatting informally to a few admirers, her boyfriend Conrad at her side, the setting sun lending her pale skin a rosy hue, Beth saw Pravesh. He was hoping to get a place at the front for Candy K's performance later that night, and had decided – in a state of near-desperation and with the hope that she would notice him again – to wear nothing but Candy K treasures: socks, boxers, T-shirt and cap. He looked like a walking CK merchandise mannequin, and had been the butt of many a snigger as he hurried into the stadium. He was impervious to the snide looks, however: his pride was dead.

It took him a good few minutes to recognise Beth.

Rule #17 in Relationship Physics states that when one dumps someone, one assumes that the dumpee must inevitably end up worse than oneself. Similarly, when one is dumped by someone, one assumes that the dumper must be superior, successful in every way.

Pravesh, in Beth's mind (when she thought of him) was a handsome, dashing, successful man (if a little on the slim side). Beth, in Pravesh's memory (he hadn't thought of her directly since the break-up) was a snivelling waste of personality.

So that when Pravesh saw a glowing, successful, obviously revered woman surrounded by a circle of admirers, and Beth saw a strange little man dressed up in a teen pop star's hideous merchandise, neither made the connection.

Until they were only two feet away from each other and their eyes met.

It was odd, as all first-meetings-after-a-break-up are. The air around them condensed into liquid humidity, and small drops of sweat sprung up on their top lips. Neither knew quite what to say, both briefly remembering the other's naked body, the daily intimacies, the shared secrets.

To heighten the awkwardness, Conrad was standing with his arm around Beth, looking confusedly at Pravesh. Why was this peculiar little man in a gaze-lock with his Beth?

'Hi, Beth. You look great,' Pravesh managed at last, his voice cracking a little, his stomach churning in an entirely unfamiliar way. He licked his lips nervously.

'Thanks, thanks. I've been well, life's been good.' She paused, wondering if her eyeliner was smudged, and if her hair had been mussed by the breeze.

'Oh,' she added, 'this is my boyfriend, Conrad.'

The two men shook hands slowly, Pravesh's eyes dropping quickly under Conrad's forthright stare.

'How are *you?*' Beth asked, not quite sure how to converse with a man whose knees stuck out from boxers that read ... *I Could Puke!*

'Oh, you know ...' Pravesh trailed off uncertainly.

Seeing Beth was bringing back an uncomfortable rush of memories.

'How's ... what was her name again? The girl with the wig?'

Beth held her breath, chastising herself for caring, but caring nonetheless.

The temperature rose two degrees as she waited for his reply.

'We … uhmm …' Pravesh coughed nervously, 'we broke up. A while ago already.'

Beth tried not to smile, but she couldn't help feeling rather pleased. She kept her disposition admirably.

'Oh, I'm sorry. So, you're here for Candy K's concert? Are you bringing a nephew or niece?'

'What?' Pravesh looked confused. 'Oh … no … I'm a fan.'

'Oh! Of course, I'm sorry, I just thought she had a … uhm …'

Beth swallowed, clearly taken aback. 'Uhm … quite a *young* fan base. None of my business anyway. I should be going, I have a busy day tomorrow.'

The echo of that remembered sentence hung mockingly in the air between them.

'Yes, I'm sure. Well … it was really nice seeing you, Beth.'

He nodded at Conrad.

'You, too, Pravesh. Look after yourself … bye now.'

As Pravesh walked away, he heard Conrad ask with a thinly disguised note of scorn, 'Who was *that*?'

'Oh, just an old boyfriend,' Beth replied casually, feeling a muddy patch in her heart finally clear.

She felt, in that moment, as if her ugly, unhappy fourteen-year-old self was finally leaving the disco, only this time she wasn't alone. Yes, it does sound rather like the concluding scene of a cheesy romantic comedy, loosely based on the Ugly Duckling fable. But human nature is the source of all bad romantic comedies: we keep perpetrating the same old sorry circumstances that they revolve around.

Beth, walking away from the last vestiges of her poor self-esteem, finally understood that Pravesh hadn't dumped her because she was not as good as the wig-wearer.

He had dumped her because he had no taste.

The air suddenly smelt like sunflowers.

The sunset glowed with an orange luminosity.

☼

Later that evening, while driving to the airport and a speaking engagement at the Johannesburg Jugglers Convention, Beth couldn't help feeling that her life was an unqualified success. She grinned as she parked her car, and when the check-in lady said, 'Good evening, and how are you today?' Beth replied, 'Better than ever!'

Pravesh, naturally, wasn't quite so thrilled. In fact, he felt a bit of a fool. Dressed like a teenager without any fashion sense, he had stumbled upon a Hollywood-type success. The woman he had always thought of as a bit of a sponge, only good enough to absorb his issues, turned out to be a local superstar.

There was only one chocolate chip left in his cookie – the prospect of seeing Candy K performing in a few short hours.

But alas, even that treat was to be withheld. About an hour before the concert, a man of around thirty-five (closer to Pravesh's age than anyone else there) came pushing towards the front. He, too, wore the Candy K T-shirt and cap, but not the boxers and socks. As he shoved past a particularly rowdy group of teenagers, they started ragging him, snatching the cap off his head and playing Piggy in the Middle with it.

There was nothing the poor man could do but follow the cap with his eyes, looking like a distressed tennis fan. Every so often he gave a little jump to try and catch it, but the kids were always one step ahead of him. To add to the man's grief, the pack of teenagers taunted him mercilessly, calling out, 'What you doing here, old man? Don't you know Candy's only eighteen? Why are you such a pervert? Couldn't you find any babies at the hospital for a date tonight? Go home, you old freak, you're not fooling anyone!'

Perhaps it was the word *freak*, a particularly painful insult for Pravesh, which mobilised him into action. Not for a moment doubting his place in the loving family of Candy K fans, Pravesh stepped forward and said peaceably, 'Come on now, guys, is that really necessary? Give the man his cap back.'

Big mistake.

Keen for a new victim, the pack turned on Pravesh. He thought he saw them snarl. Then they leapt in for the kill. 'Oh *please* Grandpa, are you really trying to defend him?! It's not as if you're not a fucking pervert, too! Get a life, old man, and stop perving over someone half your age!'

Pravesh stood his ground. 'Candy K loves me!' he said proudly, but that only provoked further gales of taunting laughter.

With a look so scornful it would have withered plastic flowers, the leader of the pack threw out, 'If she loves you, then why is she backstage with another man? Answer me that, Grandpa!'

Satisfied that they had marked their territory, the teenagers moved off, leaving Pravesh dumbstruck. He had seen a man posing next to Candy K, his arm around her in all the tabloid photographs, but naturally assumed it was her brother. The air echoed with a stunned silence as he realised the improbability of a brother with quite so much affection for his sister.

Pravesh didn't know who to blame for the growing feeling of dread in his stomach – the teens, Candy K or his own stupid faith in love.

He stumbled to his car, pushed forward by the taunts of the prepubescent fans, and somehow managed to manoeuvre out of the parking lot. His hands grew hot on the steering wheel, burning through the plastic; his mind spun on the thought that his love had been discarded, again.

Fiery tears left red streaks on his cheeks, streaks that never faded.

It took three hours to drive home, three hours of crying so hard his eyes felt raw and swelled up like blisters, three hours of jumping every time a flash of lightning lit up the night sky.

A powerful lightning storm followed Pravesh the whole way home – silent and rainless, streaking across the clouds like threads of fire.

It had all been a facade, Pravesh realised. All those hours and days spent worshipping Candy K, attributing his life's meaning to her and assuming she would one day return the favour, all of it had been a smokescreen to hide the ugly truth: he was just another pathetic fan.

By the time he pulled into his parents' complex, Pravesh had managed to forgive the rowdy teenagers a little. But he would never, ever forgive Candy K for cheating on him.

It was unforgivable.

Back in his room, Pravesh tore down all his Candy K cut-outs (they covered one whole wall of his bedroom) and burned them in the back garden. All he had to do was touch them: his hands scorched everything they came into contact with. His knees were suddenly tingling so fiercely he couldn't stand up straight, and his ears were hotter than they had ever been. The death of his Love (and his hope and his purpose and his meaning in life) had reactivated Pravesh's radar with alarming force. A hot berg wind – tinged with despair – was blowing furiously, and all the ash from his burnt love blew onto his face and clothes and clung there, covering him in a fine dust.

Drained of all motivation, Pravesh couldn't even find the strength to crawl back inside, and spent the night in the back garden, sleeping fitfully. He woke once during the night and again in the early morning, thinking that he had fallen asleep in the shower. The rain that had started falling (and did not stop) was hot, hot like a tap that's been running for ten minutes. So hot it left raindrop-sized burns all over his skin, steaming as it fell. When his mom's best friend, Mrs Chetty, scurried past, she found Pravesh lying in a steaming, muddy pool.

'Wake up sleepy-head!' she sang in an annoyingly cheerful voice. 'How are you doing, and all? Why you lying out here in the rain? It's hot, hey?' She nudged him with her shoe.

'Did you feel like camping, is that it? You felt like getting out of town?'

Mrs Chetty carried on nattering as Pravesh rolled over and lifted himself to his feet. Without so much as a glance in her direction, he stumbled past her and into the house, climbing the stairs to his bedroom and locking the door. He could hear his mom's voice from the bottom of the stairs.

'Pravesh! There you are! Come down and have some tea, I'm in the middle of making you some nice samoosas for a snack. I have a few friends coming over, they haven't seen you for *days*, and they want to catch up.'

With a groan, Pravesh slid under his bed, staring disconsolately at the dusty bed frame, three inches from his face. The heat of the night before had burnt itself out, and Pravesh was filled with ash. He coughed weakly, and a powdery cloud settled on his face.

Those were the last dying days of summer; the hottest summer Durban had ever known, and it seemed as if the full weight of all those muggy, oppressive days weighed down the atmosphere, making breathing almost impossible.

The air outside stank of sweat and garbage and hopelessness.

Pravesh did not move. Twice a day he slid out from under the bed to use the toilet, and twice a day his mom waited outside the bathroom door to talk to him as soon as he emerged.

'How about coming downstairs, hey?' she would ask. 'We could have something to eat, maybe a bit of a chitchat, you could get some fresh air. Maybe I should call your girlfriend, maybe Candy can come for dinner?'

Pravesh never even paused to listen to her, he just walked despondently back to his room and slid under the bed again. His mom vacuumed the ash-covered floor of his bedroom twice a day, but her attempts were in vain; nothing could eradicate the path of Pravesh's dejected footsteps to and from the toilet.

After a day or two, his mom started slipping things under his bed to cheer him up. The first few days it was curry – chicken, vegetable or beef – with little notes saying *Eat this! You'll feel better!* but when the plates were left untouched, she started moving on to other, more cunning forms of encouragement.

One morning it was a miniature trampoline.

Then a skipping rope.

Then a carefully cut-out page of the Classifieds section of the newspaper, with a list of promising jobs circled in red. (Pravesh could work from home filling envelopes, be a pastry chef, an adult companion, double his income in just two weeks, sell pepper-spray guns door-to-door or pack fish in Iceland.)

One by one, each of his mom's friends came upstairs to try to coax him out from under the bed. Pravesh stared straight ahead at the bedsprings, and hummed Chopin's 'Funeral March'. The only time his knees tingled and his heart raced these days was when cockroaches died, and that didn't happen nearly often enough.

Eventually, in despair, Pravesh's mom tried to drag him out from under the bed. She held his feet and pulled until his bottom half emerged, but as soon as she stood up to catch her breath Pravesh slid under the bed again.

When he next surfaced to use the toilet, she locked his bedroom door, but Pravesh just slid under the sofa in the lounge, and carried on humming the death march.

After a month of this behaviour – eating only scraps of the food his mother left next to the pink velour sofa, in the hopes that his death sensor would soon start its last furious tingling as his own body slowly shut down – Pravesh awoke one morning to a quiet house.

No noise, no people.

Nothing but a CD player.

After a few hours of staring at the sofa springs, Pravesh leant over and pressed PLAY.

'Hello,' said a voice Pravesh recognised, as if from a nightmare, 'my name is Beth Ann Walters, and I am about to expose you to the wonders of my second book, *Extraordinary Means Extra-Ordinary*. Yes, that's you. You are extra-ordinary, out of the ordinary, in all ways wonderful. You don't believe me? Well, let me tell you something! After you have listened to this fifty-minute CD, you will. Before we begin, I want you all to say it with me – I am extraordinary, because I am extra-ordinary! All together now ...'

With a loud groan Pravesh closed his eyes. His death radar started tingling.

On the first night of their journey, Mdu and Aisha camped at Golden Gate, the mountainous region a few hours outside Durban. They hiked the surrounding trails, breathing in the pine-scented air as they climbed through woods, and gulping great mouthfuls of icy water as they hopped over streams. A hot berg wind, pregnant with a thunderstorm, had sent them sliding into a narrow fissure that led to a cave, older than the sun.

There, in the dank coolness littered with baboon droppings and forgotten drifts of leaves, they paused, sipping water and eating apples, each with a sketchbook, each hesitant to begin.

'It's not easy, hey,' Mdu laughed, glancing over at Aisha with a playful grin.

Aisha laughed back, relieved not to be the only one feeling uncertain.

'I can't remember the last time I did anything really creative,' she admitted softly. 'I'm scared that once I start, I won't be able to stop.'

Then, with a devilish grin, she said, 'Fuck it, let's go!' and began drawing.

Mdu laughed out loud, a carefree laugh that echoed around the cave, and started writing.

Between them, they seemed to capture not only the mountains and valleys they could see from their hide-out in the cave, but the strange yellow light before the storm, the gathering expectation that flashed like lightning, and the ineffable freedom of that solitary hour.

That became the first Golden Moment they recorded on their adventures; their first honeysuckle-scented slice of love.

The relentless summer sun beat down on Aisha and Mdu from clear, cloudless skies that swelled as the days ended, swelled into white clouds, then grey, then black, erupting violent summer storms. The heat would lift then, just momentarily, before pressing down on them again with stifling humidity.

They trekked around the country, slicing through the summer heat to taste, see, smell and touch everything they could.

Aisha and Mdu climbed the Drakensberg mountains, camping in narrow crevices, sunning themselves in the hot sunshine by day and lying on top of each other for much-needed warmth when the sun set and the temperature dropped. In the mornings – their noses raw from such pure oxygen, their senses invigorated from sleeping in the open – they would discover secret springs to skinny dip in, their teeth chattering involuntarily from the icy brown water, their skin goose-bumping and then slowly warming up as they lay naked on the large rocks bordering the spring.

They hiked through the desolate valleys of the Karoo, lying awestruck under the millions of stars that burnt holes through the night sky, parking their car and walking and walking and walking until there was no sign of life on any horizon. They wandered deep into nothingness, reluctant to talk or sing or make any noise to disrupt the deep quiet.

They paused to meditate in the stillness of Ixopo, the grassy hills undulating like green waves, crisscrossed with footpaths walked into the earth, dotted with Nguni cattle and young barefoot boys carrying sticks.

They camped in the wild grounds of the Kruger National Park, cooking sausages on a small fire and scanning the bushes nervously for yellow eyes reflected in their torchlight. They woke, alarmed, in the middle of the night, their nostrils flaring from the smell of fresh elephant dung, their hearts racing from unfamiliar sounds.

They kayaked down the swollen Orange River and explored its surrounds, captivated by every creature, every plant, every old man and bull, drunk on the smell of kraal fires and roasting meat that rose as the sun set.

Together, Mdu and Aisha ate samp and beans cooked in tin cans on wood fires in tiny villages, invited in by the village elders and asked to tell stories in return for the meal. They ate cordon bleu cooked on state-of-the-art stoves in five-star hotels, fast food from Speedy Gonzales, Galloping Goose Fast Grub and Speedy's Quick-Quick Foods, and fried chicken cooked in the glut of chicken take-outs that dotted the countryside, all with names like Africa Fried Chicken or Chicken Licken or Get Lucky Fried Chicken, none with nutritional information anywhere to be seen.

They fasted for days on nothing more than fruit, water and chocolate biscuits, and then feasted on bean biryani in small Indian restaurants set up in family homes. They picnicked in campsites, on look-out points and at the strange green cement tables and chairs plonked by the side of the road throughout the country. They cooked two-minute noodles and instant soup in a tin kettle on a tiny gas stove, tried frying eggs on the bonnet of the car (it didn't work), and ate nothing but bread and cheese for a week.

They drove and they drove and they drove, past huts made of cow dung, and office blocks made of aluminium, past lush green vineyards and bare, endless scrubland, past flocks of sheep and herds of springbok, through cities and towns and vast patches of emptiness. They flew past small make-shift *padstalletjies* selling elephant and rhino biltong, tables under trees surrounded by boxes of grapes, container shops full of koeksisters and rusks. They braked slightly for an avenue of coloured windmills leading to a tiny tea garden.

They watched soccer matches played on dirt pitches – young barefoot boys racing around kicking deflated soccer balls through un-netted goalposts, until the yellow light from the streetlights called them home for supper.

Aisha and Mdu trekked the country like two *umgodoyi* township dogs, sniffing this way and that, wanting to see and smell everything. And they did – kilometres of farmland that stank of manure stood gracefully next to orchards of peaches with the sun-warmed scent of growth, cities impregnated with urine rubbed shoulders with kraals infused with wood smoke, and mine workers reeking of sweat walked down the same streets as socialites fragranced with perfume. Each time they stopped, Mdu would spend an hour trying to capture the place in a long prose poem, while Aisha searched for the perfect angle to encapsulate all that she could see and feel.

By mutual agreement, they avoided the many glitzy shopping centres and flashy casinos, entertainment worlds, malls and arcades, and the gated communities that spread like fungus around the country. Some of Mdu's poems spoke of the particular brand of heartache that comes from spending time only in artificial light.

Mdu and Aisha took to waking early, before sunrise, so that they could be driving before the morning heat turned the road ahead into a mirage. They tried to sleep as the midday sun put aside all semblance of good manners and burnt with reckless ferocity, tried to sleep in whatever scrap of shade they could find, sweat-soaked and headachey from heat. They cooled down in rivers and streams and swimming pools and bathtubs, and sometimes even in the sinks of public bathrooms.

And somehow, despite the heat, they found the strength to make love every day – sometimes slow and sweet, sometimes passionate and rough, sometimes quick and surprising. They made love in their tent, in hotel rooms, on trails and under the open sky. They made love in vineyards, in sugar-cane fields, on the side of the road in their car and in dry riverbeds. They were more than a little reckless at times. They were in tune with each other, in synchronised rhythm.

And some days, out of tune. Aisha would wake up grumpy, or Mdu moody; they would both take offence at little things, or disagree over where to stay, who should be driving, whose fault it was that they ran out of petrol one-hundred kilometres from the nearest town with no cell-phone reception. They passed whole mornings in tetchy silence, whole afternoons in aggrieved sulks. But always, before they went to sleep, they made it all right again. There was always a goodnight kiss, always a soft, 'I love you.'

One evening, as they stood on top of a hill watching the sun set over the Magaliesberg Mountains, the wind buffeting them like paper dolls, Aisha turned to Mdu with sparkling eyes and an uncontainable grin.

'This is it!' she called to him over the sound of the wind as it whistled past their heads, catching their words and tossing them into the valley. 'This is how life's supposed to be!'

'I know!' he called back, the corners of his eyes crinkling. 'Isn't it wonderful?'

It was in moments like these that Mdu felt a tight band across his chest loosen. His plan had worked. She was loving it! He had nothing to worry about.

They were living an extraordinary life.

❁

He wasn't the only one who thought so. Within a month, the entire country had been captivated by the romantic couple, as they submitted their poems and illustrations to four major newspapers on a weekly basis.

In their second week of publication, Mdu pulled into a small petrol station with a Quick Shop, and bought a copy of *The Star* to check on the reproduction quality. Aisha was trailing the aisles in search of sunflower seeds when she heard Mdu laughing.

'What is it?' she asked, worried, and hurried over. 'Have they made a mistake?'

Mdu shook his head and pointed to a bold headline on one of the pages: 'But Who Are They Really?'

'Listen to this,' he said. 'Mdu's parents, Mr and Mrs Shabalala, are very proud of their son. "We always knew he was something special," they said when interviewed yesterday. "Ever since he was a young boy, we've supported his creative writing." '

'What a joke! They only ever wanted me to be a lawyer or a doctor! Oh, look, here's something about you.' He lowered the paper. 'Who's Edna?'

Aisha shook her head, wondering why the name sounded familiar. It felt as if she could once have had a dream about a girl called Edna.

'Listen, they've also interviewed her. "Aisha and I were really close friends, as well as colleagues. We used to go out together all the time." Any idea?' Aisha shook her head again, faintly aware of a whispering memory of smoke and loud music.

'Oh, this is the best!' Mdu exclaimed. "They have so captured the hearts of the public, that local pop star Candy K has written a song just for them: 'Love Will Lead You Home.' 'I just love them!' she is quoted as saying. 'I would love to meet them as soon as they come home. We have so much in common, I just know we'll be best friends!' " '

Even Aisha had to laugh at that.

Mdu grinned his special grin, and paid for the paper.

They called their chronicle 'Follow the Scent of Honeysuckle', because wherever they went, small white flowers seemed to follow them, floating on the air current behind them.

They left a trail throughout the country; their blossoms soon became coveted collector's items.

Forever after, wherever their love went, sweet honeysuckle hung in the air.

Mdu and Aisha's lovemaking continued to be intense, a merging of their two souls. Often, Aisha started sobbing the moment their bodies separated, curling into a ball and hugging her knees. Once the sobs receded, she uncurled slowly and rolled over to face Mdu's worried eyes.

'I never knew I could feel this way,' she explained, taking a quavering breath, her dark eyes shining with tears. 'It's as if we're not even two different people any more.'

A flash of fear skated through her eyes as Mdu reached out an arm to draw her to him, kissing the top of her head gently, and holding her so tight she had to pull away to breathe.

Sometimes the intensity of his love for Aisha alarmed him.

It felt too powerful to be true, like the love that characters felt in movies, or in old Victorian novels.

A devastating kind of love.

Aisha, too, sometimes felt distressed by their passion.

She never doubted her love for Mdu; she loved him intensely and desperately and with a single-mindedness that terrified her. It was too visceral for comfort.

If anyone had told Aisha that one day she would feel so strongly about someone that she wouldn't be able to find where she ended and he began, she would have labelled them a lunatic.

But it was true.

Somehow, she had turned into a person she could never have imagined, a person she never thought possible.

Aisha – who hated even the idea of needing anyone – needed someone for the first time in her life.

※ ※ ※

Isn't it funny how obvious the flaws of a relationship are when you're looking at it from the outside? Take this one, for example. Surely this kind of love is unhealthy, too obsessive, even a little unbalanced?

Then again, maybe a little-known side-effect of Great Passion is a feeling of desperation in every moment, a constant fear of total destruction, a certain knowledge that a fire that burns so brightly cannot be sustained.

Maybe too many of us are accustomed to the microwaved version of love, without any thrill or danger of spontaneous combustion.

Maybe we even prefer it.

Mdu was not interested in anything less than utter infatuation. Had he been able to attain some perspective on their relationship, he would probably have picked up on the one or two aspects of Aisha's personality that didn't quite fit with his picture of her. Aren't there always one or two things that don't quite fit?

But perspective and insight were not what Mdu was after.

In his eyes, everything Aisha did was perfect. Even sobbing most times they made love. Once he was sure they were not tears of pain, Mdu felt profoundly relieved by Aisha's copious weeping. Not one tear had escaped from his eyes since his fifth birthday, when he was slapped for cheeking the parent of one of his friends.

Even as a five-year-old, he knew that only weak boys cried.

His views hadn't changed. For Mdu, cloaked in the multitude of self-imposed rules he wore like body armour, crying was simply not an option. His expectations allowed him a rigid modus operandi; he walked it as carefully as an electrified labyrinth.

※ ※ ※

Both creatures of habit, Aisha and Mdu soon crafted a tandem routine that fitted loosely around their days. It was comforting. It helped.

Mdu woke up first every morning, and gently shook Aisha's shoulder and kissed her on the cheek till she stirred. Then he started making tea, watching her as she tried to wake up. It took a few minutes, until, as if emerging from a wrestling match with her dreams – the dreams that no longer surrounded her like a shimmering layer, but still would not just slip off, politely, as they are meant to do – Aisha smiled at Mdu.

Her cup of tea would be ready then, just as she liked it (scalding hot, milky, three sugars), her bag unzipped and open (ready for her to choose that day's clothing), her toothbrush prepared for brushing (the toothpaste squeezed carefully on to the bristles).

As Aisha sleepily showered and dressed, Mdu packed up their belongings and pored over the map, deciding where to go that day. They drove the first few hours in silence, but by midmorning Aisha was completely awake, free of her dreams, and usually singing along to the radio, or holding a blue silk scarf out the window to watch it stream out behind her.

Lunch was her responsibility, and no matter where they picnicked, as they did every day, she was meticulous in her preparation. There was always a big, red blanket, always some fresh, wild flowers (or weeds) in an old water bottle, always paper serviettes (sometimes patterned).

Mdu would lie on the blanket in the dappled sunlight and listen to Aisha humming softly under her breath. These were the moments he wanted cryogenically frozen.

He did not want them ever to die.

In the afternoons, Aisha drove while Mdu hung his long legs out of the passenger window, leaning back against the seat and feeling the wind rushing between his toes.

'You know if we pass a road sign, it'll take your legs off,' Aisha warned almost every day, keeping her eyes on the road. 'I once read about this boy whose arm got ripped out of its socket 'cause he was holding it out of the school bus window.'

'That's an urban myth, and you know it!' Mdu invariably replied. But he reached out to stroke the back of her neck lightly as he spoke, tickling her and sending shivers down her spine.

Mdu loved that someone cared whether or not his legs remained attached to his torso.

In the evenings they separated for an hour or so. Mdu told Aisha he liked to meditate as the sun set, but in reality he liked hunting down a television set so that he could watch one of his talk show reruns. He watched *The Ricki Lake Show* in a hut on a tiny black-and-white TV, *Judge Judy* in the *voorkamer* of an old Afrikaans couple living in the Free State, *The Jerry Springer Show* in a tiny deserted bar in a tiny deserted town on the outskirts of the Drakensberg mountains.

Mdu could never admit to Aisha that he loved these shows; they were the antithesis of everything she stood for, the very demon of ugliness and reality that she had tried so hard to escape as a child. But he remained hooked. That daily hour of indulgence gave him the strength to be the man he wanted to be for the other twenty-three hours a day.

Aisha, for her part, spent her solitary time napping. She curled up wherever they were staying – tent, hostel, hotel or hut – curled up with one pillow to hug, and another between her knees, and slept.

She always set her cell-phone alarm for ten minutes before she knew Mdu would return, and pretended that she had spent the hour sketching.

It wasn't that she needed to escape by sleeping, not really, not exactly.

It wasn't the kind of sleep she used to indulge in, in her little flat where she did nothing but eat and sleep and read.

But it was not vastly different.

In a part of her heart that she didn't care to visit, Aisha kind of missed those days. Sometimes, as she slipped off to sleep, she talked to herself like she used to on the veranda of her little house, gently murmuring as she drifted off, 'It's not that I would trade this for that, it's just that sometimes it gets a little bit tiring. I'd like to have a rest, sometimes, just to sleep and read and not have to be discovering new things every moment.'

She breathed in deeply, and sighed, three-quarters asleep already. 'It would just be nice to be a little bit by myself again.'

And then she would fall fast asleep, waking only when the insistent beep of her alarm warned her that Mdu was on his way.

So Aisha and Mdu both kept their secrets, although neither believed the other could possibly have anything to hide. Isn't that often the case? We imagine our insides are far more mixed up than anyone else's could ever be.

☼

Week after week after week they travelled through the heat of that sweltering summer.

Of course, there was an underlying tension.

There is always an underlying tension.

And not only the pressure of Mdu meeting all of Aisha's expectations. Not only the fact that both felt they needed a little breathing space from the relationship, even as they professed only to be able to breathe in each other's company.

Not only that the ceaseless trekking Mdu had devised as a method to keep Aisha engrossed, actually wore her out.

Not only that.

Unbeknown to her, Aisha was an incessant sleep-talker. Every night as she slept, she spoke of the ocean with such intense longing that it brought tears to her closed eyes. Those tears trickled slowly down her cheeks and gathered around her head in an incandescent halo. Mdu would wake in the middle of the night and look over at Aisha – her forehead crumpled in despair, the pearls of her tears glimmering at him accusingly – and his heart would ache. Quietly, so as not to wake her, he collected the tears that escaped and scattered them in the bottom of his suitcase, hiding them so that she had no way of knowing about her nightly yearnings.

But she knew.

Of course she knew.

It was in her blood. She had lived as one with the ocean, and somehow it seemed that its salt had seeped through to her soul. Still, she spoke no word of it during the day, and to the casual eye she seemed entirely happy, carefree, even.

Mdu's eyes were as finely tuned as his ears, but it is amazing what you can choose to ignore if the desire is strong enough. Aisha kept her murmurs of discontent to such a soft whisper that Mdu could simply choose not to hear.

As a result, by some unspoken agreement, Mdu and Aisha never set foot on the coast. The newspaper reporters, who continued to follow their journey, found it strange – especially in a country with not one, but two coastlines, not one, but two oceans. They clamoured for the wild ruggedness of the West Coast, the gentle beauty of the Western Cape, and the tropical beaches of the Hibiscus Coast to be translated by Aisha and Mdu.

But Mdu was adamant in his refusal: he felt too guilty about betraying the whales. At least that's what he told himself, and Aisha, and the newspapers.

In deep truth (that cavern that one rarely bothers to enter) he was afraid, more afraid than he had ever been in his life, that if he took Aisha to the ocean she would once more swim out, never to return.

Lost, forever, in depths he could not reach.

Aisha's love was Mdu's greatest triumph.

Failure was not an option.

It was as this tension was building, causing the air between the two to crackle with electricity, that Aisha and Mdu pulled into the outskirts of Johannesburg, a city constantly busy, bustling and brightly lit, filled with people working like hamsters on the wheel of capitalism. They decided to spend the night in a hotel – after ten days under the stars with just a thin tent and the honeysuckle cloud of their love for protection, Aisha and Mdu felt ready for the comfort of a bed.

They had grown accustomed, in their travels, to the rare sleep of those in tune with nature's rhythms – going to bed soon after sunset, and waking before the sunrise. As soon as they entered the city, however, this rhythm was thrown off entirely. Bright lights created artificial noon, and the traffic was so bad that it took them an hour to travel five kilometres. Constant noise thrummed in their ears, and giant billboards emblazoned with half-naked women and screaming slogans imprinted on their retinas, so that everything they looked at had a screen of advertising before it.

After an hour and a half of city traffic, they drove past a Holiday Inn, an ugly block-shaped hotel famous for its reasonable prices and rabbit-like proliferation throughout the country. Unable to bear the thought of more bumper-to-bumper traffic, they pulled into the large parking lot.

They had grown used to the intense stillness of open spaces, and the harshness of the hotel's cheery decor and fake hospitality jarred Aisha and Mdu; it felt so bright and false, the potted plants so obviously plastic. The constant jabber of the television in the lobby and the stale cigarette smoke that hung in the air like unspoken words set their teeth on edge.

Too weary to find another option, Aisha and Mdu were quietly eating a late supper (of reheated, recooked food) in the hotel dining room, when an effervescent woman with permed brown hair came bustling in from the ballroom where she had been giving a speech of some sort. She spotted them straight away, and headed towards their table with a purposeful smile. Mdu sat speechless. How had the cashier of Handy Green Grocers managed to find him here, of all places? Was she going to chastise him for his cowardice? Turn him in to the police? Tell Aisha?

The past few months had almost allowed Mdu to bury the incident, but seeing the cashier again exhumed it all in one horrible minute. To his relief she did not mention it, only gave him a small wink that Aisha didn't notice, a sweet smile and a brief nod.

Aisha looked up from her vegetarian lasagne, wondering why a strange woman was standing silently in front of their table.

'Look at my manners!' the woman said. 'I'm so delighted to finally be meeting you two, that I can't get a word out!'

She beamed at them, vigorously shaking each of their hands in turn, 'My name's Beth, and I've got to tell you, I'm a huge fan! Huge!'

Beth paused, waiting for them to reciprocate the compliment. Neither seemed to know who she was. She leaned forward confidentially.

'Beth Ann Walters? I'm here promoting my new workshop – (Wo)men: The (Wo)w! Factor in Any Relationship?'

There wasn't the slightest flicker of recognition on either Aisha or Mdu's faces. Beth giggled.

'How refreshing! You don't know who I am! I tell you, it gets a little exhausting being recognised everywhere I go.'

She paused again, waiting for an invitation to sit down. Mdu leapt up and fetched a chair.

'Please, join us,' he said politely. Aisha sighed deeply. She had no interest in motivational speakers.

Mdu, however, did.

'So, tell me, do you think people actually implement the skills you teach them?' he asked, fascinated.

Beth launched into the details of a research study she had been conducting on the effects of her speeches on males and females between the ages of twenty and thirty-five. Mdu leaned forward in his chair, enthralled, nodding his head and saying, 'Huh! Fascinating!' whenever Beth made a particularly interesting point. Something in him that had always aspired to greatness was being woken up by Beth's unfailing enthusiasm, and although each cheery word seemed to visibly wound Aisha, denting her fragile skin with its unabashed vivacity, Mdu seemed not to notice.

For the first time since he had met her, in fact, Aisha was not the prime focus of his attention.

She didn't like it, didn't like it at all.

She loathed it, in fact.

And then Mdu said it.

Beth had just finished a story about how, after she'd spoken to a group of women prisoners, they had started an income generation project knitting tea cosies, when he leaned back in his chair and said matter-of-factly, 'You know, I've always fancied myself as a motivational speaker.'

Aisha's mouth dropped open in disbelief. Stricken, she turned to look at Mdu, hoping that he was joking, but he just grinned and nodded his head vigorously in response to Beth's delighted, 'You should!'

In that moment, Aisha's feet fell through the floor. The weight holding the gravity of her life the right way around swung out, and she could not, not for anything, imagine how Mdu could say such a thing.

His comment was so far outside the lines of how she had drawn him that it rendered the whole picture meaningless. It felt as if the person she knew inside out, had, all this time, only existed in her head.

Perhaps she had made him up.

Aisha felt sick.

☼ ☼ ☼

How often, in love, do we fall for the idea of a person? We have a very clear picture of them in our heads, and they fit it. And the parts that don't fit, we conveniently ignore, turning the volume down when they have conflicting ideas, pretending we do not notice their free will when it asserts itself.

Only it turns out our version is not always the real version.

And the space between the two is where hearts are broken.

Aisha's heart was breaking.

Silently.

Slowly.

Irrevocably.

❁ ❁ ❁

After thirty minutes of animated conversation, an admiring fan called Beth away from their table. Aisha had not said a word, stunned and sick to her stomach at the thought that she could have based her entire reality on this impostor, this man who wasn't who she thought he was at all.

Mdu, all pumped up from his motivational meeting, didn't notice Aisha's distress.

'Wow! She's a firecracker, isn't she, love?' he asked as they climbed the stairs to their bedroom. Had he taken a moment to quiet down, he would have heard Aisha's loud thoughts of despair. But Mdu was too busy enthusing about Beth to listen.

'She's really got me thinking … I've always wanted to do that kind of work.'

Aisha breathed in and out through her nose to keep from bursting into tears.

Their bedroom, on the seventeenth floor, felt like a large cardboard box decorated by a young child – two beds, a miniscule bathroom that reeked of cigarette smoke, a big TV hanging over the bed, and a window that refused to open.

An enlarged photograph of the ocean – framed in cheap, pink plastic and showing nothing but wave after endless wave – took pride of place in the centre of the room.

Mdu parted the curtains and stared out at the city skyline, a lightning storm flashing on the horizon, lighting up the clouds like little bombs.

He watched it, mesmerised.

'Aisha, look at this,' he said, turning to her.

But she was already asleep with her back to him, curled in on herself, her thoughts locked away in dreams so that even had he tried, he would not have been able to listen to her. Too deflated and distraught to make love, Aisha had quickly fallen asleep on the far side of the bed. He stroked her back for a few minutes, assuming she was just over-tired from that day's driving, then kissed her softly on the cheek and lay down to sleep.

But he could not. All through that night Aisha talked incessantly. Within minutes of falling asleep, she started crying, and the tears flowed down her cheeks and formed an outline around her whole body, an outline that was far more luminous than anything Mdu had ever seen. He tried to collect the pearls of her tears as he had done every night, but she cried with such intensity that he could not keep up.

Eventually, Mdu stopped trying.

He lay, painfully awake, listening to her sighs with an aching heart.

And then it started to rain, pouring down onto the sleeping city, drowning it.

Mdu knew that a braver love would have taken Aisha to the ocean. If she truly loved him, she would be able to resist its call, and then he could stop living every moment afraid that he would lose her, afraid that he was already losing her, afraid that he had had no right to have her love in the first place.

But his fear immobilised him.

If only Mdu had spent some time studying quantum physics in high school, he would have learnt that the Law of Attraction is one of the most powerful laws in the universe. Whatever you place too much attention on is attracted to you.

Fear attracts fear.

Aisha leaving him was such a constant, vivid image in his mind that there was no way it could not manifest.

At last, as the red flashing numbers of the alarm clock clicked to 05:00, his burning eyes conceded defeat, and he fell deeply asleep. A short hour later, the smell of tea brewing woke him up. It was the first time Aisha had ever woken before him, and it disorientated Mdu. She made no mention of the pool of tears she had woken up in, but he sensed a change in her, a slight scent emanating from her silence, a familiar scent that reminded him of the sea.

And, just as before he first woke her, Mdu could not hear any of the words she was not saying aloud.

Aisha was once again wordless.

☼

That day Mdu was too exhausted to drive – his eyes raw and scratchy on the inside, his mind blurry and hot. All the colours and noises of the city seemed too garish, too loud, too frantic that morning, made worse by the constant thrumming of the rain, a strange, hot rain that smelt like sulphur and fogged up the windows from the outside. It made driving near impossible.

With no more than a few cautionary words, Mdu curled his body away from the window and fell asleep, his head on his knees, before they even reached the outskirts of Johannesburg. They were heading for the Waterberg Game Park, three hours to the north, and Mdu, so used to whole days spent in silence with Aisha, did not take her morning reticence as a danger sign.

In the days that followed he would curse himself for this slight of attention.

As she slowly drove out of the city, Aisha wound down her window a little, holding her hand out in the hot rain, letting it scald her skin. Their encounter with Beth the night before had changed the chemical compounds of Aisha's thinking. A warning bell was sounding in every one of her nerves. She muttered softly to herself as she drove, trying to find some ladder of reasoning down which she could climb, so that she could once again recognise Mdu.

Her Mdu. The man she loved.

'Maybe I'm overreacting,' she murmured. 'Maybe he was just being nice to her. It doesn't mean that he doesn't speak my language. Of course he speaks my language. We're not even two people anymore ...'

Somehow the sentence that had seemed so reassuring before now sounded like a death knell.

'How is it that all my happiness depends on this one man?' she asked herself, glancing in the rear-view mirror.

'This one man who isn't even who I thought he was ...'

Perhaps this whole 'life' she had constructed was nothing more than a facade, she thought sadly. Perhaps things were actually the same as they had always been, and she had just been duped into thinking everything was different.

These thoughts left Aisha's mind, and swirled around her, blue-grey in colour and smelling strongly of seaweed and salt. Combined with Mdu's sleeping breath, they conjured up the longing she had felt the night before and slow tears started trickling down her cheeks, gathering like offerings at her feet. She wound the window all the way down, welcoming the hot rain that still fell, and slipping into a lucid dream; a waking dream unimpeded by confusion.

She knew exactly what to do.

Although Johannesburg was not near the coast, Aisha drove with such speed that it only took four hours to reach Sodwana Bay. Mdu, exhausted from his sleepless, worried night, slept soundly the whole way.

As Aisha rounded the last corner, surrounded by high cliffs on both sides, she could sense the sea. The air smelt sharp and she thought she could detect, ever so faintly, the crash of waves on the rocks. The sound sent a thrill down her spine. All of a sudden, stretching out in a vast sweeping curve, there it was. The torrential rain blurred the line between horizon and sky, turning everything silvery. The hot wind was scented with seaweed and wildness.

Aisha's heart leapt as she speeded up their descent.

Mdu, in the beginning stages of a nightmare, murmured something in his sleep. As she eased the car to a slow halt so as not to wake him, Aisha felt herself being pulled by a force much stronger than anything she had ever felt in her waking life. Only half-conscious of what she was doing, she took off her shoes and socks and folded her sweater on top of them in a neat little pile on the scrubby grass.

Then, wearing only a dress and the moonstone necklace that Mdu had given her a lifetime ago, drenched by the hot rain and more alive than she had felt in months, Aisha walked down the sandy bank and along the beach to the ocean's edge. As she reached the water, her whole body shivered, once, as if to warn her of the significance of what she was about to do. She shook her head clear, took a deep breath and started wading into the cold water. Once it reached her waist, she dived in, submerging herself again, at last, in the ocean and swimming out in the stroke her body remembered so well. The water flowing over her skin caressed away the vague remnants of reality that had clung to her, washing off the travels, the newspapers, the food, the smells, the sounds, the sex.

Washing off Mdu.

With each sure stroke the nerves connecting Aisha's body to her mind seemed to dissolve, one by one, and drop away.

Her dreams came rushing back. Reality said a fond farewell.

It was only when she was far out in the deep water past the pier that Aisha heard her name being shouted.

Mdu – in the throes of a sickening nightmare where he had lost Aisha forever – gasped awake, looked out the window and immediately hurtled down the beach, the rain stinging his face. He recognised Sodwana Bay straight away, his mind reminding him cruelly that in Zulu the name meant 'little one on its own'.

Too late, Mdu saw Aisha's bobbing head in the distance, and threw himself into the waves, shouting her name as he swam. Gasping for breath, swallowing sea water, he forced himself to swim faster than his arms and legs could move. The anguish he felt as he battled the waves was so great that it closed up his throat, and would not let him call to her. Summoning every ounce of willpower, Mdu plunged forward, rain pelting his eyes and mouth whenever he surfaced for air, the ocean trying to sweep him off course with a fierce undertow.

Aisha, in turn, looked back at the only man she had ever loved, treading water as she did so, and fresh tears welled up in her eyes. Mdu took advantage of the lull in her swimming to try to get closer to his only love, pushing through the burning in his arms and legs, through the raw ache in his lungs.

It was only when he was within reaching distance that Mdu saw how pale Aisha was. Her face and body had reverted to the flat colourlessness he had noticed in her that first day and which he'd spent months colouring in with his love. Mdu searched in vain for a glimmer of recognition in Aisha's eyes, but he knew she had already slipped back to where he had first found her, where she belonged.

Suddenly overcome with grief, he realised how far he was from the shore and started to panic. All of a sudden his arms and legs felt too heavy to float, and he began to sink, flailing desperately, gasping for breath between sobs, his limbs leaden, his heart raw. As Mdu turned to look at Aisha one last time, an enormous wave appeared out of nowhere, catching him unawares and forcing him underwater.

For a moment, everything became still.

Mdu tumbled round and round, watching his breath disappear in bubbles, deeper than he had ever been. He thought about dying, knew that for the first time it was within his grasp, knew that there was no life after this.

And then he started fighting to reach the surface.

That first breath he took as his head broke through was like his very first breath of life – raw, desperate, gasping. Mdu opened his stinging eyes and found himself near the shore, deposited by the ocean that had stolen his love, but wanted nothing of him.

The hot rain needled into him as he crawled up the beach. His lungs were burning, raw from lack of oxygen. ·

When he looked out over the water, Aisha was gone.

☼

That same afternoon, Mdu went out and bought a small boat. He was determined not to let go of the only love he had ever known, certain that if he could only wake her up and convince her that life was worth living – as he had done once before – she would come back to him.

He refused to give up.

So Mdu tuned his speech to the frequency that whales respond to, and set out in search of Aisha. He sailed through the night, and all the next day. It seemed obvious that if she had chanced upon a pod of whales the last time she began swimming, the same thing would happen again. And indeed, every whale he spoke to had seen the strange girl and guided him on his search.

What he feared, though, was that Aisha had rejoined a transient pod of whales, and his extensive knowledge told him that the routes she would travel were extremely unpredictable.

Sometimes they were only seen once in an area, and never again.

As he sailed, Mdu's body continued to release the scent of honeysuckle, and behind his boat a trail of small white flowers floated in its wake. The scent and the flowers confused many a wandering sailor, many a surfer, many a yachtsman, and many a cruise-ship passenger.

For many years.

 and

The day after Meryl's first night with the Undertaker (she didn't like the name Pravesh) Meryl met Harry for an after-dinner coffee and a Talk. She was well prepared. Earlier that afternoon she had spent a full hour typing out a list of what she expected from a relationship, the things she had always hoped for in love (and had not yet found).

'It's not necessarily for him,' she argued softly with herself as she waited for the list to print, 'but a good thing to have, for future reference.'

She saved it on her computer (necessary-for-love.doc) and wondered why she was being such a softy. Before their coffee date, Meryl made sure to take a long shower; she didn't want any trace of the Undertaker's scent on her.

You may wonder why she bothered to take this precaution for a man she was trying to dump.

Yes, you may.

They met at Mama Cappuccino's again, and sat at the same table, smothered in pink. Meryl had designed the talk to terrify Harry into retreat, and she was quite excited about it.

At last! she thought, an opportunity to be her most demanding and impossible, to test out all her ammunition.

What a rare treat.

She felt a twinge of remorse when Harry walked in, smiling sweetly and kissing her full on the lips before giving her a big hug and saying, 'It's lovely to see you, my Meryl. How was your day?'

But it was only a small twinge, and easily ignored.

Meryl's corset felt like two hands squeezing tightly around her waist as she watched Harry perusing the menu. She was certain this conversation would mend the troublesome rip nicely. With superglue, if necessary.

She ordered a double espresso, no milk; he ordered green tea.

And then she launched the first attack.

'Listen, Harry, there are a few things I have to get clear with you –'

Meryl paused, took a deep breath and then machine-gun rattled off everything she thought he needed to know:

'I'm living with a woman who has been my lover for the last year, but I'm breaking it off with her this week.

'My parents had a great marriage, so I expect the same.

'My mom died of cancer three years ago.

'My dad went crazy, and now lives in a mental institution.

'My brother deserted the family.

'I expect more from you.'

She said it all so matter-of-factly that Harry knew the pain was still as fresh as the first day. He felt the same way about his parents' death.

Meryl was starting to feel a little concerned. With more than half her ammunition expelled, she had expected Harry to be looking at least mildly flustered. Instead, his expression could only be called serene.

She was going to have to bring out the big guns.

'I've typed up a list of my requirements, things that I expect from a good relationship,' she said, handing him a sheet of white paper completely filled with sentences set out in point form.

'Thanks,' he said, glancing at it fleetingly.

'I won't live near the dump, Harry. Sorry.'

He did not say a word.

'And I won't have all that random, broken crap lying around my house.'

Harry squeezed her hand.

'Anything you bring home will have to be inspected by me first, and if I don't like it, you'll have to take it back.'

Harry smiled.

'You'll probably have to get rid of two-thirds of the things you own.'

Not even a flinch! This guy was made of stronger stuff than she had anticipated. He was like a hostage offering his fingernails to be pulled out one by one, meekly laying down his head so that she could burn his nostril hairs.

It was unheard of!

A thrill of anticipation ran down Meryl's spine. She had one more demand. Unquestionably, this would be asking too much.

'I don't want to work, because I'm a poet at heart, and I want to write full-time.'

She threw the sentence at him like a hand grenade, and then looked up as though expecting Harry to object, but he continued smiling calmly, nodding his head as if he expected nothing less.

Well!

That little scheme certainly backfired.

Breaking up with Harry was going to be a lot trickier than she had hoped.

But, in that moment, something strange happened to Meryl. A new path opened up for her, just like that. It wasn't glowing or angel-lined. She wasn't dying. It was simply that the possibility of marrying Harry – with the house and the junk and the smell – became real.

For the first time, she could see it. In vivid, split-second detail. He would work all day while she wrote, and in the evenings they would have dinner together and read and watch TV.

Meryl squinted incredulously at the cosy scene in her mind. She had never, not even once, not even before her mom died, not even when all her innocence was still intact, never, ever considered being looked after.

And there it suddenly was – her chance for a peaceful, loved life.

She blinked, and the vision disappeared.

'Is that all, my darling?' Harry asked sweetly, reaching out to smooth back a stray piece of hair behind her ear.

'Yes,' Meryl said. 'Oh, by the way, your Guinness World Record claim went through – you're going into the next edition. You can stop eating green food now.'

'*What?! What?!*' Harry's eyes widened and his mouth dropped open.

'I thought I'd failed, 'cause I hadn't heard from them! Oh! This is fantastic! Grandpappy and Ma would be so proud!'

He leapt up from the table, grabbed Meryl's hands and started dancing clumsily with her, looking just like he was doing a poor imitation of a flamingo. There was a light smattering of applause from the patrons at the surrounding tables. They thought he was a slightly odd young man hired by the coffee shop to entertain.

Meryl, embarrassed beyond recognition, her hair all jumbly and her skin flushed, snatched her hands away from him and sat down again, but the shadow of a smile remained on her face.

'I thought you'd be pleased,' she said demurely.

Harry was more than pleased, he was ecstatic.

He hadn't felt this happy since before that Fated Kettle Day.

He felt like planting a jacaranda tree.

It was only when Harry woke up the next morning (a Saturday, so he didn't have to go to work) that he remembered the piece of paper Meryl had given him, and took it out of his pocket where he had put it for safekeeping.

MERYL'S LIST OF REQUIREMENTS

1. You must treat me well. I don't ever want to feel as if I have made a mistake, and that someone else would have been better for me.
2. You must always be affectionate. I like being hugged and kissed and cuddled. I also like massages.
3. You must never, ever cheat on me. That is unforgivable.
4. You must never lie to me. All good relationships are built on honesty.
5. We must have sex at least four times a week, preferably more. We must devote time to learning the Art of Great Sex.
6. You must be kind and thoughtful. Little gifts are a good idea, as are small love notes, surprise dinners and candlelit baths.
7. You must respect me. I am an independent woman with valuable insights.
8. You must allow me the freedom to do what I want within this relationship. You, too, must have a life outside our relationship, or you will stifle me.
9. We must go on holiday at least twice a year, somewhere we haven't been before.
10. You must love me, as much as you can.

Harry read through the requirements once, slowly, and then he read them again, a little faster. Without saying a word he folded the list, put it back in his pocket and left the house.

His first stop was the small shopping centre down the road. The sun was baking the shops that day, and they exhaled customers in warm blasts. Harry headed straight for the Captain Video DVD store where he rented three James Bond movies for later that day – *Live and Let Die*, *Tomorrow Never Dies* and *Die Another Day*.

Then he popped next door to Rhythmic Rhythms where he bought *The Entire Collected James Bond Soundtracks*, condensed onto a triple CD. He spent the day in a continuous loop around all the Mike's Kitchens within a two-hour radius of the dump, listening to his Bond songs on his Discman.

Thinking of the list in his pocket made him itch for some stress-relief. Some of Meryl's demands seemed entirely too much to ask of him (Massages? Holidays? The Art of Great Sex?)

He'd only ever had sex once, he was hardly ready for it to be turned into an art form!

Ever since Harry met Meryl – albeit only a week and a half ago – he had not had the urge to steal tips. Now the urge came flooding back with un-paralleled force.

Harry felt a little panicked. It was as if his loud-knocking-on-the-front-door nightmare was about to come true, and he would be exposed as a cheater.

He did not feel equipped to handle the situation.

Whenever he felt like this, his palms and scalp sweated uncontrollably, making his hair stick to his head and his hands slip off anything he touched. The only cure for this panic-driven affliction was to hum the Bond theme tune and steal tips.

It made him feel dangerous and Zen at the same time: a heady combi-nation.

Even though he knew, on some level, that it was wrong, and that his parents wouldn't have approved (a knowledge that would usually have stopped Harry doing just about anything), some small part of him con-tinued to feel convinced that he was in fact just cleaning things up for the waitresses. They didn't want spare change lying around their tables, making them look messy and unprofessional.

He was only helping out.

Oh, the great depths the human psyche will go to, to justify addictive behaviour!

It wasn't that Harry didn't feel ready to commit to Meryl, not at all. He felt totally ready to start living the life he had been living in his head, complete with wife and new home, and no more stray cats to assuage the loneliness. It's just that he didn't quite expect it all to change so fast.

'I'm ready to give up my dump and my house and my treasures,' he said to himself as he drove to the first restaurant, all the windows open to let in the tumble-dryer-hot breeze.

But his voice sounded unconvinced, even in the small inside space of the car.

He tried again. 'I *am* ready to give up my dump and my house and my treasures.'

Still it sounded thin and feeble.

Perhaps, at heart, in a deeper place than Harry knew how to access, it was simply that he was used to being kind to broken things, but not used to them staying. He always set them on the path to wholeness, but never had to walk it with them. And although he wanted Meryl to stay, wanted her right there with him twenty-four-seven, baby, three-sixty-five, her presence would definitely limit his previously unlimited lifestyle.

He wouldn't be able to just think of himself anymore.

The thought took his breath away.

The idea of growing up appealed to Harry enormously. The reality of it felt like juggling knives, and not butter knives, either! Steak knives. Carving knives. Chinese karate ninja knives.

In fact, not only did it feel like he was juggling knives, but it felt as if he was simultaneously trying to ride a unicycle, and he had to keep pedalling and pedalling and pedalling so that he didn't fall off.

The only time that Harry felt he could climb off the unicycle and put down the knives was at a Mike's Kitchen.

And not, as Mike hoped, because it felt like family.

Simply because it was the only time that Harry was entirely in control – the master of his domain, the ringleader of his circus.

Not one of the clowns.

☼

For the next three weeks, Meryl meant to break up with Harry every day. She tried everything: acting clingy didn't work, acting distant didn't work, being demanding was accepted gracefully, not caring one way or the other was accepted just as gracefully.

Meryl was at the end of her tightrope.

She had written a lengthy thesis on How to Scare Men Off, she had tested out every possible flaw in relationships, and had been able to drive away legions of men in her youth, both wittingly and unwittingly.

Now, inexplicably, all her fail-safe tips were failing.

Of course, she could have just told him it was over, but for some reason Meryl found herself paralysed in that regard. She meant to, so many times. She got as far as saying, 'Harry, we need to talk' in an ominous tone. But then she froze, a fake smile plastered on her face, and he just patted her hand and kissed her on the forehead, assuming she battled to communicate the depths of her feelings for him. It was infuriating.

Things had been so simple, before, so clinical and uncluttered when she was strapped into her corset twenty-four hours a day, seven days a week, three hundred and sixty-*six* days a year (including public holidays). Being bound so tight had always been a satisfying pain, the kind of pain she felt when she didn't eat for a day to keep her weight down. A powerful, controlled pain.

Meryl longed for that familiar pain, but no matter how tightly she knotted the strings of her defence each morning, there was no denying that it was badly torn under the right armpit. And try as she might to patch it up with spite, the tear kept growing, centimetre by centimetre, until Meryl worried that others would be able to see it.

She worried, too, about the deeper effect this unbinding was having on her.

A few months ago, she would have been able to dump Harry in thirty seconds max, effortlessly crushing his self-esteem and masculinity in the process, most probably rendering him impotent for a few months, and enjoying every moment of it.

Now, all she had left were flashes of the old cynicism, sharp and unkind, and in those moments she felt in control again; she felt herself. But then, almost immediately afterwards, Meryl would be gripped by a painful remorse that felt like heartburn, and a simultaneous urge to apologise. Once, she even turned around and drove back to the petrol station where she had snapped at one of the attendants. She bought him a chocolate as a peace offering. It made her feel nauseous. Her freckles were appearing and disappearing at such a rate that people thought she had a rare case of measles.

It was as if something essential was leaking through the rip in Meryl's corset and there was no way to put it back, no way to find out exactly what she was losing. Sometimes Meryl even found herself thinking that she loved Harry's certainty in their relationship. Her whole life she had played it cool in case she came on too strong, but here was a man who bluntly and with no semblance of pretence knew exactly what he wanted, and what he wanted was her.

It was all very troubling.

Harry was one more confusion in a medley of perplexity; one more odd note in a discordant opera.

An opera that played every evening during dinner, when they met – veiled in the pretence of normality – to plan the wedding. The oppressive heat of that hottest summer added an element of pressure to those dinners. Like steam in a rice cooker, the heat that had built up each day refused to dissipate, cocooning them in humidity.

Without really intending to, Harry and Meryl fell into the rhythm of a couple who had been together for many years. Most evenings they met at a different restaurant around Durban, Harry deeply relieved to be able to eat multicoloured food, and excited to have someone to eat it with. He always arrived first, ordering a Creme Soda for himself, and a glass of chilled white wine for Meryl. They chatted about their days as they ate, or about stories they had heard on the news, or funny facts Harry had picked up in the paper, but never about their childhood, never about past pain. Over coffee (for Meryl) and green tea (for Harry, who found that he loved it, even though he no longer had to drink it) they talked Wedding Plans.

From the outside it appeared idyllic.

They ate homemade pasta at Marco's, slow-brewed curry at The Britannica, fish and chips at Something Fishy, and steaks at Havana Grill. They ate Moroccan food at Fabulous, Indonesian at Cake & Satay House, Mexican at Taco Zulu, and Chinese at Foon Lok Nien.

They splashed out and ate buffet at the Royal Grill, skimped and ate mini-pizzas at Pizzetta.

They never once ate at a Mike's Kitchen.

They ate their way around Durban, and although on the surface they looked happy – even a little in love – the tension just below the surface sucked a lot of the joy out of their dates.

Isn't that often the case?

We would all be having a much better time if only we could get out of the way.

After dinner they separated, ostensibly for Meryl to prepare her bottom drawer, and for Harry to spring clean. But in reality, both of them needed (desperately) to indulge in their Secret Stress Relievers.

☀

On the weekends they had sex. Meryl kept thinking his inexperience would mend her scepticism, but it never did. Especially not when Harry proved to be a quick learner, and a gentle, considerate lover. He would do anything she asked, for as long as she wanted. And afterwards, he would lie next to her, stroking her naked body, kissing her softly as she lay with her eyes closed, and murmuring how much he loved her.

'I never want to look at another face,' he whispered to her one night, and she could hear the sound of tearing fabric, widening the ripped inch, letting in more of his love.

In this way, the days melted into each other, one by one, surrounded by a haze of things unsaid, until the wedding day drew dangerously close, and Meryl started having anxiety attacks at work, mid-investigation.

Mr Collins was unimpressed: there was nothing quite as annoying as having his stern investigation interrupted by a woman gasping for breath, with tears in her eyes and a look of pure terror on her face.

☀ ☀ ☀

At this point, you might want to question the game Meryl was playing.

Why string the poor guy along? If you don't intend marrying someone, why continue to plan a non-existent wedding? Besides the fairly obvious heartache involved for the brideless groom, why bother going to all that bother? Why waste a significant portion of your life on what is not (as every engaged couple has discovered) a fun task?

Meryl was asking herself the same questions.

☀ ☀ ☀

The tension was startling.

Aside from her taut fear of losing control completely, Meryl was still recovering from breaking up with Edna, a debacle in all three meanings of the word:

1. Something that becomes a disaster, defeat, or humiliating failure.
2. A sudden break-up of river ice in the spring thaw, causing a violent rush of water and ice.
3. A fiasco.

Edna had not spoken a single word to Meryl since she had witnessed her first kiss with Harry, a sulk that she assumed sprang from Edna's man-hating depths.

Meryl could not have been more wrong, as Edna somehow found herself trapped in a deep sadness that she could not swim out of, no matter how much she drank or how many pretty girls she kissed. From the moment she saw Meryl kissing Harry, her mind had been playing the same single memory over and over, like a teenage girl plays 'Everybody Hurts' the first time her heart is broken.

It was the memory of the first night she met Meryl.

They had been introduced by Saveshnie, Meryl's friend and Edna's colleague, at a swanky club in Florida Road, and had connected instantly, magnetically. They spent the whole night chatting, and the conversation flowed as easily as if they were long-lost lovers reunited after a lengthy separation. Edna kissed Meryl that first night, at the top of the stairs next to the dance floor, surrounded by people dancing and laughing and drinking. Neither heard a word – they were so locked into each other that they might as well have been the only two people there.

It was instant infatuation.

The next morning Edna woke up with tender lips and the scent of Meryl on her skin. She sent her a text message as she lay in bed, still starry-eyed from the night before: *I smell like you, and I can taste you on my lips, and I don't know what you've done to me, but I'm loving it …*

The feeling was mutual. It seemed impossible to fall so hard, so fast. Three months later they moved in together.

The infatuation eroded.

But Edna could not see that now, could not see the ensuing time they had spent together when they were clearly bad for each other, obviously no longer in love. Even though it had been her philandering that sparked off the beginning of the end, now that she could sense its imminence, Edna longed for their romance again, longed for it with a fierce and wild yearning. She was hooked, she realised, on the initial falling, hooked on that feeling of delirium that comes from meeting someone new who seems to click into a part of your heart.

But this time it was more than that – she was also hooked on Meryl. She just realised it too late.

۞

Meryl knew none of this. She imagined Edna had discarded their early romance the day she picked up with Andrea, her beautiful co-worker. She could not imagine Edna and Regret ever sharing the same table.

On the morning after Harry's requirement list distribution, Meryl got up early, made a pot of coffee and woke Edna. The humidity clustered around them like paparazzi anticipating drama, and both Edna and Meryl were sweating within minutes. Opening the windows didn't help either; if anything, the air outside was more stifling than inside.

Meryl sat down at the small kitchen table, and stared into her cup of coffee.

'Listen, Edna, I think we both know it's over. I'm not gay – you know that, I know that – and although this relationship has been very fulfilling in many ways –'

She paused and closed her eyes, '– at times, it's also been quite traumatic.'

Then she took a deep breath and blurted out, 'I've been proposed to, and I've accepted.'

Meryl wondered if it was fair to leave out the part about changing her mind as soon as she had accepted. Then she remembered the beautiful girl in the wheelchair, and her lips thinned as she strengthened her resolve, pulled the laces of her corset as tightly as she could without gasping.

'Please move all your stuff out of here by this evening,' she continued. 'Good luck with your girlfriend.'

Meryl delivered her much-rehearsed speech in monotone, and when she had finished, stood up to leave for work.

Edna's torrent of furious words threw Meryl back into her seat. They covered her in muddy water, soaking her through to her underwear. She was so surprised by Edna's anger that she did not notice her shallow breathing, or the tears glistening in her eyes.

'Fuck you, Meryl. I can't believe you're leaving me for some bastard *man!* After all I've done for you. You were nothing when we met, *nothing!* I've made you what you are!'

Meryl wiped the mud from her eyes.

'But I don't like what I am, Edna! I don't like what I've become, all the lies and the cheating. That's not who I am.'

'You don't even know who you are, Meryl. You're just screwed up.' Edna spat the words out: 'I'm lucky to be rid of you.'

But she wasn't, and she knew it.

☼

And Meryl wasn't entirely finished with the lies and cheating, either, because she was still using the Undertaker every night from 8 pm till 11 pm, during her Bottom Drawer preparation time.

Her desperation time. (Meryl had yet to figure out the purpose of a bottom drawer.)

She loved the release of it, the freedom of being in disguise and not having to be herself, just being able to fuck.

That was all it was, a physical release of stress. There were less than no feelings attached, and she was pretty sure the Undertaker couldn't possibly feel anything for the shell of a person she presented to him. Their sex continued to be wild and a little dirty, and every time Meryl left the dark apartment she felt relaxed and peaceful.

It was a lot like t'ai chi, she reasoned. And if she woke up every night around 3 am feeling nauseous and guilty, with Harry's voice ringing in her ears (usually saying something sickly sweet like 'I love you, petal pie') well, that was just the side effect of too much exercise.

It happened to everyone.

Meryl had decided never to tell Harry about the affair, if she could even call it that. It would only hurt his feelings, and it didn't seem necessary – she was going to break up with him any day now, anyway. Besides, she had convinced herself that she needed her fling with the Undertaker to say goodbye to her old life, to exorcise the last little bit of infidelity that she had caught from Edna, like a virus.

A virulent STD.

Her reasoning was flawless.

☼ ☼ ☼

Sometimes in life the choices we make are conscious and well researched.

We write a list of pros and cons, and then make the best possible, informed decision.

At other times we find ourselves in situations we clearly did not choose. Or so we say.

Perhaps it has more to do with the fact that when we label something an unconscious choice, (oblivious, unaware, instinctive; also involuntary, unwitting, comatose) we don't have to take responsibility.

It just happened.

I didn't mean to.

Some things aren't planned.

How terribly convenient.

☼ ☼ ☼

Every morning, when Harry woke up at 4 am to begin work for the day, he swore that he wouldn't go tip-stealing that night.

He tried hard, he really did. After supper each evening, he began spring-cleaning the house (a mammoth task) or looked through Meryl's list of requirements again so that he would have them memorised before the wedding. But then, at around 9 pm, without fail, Harry started feeling antsy and stressed, and longed for a bit of excitement.

It was just too hot in the house; there was no oxygen, no movement in the air. Even if he had been spring-cleaning for an hour, everything still looked exactly the same, and as soon as he got halfway through the list, his heart started pounding uncomfortably (especially at #4: *All good relationships are built on honesty*).

To alleviate the pounding, Harry hopped in his car and drove around the block, listening to loud music from a certain, very famous film series. And then, somehow, without ever meaning to, Harry would find that his car was driving him to a Mike's Kitchen.

Sometimes, when he noticed the direction he was being pulled in, he would stop the car on the side of the road, take a few deep breaths and turn around. This resolve usually disintegrated after ten minutes.

However, Harry vowed to himself that a week before the wedding he would give it all up, and that if Meryl ever asked, he would tell her the truth.

But only if she asked.

Well aware from a young age that he was (in any light, under any microscope, with any magnifying glass) rather obsessive, Harry had always been very careful to keep that part of his personality entertained, so that its demands wouldn't infringe on the rest of his life.

Sometimes he succeeded.

With his Green Food Crusade officially called off, he needed something else to focus his attention on, something else to fill the minutiae of each minute. To add fuel to his obsessive fire, he was trying to downsize his garbage/treasure retrieval, an act he found extraordinarily difficult, and more of a sacrifice than Meryl could ever imagine.

It became his greatest act of love.

And it caused him a good deal of frustration on a day-to-day basis. The more he turfed things over the wall onto the dump, the more he sweated, and the more broken things he attracted. It was a tornado of temptation, and Harry had to fight against getting sucked in.

Other than his secret tip-stealing, in fact, things seemed to have reached a happy balance.

No good for Harry.

So he started hoarding something new: newspaper articles called 'Follow the Scent of Honeysuckle'. They were written by a pair of young lovers, Aisha and Mdu, travelling all over the country and recording their adventures. Harry was sure that Meryl would love them.

It was said that a trail of honeysuckle flowers followed this couple wherever they went, and that the woman was related to whales, but that sounded a little fanciful, and Harry couldn't quite believe it. He did believe in their love, though, and it inspired him to collect every one of their articles – no small task, considering he had to search the dump for each newspaper. And sometimes he'd found the right article, but it would be so badly stained that he had to throw it away and look for another one. It became a monster game of Bingo.

Each article was mounted on card and laminated, and then used to painstakingly plot and plan their honeymoon – he booked them into all the same places, and organised all the same activities.

Aisha and Mdu lived Happily Ever After, Harry was sure. How could they not?

They were in love.

Maybe if he and Meryl followed their path, they, too, would have a Happy Ending.

It was certainly worth a try.

※

Two weeks to the day after Meryl began her secret tryst with the Undertaker, he cooked her a romantic dinner, complete with black tablecloth and black candles, and told her he had left his girlfriend so that they could finally be together and pledge their love in public. She laughed at him scornfully, chastised him for ruining their last week of kinky sex, and told him about Harry.

The confused part of Meryl put up its hand and questioned why she was once again using the impending marriage as a break-up excuse, when she didn't intend going through with said marriage. Meryl rapped it on the knuckles with a wooden ruler and told it to keep quiet. Then she flounced off, pleased that that relationship had at least ended without her having to do any hard work.

Had she known how much work the Undertaker would be *after* the relationship had ended, she would never have lain down in his coffin in the first place. He followed her to work the following day and sat outside her window in the blazing heat, singing out-of-tune love songs until she threw a mug of hot coffee into his adoring eyes. The day after that he wrote her seventeen letters pledging his love, each with a small snippet of red toenail, which freaked Meryl out no end.

It took her some time to figure out why he kept sending toenails, but then she remembered she had pretended to be a beautician. Meryl burnt all seventeen letters in a small fire on her front lawn, knowing that the Undertaker was spying on her from across the street. That night she went to sleep with a small fire of satisfaction burning in her belly.

Those moments when unadulterated malice ran the show were still her absolute favourite moments of the day.

They were, regrettably, few and far between.

And then on the third day, the Undertaker went too far.

Meryl was driving to Harry's house for dinner, and had the distinct feeling that she was being followed by a hearse.

It was an unusual feeling.

Sure that the Undertaker would get lost navigating the dump, she sped up and left him at a red light. A storm was brewing on the horizon as she knocked on Harry's door; the clouds lit up with sheets of lightning, silvering across the night sky.

It was beautiful.

It set Meryl's teeth on edge.

An hour later, while they were eating, a blank, black envelope was pushed under Harry's door.

'Bit late for the postman, isn't it, my love?' Harry, ever the trusting soul, asked as he picked it up.

When he opened the envelope, he found a short braid of dark, wiry hair, tied with bows on both ends. Red bows. The only other thing in the envelope was a note. Harry read it out loud: *You used to love my pubes ... and me. A token to remember me by. Your ever-loving Undertaker.*

Meryl was repulsed. Really, this was taking it too far. What kind of a freak mailed their ex-lover a braid of their pubic hairs?

It was disgusting, and in very poor taste. She was not impressed.

Neither was Harry, but he was also thoroughly confused.

'Who's this 'Undertaker'? Any idea, my sweet?'

'Oh, he probably dropped it off at the wrong house,' Meryl lied with a straight face.

Harry still looked a bit befuddled (there were no other houses around) but quickly slipped back into adoring puppy-dog mode, asking Meryl if she had decided whether she wanted mint, vanilla or caramel icing for the wedding cake.

It was a fair question.

It incensed Meryl.

Ever since the tear in her armour started pulling open, Meryl's moods had swung more wildly than a swing-boat at a funfair, but this, *this* was too much! There was a space of about three seconds when a little voice (the same voice that had cried *Yes* to Harry's proposal) whispered to her.

Don't do this, Meryl. Please.

But Meryl taped the little voice's mouth shut.

The moment just before she said something powerfully hurtful was intense. It made her feel in control again, firmly centred, unswayable. It sewed up her corset with rope and superglue.

With a deep breath, and a curl of her lip, Meryl – her voice as smooth and cold and poisonous as mercury – asked, 'Aren't you just the tiniest bit suspicious, Harry? You don't think it's odd that a complete stranger drops his pubic hairs under your door with a love note? You don't think maybe there could be a link between that, and all the nights I've spent away from you lately?'

'Well, no ...' Harry replied, 'your bottom drawer ...'

'Christ, Harry, are you a complete idiot? What do you think I've been doing every night for the last two weeks?'

'Well, I suppose I think you've been doing what you said you've been doing ...' he replied, his forehead creasing into a frown.

'But now that you mention those nights ... I have a confession to make. Things have felt a little tense lately, and I've actually just decided to come clean, or I won't be able to marry you with a clear conscience.'

Meryl's stomach twisted. The air, suddenly, smelt like burnt toast. Had she entirely misread Harry?

'There's this thing I've been doing for a while, you could almost call it a hobby. I uhmm ... I ahhmm ... I steal tips from Mike's Kitchens. And I hum the James Bond theme tune while I do it. It's terrible, I know, and I'm going to stop, I promise ...'

Harry exhaled and smiled, relieved.

Meryl snorted.

It felt like a long time since Harry had heard a Female Derisive Snort. It sent a chill right through him.

'You think *that's* terrible? Are you kidding me, Harry?'

The demon tap-dancing on her temper started jumping up and down as Meryl stalked the cluttered room, kicking at random objects.

'Meryl, love, sit down, let's talk about this calmly.'

'No, Harry,' she retorted, coming to a standstill and looking him straight in the eyes.

'Now *I* have a confession to make. I've been sleeping with another man for the past two weeks. Not because I have any feelings for him, but because I'm totally confused and terrified of what we're about to do, and if we should even be doing it at all.'

Meryl stopped. She didn't quite know where those words had come from. But in that moment she joined the ranks of women everywhere. She had reached the point in the argument where she felt horrible and upset, and she wanted him to feel just as bad. So she used her female weapon.

She said the most hurtful thing she could think of.

'And also because I wanted some great sex with a hot guy before I chain myself to you.'

The tactic worked. She got her response.

Harry gave her a look of utter pain – his mouth ajar, his eyes full of disbelief – choked back a sob and fled from the room.

˟

Harry jumped in his car and headed straight for the closest Mike's Kitchen, all promises of never stealing tips again flying out of the window along with his shattered dreams, too broken even for him to fix.

This was *not* the way it was supposed to work out.

He opened his window to let in some air, but the rush of stale wind did nothing to clear his head. The clouds that night were heavy and ominous, pressing threateningly in on his little car.

Harry battled to breathe.

The lightning storm was now blazing – glowing cracks of electricity searing across the sky, silently and without rain.

He only just managed to get to the restaurant without crashing his car, and as soon as he walked in (sniffling and gulping, the Bond theme tune ringing in his ears) Harry was spotted.

Alas, stripped of his usual sneaky moves and inconspicuous nature, shivering violently and bumping into people, and, worst of all, without the stinky jacket that stopped broken things from being attracted to him, Harry became visible.

Very visible.

A trail of cracked mugs and plates followed him, clattering as they fell to the floor, but his violent tears kept him from noticing anything except the sick feeling in his belly. Harry was so thoroughly convinced of his

MK invisibility that he looked at the manager of the restaurant in shock when he said, 'Excuse me, sir, why are you stealing the waitresses' tips?'

Confused, traumatised and forced to lip-read because of the blaring James Bond music, Harry replied loudly, 'How come you saw me?'

Whereupon the manager took him roughly by the arm – believing him to be mentally damaged in some way – and asked the cashier to call the police.

'You can't call the cops!' Harry cried, ripping his headphones off as he deciphered what the manager was saying, 'I'm going to be in the *Guinness World Records!*'

'I couldn't care less, sir,' the manager replied, a look of scorn in his eyes.

In a moment of startling clarity, everything in the restaurant froze as Harry saw his future – he would be arrested and imprisoned, Meryl would leave him for good, his house at the dump would be liquidated to pay for the backlog of tips he owed, and all chances of happiness would disappear from his life.

Forever.

Worse yet, the Guinness people would denounce him, and his Green Food Crusade would all have been for nothing, his living monument to his parents turned to dust.

Harry dwelt in this moment longer than necessary, looking around and noticing the colour of the wallpaper (grey), the scent in the air (mothballs), the quality of the light (poor).

And then he sprang into action.

No! He could not throw it all away with such abandon! With a burst of strength to rival any James Bond, Harry broke free of the manager's firm grip, and ran for the exit. In his mind, everything slowed as he raced for the door, pushing grannies and small children out of the way with surprising force, knocking large plates of samp and beans out of waitress's hands, and leaping over yellow *Floor Slippery When Wet* signs like an Olympic hurdler.

The James Bond music blared through the headphones around his neck as Harry pushed through the swing doors, and swung round the corner to his car. Jamming in the keys, he opened the door, jumped in and sped off.

Never in his whole life had Harry lived through so much excitement in one evening, not even when his parents bought a new Scrabble set, and they stayed up all night playing, making up new words and getting wired on caffeine.

Slowly, his heart stopped pounding, he could swallow past the panic in his throat and the fizzing sensation in his veins receded a little. Harry realised that he was exhausted.

Bone-weary. Dog-tired. Pooped.

He eased his car onto the highway and drove unhurriedly in the direction of home, turning the volume of the music right down. The clouds were pressing in even lower than before, and the hot wind had grown into a hot gale, whipping the palm trees along the highway from side to side. Harry could feel the wind rocking the car, and he wound up his window to seal in the quiet.

By the time he reached the dump, he knew where to go. He wasn't quite ready to go home, so he parked his car in a secluded spot and slowly began the long climb up the slope. The clouds were now so low that Harry felt like he was climbing into them, and the hot wind stirred up the loose debris, sending objects whipping through the air.

Lightning lit up his path, exposing potential hazards, like rusty spokes and soft, oozing patches, but Harry was used to it. This was his hood. The wind grew stronger the higher he climbed, and by the time he reached the top of the slope, he had to lean into it to prevent being blown away. Lightning flashes flared around him as Harry sank into a broken-down armchair he had placed on top of the dump, his home away from home.

He sighed.

What was he to do now? The tip-stealing would have to stop, but he had already prepared himself for that. What really worried Harry was Meryl, and her strange behaviour. How could she have given him that list of requirements and then, so early on, break one of them herself? (#3, An important one.)

The thought of her being with another man was not even what bothered him the most. Harry had seen glimpses of Meryl's cynical detachment, and knew that the sex had meant nothing to her, that she could switch off her emotions as easily as you switch off a kettle, although, thinking about it, he realised that the kettle-thing was a bad example.

But he was not used to someone who loved him doing something so obviously hurtful. Even though Harry had no real friends to speak of, no living family, no ex-girlfriends and no company save the stray cats, he knew how he wanted to be treated.

And this was not good enough.

He deserved Great Love, the kind of love his ma and pa had had. Great Love did not throw away the other's emotions so carelessly. Meryl needed to know that she could not make him feel this way. He didn't ever want to feel this way again.

As Harry thought, he scribbled the main points he wanted to remember on the palm of his hand. He kept a pen in the armchair for that very purpose. *Only Great Love Will Do,* he wrote, and underlined it twice.

By the time he got up, Harry felt more than ready to lay down some requirements of his own.

☼ ☼ ☼

It might seem strange that an emotionally-stunted man like Harry could believe in something as profound as Great Love. But you have to bear in mind that Harry had lived always and only in the presence of a great love. The effect of such constancy imbues a deep sense of truth in a person, a truth that cannot be obtained by any combination of one-night stands, random relationships and multiple kissing partners.

Similar to fluoride in water, great love strengthens a person without their knowledge.

☼ ☼ ☼

Less than five minutes away, Meryl was coming undone.

In every meaning of the word (unravelled, loosened, disengaged, invalidated).

When Harry rushed out, a feeling of profound relief had washed over her. 'Thank God this is all over,' she had thought.

But not ten seconds later her eyes welled up with tears, and her heart felt as if it was being squeezed in a mammogram vice. Without intending to, the soft, exposed part of Meryl (the part she so frequently despised) had formed an attachment to Harry – to his kindness and unending patience with her, and to the love that he naturally assumed she wanted, and deserved.

Remember the old days, the cynical voice whispered cajolingly, *remember how easy things were, how comfortable and confident you were. Let's go back to those days ... get out of this dump.*

Meryl nodded, and attempted to lace and knot her fraying corset as taut as she could (almost taking her breath away). Then she started collecting Harry's treasures. She piled them all in a heap in his back garden, just behind the disused inflatable swimming pool – all the broken chairs and rusty cages and dented hubcaps and three-legged side tables, and the mounds and mounds of newspaper cuttings and comic strips and old paintings and mouldy clothing, and boxes of broken toys and cracked vases and chipped mugs, and, strangely, one whole box full of musty hats.

She threw them all onto the heap. The fierce hot wind buffeted her and tossed the papers around. She refused to draw a parallel between the wind and her feelings.

Meryl was busy hauling the thirteenth box of comic strips from under the bed when she found the laminated posters labelled *Our Honeymoon* in Harry's careful scrawl. For a moment the rip in her corset split even further, and started leaking something that smelt suspiciously like love.

She quickly read the prose poems (by a man called Mdu), glanced at the drawings (by a woman called Aisha) and scanned the photos of the two lovers. The man looked strangely familiar, and it took a few moments for Meryl to recognise him as the man from the Handy Green Grocers robbery, who had just stood there, useless, while those scumbags robbed the store.

The man whom she secretly blamed for her nightly nightmares.

The gaping hole under her right armpit starting knitting together again.

Men were useless fools.

One more reason to cast them aside, she thought, throwing the posters on top of the mound, along with a slightly torn fold-out of Candy K she had found in a dusty corner.

Meryl stood back and surveyed her handiwork. She was a little puffed. The pile of sentimental rubbish reached almost to the top of the wall surrounding Harry's house, a mishmash of all the broken things that had found their way into his life over the years, and that he hadn't been able to refuse.

Meryl, the most important broken thing of all, was not impressed.

With a derisive snort she lit a match, watching it flare and start to eat its way towards her perfectly manicured fingertips. At the last second she threw it onto the heap of junk. It landed in a shoebox full of comic strips and caught fire immediately, the thin paper crisping and burning in seconds.

Next came an old velour hat, and the arm of a broken rocking chair. The fire took delicate mouthfuls, burning with a steady contained smouldering, which, although mesmerising, was not violent enough for Meryl's tastes. With wilful abandon she lit match after match, throwing them on particularly flammable spots until the matchbox emptied and she stood back, satisfied with the roaring bonfire in front of her, oblivious to the hot wind that had picked up in the last few minutes and that was now whipping the fire into a frenzy.

It was only when Meryl started inching her way around the bonfire towards the door that a small flame of panic sparked in her belly. The bonfire had started eating the dead grass, and was spreading with frightening speed; the narrow pathway she had laid out for herself became part of a wall of fire too scorching to consider walking through. Taking a deep breath and inhaling only smoke, Meryl started coughing, and headed around the other side of the fire, towards the disused swimming pool.

Fear had erased every one of her freckles.

☀

When Harry thought about it later, he knew that they both must have seen the same thing at the same time.

Part of the beauty of sorting out his mind on top of the dump was that when he had reached a conclusion, his bed was less than five minutes away. Harry resolved to speak to Meryl the next morning. He looked at the palm of his hand, believed the words he saw there: *Only Great Love Will Do.*

He would not wash them off until after he had spoken to her. He didn't want to break off the engagement, not at all, but he wasn't willing to put up with that kind of treatment. As he stood up and stretched, a streak of lightning lit up the sky as brightly as the sun. Harry looked over at his house and saw a column of fire shoot up behind it.

He scrambled down the dump in a flash, his feet hardly touching the mounds of garbage, and flew to his house in less than two minutes (a new record).

Meryl's car was still parked outside, and with a rising wave of panic flooding his throat Harry flung open his front door. A wall of heat and ash met him. He shielded his eyes with his hand and stumbled through to the back door. The garden was ablaze, a huge pile of rubbish burning ferociously and the swimming pool filled with sun-warmed food colouring consumed by a sheet of fire.

Harry remembered, too late, that a lesser-known fact about food colouring is that it's highly flammable.

He ran as close to the fire as he could without getting burnt, and searched wildly for Meryl. His eyes were smarting from the heat and the floating ash that whirled around him in the furiously hot wind, and he struggled to see past the flames. But eventually he glimpsed her, crouched against the wall, covering her eyes with her hands.

She was trapped behind a solid wall of fire.

'Meryl!' he shouted, and she looked up, wide-eyed.

For just a moment the wind died down. When she saw Harry, she smiled her secret smile, the smile she never knew existed until she met him.

His hands limp at his sides, Harry smiled his secret smile.

The wall of fire blazed between them, the air was filled with sparks. A hot rain began to fall.

Dedicated to all those who know that
Only Great Love Will Do.

The greatest thanks go out to these dear people ...

Ron Irwin and Tris Coburn, for being the best pair of agents any writer could wish for.

Willemien de Villiers, my tireless South African editor, who took on the formidable task of unmuddling my words.

Kathleen Gilligan, whose infectious delight and belief in this book brought it to life.

I could not have done this without ...

My fantastic mom and dad, who supported me without question and never once doubted I could do it.

The boys (Bongin, Smile and Mouldy) and Ash and Dagmar, who have always been there for me, no matter what.

My favourite web designer and computer genius Smile, a master of patience.

And Aunty Nontuthuzelo for many cups of tea and kind questions.

Thanks to Jessy Pie for being a kindred spirit,

To CC for inspiring me to write a book she might actually read,

To Ugie, for putting up with wild emotion and giving me only love, and chocolate.

And of course, thanks to Squirrel, who has been right next to me from the beginning, and will be right here till the end.

All my love,
Bridget